Also by William Gray

C.S. LEWIS

DEATH AND FANTASY: ESSAYS ON PHILIP PULLMAN, C.S. LEWIS, GEORGE MACDONALD AND R.L. STEVENSON

ROBERT LOUIS STEVENSON: A Literary Life

Fantasy, Myth and the Measure of Truth

Tales of Pullman, Lewis, Tolkien, MacDonald and Hoffmann

William Gray

First published 2009
Paperback edition published 2010 by
PALGRAVE MACMILLAN

Palgrave Macmillan in the UK is an imprint of Macmillan Publishers Limited, registered in England, company number 785998, of Houndmills, Basingstoke, Hampshire RG21 6XS.

Palgrave Macmillan in the US is a division of St Martin's Press LLC, 175 Fifth Avenue, New York, NY 10010.

Palgrave Macmillan is the global academic imprint of the above companies and has companies and representatives throughout the world.

Palgrave® and Macmillan® are registered trademarks in the United States, the United Kingdom, Europe and other countries.

ISBN: 978–0–230–00505–1   hardback
ISBN: 978–0–230–27285–9   paperback

This book is printed on paper suitable for recycling and made from fully managed and sustained forest sources. Logging, pulping and manufacturing processes are expected to conform to the environmental regulations of the country of origin.

A catalogue record for this book is available from the British Library.

Library of Congress Cataloging-in-Publication Data

Gray, William, 1952–
    Fantasy, myth, and the measure of truth : tales of Pullman, Lewis, Tolkien, MacDonald, and Hoffmann/William Gray.
        p. cm.
    Includes index.
    ISBN: 978–0–230–00505–1 (alk. paper) 978–0–230–27285–9 (cloth)
    1. Fantasy fiction, English—History and criticism.   2. Literature and myth.
    3. Pullman, Philip, 1946—Criticism and interpretation.   4. Lewis, C. S. (Clive Staples), 1898–1963—Criticism and interpretation.   5. Tolkien, J. R. R. (John Ronald Reuel), 1892–1973—Criticism and interpretation.   6. MacDonald, George, 1824–1905—Criticism and interpretation.   7. Hoffmann, E. T. A. (Ernst Theodor Amadeus), 1776–1822—Criticism and interpretation.   I. Title.

PR830.F3F73   2008
823'.91—dc22   2008020949

10   9   8   7   6   5   4   3   2   1
19   18   17   16   15   14   13   12   11   10

Printed and bound in Great Britain by
CPI Antony Rowe, Chippenham and Eastbourne

For Lorna

Contents

Acknowledgements

In addition to colleagues in the English Department, University of Chichester, and students on ENL326 ('Other Worlds'), I wish to thank the following: Paul Collins, Verlyn Flieger, Jonathan Gray, Lorna Gray, Don Haase; Hans Hahn, Sue Morgan, Philip Pullman, Christina Scull, Nicholas Tucker, Jean Webb; also Brian Hulme at Northcote House for permission to rework material from my book *C. S. Lewis*.

I am grateful to the following for permission to publish extracts from their books (for abbreviations see below):

Cambridge University Press
C. S. Lewis: *The Discarded Image*; *SLE*; *SMRL*

The C. S. Lewis Company Ltd.
C. S. Lewis: *CN* (*LWW*; *PC*; *VDT*; *SC*; *MN*; *LB*); *CT*; *GD*; *LL1* (*2 & 3*); *OTOW*; *PR*; *SBJ*; *TWHF*

HarperCollins Publishers
J. R. R. Tolkien: *BLT1* (2); *LOTR*; *LR*; *MCOE*; *S*; *SD*; *SWM*; *TL*; *T&L*. Humphrey Carpenter: *Biog*

The Houghton Mifflin Harcourt Publishing Company
C. S. Lewis: *OTOW*; *TWHF* (US rights)

Oxford University Press
E. T. A. Hoffmann: *GPOT*
C. S. Lewis: *AOL*
George MacDonald: *PGPC*

Scholastic Ltd.
Philip Pullman: *HDM*

Abbreviations

ABNW	*At the Back of the North Wind*
AC	*Adela Cathcart*
AOL	*The Allegory of Love*
AOM	*The Abolition of Man*
AS	*The Amber Spyglass*
Biog	*J.R.R. Tolkien: A Biography* (Carpenter)
Blackwelder	*Lord of the Rings 1954–2004: Scholarship in Honor of R. E. Blackwelder*
BLT1 (2)	*The Book of Lost Tales, Part One (Two)*
CFT	*George MacDonald: The Complete Fairy Tales*
CN	*The Chronicles of Narnia*
CT	*The Cosmic Trilogy*
FQ	*The Faerie Queene*
GD	*The Great Divorce*
GK	*The Golden Key*
GMAW	*George MacDonald and His Wife*
GP	*The Golden Pot*
GPOT	*The Golden Pot and Other Tales* (OUP, 1992)
HDM	*His Dark Materials*
HOTW	*The House of the Wolfings*
HPS	*The Harry Potter series*
H&S2	*Tolkien Companion & Guide: Reader's Guide* (Hammond & Scull)
HvO	*Heinrich von Ofterdingen*
IM	*Interrupted Music* (Flieger)
Inks	*The Inklings* (Carpenter)
L	*Lilith*
LB	*The Last Battle*
LL1 (2 & 3)	*The Letters of C.S. Lewis, Volume 1 (2 & 3)*
LOTR	*The Lord of the Rings*
LP	*The Light Princess*
LR	*The Lost Road*
LWW	*The Lion, the Witch and the Wardrobe*
L&S	*Lenz with Scott (eds), His Dark Materials Illuminated*
MCOE	*The Monsters and the Critics and Other Essays*
MN	*The Magician's Nephew*
NATC	*The Norton Anthology of Theory and Criticism*
NCP	*The Notion Club Papers*
NL	*Northern Lights (The Golden Compass in USA)*
NS	*Natural Supernaturalism* (Abrams)

OFS	*On Fairy-Stories*
OSP	*Out of the Silent Planet*
OTOW	*Of This and Other Worlds*
PAC	*The Princess and Curdie*
PAG	*The Princess and the Goblin*
PC	*Prince Caspian*
Ph	*Phantastes*
PPL	*A Preface to Paradise Lost*
PR	*The Pilgrim's Regress*
RME	*The Road to Middle-Earth* (Shippey)
S	*The Silmarillion*
SBJ	*Surprised by Joy*
SC	*The Silver Chair*
SD	*Sauron Defeated*
SK	*The Subtle Knife*
SL	*The Screwtape Letters*
SLE	*Selected Literary Essays* (Lewis)
SMRL	*Studies in Medieval and Renaissance Literature* (Lewis)
SR	*Sartor Resartus*
SWM	*Smith of Wootton Major*
THS	*That Hideous Strength*
TL	*The Letters of J.R.R. Tolkien*
T&L	*Tree and Leaf*
TS	*Topographies of the Sacred* (Rigby)
TWHF	*Till We Have Faces*
VDT	*The Voyage of the Dawn Treader*
VTA	*A Voyage to Arcturus*

Prelude: Pullman's 'High Argument'

The aim of this book is to examine the genre[1] of fantasy or mythopoeic fiction, particularly that written for children,[2] in relation to a literary tradition that might broadly be described as Romantic. This Romantic tradition was shaped and informed by various dissident interpretations of Christian, Jewish and Platonic writings (often labelled Hermetic or Gnostic), as M. H. Abrams argued in his influential (if contested) *Natural Supernaturalism: Tradition and Revolution in Romantic Literature* (*=NS*).[3] Philip Pullman's *His Dark Materials* trilogy (*=HDM*) may be seen as in certain respects the culmination of this tradition of mythopoeic fiction infused with (or contaminated by) a particular kind of Romanticism. Whatever explicit references Pullman may provide, for example in the 'Acknowledgements' section of *The Amber Spyglass* (*=AS*) and its chapter epigraphs (in the UK version), it is apparent that the very project of *HDM* is profoundly Romantic in that it seems to offer a new mythology analogous to that called for by Romantic thinkers such as Schlegel and Schelling in Germany, and Blake and Carlyle[4] in Britain. However, in the essentially circular or spiralling movement which Abrams claims is characteristic of Romantic thought, the new mythology re-appropriates older mythologies in a new key (the musical allusion is not accidental).[5]

HDM is Pullman's 'high argument', I suggest, because by following Romantic writers such as Blake, Wordsworth, Coleridge and Shelley, it addresses some central religious questions that have major cultural implications. Not only does it present a highly negative image (indeed a caricature) of institutional religion, specifically of the Church; it also engages in a quasi-theological argument about the nature of the Christian story, or metanarrative, of the Fall. In contrast to the 'official' Church doctrine that the Fall of Adam, traditionally blamed on Eve's succumbing to the subtle words of the serpent, is the source of all evil and misery, Pullman explores the idea that the Fall was ultimately 'a good thing'. There is a long alternative Christian tradition of seeing the Fall as *felix culpa* (a 'happy fault' or 'Fortunate Fall'), since the resulting redemption through the work of Christ far outweighs the original loss. Milton's Adam contemplates this possibility in *Paradise Lost* (XII 471–8).[6] Some Romantic readings of the Fall see it as ultimately 'fortunate' in that it occasions a final (and richer) restoration of the unity of God, humanity and nature that had been split apart by the (in some sense necessary) Fall. Traditional Christian teaching sees the ultimate reconciliation towards which all Creation groans (Romans 8:22) in supernatural terms as the work of Christ through the power of the Spirit; Romantic thinkers, however, have tended to see this development towards a final reconciliation in a 'new Heaven and a new Earth' (Revelation 21:1) as an expression in *metaphorical* terms (Hegel's *Vorstellungen* or 'pictures') of a purely immanent natural process. Rather than simply abandoning the whole Christian myth as some eighteenth century rationalists had advocated, a number of Romantic thinkers preferred to reinterpret it in natural terms that retained (they thought) some of the values of Christianity without the crude and no longer believable supernatural elements. Thus the truths of religious experience and 'spirituality' could be preserved even (and especially) for 'its cultured despisers', as Schleiermacher famously put it.[7] Such a reinterpretation of Christianity was, however, in this-worldly terms. What Romanticism offered, as Abrams puts it using Carlyle's phrase, was a 'natural supernaturalism' that would 'embody the divine Spirit of that [Christian] religion in a new Mythus'.[8]

Abrams claims that this transformation of the Christian doctrine of the miraculous reconciliation of all things through God's gracious intervention into the myth of a *non-supernatural* reconciliation is precisely Wordsworth's 'high argument',[9] which boldly follows Milton's attempted theodicy in *Paradise Lost*. According to Abrams, Wordsworth is trying to show how the Fall – that is, a prevailing human sense of separation, pain, loss and despair – can be overcome and a reconciliation can be achieved not through any transcendent supernatural agency, but rather through the immanent work of the human spirit. It might thus be argued that long before Pullman tried to offer '*Paradise Lost* in three volumes',[10] Wordsworth had tried to do much the same in his own inimitable way in *The Prelude*. In his 'Acknowledgements' at the end of *AS*, Pullman makes particular mention of Kleist, Milton and Blake. However, although Pullman frequently quotes Kleist's essay *On the Marionette Theatre* approvingly for its discussion of the Fall as ultimately 'fortunate', Abrams claims that Kleist:

> merely epitomized what had become one of the most familiar of philosophical commonplaces. [Kleist] uses the figure to support his paradox (derived from Schiller) that puppets, acting by pure necessity, exhibited a grace beyond the reach of human dancers, since these latter are inescapably self-divided and self-conscious. The key to this disparity between puppet and dancer . . . lies in a just understanding of the third chapter of Genesis.
>
> (NS 221)

If Pullman cites Kleist rather than Wordsworth, it is nevertheless the case, according to Abrams, that *both* Kleist *and* Wordsworth share the same general message with a range of other (especially German) Romantic writers. Blake of course holds a particularly important place not only for Pullman, but also for Abrams, who argues that Blake actually delivered the new mythology of which writers such as Schelling announced the advent (*NS* 256).

Thus Pullman seems very much aligned with the Romantic project as elaborated by Abrams in *NS*. It remains to be seen how this can be reconciled with the fact that Pullman is often claimed to be postmodern. The continuities as well as the tensions between Romanticism and postmodernism have been much discussed. One of the most obvious affinities between Romanticism and postmodernism is the emphasis on 'the sublime' or non-representable, although how this is interpreted varies greatly. The sense of the unrepresentable or infinite is central to German Romantic or Idealist philosophy after Kant. Andrew Bowie has discussed some of the correspondences between this German Romantic tradition (including philosophers, artists and writers) and postmodernism, with particular reference to the importance of music to Romantic thought – an emphasis relevant to the discussion of Pullman.[11]

The resistance to any kind of institutional constraint or 'system', whether religious or secular, is also characteristic of the original Romantic impulse both in Germany and Britain, although there is also a tendency for the 'canonical' figures[12] in both countries to swerve away from the original radical impulse. While the generation of Romantic specialists coming after the likes of Abrams and Harold Bloom tended to be suspicious of the latters' alleged ideological complicity in the Romantic quest for transcendence and 'the high Romantic argument', more recently, according to Paul Hamilton, 'literary critics of Romanticism have mostly given up excoriating its philosophical sublimation of real issues';[13] as Michael John Kooy puts it, they 'no longer labour the point about how Romanticism occluded the historical (political, social) with aesthetic and metaphysical razmataz.'[14] Without going into Pullman's biography, it is probable that he would have studied Romantic literature before the generation of Romantic scholars who were in reaction to Abrams, Bloom and Northrop Frye – let alone 'a new generation of ideologically alert Romantic scholars (who never really took seriously Shelley's claim about "legislators of the world" in the first place)'.[15] Indeed it seems likely that on one level Pullman *does* take seriously Shelley's claim that poets – or at least storytellers – are 'the unacknowledged legislators of the world',[16] and that he does in some sense endorse Wordsworth's 'high argument'.

However, a spot of subversive postmodern intertextuality and metafictional game playing[17] can always serve to deflect criticism of political naivety (or worse). On the other hand, Pullman is on record as saying is that he is 'temperamentally ... "agin" the postmodernist position that there· is no truth and it depends on where you are and it's all the result of the capitalist, imperialist hegemony of bourgeois . . . all this sort of stuff'[18] – in other words, he claims to be instinctively against precisely the kind of cultural materialism that would suspect complicity between critics like Abrams and the 'high argument' of Romantic ideology. Pullman's ambivalence towards postmodernism is a correlate of his attraction to the 'high argument' of Romanticism; his own desire to create a new mythology is in tension with any postmodern scepticism towards grand narratives.[19]

In discussing *HDM* as a kind of myth, Millicent Lenz has invoked as an analogue Wagner's *Ring* cycle (*L&S* 4). However helpful (or not) we may find this analogy, it has the advantage of drawing attention to the profoundly Romantic dimension in Pullman's work. Wagner's music dramas are the epitome of Romanticism, both technically in his realization of the Romantic dream of a synthesis of the arts (*Gesamtkunstwerk*),[20] and also in his use of myth and legend, in which respect he has been seen as 'the heir to Romantic mythology'.[21] In the creation of a new mythology through the appropriation of older mythological material, Wagner put into practice the German Romantic programme, as articulated particularly perhaps by Novalis – both in his philosophical fragments and in his own creative writing (represented above all by *Heinrich von Ofterdingen* (=*HvO*) and the several *Märchen* it contains). The most characteristic Romantic literary form is the *Märchen* or fairytale. For Novalis (the pseudonym of Friedrich von Hardenberg), the *Märchen* or more properly the literary fairy-tale *(Kunstmärchen)* – that is, the imaginative reworking of material derived from the kind of folk-tales famously collected by the Grimm brothers – was at the heart of Romantic literary theory. The genre of the *Kunstmärchen* enjoyed an extremely high status in German literary culture – as Novalis claimed: 'POETICS. Everything is a fairy-tale [*Märchen*]'.

In terms of Pullman's 'high argument' – that is, his attempt to suggest the possibility of a reconciliation of humanity with itself and with nature in which experience re-appropriates the lost vision of innocence, but on a higher plane (the basic theme of German Romanticism, according to Abrams) – a crucial question is: from where does he derive the key elements of his new mythology? Two main sources present themselves: Milton and Blake. If the thrust of Pullman's 'high argument' seems akin to Wordsworth's, the latter does not provide much help in actually constructing a new mythology. In going back to Milton, Pullman is accessing a Christian mythology that in Wordsworth's time would hardly have been available explicitly *as* mythology, for as C.S. Lewis suggested, 'the marvellous is "romantic", provided it does not make part of the believed religion'.[22] Lewis argued this point more fully in *The Allegory of Love*:

> The decline of the [Graeco-Roman] gods . . . was not, for them or for us, a history of sheer loss. For decoration may let romance in. The poet is free

to invent, beyond the limit of the possible, regions of strangeness and beauty for their own sake. . . . [U]nder the pretext of allegory, something else has slipped in . . . something which, under many names, lurks at the back of most romantic poetry. I mean the 'other world' not of religion, but of imagination; the land of longing, the Earthly Paradise, the garden east of the sun and west of the moon.[23]

Whatever we may think of Lewis's Christian commitments (when he wrote the above passage, his heyday as a popularizing Christian broadcaster and intellectual prize-fighter at Oxford was still in the future), there seems to be truth in his insight that only when a mythology ceases to be believed in as a living religious system does it become free to be recycled as imaginative 'Romance'. In the Romantic period it was a bold spirit, such as Blake, who was willing to create a new mythology out of Christian material (the questions of how 'new' and how 'Christian' Blake's mythology was, still remain open[24]). Generally it was other, and especially Greek, mythology that was used. Wordsworth may have *alluded* to *Paradise Lost* as an analogue to his 'high argument', but he would hardly have risked explicitly plundering its mythological resources; his position *vis-à-vis* orthodox Christianity was precarious enough already (*NS* 120; 497n74). It has fallen to Pullman to use *Paradise Lost* in a fully mythological way, that is, to quarry Milton's great Christian poem in an entirely disbelieving way. For Pullman the question of the truth or falsity of *Paradise Lost* simply does not arise; or if it does, it is only in relation to the way Pullman has interpreted *Paradise Lost* in a spirit that is essentially anti-orthodox or Gnostic.

The 'regions of strangeness and beauty' created by Lewis appeared not only in the Narnia books, but also in his 'Cosmic Trilogy' written in the years following the publication of *AOL*. A key influence on Lewis at the time he was writing his 'Cosmic Trilogy' was a figure that Pullman has also cited as a significant influence: David Lindsay, author of *A Voyage to Arcturus* (1920) (= *VTA*). Lindsay managed, according to Lewis, to fuse two separate strands of fantasy writing – the 'the Novalis, G. MacDonald sort' and the 'H.G. Wells, Jules Verne sort' – into a kind of science fiction that can carry a *spiritual* weight.[25] This combination of science fiction with the Romantic/Gnostic tradition clearly points forward to the *HDM* trilogy, although Pullman has distanced himself from Lindsay's very dark (philosophically 'pessimistic') vision.[26] Another writer admired by Pullman – and one with an even deeper admiration for Lindsay – is Harold Bloom, who claimed in his essay '*Clinamen*: Towards a Theory of Fantasy' to 'write a kind of Gnostic or Kabbalistic criticism even as I write a Gnostic narrative, or as I would now say, I am a fantastic or Romantic critic of fantasy' (*Clinamen* 19). Bloom admits to an almost unbounded – and certainly obsessive – fascination with *VTA* which he claims to have read 'literally hundreds of times' (*Clinamen* 11). Though he holds fire in relation to George MacDonald, Bloom is withering in his comments on the works of the 'Neochristian Inklings':

> [D]espite all their popularity [they] are quite peripheral . . . Inkling fantasy is soft stuff, because it pretends that it benefits from a benign transmission both of romance tradition and of Christian doctrine. Lindsay's savage masterpiece compels the reader to question both the sources of fantasy, *within the reader*, and the benignity of the handing-on of tradition. Fantasy is shown by Lindsay to be a mode in which freedom is won, if at all, by a fearful agon with tradition.
>
> (*Clinamen* 15)

Bloom is here foreshadowing Pullman's later, and perhaps harsher, criticisms of Lewis and Tolkien, whose popularity by the turn of the century Bloom could hardly have guessed at in 1981. In this essay Bloom argues that:

> Fantasy is a literary sub-genre, by which I do not mean to deprecate it, but rather to state this formula: what is good in fantasy *is* romance, just as anything good in verse *is* poetry. Historically, the eighteenth century, and subsequently Romanticism, replaced the heroic genre by romance, even as the concept of the Sublime replaced theology.
>
> (*Clinamen* 2)

Here Bloom is echoing Abrams's 'high argument' about the supplanting of orthodox Christianity as a believed religion by a new (yet also ancient and heretical) Romantic myth. Pullman's acknowledgement of Bloom as an influence underscores his own indebtedness to the Romantic/Gnostic tradition. In Bloom's *Omens of the Millenium*, presumably one of the sources for Metatron and the other angels in *HDM*, Bloom explicitly offers an apologia for his Gnosticism in an introduction whose title – 'Prelude: Self-Reliance or Mere Gnosticism' – seems to allude (in pastiche) back to Wordsworth's *Prelude* and (in parody) forward to Lewis's *Mere Christianity*.[27] Such a self-positioning might also apply *mutatis mutandis* to Pullman.

A further link back to Abrams's argument in *NS* is Bloom's claim that Lindsay's *VTA* is a direct descendant of Carlyle's *Sartor Resartus* (*Clinamen* 1–2). Bloom claims that: 'In *Sartor Resartus*, the post-Calvinistic Lindsay found most of the ingredients of his Gnostic myth, presented by Carlyle however with his characteristic German High Romantic irony and parodistic frenzy of despair' (*Clinamen* 7–8). According to Bloom, it was from *SR* that Lindsay derived the Norse name of 'Muspel', one of the planets in *VTA*:

> Carlyle writes of 'the Adam-Kadmon, or Primeval Element, here strangely brought into relation with the *Nifl* and *Muspel* (Darkness and Light) of the

antique North' [*SR* 29]. Carlyle's juxtaposition is of the Kabbalistic Primal Man with the Niflheim or mist-home, the Northern night, and with Muspelheim or bright-home, the Southern realm of light. Lindsay reverses here these mythological *topoi*, in one of his many instances of a kind of natural Gnosticism. It may be, though, that here Lindsay followed Novalis, who in chapter 9, "Klingsor's Tale", of *Heinrich von Ofterdingen* placed the realm of King Arcturus in a northern region of light.

(Clinamen 9)

Earlier in this essay Bloom had subordinated Hoffmann and Novalis to Hans Christian Andersen and Lewis Carroll as 'the most inventive of nineteenth century romance fantasists'; now he claims that 'Novalis and Shelley are the two greatest masters of High Romantic fantasy-quest, and Lindsay descended from both of them' (*Clinamen* 2; 9). Bloom goes on to quote a letter from Novalis to Friedrich Schlegel which describes his own 'Klingsor's *Märchen* ' in terms that Bloom thinks are 'precisely applicable' to *VTA*: 'The antipathy between Light and Shadow, the yearning for clear, hot, penetrating aether, the Unknown-Holy, the Vesta in Sophia, the mingling of the romantic of all ages, petrifying and petrified reason, Arcturus, Chance, the spirit of life, individual strokes as arabesques, – this is the way to look upon my Fairy Tale' (*Clinamen* 9–10).

We will be exploring works by Novalis and Hoffmann in more detail below. It is important to emphasize at this point the extent to which especially Novalis epitomizes the Romantic 'high argument'. Summing up his discussion of 'a recurrent pattern in German literature', Abrams sees Novalis as 'an author who conveniently brings together almost all the elements I have been detailing – the Scriptural story of Eden and the apocalypse; pagan myths and mystery cults; Plotinus, Hermetic literature, and Boehme; the philosophical and historical doctrines of Schiller, Fichte, Schelling, and contemporary *Naturphilosophie;* the exemplary novel of education, *Wilhelm Meister's Lehrjahre* – and fuses them into the subject-matter of all his major writings' (*SN* 245–6). In Novalis's version of the Romantic 'high argument':

> the process of representative human experience is a fall from self-unity and community into division, and from contentment into the longing for redemption, which consists of a recovered unity on a higher level of self-awareness. This process is represented in the plot-form of an educational journey in quest of a feminine other, whose mysterious attraction compels the protagonist to abandon his childhood sweetheart and the simple security of home and family (equated with infancy, the pagan golden age, and the Biblical paradise) to wander through alien lands on a way that rounds imperceptibly back to home and family, but with an accession of insight (the product of his experience en route) which

enables him to recognize in the girl he has left behind, the elusive female figure who has all along been the object of his longing and his quest.

(NS 246)

This pattern is incarnated both in Novalis's novels or rather *Märchenromane*[28] ('fairy tale novels' – or 'faërie romances', to adopt George MacDonald's term) and in the shorter *Märchen* they contain. The fairy-tale 'Hyacinth and Roseblossom' ['Hyazinth und Rosenblütchen'] recounted in Novalis's *The Novices of Sais* [*Die Lehrlinge zu Sais*] offers perhaps the archetypal version of the pattern, although it is also presented more elaborately in 'Klingsor's *Märchen*' in *HvO* (with the latter *itself* also offering a version of the classic pattern). Of 'Klingsor's *Märchen*', Abrams comments: 'it is as though a script writer had fused elements from *Jerusalem, Prometheus Unbound*, and *Endymion* into the scenario for a Walt Disney fantasia' *(NS 251)*. There also seems more than a hint here of Pullman's *HDM* – though of course in the latter it is a *girl* who sets off on a quest/educational journey.

How aware Pullman is of Novalis's work in particular is uncertain. He has certainly declared a general nostalgia for German Romanticism, though without specifying precisely which German Romantic texts have influenced him.[29] There are some playful suggestions at the end of *Count Karlstein or The Ride of the Demon Huntsman* (a work which is itself based on Carl Maria von Weber's archetypal Romantic opera *Der Freischütz*). *Count Karlstein* as well as *Clockwork* simply exudes German Romanticism in general and Hoffmann in particular. This German tradition was mediated into English literature above all by George MacDonald, who frequently quotes Novalis, taking as his motto the latter's famous phrase: 'Our life is no dream, but it should, and perhaps will, become one'. MacDonald prefaced his *Phantastes: A Faërie Romance* with a lengthy quotation from Novalis on the nature of the fairy tale. The only MacDonald text Pullman admits to having read is 'The Golden Key' (=*GK*), which is as much influenced by Novalis as anything MacDonald ever wrote. *GK* certainly embodies Abrams's 'recurrent pattern' of especially German Romanticism, though for Pullman's taste it is overly spiritualized and otherworldly.[30] At this point in his letter Pullman refers to Lindsay's *VTA*, which was in fact strongly influenced by MacDonald, especially by his late fantasy novel *Lilith*. However, as already indicated, Pullman has distanced himself from Lindsay's acute pessimism (or 'Black Platonism').[31]

One of the issues to be addressed below is the ambivalence of Pullman towards the Gnostic/Platonic tradition that underlies the Romantic 'high argument'. While the Romantic impulse itself may be to celebrate the triumph of life (even through death and despair) and concrete organic existence as opposed to abstraction, the Gnostic/Platonic tradition with which it so often flirts has always had a tendency to Manichaeism, that is, to a devaluation of physical existence. Pullman criticizes this tendency wherever he thinks he finds it, and especially in C.S. Lewis. However, the Romantic impulse is nothing if not *dialectical* and its dialectic takes the form of *narra-tive*. In this it is the direct heir to Augustinian Christian Platonism, as Abrams argues in *NS*. If Pullman is presenting a form of Romanticism's 'high argument', then perhaps he might reconsider the role of Platonism (dialec-tically understood) within that argument. After all, a key Romantic impulse was precisely *against* the reductive materialism of the eighteenth century, and Pullman has implicitly taken a stand against a form of cultural materi-alism prevalent in the late twentieth century. The materialism appropriate to the 'high argument' of Romanticism is surely *dialectical* materialism, which according to Abrams – using of course the early writings of Marx repudiated by Althusser[32] – is a version of the recurrent Romantic pattern of circuitous return (*NS* 313–6).

If this prelude has, like other preludes, become rather long, it is because in its attempt to get a preliminary overview of the ground to be traversed and the issues to be addressed, it has been forced by the grandeur of Pullman's lit-erary ambitions to encounter some giants, including Wordsworth, Milton, Blake, Novalis, Carlyle and Wagner. I have discussed elsewhere the question of Pullman and 'the anxiety of influence'.[33] Perhaps, like James Joyce, Pullman wanted to write something that would keep the professors busy for a long time. Certainly he has galvanized (to use a good Romantic metaphor) a giant of a tradition, as Novalis describes in 'Klingsor's Fairy Tale':

They went round the earth until they came to the old giant, down whose shoulders they climbed. He appeared lamed by a stroke and could not move a limb . . . Fable [Poetry] touched his eyes and emptied her little jug [of Sophia-Wisdom's water] on his forehead. As the water flowed over his eye into his mouth and down over him into the basin, a flash of life quiv-ered in all his muscles. He opened his eyes and rose up in vigour . . .

'Are you here again, sweet child?' the old giant said; 'I have been dreaming and dreaming of you. I always thought you would appear before the earth and my eyes got too heavy for me. I suppose I have slept a long time.'[34]

1
German Roots and Mangel-wurzels[1]

Fairy-tales and fantasy literature were not invented by the German Romantics, but they are indelibly associated with them. While there are other collections of what came to be called fairy-tales – *contes de fées* was originally, and significantly, a French term[2] – it is the Grimm Brothers' collection of folktales, *Children's and Household Tales* [*Kinder- und Hausmärchen*] (1812–14), that has become the classic and probably most influential collection of 'fairy-tales'. The Grimms did a fair bit of rewriting of the oral 'folk-tales' that they collected;[3] indeed some of these were not originally oral at all, but were originally French literary fairy-tales that had passed into oral tradition.[4] However, it was German Romantic writers such as Tieck, Novalis, Eichendorff, Brentano, Fouqué and E.T.A. Hoffmann, who developed the so-called *Kunstmärchen* or invented literary fairy-tale in this period (1796–1830). Again, the idea of inventing fairy-tales was not itself new – the French, for example, had been inventing fairy-tales in the century before the Grimms and the Italians in the preceding centuries.[5] What was new was the set of ideas and values – the ideology[6] – that inspired German Romantic writers to take up folk material and motifs and refashion them into a literary creation that was *fairy-tale-like* [*märchenhaft*], though not itself originally belonging to folk tradition.[7]

German Romanticism is a notoriously complex phenomenon. It had a more complicated development than other Romanticisms and there are up to three distinct stages of Romanticism in Germany. Its complexity is partly due to the fact that it could be said – with some measure of agreement – that German writers and intellectuals invented the concept of 'Romanticism' as a theorized literary movement. As Raymond Immerwahr puts it:

> Although the adjective [*romantisch*] itself was of English origin and the steadily increasing prestige of 'romantic' values and attitudes was a general European phenomenon, the attempt to make them the basis of a programmatic literary and cultural movement originated in Germany.[8]

As was suggested in the Prelude above, the philosophical roots of Romanticism go back a long way, but certainly late eighteenth- and early nineteenth-century German Idealist philosophy played a crucial role in shaping the Romantic world-view. Wordsworth may have claimed to be innocent of German metaphysics,[9] but Coleridge was certainly not. Passages of his *Biographia Literaria* are notoriously plagiarized from German sources.[10] What characterizes German Romanticism perhaps above all is an emphasis on the *imagination* and on *creativity*. This emphasis derives in large measure from the philosophy of Immanuel Kant, who argued in his *Critique of Pure Reason* (1781) that, to put it very crudely, the human mind is not merely the passive recipient of information coming into it from the outside. On the contrary, argued Kant, the human mind actively *shapes* what it perceives. Every perception is always already *interpreted* within the structures of consciousness. Kant is probably the most influential philosopher in modern western thought in the sense that wherever there is talk of the *constructedness* of human knowledge and experience, there is present some residual influence of Kant's concept of philosophical *Idealism*: that is, the idea that the mind (or language itself, as later 'linguistic idealists' such as Wittgenstein and perhaps Derrida would say) plays a crucial role in creating our experience of 'reality'.

This restriction of human knowledge to the capacity of our receiving equipment – that is, to the structures of human consciousness – may be seen negatively, as some kind of loss of the real, whether material or spiritual. However, from early on, followers of Kant saw his project in more positive terms as an affirmation of the human mind in its creative role in shaping and even constructing experience. The particular part or faculty of the mind that controls this shaping, constructing process is the *Imagination* [*Einbildungskraft*]. The idea of the 'primary' or transcendental imagination is central to Romantic thought. Coleridge famously contrasts it in his *Biographia Literaria* with 'fancy', which is merely imitative, whilst the creative imagination is literally divine in origin, scope and power. Followers of Kant took up this implication of his thought and developed it in ways that went far beyond Kant himself. They saw the presence of the divine shaping Imagination in the human spirit (Coleridge's 'repetition in the finite mind of the eternal act of creation in the infinite I AM'[11]) as suggesting that humanity too was in some sense divine. While Kant himself had modestly wanted to limit religion to the bounds of reason alone, his more adventurous followers such as Fichte, Schelling and Hegel developed forms of pantheism that affirmed the ultimate identity of the human spirit with the divine Spirit.

What is relevant to the present study is the fact that these post-Kantian Idealist philosophers moved in the same circles as – and often actually *were* – creative writers in the early German Romantic school. Flourishing in the late 1790s and early 1800s, what is technically called Early German Romanticism (*Frühromantik*) not only included theoreticians such as

Friedrich Schlegel, but also creative writers such as Tieck and Novalis. The latter was also in his very distinctive way a philosopher, just as Friedrich Schlegel wrote novels. German Romantics were trying to overcome the dichotomy between literature and philosophy, and develop a 'progressive universal poetry [*Universalpoesie*]'[12] produced by a communal process of 'Symphilosophy' [*Symphilosophie*], of which the short-lived journal the *Athenaeum* (1798–1800) was the principal organ. The next stage of German Romanticism, called High Romanticism (*Hochromantik*), spanned the first two decades of the nineteenth century and includes Friedrich de la Motte Fouqué and E.T.A. Hoffmann. There is a famous essay by Heine[13] that compares the different styles of Romanticism evident in Novalis and Hoffmann. For Heine, Novalis represents, in summary, the kind of early German Romanticism that is otherworldly and 'yearning for the blue yonder', symbolized by *Heinrich von Ofterdingen*'s 'Blue Flower'. This kind of utopian Romanticism is characterised by *longing [Sehnsucht]* for the Ideal contained in some quasi-Platonic ideal realm that is our true home; what Novalis had in mind when he said: 'All fairy-tales are only dreams of that familiar world of home which is everywhere and nowhere',[14] and to which we are always going home ('Where are we going?' 'Home, always home [*immer nach Hause*]' (*HvO* 159). Although Hoffmann belongs to the High Romantic period, he was aware of 'the unspeakable bliss of infinite yearning' (*GPOT* 82) that characterizes the Early Romantic movement. This idea is also evident in MacDonald's *GK* where Mossy and Tangle spend their whole lives trying reach the 'country whence the shadows come'.[15] The present world is only a 'vale of Soul-making', in Keats's phrase,[16] from which we seek liberation through finding our true home in the other world. However, as Heine pointed out, there is in the later Romanticism of Hoffmann much more of an awareness of the pull of *this* world, and of a real *struggle* between the competing demands of this world and some other world.

This second stage of German Romanticism is also the period in which Jakob and Wilhelm Grimm produced their famous collection of 'fairy-tales'. Originally the Grimms were collecting folk material for a collection of folk-tales planned by another leading German Romantic, Clemens Brentano, as a sequel to his collection of folk songs and ballads, co-edited with Achim von Arnim, entitled *The Boy's Magic Horn* [*Des Knaben Wunderhorn*] (1805–8). However, when Brentano's folk-tale project went off the boil, the Grimms decided to publish their material themselves as *Children's and Household Tales*. Like other Romanticisms, German Romanticism had a strong interest in folk material such as ballads and folk-tales. This connects with an emphasis on the supposedly *natural* as opposed to what were perceived as the pernicious constraints of civilization. Romanticism began after all in the century of Jean-Jacques Rousseau and the cult of the noble savage, though it immediately has to be said that for German Romanticism – that most dialectical of literary movements – there was strong sense of the centrality of *art*. Novalis famously said that 'to become a human being is an art';[17] what epitomizes German Romanticism is precisely the *Kunstmärchen* [*Kunst* = art]. The idea of self-creation is also reflected in the emphasis on the *distinctiveness* both of the individual and of the nation or people [*Volk*]. This contrasts with the Enlightenment's emphasis on *Universal* Reason as the guardian of moderation and civilized values. During the Enlightenment the claim to be special, whether made of a religious revelation or a privileged caste of priests or aristocrats, was liable to be thought of as superstitious, reactionary and extreme. By contrast, the Romantics prized what was strange, individual, different and even excessive. They also flirted with religion and mysticism (there is much emphasis on Eastern ideas, which were beginning to become more widely known in the West at this time).

Romanticism was drawn to what was dark and ambiguous, as opposed to the Enlightenment ideals of rational clarity and universality; to the Gothic, as opposed to the Neo-Classical, in literary as well as architectural terms. In contrast to the Enlightenment's preference for what was clear as day, Novalis composed a set of 'Hymns to the Night' [*Hymnen an die Nacht*], translated by George MacDonald (his translation of their companion piece, the unorthodox *Spiritual Canticles* [*Geistliche Lieder*], was partly responsible for his ejection from his pastorate at Arundel). Again, in contrast to the great advances made in the natural sciences by the eighteenth century, one Romantic thinker and scientist, G.H. Schubert, wrote a book on aspects of the 'dark side' (*Nachtseite*) of science, *Ansichten von der Nachtseite der Naturwissenschaft* (1808),[18] and explored the unconscious in a way that remarkably anticipates Freud.[19] Schubert's work on the *Nachtseite* of science is one of the main sources for the mythology in Hoffmann's *The Golden Pot* (=*GP*) and *Princess Brambilla*. The Romantics in general were very interested in the unconscious and dreams; for Schubert, especially in his book *The Symbolism of Dreams* [*Die Symbolik des Traumes*] (1814), dreams were the royal road to the unconscious, which in turn led, he believed, to an awareness of the presence of God in nature.

The Romantic awareness of a supernatural power in nature was ambivalent, however. If nature could be positively overwhelming and might occasion a sense of rapture, it could also be terrifying and might reduce an individual to madness. This daemonic and disruptive side of nature can been seen in Fouqué's *Undine* (1811), while Tieck's *Eckbert the Fair* [*Der blonde Eckbert*] (1797) is a deeply unsettling study of madness, as is his *The Rune Mountain* [*Der Runenberg*] (1802), written just before Tieck himself suffered some kind of mental breakdown. The fickleness of nature and its domination by supernatural powers is also a theme of Tieck's later *The Elves* [*Die Elfen*] (1811), translated by Thomas Carlyle.[20] The literary work of Hoffmann also explores madness, not only in the essentially light-hearted manner of *GP*, but also in a very disturbing way in *The Sandman* (1816). The latter was of course the subject of Freud's famous (and famously flawed) reading in his essay 'The Uncanny'.

Undine is, according to Carol Tully, 'in many ways the ultimate *Kunstmärchen'*.[21] Certainly MacDonald claimed in his essay 'The Fantastic Imagination' that: 'of all the fairy tales I know, I think *Undine* the most beautiful' (*CFT* 5) and offered it as an epitome of the genre. As a *Kunstmärchen* or literary fairy tale it is certainly much longer and more complex than the average folk tale. It contains typical Romantic elements such as an element of the daemonic *Nachtseite* or uncanny dark side of Nature, especially in the many forms of Undine's shape-shifting uncle Kühleborn. Kühleborn would be the archetypal wicked uncle (like Uncle Andrew in Lewis's *The Magician's Nephew*) if he were human, though of course he isn't. There is also a strong flavour of the *medievalism* that was an essential ingredient of Romanticism in general, though it is perhaps particularly characteristic of German Romanticism. In this, as in most respects, *HvO* epitomizes German Romanticism, though well-known works by Tieck, Novalis, Eichendorff, Brentano, Fouqué and Hoffmann are set in a quasi-medieval world, or in an idealized sixteenth century Germany based on the revival of interest in Dürer's art in the Romantic period – a trend culminating in Wagner's *Die Meistersinger von Nürnberg*. The medievalism which characterizes the fantasy tradition explored in this book (knights, dragons, castles, damsels in distress, witches and wizards) comes not only from indigenous British traditions such as Malory's *Le Morte d'Arthur* and Spenser's *The Faerie Queene,* but also from the German fairy-tales that so impressed the Victorian writers of fantasy and fairy-tale.

Like a Grimms' fairy-tale or Tieck's *Eckbert the Fair, Undine* is contained within its own quasi-medieval fairy-tale world – as would also be the case with many later fairy-tale fantasies, from works by Ruskin and MacDonald through to (with reservations discussed below) Tolkien. In contrast to this 'one world' fairy-tale, there is in Hoffmann's *GP* a dramatic tension *between* two (or more) worlds, which is perhaps more characteristic of the fantasy tradition explored in this book, for example in *The Chronicles of Narnia* (=*CN*), *HDM* and to some extent the Harry Potter series.[22] Indeed with *GP* we can perhaps see the beginnings of the idea of 'Muggles' with the typical Romantic contempt for the bourgeois 'Philistines', a term actually coined by German students in the Romantic period. The idea of a *tension*, and indeed a kind of *negotiation*, between the pull of two worlds is a typical theme of German Romanticism, particularly of the second phase. Earlier German Romanticism often seemed only hostile to the everyday world, seeking either magically to transform it or merely to escape from it.

Typical of early German Romanticism is Novalis, who claimed, in MacDonald's favourite quotation, that '[o]ur life is no dream; but it ought to become one, and perhaps will'.[23] Novalis called his revolutionary project of transforming the world through poetry 'Magic Idealism', and sought, like other German Romantics, to create a new mythology that would express, and perhaps initiate, a social and even a cosmic revolution: a Golden Age. In the Prelude above, I suggested that whatever direct knowledge of Novalis's writing

Pullman may or may not have,[24] there seem to be parallels between the two writers, if only in the sense that Pullman seems bent on the creation of a new, essentially Romantic, mythology of the kind that Novalis sought to achieve in his writings. Perhaps the point at which the writings of Novalis and Pullman most resemble each other is in the (veiled) expression of the sexual charge that is generated by the coming of the Golden Age, or at least by the reversal of a process of catastrophic decline. At the end of *AS* the halting and subsequent reversal of the loss of Dust coincides with the beginnings of Will and Lyra's carnal knowledge of each other. There is evidently an erotic aspect to the moment when they mutually (and presumably metonymically) stroke their daemons' fur. In the fairy-tale 'Hyacinth and Rosebud' ['*Hyazinth und Rosenblütchen*'], recounted in Novalis's philosophical novel *The Novices of Sais* [*Die Lehrlinge zu Sais*] (1802), the protagonist Hyacinth embarks on a long quest for the goddess Isis, who in the end, at the moment of unveiling, turns out to be Rosebud, his childhood sweetheart:

> [O]nly a dream could lead him into the holiest of regions. The strange dream led him through endless chambers full of curious things floating on harmonious sounds and with changing chords. Everything seemed to [Hyacinth] so familiar and yet in such splendour as he had never seen. Then the last trace of earth disappeared, as if dissolved in air, and he stood before the heavenly maiden; he lifted the light shimmering veil, and Rosebud sank into his arms. A distant music surrounded the mystery of the lovers' reunion, the outpourings of yearning, and excluded all that was foreign from this rapturous place.[25]

The final words of 'Hyacinth and Rosebud' speak of 'those days' and evidently refer to a kind of Golden Age. Similarly, the conclusion to the so-called Atlantis *Märchen* in *HvO* presents the resolution of a love problem as the inauguration of a Golden Age: ' . . . that evening became a holy eve for the whole country whose life thereafter was only one long beautiful festival' (though the Golden Age of Atlantis is not destined to last, at least not 'in the sight of men') (*HvO* 52). The conclusion of 'Klingsor's *Märchen*' in *HvO* is Novalis's boldest expression of the arrival of the Golden Age as an (orientalized) erotic event:

> In the meantime the throne [of Arcturus and Sophie] had imperceptibly changed into a magnificent bridal bed, over whose canopy the Phoenix hovered with little Fable. The back of the bed was supported by three caryatids of dark porphyry, and the front rested on a sphinx of basalt. The king embraced his blushing beloved, and the people followed the example of the king and caressed one another. One heard nothing but words of endearment and a whisper of kisses.

> (*HvO* 148)

Like all true Romantic heroes, Novalis died young. The second wave of German Romantics were more aware of the need to decide between this dull, unsatisfactory world and some other, more utopian dream world. The narrator at the end of *GP* laments: 'Happy Anselmus, who has cast off the burden of daily life! . . . now you are living in joy and bliss on your estate in Atlantis! But as for poor me . . . I shall . . . return to my garret; the petty cares of poverty-stricken life will absorb my thoughts . . . ' (*GPOT* 83). However, the narrator is admonished by Archivist Lindhorst, who is also, or 'really' (that is the question[26]), a salamander or elemental spirit; he is reminded by Lindhorst that Atlantis is 'the poetic property of the mind'. Indeed, he asks, 'is Anselmus's happiness anything other than life in poetry, where the holy harmony of all things is revealed as the deepest secret of nature?' (*GPOT* 83). The suggestion of a resolution of the tension between two worlds into a this-worldly experience, transfigured but not abolished by the poetic imagination, is typical of second wave German Romanticism, and gestures ultimately towards the culture of *Biedermeier*, or middle-class conventionality, typical of nineteenth century Germany and comparable in some respects with Victorian 'respectability'. The latter is mocked by Rowling in its modern incarnation in the Dursleys, whose obsession with respectability occludes the family history of magic, though the final scene of *Deathly Hallows* shows Harry Potter himself, now a family man, looking very *Biedermeier* (his magical scar hasn't troubled him for 19 years). *Biedermeier* is a compromise-formation that distances itself from the utopian dreams of early Romanticism as leading only to madness or revolution. An unkind interpretation would call this 'selling out'. Similar tendencies have been seen in Wordsworth and Coleridge.

However, Hoffmann was far from offering in his writings any comfortable resolution of the tensions between the two worlds – that of Philistine ordinariness and that of utopian fantasy. On the contrary, he repeatedly dramatized precisely this tension, a tension that characterized his own life and that of many other middle-class artists and intellectuals in this period in Germany.[27] It is significant that at the end of *GP* the narrator explicitly appears as a writer living in a garret; Hoffmann's framing devices are often sophisticated and readers neglect them at their peril – as in the case of Freud's notoriously reductive reading of *The Sandman*.[28] Anselmus's problem is to decide between – on the one hand – a safe career in the bourgeois world of minor officials such as Sub-Rector Paulmann and Registrar (later Counsellor) Heerbrand, and marriage to the former's daughter Veronica; or – on the other hand – living in bliss in Atlantis with Serpentina, the daughter of Achivist (Salamander) Lindhorst. But Anselmus's problem is transferred (or does the transference actually work the other way?) to the narrator, who, feeling 'pierced and lacerated by . . . anguish', complains that 'the petty cares of my poverty-stricken life will absorb my thoughts, and my gaze is obscured by a thousand ills as though by a black mist, so that I doubt if I shall ever behold the lily' (which, symbolizing 'the knowledge of the holy harmony of all living things', grants 'utmost happiness for evermore') (*GPOT* 83). As Zipes has pointed out, Hoffmann himself was 'experiencing personal difficulties regarding what professional career he should pursue (musician, writer or lawyer?) and at a time when early capitalist market conditions in publishing and the absence of copyright made the process of writing for unknown audiences all the more alienating.'[29] If Anselmus goes out of his mind in the most blissful of ways (that is, into Atlantis), then the narrator of *GP*, who is 'pierced and lacerated by . . . anguish', fears going out of his mind in a considerably less happy way, ('my tormenting dissatisfaction made me ill') (*GPOT* 79). In *The Sandman* 'the tormented, self-divided Nathanael' goes out of his mind in the most terrifying way imaginable.

On another level, however, the main protagonist of *GP*, that 'Modern Fairy-Tale', is not so much Anselmus (or even the narrator) as the salamander living in early nineteenth century Dresden under the name of Archivist Lindhorst. The salamander is one of the elemental spirits about whom, in Fouqué's *Undine*, the eponymous nymph tells her new husband, the knight Huldbrand:

> You should know, my love, that there are living creatures among the elements that look quite like mortals but are seldom seen by them. Wondrous salamanders glitter and play in the flames, withered bad-tempered gnomes live deep in the earth; treefolk who belong to the air inhabit the forests; a multitude of water spirits reside in the lakes and rivers and streams.[30]

Hoffmann knew *Undine*, published in 1811, not least because he later created an opera based on it, which was successfully produced in 1816. There is even an echo of the plot of *Undine* in *GP*, insofar as the story in *Undine* hinges on the fact that elemental spirits such as Undine have no immortal soul and can only acquire one by marrying a mortal; similarly, the salamander in *GP* can only be restored to his original glory by marrying off his three serpent daughters to mortal men, of whom Anselmus is the first. All of this material is also found in *Le Comte de Gabalis* (1670) by the Abbé de Montfaucon de Villars, which is referred to in passing by 'Salamander Lindhorst' in his letter to the narrator of Anselmus's adventures; Lindhorst claims that according to Gabalis 'elemental spirits are by no means to be trusted' (*GPOT* 80). Lindhorst's claim is actually a simplification of *Le Comte de Gabalis* where there is much discussion of the advantages and disadvantages to both sides in unions between humans and elemental spirits. For example, some gnomes reckon that having an immortal soul is too big a risk given that it can be condemned to eternal punishment in Hell, of which they have some knowledge due to its underground proximity; non-existence is better than Hell, they argue, a viewpoint that is of course roundly condemned in *Le Comte de Gabalis*.

Hoffmann's main source for the myth in *GP* is, according to Ritchie Robertson, G.H. Schubert's book on the 'dark side' of science, *Ansichten von der Nachtseite der Naturwissenschaft* (1808) (*GPOT* xiiin11). Whatever its precise origins, the myth as it appears in Hoffmann's fairy-tale it is very much in the same genre as the other great fairy-tale myths of the Romantic period in Germany – Goethe's *Märchen* and Novalis's 'Klingsor's *Märchen*' in *HvO*. Though he never mentions Abrams's *NS*, Robertson's comment in his Introduction very much aligns Hoffmann's myth with Abrams's summation of the 'recurrent pattern' in Romantic thought: 'Thus the myth is dialectical. Instead of moving in a circle from original unity to its restoration, it moves in a spiral from original unity to the recreation of that unity on a higher plane, enhanced by consciousness' (*GPOT* xiv). The myth first appears in the third chapter (or 'Vigil', as Hoffmann calls them), under the ironic subtitle 'News of Archivist Lindhorst's family'. It begins with the primeval waters, and the first appearance of life and particularly of 'a black hill which rose and sank as does a man's breast when it heaves with ardent yearning'. When touched by the pure ray of the sun, the black hill in 'an excess of delight gave birth to a splendid fiery lily' (*GPOT* 15). Enter the youth Phosphorus, for whom the lily is overcome by 'passionate yearning love'. Phosphorus warns the lily that, should their love be consummated, 'the yearning that now suffuses you will be split into countless rays and will torture you, for the mind will give birth to the senses, and the supreme joy kindled by the spark that I now cast into you is the agonizing despair in which you will perish, to grow anew in an alien guise. This spark is *thought!*' (*GPOT* 15–16). This passage not only harks back to ancient Gnostic myths of the alienation of consciousness, but also perhaps points forward to Pullman's myth of 'Dust' as matter becoming self-conscious. At the kiss of Phosphorus the lily suffers a kind of *Liebestod*, or 'love-death', bursting into flames from which emerges 'an alien being which swiftly escaped . . . and roamed through infinite space' (*GPOT* 16). A black dragon appears and manages to capture the being that had sprung from the lily; this being becomes the lily once more, but 'thought remained to lacerate her, and her love for the youth Phosphorus was an agony which breathed poisonous vapours upon [her fellow] flowers . . . and made them wither and die.' Phosphorus then dons shining armour, fights and defeats the dragon with the help of the flowers who flutter round it like brightly coloured birds. The lily is freed and united with Phosphorus in 'the ardent passion of heavenly love' to general rejoicing in which the flowers, birds and 'even the lofty granite rocks' join in (*GPOT* 16). The myth that Lindhorst recounts is accused by the other characters of being 'a lot of Oriental bombast', to which Lindhorst replies that 'it is very far from absurd or even allegorical, but literally true'; the fiery lily is his 'great-great-great-great-grandmother' (prefiguring Princess Irene's 'great-great-grandmother' in MacDonald's *Curdie* books) (*GPOT* 17). Lindhorst continues with some further news about his brother who 'went to the bad and joined the dragons' and now lives in grove of cypresses near Tunis, guarding a mystical carbuncle from the attentions of an evil necromancer. The company greets this latest news about Lindhorst's family with laughter, but Anselmus has an uncanny feeling about it and the 'mysterious penetrating quality' of Lindhorst's 'strangely metallic-sounding voice' shakes him to the core (*GPOT* 17–18).

The continuation of the myth is taken up in the eighth Vigil by Lindhorst's daughter Serpentina, who mysteriously appears to Anselmus (evidently, like Harry Potter, a 'Parseltongue'), while he is copying a manuscript whose unfamiliar characters tell – as he realizes 'in an inner intuition' – 'Of the Marriage of the Salamander and the Green Snake' (*GPOT* 52). The land ruled by Phosphorus, we now learn, was Atlantis. Phosphorus was 'the mighty prince of spirits' and the elemental spirits (sylphs, nymphs, gnomes and salamanders) were his servants. Serpentina's father, the salamander we know as Lindhorst, was Phosphorus's favourite. He fell in love with a green snake, the daughter of a lily, and carried her off to Phosphorus's castle, imploring the latter to marry them. But Phosphorus refuses, telling the salamander that the lily was his former beloved, and only the victory of Phosphorus over the black dragon now bound in chains by the earth-spirits, has kept the spark that Phosphorus deposited in the lily from destroying her. If the salamander were to embrace the green snake, Phosphorus warns him, his heat will burn her up and a new being will appear which will immediately escape (this is clearly a repetition of the earlier part of the myth). However, like Phosphorus before him, the salamander cannot resist kissing the green snake; as prophesied, it crumbles to ashes, and out of them a winged creature flies away. At this the salamander goes mad with grief and lays waste the garden in his wild fury. As a punishment, the prince of the spirits banishes the salamander – his light now extinguished – to the realm of the earth-spirits. But after the intercession of the gardener (an earth-spirit), the prince of spirits declares:

> In the unhappy time when the degenerate race of men will no longer understand the language of nature, when the elemental spirits, each confined in his own region, will speak to men only in faint and distant sounds, when man will be estranged from the harmonious circle and only an infinite yearning will bring him obscure tidings of the wondrous realm that he once inhabited, while faith and love dwelt in his heart – in that unhappy time the salamander's fiery substance will catch light anew, but he will rise only to their wretched life and endure its privations. But not only will he retain the memory of his primal state; he will again live in holy harmony with all of nature, he will understand its marvels, and the power of his brothers will once more be at his command. In a lily bush he will again find the green snake, and his marriage to her will bring forth three daughters.

(*GPOT* 55)

If, however, each of the green snakes can attract the love of youth with 'child-like poetic spirit' who can shake off 'the burden of common cares' and develop, along with his love for the snake, 'a living and ardent faith in the wonders of nature, and in his own existence amid these wonders', then finally the salamander may 'cast off his weary burden and join his brothers' (*GPOT* 56).

Anselmus is of course precisely such a youth with 'child-like poetic spirit', who is indeed 'mocked by the rabble because of the lofty simplicity of [his] behaviour and because [he] lack[s] what people call worldly manners' (*GPOT* 56). He is the archetypal Romantic 'outsider' and bears a family resemblance to other specially chosen, but rather geek-ish heroes down to Bastian in Michael Ende's *Neverending Story* and even perhaps Harry Potter (or the youthful Severus Snape). The fact that Anselmus has been chosen finally to attain Serpentina (and Atlantis) does not mean, however, that he will be spared a long and testing struggle to achieve this lofty destiny. The testing of Anselmus is partly based on that of Tamino in *The Magic Flute* by Wolfgang Amadeus Mozart, whose middle name Hoffmann appropriated as a mark of his admiration for the composer. *GP* has many similarities to Mozart's fairy-tale opera that Hoffmann knew well from his work as an orchestra conductor. Lindhorst resembles the wise old man Sarastro, while the main antagonist in both works is an evil female figure, the Queen of the Night in *The Magic Flute*. In *GP* the evil female is the old apple-woman with whom Ansemus collides in the first sentence of the story and who pursues him for the rest of the narrative.

The old woman owes her malign existence to the fact that the black dragon, defeated by Phosphorus in the first part of the myth, managed to escape after a hideous battle with the salamanders and earth-spirits. Although the dragon was recaptured and is once more heaving and groaning in chains, black feathers from his wings fell to earth during the struggle and brought about the birth of malign spirits. The union between one particular feather and a mangel-wurzel gave birth to the evil old woman. She derives much of her power from the captive black dragon (in a sense her grandfather); she works her black magic ceaselessly to oppose the salamander, and in particular, to capture the eponymous golden pot. Anselmus is warned by Serpentina to beware of the old apple-woman who is his foe, because his 'innocent child-like spirit has already foiled many of her evil spells' (*GPOT* 57). The old woman finally succeeds in grabbing the magic pot, but Lindhorst foils her escape – she and her cat are brutally destroyed by the salamander and his screech owl:

> Thick smoke was rising from the spot where the old woman had been lying under [Lindhorst's] dressing gown. Her howling, her terrible piercing yells of lamentation, were dying away in the distance. The clouds of smoke evaporated, along with their penetrating stench. The Archivist raised the dressing gown, and beneath it lay a nasty mangel-wurzel.
>
> (*GPOT* 72)

The myth is continued when Lindhorst the salamander contacts the narrator, who is in despair at his inability to complete the story of Anselmus. Anselmus has now of course been drawn into the salamander's story and is himself part of the myth. Lindhorst invites the narrator to the very scene of writing, the purple desk where Anselmus had worked. Here the salamander produces a goblet of fire, or at least of flaming arrack, into which he jumps, to the narrator's astonishment. The latter, however, is undeterred; he writes: 'I blew the flames gently aside and took a sip of the drink. It was delicious!' (*GPOT* 81). Without more ado, the final part of the myth suddenly appears on *our* page. There is nothing said in the text about whether the narrator copied a manuscript, wrote to the salamander's dictation, or indeed found the text magically appearing as he wrote (as had once happened to Anselmus). The act of writing is in this case simply invisible. This is intriguing not least because in other cases, Hoffmann's (or at least the narrator's) act of writing has been *made* invisible – that is, it has been occluded – by *readers*, most notably by Freud in his essay on 'The Uncanny' which simply ignores the frame of *The Sandman*. The myth produced by this invisible act of writing depicts Anselmus as leading an idyllic life in Atlantis. Emerging from a magnificent temple, Serpentina appears, bearing the golden pot: the gift of the earth-spirit who was Phosphorus's gardener. The golden pot now contains, as prophesied, a magnificent lily. At this point, we are told:

> Anselmus raises his head, as though transfigured by radiant light. Is it his gaze, his words, his song? It rings out clearly: 'Serpentina! Faith in you, love for you has disclosed to me the innermost being of nature! You brought me the lily which sprang from the gold, from the primal force of the earth, even before Phosphorus awakened thought. The lily is the knowledge of the holy harmony of all living things, and in this knowledge I shall live in the utmost happiness for evermore. Yes, I am a supremely happy man who has been granted supreme knowledge.'
>
> (*GPOT* 82–3)

If Anselmus has reached the pinnacle of knowledge and happiness for which philosophers (Gnostic, Hermetic and Romantic) had all been searching, it is little wonder that when the narrator comes down from his trip to Atlantis, he feels 'pierced and lacerated by sudden anguish'. As was noted above, this split between a yearned-for supreme happiness and an actual wretched reality, seems to have been particularly acute in Germany in the years following the French Revolution, though there is also something universal in this particular expression of what used to be called 'the human condition'. The consolation offered to the narrator by the Salamander Lindhorst – 'Weren't you in Atlantis yourself a moment ago, and haven't you at least got a pretty farm there, as the poetic property of your mind?' (*GPOT* 83) – seems at best ambiguous. It looks very like a case of Romantic Irony.

Hoffmann also embodied myths in others of his works than *GP*, for example in *Princess Brambilla* (1820) and *Master Flea* (1822). *Princess Brambilla* is styled by Hoffmann as 'A Capriccio after Jacques Callot'. He elsewhere defined 'the manner of Callot' as that of: 'a poet or writer [i.e. Hoffmann] to whom the figures of ordinary life appear in his inward romantic spiritual realm, and who portrays them in the light that there plays around them as though strange and curious finery'(*GPOT* xxii–xxiii). This capacity to see and represent simultaneously the ordinary external world and a vividly imagined magical inner world is also called the Serapiontic principle by Hoffmann. This was named after St. Serapion on whose feast-day the so-called 'Serapion Brethren' was founded: an informal circle of writers in Berlin to which Hoffmann belonged. In Hoffmann's collection of stories *The Serapion Brethren* there is an account of a hermit in a wood near Bamberg, who believed he was Serapion, was living in the Egyptian desert and that the towers of Bamberg were actually those of Alexandria. The hermit's failure, according to the Brethren, was not so much his powerfully vivid imagination, as the fact that he did not recognize that there is *also* a real external world in tension with the imagined (*GPOT* ix–x). An inextricable mixture of dream and reality pervades *Princess Brambilla* to such an extent that it is never entirely clear whether the protagonist is actually Giglio Fava – a struggling actor in eighteenth-century Rome – or Prince Cornelio Chiapperi, or indeed King Ophioch of Urdar (Giglio's lover similarly fluctuates between being the dressmaker Giacinta Soardi, Princess Brambilla and Queen Liris of Urdar). Just as the plot of *GP* alternates between contemporary Dresden and the myth of the salamander, so the plot of *Princess Brambilla* weaves in a complex series of arabesques between theatrical intrigues in eighteenth-century Rome and the myth of King Opioch and Queen Liris of Urdar (the names are predictably derived from G.H. Schubert).

There is, if anything, an even more complicated series of permutations of identity in *Master Flea: A fairy-tale in seven adventures of two friends*. The eccentric hero Peregrinus Tyss is also identified with King Sekakis of Famagusta whose daughter Gamaheh is murdered by the Leech Prince and reincarnated in the beautiful Dörtje Elwerdink and later as a tulip. The reader is, moreover, given to believe that she is also somehow identified with Peregrinus's old servant Aline. All of this is held together in a bizarrely complicated plot that includes the exploits of the eponymous Master Flea. There is a great deal going on in this tale, including a politically subversive satirical interlude (the Knarrpanti episode) that was still the subject of legal proceedings when Hoffmann died in 1822. The myth running through the tale is also heavily influenced by Novalis's *Novices of Sais* and echoes the polemic in that tale about the dangers of a reductive and mechanistic approach to scientific research. The myth concludes with a paradisiacal vision similar to the vision of Atlantis at the conclusion of *GP*.

Typically, then, the protagonists in Hoffmann's fairy stories are, or are fantasized to be, participants in a much grander narrative or myth. Freud's work on 'Family Romance' is arguably relevant here,[31] as well as perhaps his work on the hysterical fantasies of Schreber. Myths in Hoffmann have a highly ambiguous and problematic relation to 'reality'; it is quite arguable that Anselmus or Giglio Fava or Peregrinus Tyss (in *GP, Princess Brambilla* and *Master Flea* respectively) are simply mad. Certainly this seems a strong likelihood in the case of Nathanael in *The Sandman*. Maria Tatar has argued convincingly that Hoffmann was familiar with, and used, the contemporary discourse of madness.[32] Analogously, it could be argued that Harry Potter's adventures are the fantasies of a marginalized and clinically depressed teenage misfit (and/or single parent?). Psychoanalytical readings of the fantasy tradition really began with Freud's analysis of works by Hoffmann, especially *The Sandman*, though as Calhoon has suggested, the traffic between Freud and Romanticism is by no means one way: Freud's work only makes sense, he suggests, within the discourse that Romanticism helped to constitute.[33] The fantasy writings of MacDonald, Lewis Carroll, C.S. Lewis and J.R.R Tolkien are eminently susceptible to psychoanalytical readings, as arguably are those of J.K. Rowling and Pullman.

The fantasy tradition stretching back to Romanticism seems to invite not only psychoanalytical, but also political readings. In *NS*, Abrams argues that Marx, like Freud, is a product of German Romanticism; he rests his case largely on Marx's early *Economic and Philosophical Manuscripts* (1844) (*NS* 313–16). In Nietzsche's case, Abrams argues for a Romantic genealogy as well, though here his argument is tenuous and based entirely on *The Birth of Tragedy* (1872) (*NS* 316–18). A much stronger case could be made for exploring Nietzsche in terms of the horizon of German Romanticism, not least with reference to Richard Wagner, about whom Abrams remains strangely (and noticeably) silent. Certainly the fantasy tradition from German Romanticism onwards has been from the beginning a matter of political debate. Heine was aware of such issues in his *The Romantic School* [*Die Romantische Schule*] in the 1830s. The question has always been whether German Romanticism in general – and in particular the myths which it created (especially those by Novalis and Hoffmann) – are, on the one hand, the expression of a radical Utopian subversiveness or, on the other, the products of a political apathy or conservatism finding solace in escapist fantasy. Some critics, such as Rosemary Jackson, are scathing of the particular tradition of fantasy that is the focus of the present book, seeing it as fundamentally reactionary. She calls it 'transcendentalist' and expressive of a 'nostalgic, humanistic vision' that looks back to a 'lost moral and social hierarchy', and seeks to 'expel' and displace desire into 'religious longing and nostalgia', thereby defusing 'potentially disturbing, anti-social drives' and retreating from confrontation.[34] Jack Zipes, on the other hand, makes considerable claims for the subversiveness of the fairy-tale and fantasy tradition.[35] Zipes and others are, however, scathing about 'the Harry Potter phenomenon' as implicitly reactionary and certainly an expression of rampant capitalism.[36] The issue of the politics of Pullman's *HDM* is more complex.

These are issues to which I shall return. The use, especially by Novalis and Hoffmann, of *myths* to embody spiritual as well as political aspirations has been discussed with an eye to the related use of myth by later writers such as Tolkien, Lewis and Pullman. In contrast to the Utopian other-worldliness of the early German Romantics, and their tendency to create a single self-contained, fairy-tale-like world (or 'chronotope') of the *marvellous* (in Todorov's definition),[37] there is in the *fantasy* works of later German Romantics, such as Hoffmann, a greater sense of *ambiguity* and *tension* between the competing demands of this world and other possible worlds. Particular attention has been given to Hoffmann's *GP* as a paradigm of fantasy literature 'for children of all ages', from MacDonald's work through to the Harry Potter series. The characteristic theme of German Romantic literature, that is, the discrepancy (and complex relationship) between the fantastic world of the (possibly Utopian) imagination, and the 'real' world of the bourgeois 'Philistines' (the Dursleys, if not 'Muggles' as such) will inform the remainder of this study.

2
George MacDonald's Marvellous Medicine

Whatever truth is in the (suitably Romantic) theory that a remote Scottish castle was the site of MacDonald's first encounter with works by Novalis, Hoffmann and other German Romantics in the original German,[1] he would certainly also have encountered them in the translations of Carlyle. In 1827, two years after MacDonald's birth, Carlyle published his two-volume *German Romance: translations from the German with biographical and critical notices,* which contained: five tales by Tieck, including 'The Fair-Haired Eckbert', 'The Runenberg' and 'The Elves'; Fouqué's 'Aslauga's Knight' (Carlyle notes that *Undine* and *Sintram* had already been translated); some tales by Museus and Jean Paul Richter; and Hoffmann's *GP.* Tieck and Schlegel's edition of the collected writings of Novalis had appeared in Germany the previous year, and in 1829 Carlyle produced a long review-article entitled 'Novalis' that contained lengthy translated extracts both from Novalis's philosophical fragments and from his novels, including *HvO.* Carlyle's essay contextualizes Novalis's thought within 'the then and present state of German metaphysical science', referring particularly to Fichte's *Wissenschaftslehre,*[2] and summarizing the connections between Romanticism and Idealist philosophy. Although the citations from Novalis in MacDonald's *Phantastes* (1858) are given in the original German, and though the translations sometimes added by MacDonald may differ slightly from Carlyle's versions, nevertheless it is Carlyle's translations that would almost certainly have paved the way for MacDonald's assimilation of the German Romantic tradition. In a letter to Carlyle of 1877, MacDonald presumed to address his fellow Germanophile Scot – the so-called the 'Sage of Chelsea' – as 'my big brother'.[3]

It was during MacDonald's convalescence after a lung haemorrhage in 1856, two years before the publication of *Phantastes,* that he wrote to his wife that he was re-reading Hoffmann's *GP* and finding it 'delightful'.[4] In his biography of his father, Greville MacDonald speculates that it was Carlyle's translation that his father read on this occasion, since he had found this version among his father's books – though he hastens to add that Carlyle's translation had doubtless led his father 'to the original'.[5] On reading Carlyle's translation for himself, Greville MacDonald comments:

> I cannot but think that it made an arresting impression upon [my father]. It is splendid, dazzling in colour, very mad in a sort of riotous detail, but with a *meaning* which is stated at last when there can no longer be any need for it. . . . [T]he story is greater than its writer knows: it transcends its apology. Its very madness, its rampant magic, its wit and tragic humour, its gentle touches of pathos, its faculty of *bi-local existing* . . . must fascinate the imaginative reader.
>
> (*GMAW* 298)

His conviction that the meaning of *GP* is 'stated at last' in an 'apology' suggests that Greville may have missed Hoffmann's narratological games. He would not be the first to reduce Hoffmann's work to some enunciated meaning (or 'content') and overlook its problematic enunciation (or narrative form); Freud had done something similar five years earlier in his 1919 essay 'The Uncanny'. Certainly MacDonald *fils* does not seem very alert to the Romantic irony at work in Hoffmann.

If he is on shakier ground than he seems to realize when finding a moral at the end of *GP*, Greville MacDonald is on safer ground when he draws attention to the similarities between the beginnings of *GP* and *Phantastes*, and the way that 'both Celtic and German poet would have us understand that quite easily and unexpectedly we may also step – not *if we will*, but rather *if we are led* – out of the common tangible world into that truer land of faerie and imagery' (*GMAW* 298). Or as he put some years earlier in his introduction to the 1915 edition of *Phantastes* published by Everyman's Library in their series 'For Young People' (presumably the edition purchased by a young person named C.S. Lewis): 'When Anodos steps from his bed into Fairyland, we know that Fairyland was always about him waiting to be stepped into.'[6] Indeed Fairyland is actually 'much more real than the vulgar world that will not let us step outside its heavy bars' (*Ph* vii). Such a claim is founded on the high view of the imagination ascribed by Greville MacDonald to his father:

> To him, the imagination stood highest of all the faculties. It is the soul of Art – the power of creating symbolic utterance for Ideas, which, without it, could have no means of presentation . . . Granted this high office of the imagination, then the fairy-tale is, in so far as it is Art, revelation; even though its significance is not to be defined in terms of precise allegory, parable, or fable.
>
> (*Ph* vii)

Such revelation is, however, by no means to be equated with the revelation of Christian doctrine. Greville MacDonald resists any assimilation of his father's writing to religious dogma: 'The unbeliever, who is incapable of finding fairy-tale in the mustard seed, asks for Truth in a nutshell. Dogma, however serviceable as an algebraic sign, becomes anti-Christ as soon as it claims to *contain* the unknown quantity'. (*Ph* viii)

Whether Hoffmann saw any overlap between the Christian and the magical 'Other World' (and like the contemporary chroniclers of Faerie – Neil Gaiman and Susanna Clarke – he apparently did not[7]), there is in MacDonald a hope that Faerie can fuse with Christian faith into what Greville MacDonald calls his father's 'fairy-faith' (*GMAW* 378). As the he puts it in his biography:

> *Phantastes*, in a word, is a spiritual pilgrimage out of this world of impoverishing possessions into the fairy Kingdom of Heaven. As . . . George MacDonald compels us to fresh adventure beyond the common arid concepts of a wholly undesirable future life, so does *Phantastes* bring home to us in allusive burgeoning the celestial purpose of our daily existence. Its very religion is fairyland – and how much more George MacDonald would have ourselves set out and discover.
>
> (*GMAW* 299)

A Romantic synthesis of 'natural' simplicity and spirituality, expressed in the form of the *Märchen*, lies at the heart of MacDonald's work. Greville MacDonald comments on the folk element in *Phantastes*, written within a couple of years of his father's therapeutic reading of *GP*:

> As the inspiration of his fairy-tale [*Phantastes*] was the spirit of the *volk-märchen* [*sic*], so the soul of folk-music took possession of his muse. Without the thatched cottage no cathedral had ever soared; without the folk-song no oratorio; without ballad no ode or sonnet. The child is father to the man; and from now onwards we find the child's simple faith dominating all his writings as surely as in his youth it first took control of his theology.
>
> (*GMAW* 299)

Essays on the imagination

The Romantic synthesis of undogmatic and *experiential* Christian faith with pantheistic speculation had taken root in Britain as well as in Germany. Behind the Victorian religious thinkers who influenced MacDonald (for example, F.D. Maurice and A.J. Scott) lay the great English Romantics, whose work MacDonald had discovered at about the same time as he discovered the German Romantics.[8] MacDonald's adherence to the Romantic cult of the creative imagination is evident in virtually everything he wrote, but is given explicit formulation in two essays collected in *A Dish of Orts* (1893). 'The Fantastic Imagination' is the later, lighter and more attractive piece – partly no doubt because of its anticipation of reader-response theory.[9] It served as the introduction to an 1893 American edition of *The Light Princess and Other Fairy Tales*. 'The Imagination: Its Function and its Culture', originally appearing in 1867, is an altogether weightier piece, which develops MacDonald's theory of the imagination with reference to Coleridge, Wordsworth and Shelley. It begins with a formal definition of 'imagination':

> The imagination is that faculty which gives form to thought – not necessarily uttered form, but form capable of being uttered in shape or in sound, or in any mode upon which the senses can lay hold. It is, therefore, that faculty in man which is likest to the prime operation of the power of God, and has, therefore, been called the *creative* faculty, and its exercise *creation*.[10]

It is interesting, however, to note how MacDonald's attraction to the Romantic emphasis on quasi-divine creativity is tempered by a residual Calvinist insistence on the *difference* between the human and the divine (this despite MacDonald's repudiation of the 'puritanical martinet of a God' of Calvinism[11]):

> It is better to keep the word creation for that calling out of nothing which is the imagination of God; except it be as an *occasional symbolic expression, whose daring is fully recognized*, of the likeness of man's work to the work of his maker. The necessary unlikeness between the creator and the created holds within it the equally necessary likeness of the thing made to him who makes it, and so of the work of the made to the work of the maker.
>
> (*Orts* 2, emphasis added)

MacDonald is thus wary of using the term 'creation' for human artistic activity. In seeking to resist the blurring of ontological boundaries that characterizes the Romantic assimilation of neo-Platonic mystical pantheism and its *analogia entis* (analogy of being), MacDonald seems to approach the notorious claim of the twentieth-century theologian Karl Barth that the *analogia entis* (analogy of being) is 'the anti-Christ'.[12] Barth proposed instead an *analogia fidei* (analogy of faith) that gives priority to divine *revelation*, and according to which human attributes may be compared to *revealed* divine attributes. MacDonald appears to anticipate Barth's position on this issue by agreeing to compare the human and the divine imagination only on the basis of the former's derivative resemblance to the latter, and not vice versa.

> The imagination of man is made in the image of the imagination of God. Everything of man must have been of God first; and it will help much towards our understanding of the imagination and its functions in man

if we first succeed in regarding aright the imagination of God, in which the imagination of man lives and moves and has its being.

(*Orts* 2)

So wary is MacDonald of any kind of presumption in linking the activity of the divine and the human imaginations, that he is uncomfortable even with the term 'poet' or 'maker', preferring the old French term 'trouvère': 'Is not the *Poet*, the *Maker*, a less suitable name for him than the *Trouvère*, the *Finder?* At least, must not the faculty that finds precede the faculty that utters?' (*Orts* 13). In a curious way MacDonald seems to anticipate not only Karl Barth but also Roland Barthes. For Barthes as well as Barth, the overweening yet fragile human subject is really only the site for the free play of 'the Word'. The position of Barthes within post-structuralism is evident, while arguments linking Barth to postmodernism are pretty well established.[13] The extent to which MacDonald might also be considered postmodern has received some discussion. However, it is perhaps not so much MacDonald's tricky metafictional games that qualify him for the designation 'postmodern', as his immersion in the philosophical world of German Romanticism. As Andrew Bowie has convincingly argued, MacDonald's hero Novalis was, like other German Romantic thinkers, well aware of issues that are now said to characterize postmodernism.[14] And behind the central Romantic thinkers, as well as behind the main postmodern thinkers, looms the giant figure of Hegel.[15]

These issues will re-emerge below in relation not only to Tolkien's and Lewis's theory of mythopoeia, but also to Pullman's approximation of mystical pantheism in *AS*. Moreover, in addition to MacDonald's quasi-Calvinist (and proto-Barthian) emphasis on divine transcendence, there is also in his writings the anticipation of an altogether different kind of thinking that would later develop under the influence of Freud. While Freud invented psychoanalysis, he certainly did not invent the idea of the unconscious. MacDonald would have found the idea of the unconscious already in the English and German Romantics, but it is actually Ruskin he mentions when introducing it:

[A]s to this matter of *creation*, is there . . . any genuine sense in which a man may be said to create his own thought-forms? Allowing that a new combination of forms already existing might be called creation, is the man, after all, the author of this new combination? Did he, with his will and his knowledge, proceed wittingly, consciously, to construct a form which should embody his thought? Or did this form arise within him without will or effort of his – vivid if not clear – certain if not outlined? Ruskin (and better authority we do not know) will assert the latter, and we think he is right . . . Such embodiments are not the result of the man's intention, or of the operation of his conscious nature. His feeling is that they are given to him; that from the vast unknown, where time and space are not, they suddenly appear in luminous writing upon the wall of his consciousness. Can it be correct, then, to say that he created them? Nothing less so, as it seems to us. But can we not say that they are the creation of the unconscious portion of his nature?

(*Orts* 16)

MacDonald was not naïvely optimistic in relation to the productions of the unconscious, as even a cursory glance at the horrors of *Phantastes* (not to mention his late work *Lilith*) would reveal. Rather, his faith in the unconscious is precisely an *act of faith* that:

God sits in that chamber of our being in which the candle of our consciousness goes out in darkness, and sends forth from thence wonderful gifts into the light of that understanding which is His candle. . . . If the dark portion of our own being were the origin of our imaginations, we might well fear the apparition of such monsters as would be generated in the sickness of a decay which could never feel – only declare – a slow return towards primeval chaos. But the Maker is our Light.

(*Orts* 16–17)

Again, MacDonald might seem closer to Calvin (and Barth) than we might expect when, in contrast to any sunny liberalism, he emphasizes the capacity of the human unconscious to produce monsters of the imagination (MacDonald is after all writing from the same tradition that produced Hogg's *Confessions of a Justified Sinner* and Stevenson's *Strange Case of Dr Jekyll and Mr Hyde*[16]). In contrast, however, to the 'miserable, puritanical martinet of a God' of the Calvinists, who have taken 'all the glow, all the colour, all the worth out of life on earth', and reduced it to 'a pale, tearless hell', MacDonald affirms 'the Ancient of Days', 'the glad creator'.[17] This emphasis will become relevant later when we discuss Pullman's implicit and explicit criticisms of Christianity, especially in the *HDM* trilogy. The latter contains a sustained attack on the Church (in Lyra's world) that was established by Pope John Calvin (one can imagine MacDonald chuckling over this). 'The Ancient of Days' appears in Pullman's trilogy not as (MacDonald's) antitype to the 'miserable, puritanical martinet of a God', but rather *actually as* the last pathetic vestige of the latter usurping imposter.

MacDonald's work has always attracted various kinds of psychoanalytical readings, most notoriously the 'vulgar' Freudian readings in Wolff's *The Golden Key*. Over a decade ago I criticized Edmund Cusick's apologia for a Jungian interpretation of MacDonald,[18] defending the neo-Freudian 'Object-relations' approach of David Holbrook, and proposing a reading of *Phantastes* in terms of Julia Kristeva's psychoanalytic work.[19] I now accept that there is more to be said for a Jungian approach than I was willing then to concede. Jung and MacDonald certainly shared a common interest in the Gnostic and Hermetic traditions, and, like the Romantics, both had drunk deep of Platonism. This interest in (and broad sympathy with) the Gnostic tradition is also shared by Pullman, though he criticizes (and arguably misrepresents) 'Platonism'.[20] Pullman's advocacy of 'the necessity of atheism' and his depiction of the literal 'death of God' in *AS*, have arguably more to do with the Gnostic demiurge than with 'the Ancient of Days' and 'glad creator' whom MacDonald worshipped.

MacDonald's recognition that the fantastic imagination can breed monsters as well as archetypes of beauty, truth and goodness does not entail the view that young people should be protected from 'those wild fancies and vague reveries in which [they] indulge, to the damage and loss of the real in the world around them' – a repressive view presumably held particularly by those 'Calvinists' with 'their miserable, puritanical martinet of a God'. On the contrary, MacDonald argues, we need more, not less, imagination, for if you '[k]ill that whence spring the crude fancies and wild day-dreams of the young, and you will never lead them beyond dull facts – dull because their relations to each other, and the one life that works in them all, must remain undiscovered' (*Orts* 18). MacDonald is here intervening in the debate about the educational usefulness of fairy tales and fantasy. The argument he mounts in this essay is that literally *everything* (from science to morality to language itself) ultimately derives from the free exercise of the creative imagination; in the first place from the divine imagination, and subsequently, though no less necessarily, from the fallible activity of the human imagination. Here we have one of the sources of the arguments that will later be run by Lewis and Tolkien for the central importance of the mythopoeic imagination.

MacDonald's later essay 'The Fantastic Imagination' provides many of the key ideas encountered in Tolkien's 'On Fairy-Stories' and Lewis's various writings on fairy-tales and fantasy: the dislike of allegory, the requirement to abide by the internal laws of the invented fantasy world (the 'sub-creation') and the rejection of the idea that fairy-tales are primarily for children. MacDonald's reaction to the latter prejudice virtually provides the slogan for so-called 'crossover' fantasy fiction: 'For my part, I do not write for children, but for the childlike, whether of five, or fifty, or seventy-five' (*CFT* 7). As was suggested above, 'The Fantastic Imagination' also contains ideas that sit comfortably with modern reader-response theories. For example, to the interlocutor's question about how she can be assured that she is not reading her own meaning into MacDonald's fairy-tale, rather than his out of it, he replies: 'Why should you be so assured? It may be better that you should read your own meaning into it. That may be a higher operation of your intellect than the mere reading of mine out of it: your meaning may be superior to mine' (*CFT* 7). In an simile that gestures back to especially German Romanticism, as well as perhaps forward to Kristeva,[21] MacDonald compares the fairy tale to a sonata which should be 'mood-engineering

[and] thought-provoking' rather than conceptually precise (*CFT* 9). Words are 'live things' which have the capacity not only to 'convey a scientific fact', but also to 'throw a shadow of her child's dream on the heart of a mother' (*CFT* 8). However, MacDonald resists the relativistic inference drawn by his interlocutor that therefore: 'a man may then imagine what he please, what you never meant' by inserting a moral caveat at this point: he welcomes multiple readings by a 'true' reader, but dismisses the interpretations of reader who is not 'true', since the latter 'will draw evil out of the best' (*CFT* 9). In a (fundamentally theological) move which anticipates more recent theories of polysemy, MacDonald claims that: 'while God's work [or word?] cannot mean more than he meant, man's *must* mean more than he meant'. (ibid., emphasis added). Because, according to MacDonald, human creation is necessarily based on the divine work of Creation, the meanings of any text will always exceed what the author consciously seeks to embody in such a creation. Indeed, says MacDonald, the author 'may well himself discover truth in what he wrote; for he was dealing all the time with things that came from thoughts beyond his own' (ibid.). MacDonald here offers an image of the writer caught between two unknowns: both the origin and the destiny of a text lie far beyond any authorial control (the Barthesian notion of the 'scriptor' comes to mind[22]). If the second of these unknowns, the reception of a text, is subject to the moral and spiritual capacities of its recipients (they can be 'true' readers, or not), then the first unknown – the unconscious – is firmly in the hands of God, MacDonald believes. He has to believe this, since for him the alternative is almost unthinkable.

In his earlier 'Imagination' essay MacDonald had raised the spectre of this alternative possibility that 'if the dark portion of our own being were the origin of our imaginations, we might well fear the apparition of such monsters as would be generated in the sickness of a decay which could never feel – only declare – a slow return towards primeval chaos'[23] (*Orts* 16–17). He avoids mentioning such monsters in his later essay 'The Fantastic Imagination', perhaps because is inappropriate in the introduction to a collection of fairy-tales for the childlike of all ages. Ironically, however, MacDonald had been confronting his own legion of horrors in the process of writing his final work, the fantasy novel *Lilith*, whose composition overlapped with the production of 'The Fantastic Imagination'. The disturbing material in *Lilith* distressed MacDonald's wife, who read extracts of the work-in-progress and wanted him to give it up (*GMAW* 548). There are horrors, too, in MacDonald's first fantasy novel *Phantastes*, for example the carnivorous Ash, the gruesome 'back side' of the Alder-maiden and the ogre in the Church of Darkness. MacDonald's earlier essay on the Imagination is helpful in interpreting *Phantastes* – a work that seems simultaneously to compel and resist interpretation. Indeed, although *Phantastes* predates the earlier 'Imagination' essay, one might argue that in a sense the former almost *is* the essay, expressed in the form of fantasy fiction.

Phantastes

In his introduction to the 1915 edition of *Phantastes*, Greville MacDonald finds the title 'quite puzzling', while the novel's epigraph – 'Phantastes from "their fount" all shapes deriving / In new habiliments can quickly delight'[24] – is 'not wholly illuminating' (*Ph* viii). However, the context leaves no doubt, he suggests, that Fletcher's Phantastes stands for the imagination (ibid.). Indeed *Phantastes*, it might be claimed, is not only a work *of* the Romantic imagination, but also a work *about* the Romantic imagination. The epigraph to the first chapter is from Shelley's 'Alastor', which is in part a response to Coleridge's 'Dejection: An Ode' (John Docherty has argued that the *whole* collection entitled *Alastor; or, the Spirit of Solitude: and other poems* (1816) is relevant[25]). MacDonald quotes Coleridge's 'Dejection Ode' as the epigraph to Chapter IX of *Phantastes*, where Anodos first begins to experience the blighting effects of his Shadow (his 'black sun'[26]). The novel as a whole has been interpreted as – like Coleridge's 'Dejection Ode' – the representation of a struggle between 'Dejection' and 'Joy'.[27] The decisive factor in this struggle is the subjective contribution we can (or cannot) make to our experience, as the epigraph from Coleridge makes clear:

> O Lady! We receive but what we give,
> And in our life alone does nature live:
> Ours is her wedding garment, ours her shroud.
> . . . .
> Ah! From the soul itself must issue forth,
> A light, a glory, a fair luminous cloud,
> Enveloping the Earth –
> And from the soul itself must there be sent
> A sweet and potent voice, of its own birth,
> Of all sweet sounds the life and element!

As is made explicit a couple of stanzas later, the real subject of Coleridge's ode is the threatened loss of his 'shaping spirit of Imagination'. Arguably, this is also the central theme of *Phantastes*. It is Anodos's creative imagination that transforms his bedroom into Fairyland and the failure of that creative imagination that exposes Anodos to his corrosive Shadow. This failure of the creative imagination is presented by MacDonald as essentially a *moral* failure. Anodos disobeys the admonition of the woman in the Church of Darkness not to enter the backless cupboard (later to appear in *LWW*) where he meets his Shadow. The woman (actually an ogre) subsequently tells Anodos that this act of disobedience is linked to his liaison with the Alder-maiden in the forest. He had been warned against the dangers of 'the Maiden of the Alder-tree' by the crest-fallen knight, who reminds Anodos of Sir Percival in the story he has just read in an old volume of fairy tales (a pastiche of Malory concocted by MacDonald). The knight whom Anodos meets in Fairy Land is of course *not* Sir Percival, although the same fate has befallen him that will in turn befall Anodos. This is similar to Anodos's reading experiences in the library of the Fairy Palace, where he temporarily *becomes* a character so that 'his story was mine' (*Ph* 95). In the present case there is a triple identification: Sir Percival, the knight and Anodos (not to mention the implied reader and author).

In a sense, then, it is Anodos's failure to learn the lessons to be found in fairy tales that precipitates his downfall, which is essentially a failure in imagination. Coleridge himself wrote about the nourishing effect of fairy-tales on his imagination; to come full circle, it is the debilitating effects of his failure of imagination which he laments in 'Dejection: An Ode' and to which the poems published with 'Alastor' are arguably Shelley's riposte. While 'Alastor' itself may provide the epigraph for *Phantastes*, Docherty argues that it is lines from Shelley's poem (probably) to Coleridge ('Oh! there are spirits of the air') that seem most relevant to *Phantastes*:

> Thine own soul still is true to thee,
> But changed to a foul fiend through misery.
>
> This fiend, whose ghastly presence ever
> Beside thee like thy shadow hangs,
> Dream not to chase. . .

Such plot as *Phantastes* has centres round Anodos's attempts to escape from the 'ghastly presence' of his 'Shadow', and its attendant misery (a soul-destroying anticipation of Pullman's 'spectres' and Rowling's 'dementors'?).

The lengthy main epigraph to *Phantastes* is provided, however, by Novalis. There is a minor misquotation and some omission on MacDonald's part, and some inaccuracy in the German edition of Novalis that MacDonald was using[28] (the same edition that Carlyle had reviewed in his Novalis essay thirty years earlier). The main omission occurs when MacDonald drops Novalis's claim that 'the true fairy-tale-teller [*Märchendichter*] is a seer of the future'. Apparently MacDonald was uncomfortable, in mid-century Victorian England, with assuming the mantle of the visionary prophet of early German Romanticism. MacDonald's mistakes in transcription are hardly important, but there is one glaring mistake in Tieck and Schlegel's edition, which MacDonald perpetuates, seemingly unaware of the problem. The passage from Novalis begins: 'One can imagine stories without coherence [*ohne Zusammenhang*], but rather with association [*Association*], like dreams'; it continues some lines later: 'A fairy tale [*Märchen*] is like a dream-image [*Traumbild*] without coherence [*ohne Zusammenhang*]. A collection of wonderful things and events, like, for example, a musical fantasy, the harmonic sequences of an Aeolian harp, or nature itself'. The epigraph then declares: 'In a genuine fairy-tale [*Märchen*] everything must be wonderful, mysterious and *coherent* [*zusammenhängend*]'. This contradiction of requiring both coherence and incoherence in a fairy-tale is not mere inconsistency on Novalis's part; nor is it, more interestingly, a paradox of the kind that Novalis was capable of producing; it was in fact the result of a mis-transcription by Tieck and Schlegel of Novalis's original '*in*coherent' [*unzusammenhängend*].

Ironically, what turns out to be merely Novalis's merely apparent demand for both coherence and incoherence in a fairy-tale is nevertheless emblematic of the tale for which it serves as epigraph; there has in fact been much discussion of whether or not *Phantastes* is itself 'like a dream-image without coherence'. In her article 'The Structure of George MacDonald's *Phantastes*', Adrian Gunther claims that there are two camps on the question of the narrative coherence of *Phantastes*.[29] Critics such as Wolff, Reis, Manlove and Raeper see the novel as merely episodic and unstructured, whereas critics writing slightly later, such as Docherty and McGillis,[30] have argued for the presence of what Gunther calls 'elaborate and extraordinarily self-conscious . . . principles of structural form underlying this book'.[31] Advocating the latter approach, Gunther argues that the centre of *Phantastes* is dominated by the sequence in the Fairy Palace, and the centre of that sequence by Anodos's stay in the palace library.[32] Not just in terms of chapters, but also rather uncannily in terms of pagination, Chapter XIII sits right at the centre of *Phantastes*. This central chapter is the story of Cosmo, the student of Prague. Due to the reading-effect at work in the library of the Fairy Palace, Anodos feels that he *becomes* Cosmo while reading this story:

> Of course, while I read it, I was Cosmo, and his history was my history. Yet, all the time, I seemed to have a kind of double consciousness, and the story a double meaning. Sometimes it seemed only to represent a simple story of ordinary life, perhaps almost of universal life; wherein two souls, loving each other and longing to come nearer, do after all, but behold each other as in a glass darkly.
>
> As through the hard rock go the branching silver veins; as into the solid land run the creeks and gulfs from the unresting sea; as the lights and influences of the upper worlds sink silently through the earth's atmosphere; so doth Faerie invade the world of men, and sometimes startle the common eye with an association as of cause and effect, when between the two no connecting links can be traced.
>
> (*Ph* 106–7)

Already it is intimated that the uncanny love story of Cosmo is no simple affair (the very name 'Cosmo' hints that something world-shaking is underway). Cosmo, who has a taste for solitary reverie and esoteric literature, lives in a garret in the old city of Prague. In a scene foreshadowing Rowling's 'Diagon Alley', Cosmo ventures down a narrow alley, through a dirty little court and in a suitably Gothic junk shop discovers (or is it vice versa?) a strange old mirror with some curious carving. Cosmo's desire to possess the mirror increases 'to an altogether unaccountable degree' when he is made a strange offer he cannot refuse by the Hoffmannesque shop-owner, 'a little, old, withered man, with a hooked nose and burning eyes constantly in slow restless motion', who evokes in Cosmo 'a kind of repugnance . . . mingled with a strange feeling of doubt whether a man or a woman stood before him' (*Ph* 110–11) – an interesting blend of anxieties about race and gender. Back in Cosmo's garret, the mirror begins to work its magic, prompting him at first to muse on the kind of artistic and philosophical question that was *de rigueur* for any self-respecting young German Romantic:

> What a strange thing a mirror is! And what a wondrous affinity exists between it and a man's imagination! For this room of mine, as I beheld it in the glass, is the same, and yet not the same. It is not the mere representation of the room I live in, but looks just as if I were reading about it in a story I like. All its commonness has disappeared. The mirror has lifted it out of the region of fact into the realm of art; and the very representing of it to me has clothed with interest that which was otherwise hard and bare; just as one sees with delight upon the stage the representation of a character from which one would escape in life as from something unendurably wearisome. But is it not that art rescues nature from the weary and sated regards of our senses, and the degrading injustice of our anxious everyday life, and, appealing to the imagination, which dwells apart, reveals Nature in some degree as she really is, and as she represents herself to the eye of the child?
>
> (*Ph* 112–13)

Such a transformation of 'this room of mine' though the creative imagination echoes the beginning of *Phantastes* where Anodos's room literally dissolves into Fairy Land (*Ph* 7–8); it also points towards the end of the novel where, back in his own castle and grounds, Anodos wonders whether he can 'translate the experiences of his travels [in Fairy Land] into common life' (*Ph* 236). Mediating between, on the one hand, 'our anxious everyday life' and, on the other, the realm of Faerie that is always ready to 'startle the common eye' and 'invade the world of men', is the magic mirror of art or the imagination.

As he continues to gaze into the looking-glass, Cosmo concludes with a wish of considerable intertextual significance, given that one of the earliest readers of *Phantastes* was MacDonald's friend C.L. Dodgson: 'I should like to live in *that* room if only I could get into it' (*Ph* 113). Alice's corresponding wish in *Through the Looking-Glass* is: 'Oh, Kitty, how nice it would be if only we could get through into Looking-glass House!'[33] The magic mirror reveals, in the reflection of Cosmo's own room, a sad beauty with whom he falls obsessively, but hopelessly in love (again, a curious anticipation of Dodgson's hopeless love for Alice Liddell, and his attempt to capture her in the imaginative magic mirror of a *Kunstmärchen*). The lady in the mirror of course turns out to be an enchanted princess, whom Cosmo can only save by breaking the mirror, although at the cost of his own life. Like a true Romantic hero, Cosmo has his *Liebestod*, and dies happy.

The imagination, then, symbolized by the magic mirror, stands at the very centre of *Phantastes*, which is thus literally *about* the imagination. There are slightly different, although ultimately congruent, arguments for a coherent structure in *Phantastes* offered by Docherty, McGillis and Gunther. What they have in common is an insistence that the problem of coherence in *Phantastes* is really to do with a misguided expectation of some kind of *linear* order in the narrative. Anodos himself admits that he 'can attempt no *consecutive* account of [his] wanderings and adventures' (*Ph* 72, emphasis added). However, the narrative is structured in terms of centre and circumference, rather than any kind of linear progression; in linear terms, the narrative is actually characterized by *lack of progress* and by repetition – in *Phantastes* it often seems that our hero's progress consists of two steps forward and one step back. The other central chapter in *Phantastes*, Chapter XII, also contains a tale from the palace library that is about desire, death and reflection, although in the other world of this tale water does *not* give any reflection; only the sky, concave like an inverted sea, offers distorted reflections. MacDonald's highly imaginative account of life on this 'far-off planet' anticipates some later science fiction, particularly Lewis's 'Space Trilogy'. In this strange other world, desire is as lethal as in Cosmo's Prague, though on this planet the idea of fatal attraction has been generalized into a kind of law of nature:

> When a youth and a maiden look too deep into each other's eyes, this [indescribable] longing seizes and possesses them; but instead of drawing nearer to each other, they wander away, each alone, into solitary places, and die of their desire. But it seems to me, that thereafter they are born babes on our earth.
>
> (*Ph* 102–3)

Although quite different from the Cosmo chapter, this chapter nevertheless strangely echoes it. It is almost as if the centre of *Phantastes* is actually an ellipse, containing two complementary stories, 'a self-encircling twin star', as in the following passage from the beginning of Chapter XII that seems to relate not only to this chapter, but also to the following chapter about Cosmo, as well as to *Phantastes* as a whole:

> They who believe in the influences of the stars over the fates of men, are, in feeling at least, nearer the truth than they who regard the heavenly bodies as related to them only by a common obedience to a common law. All that man sees has to do with man. Worlds cannot be without an intermundane relationship. The community of the centre

of all creation suggests an interradiating connection and dependence of the parts.

No shining belt or gleaming moon, no red or green glory in a self-encircling twin star, but has a relation with the hidden things of a man's soul, and, it may be, with the secret history of his body as well. They are portions of the living house wherein he abides.

(*Ph* 97)

In her article on the structure of *Phantastes*, Gunther quotes this passage in its entirety; it also provides McGillis with the title of his chapter: 'The Community of the Centre'. The idea of 'an interradiating connection and dependence of the parts' of creation coming together in the mind, and even in the body, of a human being is a Romantic concept. It therefore comes as no surprise when McGillis, at the key point in his argument, refers to Abrams, who 'has taught us to read Romantic works as spiral journeys beginning where they end, but ending on a higher level of consciousness . . . The structure [of *Phantastes*] I suggest is apparent in such Romantic texts as *The Rime of the Ancient Mariner*, *The Prelude*, *La Belle Dame Sans Merci* and *Heinrich von Ofterdingen*. MacDonald undoubtedly got his structure from Novalis's unfinished romance where it is both clearer and more complex than in *Phantastes*'.[34] Thus in the 'high argument' of MacDonald's first novel *Phantastes* – which like *Paradise Lost* and *The Prelude* is a kind of theodicy – there emerges the spiralling or dialectical pattern traced by Abrams in his classic account of English and German Romanticism.

Adela Cathcart ('The Light Princess', 'The Shadows', 'The Giant's Heart')

When the opening sentence of Chapter XII of *Phantastes* suggests that everything 'has a relation with the hidden things of a man's soul, and, it may be, with the secret history of his body as well', another aspect of Romanticism comes into view. Romantic thinkers (in a broad sense) have been drawn to esoteric traditions of alchemy and the theory of correspondences, including the macrocosm/microcosm idea associated with nature mysticism. Such thinking links with the development (originally in Germany) of alternative approaches to medicine, including homeopathy. The figure usually credited with founding homeopathy is Samuel Hahnemann (1755–1843), whose life overlapped with German Romanticism. While Hahnemann, as a scientist, could be sharply critical of the excesses of *Naturphilosophie*, there are nevertheless obvious correspondences between homeopathy and the holistic emphases typical of Romanticism. These points are relevant because following *Phantastes*, MacDonald's next book containing fantasy writing was dedicated to a well known homeopathic doctor, John Rutherfurd Russell. MacDonald discussed Russell's account of homeopathy in his review of Russell's *The History and Heroes of Medicine*, later published in *A Dish of Orts*. Without being enthusiastic, MacDonald quietly approves of Russell's sober defence of home-opathy's historical credentials, which eschews the kind of 'elaborate theories of . . . popular physicians, which have owed their birth to premature general-ization and invention', and argues the case for homeopathy in an 'honest and dignified manner' (*Orts* 156–8). Russell actually appears in MacDonald's *The Portent*, thinly disguised as Dr Ruthwell,[35] who according to the narrator 'was one of the few [in the medical profession] who see the marvellous in all sci-ence, and, therefore, reject nothing merely because the marvellous may seem to predominate in it. Yet neither would he accept anything of the sort as fact, without the strictest use of every experiment within his power.'[36]

A further reason to note that MacDonald's *Adela Cathcart* (=*AC*) is 'affec-tionately dedicated' to Russell is that a central theme of the novel is alter-native approaches to healing, including those in which 'the marvellous may seem to predominate'. Adela is suffering from the kind of 'mysterious ail-ment' to which young women were so notoriously prone in Victorian times.[37] The medicine provided by the stuffy Dr Wade ('steel-wine and qui-nine') is failing to make any headway with Adela. Her uncle, the narrator John Smith (usually reckoned to be a *persona* of MacDonald himself), is inclined to try 'the homeopathic system – the only one on which mental distress, at least, can be treated with any advantage'.[38] Hahnemann had advocated that 'to identify the most appropriate treatment, homeopathic physicians should take into account not just the disease, but, rather, the patient as a whole with all their characteristic traits'.[39] The handsome young Dr Armstrong, who is also a gifted musician, is more to the narrator's taste: '"A wonderful physician this!" thought I to myself. "He must be a follower of some of some of the old mystics of the profession, counting harmony and health all one"' (*AC* 47). Dr Armstrong agrees that working from the inside out may be better for Adela than any 'physical remedies'; he suspects that the cause of her illness is 'a spiritual one', and expresses the belief that many women 'go into a consumption just from discontent' (*AC* 52). The alterna-tive therapy proposed by Adela's uncle, and seconded by the young doctor, is a diet of stories to 'bring her out of herself'; thus a sort of 'narrative therapy group' is set up (*AC* 50–1). This 'story club' forms the narrative frame within which MacDonald can present a series of stories. In this 'cure' arranged for Adela, 'the marvellous' predominates, since fairy-tales constitute a major ingredient in the narrative medicine prescribed.

Smith himself starts the story-cycle with 'The Light Princess' (=*LP*), a tale he has 'just scribbled off', with the subtitle 'A Fairy-Tale without Fairies'. Even before he can begin, he is interrogated by the unpleasant Mrs Cathcart, Adela's aunt, who has already dismissed the morning's sermon as 'pantheism' (*AC* 54). When Smith announces that his contribution is 'a child's story – a fairy-tale, namely; though I confess I think it fitter for grown than for young children', Mrs Cathcart asks insinuatingly whether he approves of fairy-tales for children – especially on Sundays. Smith's reply to

Mrs Cathcart, as representative of mid-Victorian puritanical Evangelicalism, is that fairy-tales, of which he is confident God approves, are 'not for children alone . . . but for everybody that can relish them' (*AC* 56). Here Smith represents MacDonald's own struggle to get a hearing for his fairy-tales, in the face of an (at best) indifferent mid-Victorian audience. The very fact that he had to resort to the device of the frame-narrative of *AC* to get his fairy-tales published indicates the indifference, if not hostility, he faced.

Ironically, and rather bizarrely, Mrs Cathcart may also represent John Ruskin, whose *The King of the Golden River* had pioneered the *Kunstmärchen* or literary fairy-tale in England. Ruskin, like C.L. Dodgson, had seen *LP* prior to publication, and in a letter to MacDonald in July 1863 had complained that it was 'too amorous throughout – and to some temperaments would be quite mischievous'.[40] On reading *AC* the following year, Ruskin wrote to MacDonald, either in a state of what Raeper calls 'mock-fury', or in a state of incipient paranoia foreshadowing the mental breakdown he was subsequently to experience:[41]

> You *did* make me into Mrs Cathcart – She says the same things I said about the fairy tale. It's the only time she's right in the whole book, you turned me into her, first – and then invented all the wrongs to choke up my poor little right with. I never knew anything so horrid.[42]

Ruskin is right that there *is* an unmistakable aura of sexuality in *LP*, though whether this is in any sense 'mischievous' is another matter. Glancing back to the element of eroticism – even 'sexual healing' – in the work of Novalis, as well as forward to the climax of Pullman's *HDM*, there is a definite sexual charge in some of the scenes between the prince and the princess, especially the swimming scenes that Ruskin thought particularly *risqué*. But as MacDonald says in his fairy-tale: 'Perhaps the best thing for the princess would have been to fall in love' – a suggestion echoed in the not entirely disinterested second opinion of Dr Armstrong in the strange case of Adela Cathcart: 'Isn't there any young man to fall in love with her?' (*AC* 53–4).

Although *LP* does not contain any actual fairies, it is very much in the fairy-tale tradition, and does contain a witch, Princess Makemnoit, who 'beat all the wicked fairies in wickedness'. In its opening sequence, which plays on the beginning of 'Sleeping Beauty', Makemnoit pronounces a baptismal curse that condemns the princess to eternal levity. This is the mirror image of Adela being condemned to the depression of which she gives a powerful description that recalls the effects of MacDonald's 'black sun' as well as Pullman's 'spectres' and Rowling's 'dementors':

> I woke . . . with an overpowering sense of blackness and misery. Everything I thought of seemed to have a core of wretchedness in it. . . . It was as if

> I had awaked in some chaos over which God had never said: "Let there be
> light". . . . I began to see the bad in everything . . . Nothing seems worth
> anything. I don't care for anything
>
> (*AC* 25)

Both Adela's depression and the princess's levity could be seen as 'hysterical'
in various senses; both can be seen not only as curses, but also as obstacles,
even resistances, to growth into full womanhood, including sexual maturity.
Both *AC* and *LP* end with the lovers' union. The fairy-tale's happy ending is
engineered (literally, since the prince stops the drainage of the lake by using
his own body as a plug) by the prince's death and resurrection. The resusci-
tation is performed by the princess's old nurse, who turns out to be a 'wise
woman', and 'knew what to do'.

This is one of the series of 'wise women' who figure so prominently in
MacDonald's fantasy writing; she is preceded by the old woman with the
young eyes in *Phantastes*, and succeeded by Princess Irene's great-great-
grandmother in *The Princess and the Goblin* (=*PAG*) and *The Princess and
Curdie* (=*PAC*), as well as by the eponymous 'Wise Woman'. The nurse's contribution is crucial to the outcome of *LP*, yet she is mentioned almost in passing.
The prince's redeeming death is presented both as Christ-like (complete with
Eucharistic wine and biscuit) and also as highly Romantic (with echoes of
Fouqué and Andersen); it is indeed a kind of *Liebestod*, only on this occasion
it is the male lead who dies – a reversal of gender stereotypes underlined by
the fact that in *LP* it is the prince who needs the kiss. Here MacDonald
achieves a synthesis of Christian teaching and the Romantic fairy-tale that
exemplifies what Greville MacDonald called his father's 'fairy-faith'. Such a
synthesis flies in the face of the likes of Mrs Cathcart, who would keep their
evangelical creed pure of the inappropriate levity of fairy-tales like *LP*. It is
largely from MacDonald that Lewis learned to use fairy-tale material in order
to slip Christian ideas past watchful dragons such as Mrs Cathcart.[43]

There is a fairy-tale in all three volumes of *AC*, each told by the narrator
'John Smith' and each dealing with a particular stage of life. *LP* in Volume
One is primarily concerned with adolescence and growing up, and with young
love. 'The Giant's Heart' in Volume Three seems appropriate for younger
children. 'The Shadows' in Volume Two appears particularly related to old
age, as implied by the fact that its hero is called 'Old Ralph Rinkelmann'.
Rinkelmann, who is a writer, has been chosen to be 'king of the fairies'. The
fairies wait until he is 'dreadfully ill', 'hovering between life and death',
before taking him off to their country – something they can only do when
grown-up mortals are in such a liminal state. 'The Shadows' was apparently
the first of MacDonald's fairy-tales to be written; it was composed during the
writing of *Phantastes*, when MacDonald himself was ill.[44] He was at that time
much influenced by Hoffmann, though echoes of Andersen can also be
detected. Adela interjects that this seems to be yet another fairy-tale, but is

told that despite the opening, the fairies do not actually figure much in this tale. The tale is really about the Shadows, also subjects of Rinkelmann, whom he had overlooked at his coronation. Rinkelmann is able to see the Shadows better after one of them draws a finger across the ridge of his forehead, a well-known device for inducing the mesmeric state, according to Broome.[45] The Shadows place Rinkelmann on a litter or bier 'covered with the richest furs, and skins of gorgeous wild beasts, whose eyes were replaced by sapphires and emeralds, that glittered and gleamed in the fire and snow-light', and transport him to their Church in Iceland (*AC* 191–2; *CFT* 58). The journey to the Church of the Shadows is perhaps the best feature of the tale, evoking the piercing mystery of the 'Northerness' which later overwhelmed Lewis, and which also appears in Pullman's *Northern Lights* (MacDonald's description of the *aurora borealis* is of course based on the experience of someone born and bred in Aberdeenshire). The 'human Shadows', as they insist on being called, spend the remainder of the story mingling on the frozen mountain-lake, which is not only their church but their 'news-exchange', their 'word-mart and parliament of shades' where they tell each other about the various ways they have unobtrusively intervened in human lives. Far from having any malign intent of frightening people, the Shadows wish 'only to make people silent and thoughtful; to awe them a little' (*AC* 196; *CFT* 62). In the silence that follows 'The Shadows', Adela asks her uncle about the different kinds of shadows and puzzled by his reply, accuses him:

> I do believe, uncle, you write whatever comes into your head; and then when anyone asks you the meaning of this or that, you hunt round till you find a meaning just about the same size as the thing itself, and stick it on.
> (*AC* 217; *CFT* 347n18)

To which MacDonald/Smith replies: 'Perhaps *yes*, and perhaps *no*, and perhaps both' (*AC* 217). Smith's laid-back attitude to meaning not only prefigures 'The Fantastic Imagination', but also echoes the Shadows' intention 'only to make people silent and thoughtful; to awe them a little'.

The final fairy-tale in *AC*, 'The Giant's Heart', is 'only a child's story', says Smith and 'absurd to read . . . without the presence of little children', so some local children are drummed up as an audience (*AC* 315). Ironically, however, what is presented as the slightest of stories receives the weightiest of introductions. In a passage which, with its contrast between fancy and the imagination, seems close to the Romantic 'Imagination: Its Function and its Culture' published three years later, MacDonald/Smith reflects on 'the wondrous loveliness with which the snow had at once clothed and disfigured the bare branches of the trees' (*AC* 312). His meditation continues:

> This lovely show . . . is the result of a busy fancy. This white world is the creation of a poet such as Shelley, in whom the fancy was too much for

the intellect. Fancy settles upon anything; half destroys its form, half beautifies it with something that is not its own. But the true creative imagination, the form-seer, and the form-bestower, falls like the rain in the spring night, vanishing amid the roots of the trees; not settling upon them in clouds of wintry white, but breaking forth from them in clouds of summer green.

(*AC* 312)

In contrast to the artificial world, seemingly of marble, created by the snow, there is something very earthy about 'The Giant's Heart'; it harks back to folk-tales such as 'Jack and the Beanstalk', as well as forwards, perhaps, to Roald Dahl's *BFG*. It is difficult to draw any 'uplifting' message from 'The Giant's Heart'. As McGillis has shown in his analysis of the tale,[46] there is a system-atic subversion of any kind of 'moral' to be drawn. MacDonald uses a highly conventional form to subvert conventional expectations. The children in *AC* do not seem to know what to make of 'The Giant's Heart'; nor do subsequent critics, as McGillis shows. Yet the tale is so free from any kind of saccharine Victorian sentimentality, as well as so ruthless in its exposure of cruelty and hypocrisy, and of how ambivalently *interlinked* they can be, that it can pro-voke a sardonic delight. If the tale does have a message, it perhaps lies in the final sentence: 'A fountain of blood spouted from [the giant's heart]; and with a dreadful groan, the giant fell dead at the feet of little Tricksey-Wee, who could not help being sorry for him after all' (*AC* 337; *CFT* 98). By leaving the last word to a female response to male violence, perhaps a gesture is made towards the moral that Smith draws at the end of the chapter, when he reflects (or hopes) 'how much more one good woman can do to kill evil than all the swords of the world in the hands of righteous heroes' (*AC* 338).

Dealings with the Fairies ('Cross Purposes', 'The Golden Key')

The year after MacDonald managed to get his fairy-tales published by including them in his novel *AC*, his friend C.L. Dodgson saw the publica-tion of his own fairy-tale, originally entitled *Alice's Adventures Underground*. MacDonald, together with his family as trial audience for the manuscript version, famously contributed to the appearance in print of *Alice's Adventures in Wonderland* in 1865 (*GMAW* 342). The tremendous success of *Alice in Wonderland* (as the fairy-tale by 'Lewis Carroll' came popularly to be known) opened up a market for fairy-tales. MacDonald was therefore able to secure the publication of his own volume of fairy-tales, *Dealings with the Fairies*, in 1867. This volume included the three fairy-tales from *AC*, plus two new tales, 'Cross Purposes' and 'The Golden Key' (=*GK*). 'Cross Purposes' thus in a sense owes its existence to *Alice in Wonderland*, and in his fairy-tale MacDonald makes a series of intertextual jokes about this literary indebtedness. The hero-ine is named 'Alice', though unlike the original Alice, she has a 'buddy' named 'Richard' – 'name enough for a fairy story', comments the narrator

(*CFT* 106). The adventures of MacDonald's Alice echo those of Dodgson's, though they also repeat motifs from *Phantastes*, which, ironically, Dodgson had himself imitated in his *Alice* book.

Like her namesake, MacDonald's Alice shrinks to the size of the fairy Peaseblossom, who then, like Anodos's fairy great-great-grandmother in Chapter I of *Phantastes*, transforms herself into 'a tall slender lady'; then the tufts of Alice's counterpane become 'bushes of furze' (*CFT* 105), much like the transformation of Anodos's bedroom into a wood in Chapter II of *Phantastes*. The latter chapter's epigraph is from Novalis's *HvO* ('"Seest thou not the blue waves above us?" He looked up, and lo! the blue stream was flowing gently over their heads.') – lines which seem at least as relevant to the present chapter of 'Cross Purposes' where MacDonald's Alice follows her namesake 'down and down', ending up under water at the bottom of a pool. 'Cross Purposes' perhaps resembles *Alice* more than any other of MacDonald's stories, with its hallucinatory sequence of anarchic metamorphoses, from umbrellas to geese to 'a flock of huge mush-rooms and puffballs', with one goose turning into a hedgehog when picked up. The sudden appearance of a hedgehog recalls the croquet game in *Alice*, as Knoepflmacher points out (*CFT* 349n7); however, the bizarre metamor-phoses in 'Cross Purposes' perhaps resemble more than anything else the sheep [?] in the shop [?] sequence in Chapter 5 of *Through the Looking-Glass*, published four years after MacDonald's *Dealings with the Fairies*.

'Cross Purposes' contains allusions to, and swipes at, the rigidity and imper-meability of Victorian class boundaries; for example, on returning home, Alice and Richard feel they must part, despite the bond they have developed in Fairy Land. (*CFT* 119) However, Hastings's argument that such class issues are similarly apparent in *GK* is unconvincing, as is his claim that 'Cross Purposes' is 'an early attempt at the visionary fairy-tale perfected in *GK*'.[47] There is almost a quantum leap between 'Cross Purposes' and *GK* in terms of imagina-tive power and scope. Michael Mendelson highlights the sheer scope of *GK*:

> In a purely geographical way, this unique fairy-tale has enormous breadth, moving as it does through an entire continent of symbolic ter-rain. At the same time, it traverses a literary route from traditional folk tale to the apocalyptic epic of salvation, so that both 'Hansel and Gretel' and Dante's 'Paradiso' can be cited as precedents. . . . Indeed, we might well raise the question whether this is really a fairy-tale at all, since it also borrows so heavily from the narrative formulas of romance and the the-matic ambitions of prophetic myth.[48]

GK is a *Kunstmärchen* on a grand scale; another influence that MacDonald himself cites in a footnote (a curious procedure for a fairy-tale) is the work of Novalis. MacDonald notes in relation to his account of Tangle's encounter with the Old Man of the Fire, the oldest man of all, who is also 'a little naked child . . . playing with balls of various colours and sizes, which he disposed in strange figures upon the floor beside him' (*CFT* 139): 'I think I must be indebted to Novalis for these geometrical figures' (*CFT* 350n14). Tangle's response to this strange experience is to feel that 'there was something in her knowledge which was not in her understanding. For she knew that there must be an infinite meaning in the change and sequence and individual forms of the figures into which the child arranged the balls, as well as the various harmonies of their colours' (*CFT* 139). Here MacDonald is not only drawing on Novalis, but also on Kant, whose distinction between Reason (*Vernunft*) and Understanding (*Verstand*), or (roughly) between intuitive knowledge and logic, lies behind most varieties of Romantic philosophy. This distinction has a long history in religious and mystical (especially neo-Platonic) thought. Another name for 'knowledge which is not in the under-standing' is *gnosis*. Tangle has a kind of mystical experience on entering the cave of the Old Man of the Fire:

> [S]he had a marvellous sense that she was in the secret of the earth and all its ways. Everything she had seen, or learned from books; all that her grandmother had said or sung to her; all the talk of the beasts, birds, and fishes; all that had happened to her on her journey with Mossy, and since then in the heart of the earth with the Old man and the Older man – all was plain: she understood it all, and saw that everything meant the same thing, though she could not have put it into words again.
>
> (*CFT* 139)

For a full seven years, though it only seems like seven hours to Tangle, she continues to gaze at the (by implication) divine child diligently shifting and arranging the coloured balls, and '[f]ashes of meaning would now pass from them to Tangle, and now again all would be not merely obscure, but utterly dark. . . . [T]he longer she looked the more an indescribable vague intelli-gence went on rousing itself in her mind. . . . [T]he shape the balls took, she knew not why, reminded her of the Valley of Shadows' (*CFT* 139). Here we see a kind of Platonism: the coloured balls arranged by the child in the cave seem symbolic of Platonic forms of which the shadows in this world remind us. The child, endlessly 'playing his solitary game', is evidently in some sense divine: 'There was such an awfulness of absolute repose on the face of the child that Tangle stood dumb before him. He had no smile, but the love in his large grey eyes was deep as the centre. . . . For the heart of the child was too deep for any smile to reach from it to his face' (*CFT* 140).

MacDonald's veneration of the child is not merely the expression some generalized Romantic privileging of childhood. It is a specific theological point that he argues in his sermon 'The Child in the Midst' (based on Mark 9:33–7), contained in the first volume of his *Unspoken Sermons*, published in 1867, the same year as *Dealings with the Fairies* (including *GK*). He sums up as follows: 'God is represented in Jesus, for that God is like Jesus: Jesus is represented in the child, for that Jesus is like the child. Therefore God is represented in the child, for that he is like the child. God is child-like. In the true vision of this fact lies the receiving of God in the child.'[49] MacDonald develops this truth he believes he has found in Scripture:

> In this, then, is God like the child: that he is simply and altogether our friend, our father – our more than friend, father, and mother – our infinite love-perfect God. Grand and strong beyond all that human imagination can conceive of poet-thinking and kingly action, he is delicate beyond all that human tenderness can conceive of husband or wife, homely beyond all that human heart can conceive of father or mother (ibid.).

In contrast to this emphasis on the childlikeness of God, stands the 'martinet' view of God that MacDonald deplores:

> How terribly . . . have the theologians misrepresented God . . . Nearly all of them represent him as a great King on a grand throne, thinking how grand he is, and making it the business of his being and the end of his universe to keep up his glory (ibid.).

It is worth stressing MacDonald's theological views at this point because, as I will discuss below, Pullman's atheism is partly based on a view of God that MacDonald equally detests, a detestation that has been largely occluded due to the influence of Lewis. As I have argued elsewhere: 'Pullman's idea of "the republic of heaven" depends precisely on his opposition to the idea of God as king (an opposition which MacDonald shared, but Lewis edited out).'[50]

However, as Rolland Hein has pointed out (echoing the Kantian 'knowledge which is not in the understanding'), while the sermon 'The Child in the Midst' gives a 'compelling exposition' of the *concept* of the childlikeness of God, the *idea* is given imaginative expression in the powerful myth of a fairy-tale.[51] For *GK* is in the beginning a fairy-tale. It starts with fairy stories: we are told that on the day before their awfully big adventure starts, Mossy – whose name derives from the mossy stone on which he sits for whole days reading – was as usual listening to his great-aunt's stories; and Tangle had been reading 'Silverhair' ('Goldilocks') all day. However, this fairy-tale beginning quickly moves on to something much more ambitious. As Mendelson espresses it, citing Carlyle: 'these familiar narrative elements [of the fairy-tale] are here put to work in the service of a 'new mythus', so that the fairy tale becomes a means of symbolic discourse in which MacDonald attempts to expound his own, unique vision.'[52]

MacDonald thus stands on the trajectory that I have suggested runs from Romanticism to Pullman. For all its relative brevity, MacDonald has sought in *GK* to create a new myth, the cosmic proportions of which he will hardly approach again until his last work, *Lilith*. *GK* is the only work by MacDonald that Pullman admits to having read.[53] Other than the grand, if not grandiose, ambition to create a 'new mythus' in the great Romantic tradition, and a particular veneration for John Milton (*GK* is considerably indebted to *Comus*[54]), the most evident similarity between *GK* and Pullman's *HDM* is the partnership of Tangle and Mossy, which foreshadows Lyra's and Will's. Some analogy might perhaps be seen between Mossy's 'golden key' and Will's 'subtle knife'. Both magical objects have obvious phallic overtones, though even Wolff himself admits that his notoriously reductive Freudian reading is 'banal', and suggests other interpretative possibilities for the key, such as 'the poetic imagination' or 'religious faith'.[55] And even if the golden key is not phallic in a vulgar Freudian sense, it still raises issues for a feminist approach, in that its possession seems to privilege Mossy in terms of the length and difficulty of the different journeys he and Tangle have to make. However, as Cynthia Marshall has argued, such a reading may oversimplify the narrative complexity of *GK* by assuming that the tale is linear and teleological; it is after all Tangle, and not Mossy, who has the numinous experience with the Old Man of the Fire that lies at the heart of the work.[56] Mossy's 'golden key' and Will's 'subtle knife' both enable entry into other worlds, although the difference between the attitudes of MacDonald and Pullman to Platonism is evident in the different reasons Will and Mossy have for leaving behind their magic objects. Will renounces the 'subtle knife' because of the damage caused by using it to gain entry into other worlds; Mossy simply no longer needs the 'golden key' after it has unlocked the door into the rainbow containing the great spiral staircase which will lead him and Tangle up to the other world, 'the country whence the shadows fall' (*CFT* 144). Whether MacDonald's Platonism is of the same 'world-hating' variety that Pullman thinks he finds in the work of Lewis, is a matter for further discussion.

At the Back of the North Wind

In 1868, the year after the publication of *Dealings with the Fairies*, the first instalments of *At the Back of the North Wind* (=*ABNW*) appeared in the magazine *Good Words for the Young*. The following year, MacDonald himself became editor of the magazine that in 1870 was to begin the serialization of *PAG*. These fantasy novels represent a development of MacDonald's work from the (in the case of *GK* admittedly lengthy) fairy-tale, to something altogether larger in scope. However, *GK* had been a very ambitious work in all but length, and in several respects *ABNW* is a continuation of its mythopoeic programme. The Christ-like Wise Child is as central to the novel as it was to the fairy-tale and there is again some literary name-dropping. If Novalis appeared – perhaps rather incongruously – in a footnote to *GK*, then *ABNW* includes explicit references to Herodotus, Dante (thinly disguised as 'Durante') and James Hogg, 'the Ettrick Shepherd', whom MacDonald simply refers to as 'the shepherd' when introducing an extract from Hogg's poem 'Kilmeny'. 'Kilmeny' was published in 1813 as part of Hogg's *The Queen's Wake*; it is modelled on traditional

Scottish ballads such as 'Tam Lin' and 'Thomas the Rhymer', which depict an abduction to Faërie – a theme used MacDonald in his fairy tale 'The Carasoyn', originally published in 1866 as 'The Fairy Fleet' in *The Argosy*. In his essay 'On Fairy-Stories' Tolkien quotes some stanzas from 'Thomas the Rhymer', omitting the title, doubtless assuming that the original audience of his Andrew Lang Lecture at St Andrew's University would get the reference. The stanzas illustrate the idea that Faërie is *neither* Heaven *nor* Hell but a third, *other* place that the ballad calls 'fair Elfland'.[57] Raeper picks up this idea in his essay 'Diamond and Kilmeny: MacDonald, Hogg and the Scottish Folk Tradition', arguing that 'the bright third way of the imagination' was suppressed by Calvinism in Scotland, though it lived on in the folk traditions which were revived during the Romantic period.[58] The appearance of Hogg's 'Kilmeny' in *ABNW* shows how ready MacDonald was to synthesize Scottish folk traditions, Romantic ideas about the potency of the imagination and his own version of Christian belief, in order to create what Greville MacDonald called his father's 'fairy-faith' (*GMAW* 378).

The precise identity of 'North Wind' and the nature of the country that lies at her back, remain mysterious. Humphrey Carpenter is confident that the land at the back of the North Wind is Purgatory.[59] Certainly *ABNW* alludes to Dante and it is true that MacDonald's veneration for Dante can be detected in other of his works, such as *GK* and *Lilith*. And certainly MacDonald entertained what might now be termed 'ecumenical' ideas about the after-life that had worried his evangelical congregation at Arundel (he was ejected partly on account of his willingness to entertain the possibility that animals, and worse still, Roman Catholics, might have some hope of a blessed afterlife). Nevertheless, as Knoepflmacher has pointed out, Diamond's experience of the country at the back of the North Wind seems closer to that of Bonny Kilmeny, the Scottish peasant girl, than that of 'the great Italian of noble family'.[60] North Wind herself is equally resistant to identification. Carpenter is doubtless correct to see her as partly a personification of the will of God. Such personifications (or hypostases) of God's inscrutable wisdom and activity are not uncommon in the Judeo-Christian tradition;[61] they are particularly characteristic of the Gnostic and Kabbalistic traditions, running from ancient times through Boehme to Swedenborg, and were of great interest to Romantics such as Novalis and Coleridge, as well as MacDonald. The figure of Wisdom-Sophia has been related especially to the great-great-grandmother in MacDonald's *Princess* stories.[62] North Wind could be seen as a slightly earlier incarnation of this great-great-grandmother figure. She shares the shape-shifting capacity of the latter, her appearance being determined in large measure by the moral capacity of the person she is encountering. In the chapter entitled 'What *is* in a name?' in *PAC*, Irene's great-great-grandmother explains to Curdie that the mode of her appearance to the miners and their families – whether as the radiant 'Mother of Light' or the witch-like 'Old Mother Wotherwop' – depends on their moral state. And in the following chapter, Curdie acquires the ability (through plunging his hand in great-great-grandmother's fiery roses) of actually *feeling* 'the beast within'. We first see both of these ideas when North Wind appears as a wolf to an abusive, gin-swilling nurse; the wolf is the only form in which the nurse could have seen North Wind, the latter tells Diamond, since 'that is what is growing to be her own shape inside of her'.[63] As a result of falling over in fright at North Wind's attack on her in the form of a wolf, the nurse will lose her job – and not before time, comments North Wind (*ABNW* 44).

We see here in miniature the issue that will loom large a few chapters later, when North Wind sinks a ship – with the loss of many lives – in order to teach Mr. Coleman a lesson about financial dishonesty. The relativity of North Wind's shifting appearances shades into a moral relativity, or confusion, when Diamond asks North Wind how she can with one arm take care of a poor little boy and with the other sink a ship. This is in a nutshell the old problem of evil: how can the same all-loving and all-powerful God be responsible for both the evil and the goodness in the world? The dualist option taken by the Gnostic tradition is ruled out when North Wind gets Diamond to accept that she cannot be two selves – 'the kindest, goodest, best me in the world' and the 'me' who sinks ships. Diamond must just take it on trust that the 'me' who sinks ships is the same 'me' who chooses to be good to Diamond. Diamond is so attached to the kind 'dear North Wind', and so fearful that she might really be the cruel other North Wind, that he declares: '"I love you, and you must love me, else how did I come to love you? How could you know how to put on such a beautiful face if you did not love me and the rest? No. You may sink as many ships as you like, and I won't say another word"' (*ABNW* 80). Here love seems to turn into mere submissiveness. This seems a version of the ultimately brutal theodicy proffered, or imposed, in the book of Job, when God's answer to Job out of the whirlwind appears to be the mere exertion of power: '"Who are you to question my wisdom with your ignorant, empty words? . . . Where were you when I made the world?"' (Job 38:2–4). Once again there is in MacDonald a residue of the Calvinistic stress on the sheer transcendence and omnipotence of God. North Wind is neither willing, nor obliged, to provide any explanation of her apparent cruelty. She is, she says, merely following orders. Admitting that sinking the ship is 'rather dreadful', she continues: '"It is my work. I must do it"' (*ABNW* 66). However, her cruelty is merely apparent, she claims: '"I can do nothing cruel, although I often do what looks like cruel to those who do not know what I am really doing. The people they say I drown, I only carry away to – to – to – well, the back of the North Wind – that is what they used to call it long ago, only *I* never saw the place"' (*ABNW* 67). And North Wind can only bear carrying out her gruesome work, she says, because:

I am always hearing, through every noise, through all the noise I am making myself even, the sound of a far-off song. I do not know exactly where it is, or what it means; and I don't hear much of it, only the odour of its music, as it were, flitting across the great billows of the ocean outside this air in which I make such a storm; but what I do hear, is quite enough to make me able to bear the cry from the drowning ship.

(*ABNW* 83–4)

Such synesthetic delights are doubtless a comfort to North Wind. They will not, however, do much for the drowning people, Diamond insists. North Wind replies: '"But you have never heard the psalm, and you don't know what it is like. Somehow, I can't say how, it tells me that all is right; that it is coming to swallow up all cries"' (*ABNW* 84). But that still won't help the drowning people, Diamond persists, pushing North Wind to reply 'hurriedly': '"It must. It must . . . It wouldn't be the song it seems to be if it did not swallow up all their fear and pain too . . . I am sure it will"' (*ABNW* 84).

Apart from North Wind's evident need to protest rather too much, what is significant here is MacDonald's confidence in the redemptive power of song. This was already a feature of *Phantastes* when Anodos's song releases the lady locked in the block of alabaster, and when the song of the young girl, whose globe Anodos had shattered, sets him free from the tower where he is imprisoned. The magical power of song will also feature in the *Princess* books. It appears in *ABNW* as the endlessly repetitive nonsense verse in the book that Diamond and his mother find on the beach at Sandwich, which is almost identical, Diamond says, to the tune sung by the river at the back of the North Wind (*ABNW* 151) – though the tunes sung by the latter were not in people's ears but in their heads, he insists (*ABNW* 122). The way in which, particularly in *ABNW*, song is related to nonsense verse as well as to natural sounds such as running water is suggestive of Kristeva's idea of the semiotic.[64]

If the atmospheric conditions in the country at the back of the North Wind (neither wind nor sun, only a rayless light, apparently emanating from the flowers) and the way into it (through North Wind's body) are extraordinary, then the *effects* of having been at the back of the north wind seem rather more ordinary. They result in Diamond becoming what some readers may feel is a kind of plaster saint, a priggish little 'do-gooder' typical of didactic evangelical fiction in the Victorian period. *ABNW* did after all first appear in the evangelical magazine *Good Words for the Young* in 1868, the year after Hesba Stretton's *Jessica's First Prayer* was serialized in *Sunday at Home*. Nanny, the little crossing-sweeper whom Diamond rescues, resembles a street Arab out of a Stretton story. She is an orphan, admitting that she would prefer be beaten by Old Sal if only the latter were her mother, rather than the exploitative crone who shuts Nanny out of the squalid den they share and cackles to hear her crying outside in the cold and dark. Old Sal not only recalls a Dickensian grotesque, but also points forward to Pullman's fearsome Mrs Holland in *The Ruby and the Smoke*, also set in Victorian London, who brutalizes the young, presumably orphaned, Adelaide.[65]

As well as rescuing Nanny when she falls ill and getting her into the Children's Hospital with the help of the philanthropic Mr. Raymond, Diamond also intervenes in the dysfunctional family next door, figuring as a ministering angel straight from the pages of evangelical fiction: 'The little boy was just as much one of God's messengers as if he had been an angel with a flaming sword, going out to fight the devil' (*ABNW* 186). However, in contrast to the 'very stupid' philanthropists of the narrator's acquaintance, who would have scolded the drunken cabman as well as his wife, and left them some 'ill-bred though well-meant shabby little books . . . which they were sure to hate the sight of' (*ABNW* 187), Diamond goes straight to the wailing baby lying neglected as the father sits in a drunken stupor after having beaten his wife. Diamond first sings to the baby, 'song after song, every one as foolish as another' (*ABNW* 188), and then delivers a two-page temperance sermon to the baby that puts it to sleep. After Diamond has slipped away, the drunken cabman says to his stunned wife (they have both been watching Diamond and the baby): ' "I do somehow believe that wur an angel just gone. . . . He warn't very big, and he hadn't got none o' then wingses, you know. It wur one o' them baby-angels you sees on the gravestones, you know" ' (*ABNW* 191). While singing to the baby, Diamond had literally shown him the light, a 'very dingy and yellow light' from a dirty lamp in the yard, but light nevertheless, enough to make the baby smile, if also to reveal the 'wretched room . . . so dreary, and dirty, and empty, and hopeless' (*ABNW* 187). After Diamond's visit, the cabman too has metaphorically seen the light; he manages not to go near the public house for a whole week, and some time later really begins to reform (*ABNW* 192).

If this sequence is formulaic and sentimental to the point of mawkishness, what distinguishes it from other temperance fiction is Diamond's bond, and indeed identification, with the baby. In an apparently mad inversion of the desperately inadequate real situation, Diamond tells the baby: ' "you *do* take care of them [the parents], baby – don't you, baby? I know you do. Babies always take care of their fathers and mothers – don't they, baby? That's what they come for – isn't it, baby?" ' (*ABNW* 190). Such a role reversal that turns the baby into the nurturer, is an extreme version of the Wordsworthian dictum 'The Child is father of the Man'. It can be seen in the final lines of one of Diamond's songs, the opening lines of which many people will probably recognize, even if they have never heard of George MacDonald, let alone Diamond:

> Where did you come from, baby dear?
> Out of the everywhere into here.

(*ABNW* 336)

The final lines run:

> But how did you come to us, you dear?
> God thought about you, and so I am here.

(ABNW 337)

This sense that the baby is there *for* the parents is grounded in MacDonald's theology of the childlikeness of God, presented in his sermon 'The Child in the Midst', discussed above in relation to *GK*. Diamond can only produce his nonsense songs derived from the back of the North Wind with the assistance of a baby. He tells Mr. Raymond: '"I couldn't make a line without baby on my knee. We make them together, you know. They're just as much baby's as mine. It's he that pulls them out of me"' (*ABNW* 221). This prompts Mr. Raymond, 'the poet', to muse: '"I suspect the child's a genius . . . and that's what makes people think him silly"' (*ABNW* 221).

Nanny and her friend Jim, both of whom owe their much-improved life in the country to Diamond, rather exclude him towards the end of the novel, saying he is 'silly' and 'has a tile loose'. Another description of Diamond is 'God's baby', who, the narrator suspects, still exerts a positive 'unconscious influence' on Nanny and Jim despite their desertion of him. In fact Nanny and Jim look more like the typical heroes of a children's story than Diamond himself; they suggest more modern children's literature in that MacDonald doesn't duck from the probable sexual attraction between them. Diamond is a strange figure, verging on the Romantic crazed isolate: he is happiest either with what he regards as *his* baby Dulcimer or alone in his tree-top nest where he is closest to the sky, and thus North Wind. Indeed Diamond seems happiest at the extreme margins of human experience: with the baby, fresh from 'the everywhere'; or with North Wind, the ultimate mother figure who is also the figure of death, and who is thousands of years old. Both baby and Mother/Death speak a language that is outside of the human, or at least outside normal human language, but which seems associated with the back of the North Wind. We will come across beautiful mother figures thousands of years old, and language that is outside of ordinary human language, in later works by MacDonald, especially the *Princess* books; we have already met with them in *Phantastes*.

The Princess and the Goblin and *The Princess and Curdie*

MacDonald was himself editor of *Good Words for the Young* when *PAG* began its serialization in November 1870, running until June 1871; the book version appeared in 1872. *ABNW* had been set in mid-Victorian London and Kent, with actual places, street names and districts of London mentioned; in this sense it is more like Hoffmann's *GP* where the fantasy dimension mysteriously irrupts into a real, precisely located historical context. *PAG* is by contrast much more in the fairy-tale tradition, beginning: 'There was once a little princess whose father was king over a great country full of mountains and valleys.'[66] *PAG* is thus more like one of the fairy tales contained *within* both *AC* and *ABNW*, only much longer. Unlike *ABNW*, with its single main protagonist Diamond, *PAG* and its sequel focus on a duo: a partnership of two children (young adults in *PAC*) who have a relationship with an increasingly sexual undertone. Princess Irene and Curdie are not always physically together, but they are the twin heroes of the books, even when the reader's attention is shuttled between them. Like *ABNW*, the *Princess* books are dominated by a numinous mother figure, thousands of years old, who has an intimate if unspecified relationship with the divine. This quasi-divine female figure is also incarnated in the eponymous 'Wise Woman', published in 1875 in between *PAG* and *PAC*. The latter was serialized in 1877 in *Good Things* (the successor of *Good Words for the Young* after the latter's demise), but did not appear in book form until 1883.

What North Wind and Irene's great-great-grandmother have in common is that the messages they communicate to Diamond and Curdie respectively come in a non- (or barely) linguistic form, in songs whose meaning it is not quite possible to grasp. In Diamond's case the song is mixed in with the sound of the river at the back of the North Wind; in Curdie's case, the message appears in the singing of great-great-grandmother Irene's spinning wheel. It is worth quoting *in extenso* one of MacDonald's most evocative passages:

No sooner was [Curdie] in [great-great-grandmother's] room than he saw that great revolving wheel in the sky was the princess's spinning wheel, near the other end of the room, turning very fast. He could see no sky or stars any more, but the wheel was flashing out blue – oh such lovely sky-blue light! – and behind it of course sat the princess, but whether an old woman as thin as a skeleton leaf, or a glorious lady as young as perfection, he could not tell for the turning and flashing of the wheel.

'Listen to the wheel,' said the voice which had already grown dear to Curdie: its very tone was precious like a jewel, not *as* a jewel for no jewel could compare with it in preciousness.

And Curdie listened and listened.

'What is it saying?' asked the voice.

'It is singing,' answered Curdie.

'What is it singing?'

Curdie tried to make out, but thought he could not; for no sooner had he got hold of something than it vanished again. Yet he listened, and listened, entranced with delight.

'Thank you, Curdie, said the voice.

'Ma'am,' said Curdie, 'I did try hard for a while, but I could not make anything of it.'

'Oh yes, you did, and you have been telling it to me! Shall I tell you again what I told my wheel, and my wheel told you, and you have just told me without knowing it?'

'Please, ma'am.'

Then the lady began to sing, and her wheel spun an accompaniment to her song, and the music of the wheel was like the music of an Aeolian harp blown upon by the wind that bloweth where it listeth. Oh, the sweet sounds of that spinning wheel! Now they were gold, now silver, now grass, now palm trees, now ancient cities, now rubies, now mountain brooks, now peacock's feathers, now clouds, now snowdrops, and now mid-sea islands. But for the voice that sang through it all, about that I have no words to tell. It would make you weep if I were able to tell you what that was like, it was so beautiful and true and lovely. But this is something like the words of its song.

(*PGPC* 216–17)

In an evasive strategy typical of MacDonald, we are then offered 'something like' the princess's song, after which '[t]he princess stopped and she laughed. And her laugh was sweeter than song and wheel; sweeter than running brook and silver bell; sweeter than joy itself, for the heart of the laugh was love' (*PGPC* 217). Almost the whole thesis of the present book is implicitly present in this passage. The Aeolian harp is an archetypal Romantic motif, widespread in both English and German Romanticism; it was present in the passage from Novalis that MacDonald had quoted as the epigraph to *Phantastes*. A perhaps less obvious Romantic echo in the passage is of Hoffmann's *The Sandman*, when Nathaniel's madness is epitomized in his vision of a wheel of fire. It is almost as if in *PAC* MacDonald is transmuting what might be described as Nathaniel's very bad psychedelic trip into the best of all trips – into the divine love at the heart of the princess's delicious laugh. However, the whirling wheel in MacDonald's text flashes out blue – 'oh such a lovely sky-blue light' – not only the blue which intoxicated Novalis, but also the colour that Kristeva claims in her essay 'Giotto's Joy' is quintessentially that of 'the semiotic'.[67] The presence of the semiotic has been noted in MacDonald's work,[68] but usually in an oral and/or aural form, as it is evident in the present passage with the song of the great-great-grandmother's wheel whose meaning Curdie can never quite get hold of conceptually, though, as the princess insists, he knows it 'without knowing it' (*PGPC* 216). The reference to 'joy itself' in the passage not only links back to Wordsworth's (and perhaps Schiller's) poetic invocations of joy, but also forward to discussions of joy by Tolkien (in *OFS*) and Lewis (especially in *Surprised by Joy* – the autobiography whose title he stole from Wordsworth). Indeed, Pullman's dispute with Lewis might be seen as essentially a dispute about joy, with Pullman insisting on the this-worldliness of joy in opposition to the views of Lewis, who, according to

Pullman's interpretation, postpones or relegates joy to some other, future world.

Although we find at the core of *PAC* a laugh 'sweeter than joy itself, for the heart of the laugh was love', this fairy-tale has no happy ending. There may be royal wedding between Princess Irene and Prince Conrad (as Curdie, who turns out to have royal blood, is henceforth known); but in contrast to the *Märchen* by Novalis discussed above, this marriage is not followed by children and a Golden Age. The subsequent reign of Irene and Curdie, after the death of the old King-Papa, is dismissed in one short sentence. Irene and Curdie are succeeded by a bad king whose greed, together with the recidivism of the people, bring about the literal undermining of the city of Gwyntystorm, which '[o]ne day at noon . . . fell with a roaring crash. The cries of men and the shrieks of women went up with its dust and then there was great silence' (*PGPC* 341). Finally, as we are told in the last sentence of the story, the very name of the city is forgotten. There has been some discussion of the apparent bleakness of this conclusion. Against the widely-held view that MacDonald here reveals a strain of pessimism, McGillis argues that the apocalyptic ending of *PAC* is actually 'exhilarating', since the wilderness which replaces the city represents renewal and new beginnings (*PGPC* xvii–xviii). He adduces as evidence the final chapter of *Lilith* entitled 'The Endless Ending'. This, however, might be a case of explaining *obscurum per obscurius* or attempting to enlighten darkness through even deeper darkness. For *Lilith* is a notoriously 'dark' work, emerging late in MacDonald's writing career before he lapsed into the literary – and ultimately literal – silence of his final 'long vigil' (*GMAW* 560–1).

Lilith, 'The Wise Woman', 'Photogen and Nycteris'

Although *Lilith* is hardly a children's book, it is important to the 'crossover' fantasy genre because of its direct influence on Lewis, and its indirect influence on Pullman via Lindsay's *VTA* that builds on the pessimistic reading of which *Lilith* is susceptible. There are also a couple of 'crossover' fairy-tales by MacDonald, written between the *Princess* books, which have a decidedly grim strain to them. What Knoepflmacher calls these 'darker-hued' tales (*CFT* 187) are 'The Wise Woman' (or 'The Lost Princess') and 'The History of Photogen and Nycteris' (or 'Day Boy and Night Girl'). Each contains a dominating female figure with supernatural powers whose actions could be seen as vindictive. 'The History of Photogen and Nycteris' begins by telling us that the witch Watho 'had a wolf in her mind' that made her cruel (*CFT* 304). Watho is a forerunner of Lilith in several respects: she is cruel, physically magnificent and able to change her shape into that of a predatory animal. The case of 'The Wise Woman' is more complex, because we are asked to believe that the eponymous Wise Woman is only being cruel to be kind. She is a quasi-divine figure and like North Wind acts with apparent cruelty only with the best of intentions. While Princess Rosamond and Agnes's father are 'chosen' ('plucked out' in Augustinian/Calvinist terms), the peasant-girl Agnes is consigned to a series of almost unbelievably harsh tests in order to 'improve' her. Here George MacDonald's marvelous medicine is bitter indeed. For her own good, we must understand, Agnes is placed naked in a 'cunningly suspended' hollow sphere. She cannot escape, for wherever she walks, she remains in the same place 'like a squirrel in his cage'. Space is thus effectively abolished for Agnes; suspended in a sensory void, she also loses any sense of time:

> [N]othing to see but a cold blue light, and nothing to do but see it. Oh, how slowly the hours went by! She lost all notion of time. If she had been told that she had been there twenty years, she would have believed it – or twenty minutes – it would have been all the same: except for weariness, time was for her no more.
>
> (*CFT* 260)

In this timeless void, Agnes is confronted by herself in the form of an uncanny double, whom Agnes hates 'with her whole heart'. Discovering that she appears to be shut up with her own Self forever, Agnes falls asleep in 'an agony of despair' (*CFT* 261). She awakes 'sick at herself' and 'would gladly have been put out of existence' (ibid.). After three days of wrestling with a self she finds 'despicable', Agnes awakes in the arms of the Wise Woman, with 'the horror' (that is, her Self) vanished. However, despite the Wise Woman's attentions, Agnes soon lapses and fails further tasks she is set. At the end of the story the Wise Woman delivers the following (not quite) damning verdict to Agnes's mother: '"She is your crime and your punishment. Take her home with you, and live hour after hour with the pale-hearted disgrace you call your daughter. What she is, the worm at her heart has begun to teach her. When life is no longer endurable, come to me"' (*CFT* 302). Agnes's only hope is 'the worm at her heart'; in this she prefigures the fate of Lilith.

As in the case of Agnes, the only hope for Lilith lies in suffering. At the climax of *Lilith*, after she has been captured and taken for correction in the 'House of Bitterness', a 'worm-thing', 'white-hot, vivid as incandescent silver, the live heart of essential fire', penetrates into the 'secret chamber of her heart' (*L* 201). The Princess gives a 'writhing contorted shudder' as she is tortured: 'Her bosom heaved and sank, but no breath issued. Her hair hung and dripped, then it stood out from her head and emitted sparks; again hung down, and poured the sweat of her torture on the floor' (*L* 201). It is of course possible to interpret this sequence as showing Lilith being tortured into submission to the patriarchal order.[69] Such torture is intended as purgatorial, however. In MacDonald's great drama of redemption, in which he sought to echo Dante's *Divine Comedy*, Lilith's suffering is presented as ultimately a means of grace. Lilith may be beyond human help, we are told by Mara (the daughter of Adam and Eve), but not beyond salvation:

> She is far away from us, afar in the hell of her self-consciousness. The central fire of the universe is radiating into her the knowledge of good and

evil, the knowledge of what she is. She sees at last the good she is not, the evil she is. She knows that she is herself the fire in which she is burning, but she does not know that the Light of Life is the heart of that fire. Her torment is that she is what she is. Do not fear for her; she is not forsaken. No gentler way to help her was left.

(*L* 201–2)

There are certainly echoes of the Catholic doctrine of purgatory in MacDonald's views on the redemptive power of suffering, both before and after death. However, his beliefs went beyond the pale of Catholic as well as Protestant orthodoxy, and tapped into an ancient and heretical tradition of theological universalism, according to which all would finally be saved, including Satan. In *Lilith* MacDonald explicitly affirms the ultimate salvation of the Shadow (named Samoil, a corruption of Samael, the Satan of the Kabbalah) (*L* 218). This universalist tradition, a watered-down, sentimentalized nineteenth century version of which *Lilith* was apparently intended to criticize (*GMAW* 551–2), runs back to the formally anathematized teachings of Origen, and reappears in the heretical neo-Platonism of late medieval German mysticism and Boehme (to whose works MacDonald returned in old age, when writing *Lilith*); it resurfaces in German Romanticism. Also central to *Lilith*, 'The Wise Woman' and other works by MacDonald, is the idea that salvation demands the 'annihilation of Self (*Selbsttödtung*)', in the phrase of Carlyle (*SR* 142), who derived the idea partly from MacDonald's hero Novalis. While the necessity of 'dying to live' – a belief expressed with disconcerting literalness in *Lilith*, with Adam appearing as the sexton of a vast graveyard – is something few Christians, or indeed adherents of other religious traditions, would dispute, MacDonald's insistence on the universality of redemption is something that many religious groups (whether mainline or not) have felt compelled to reject. Someone who did not so much reject MacDonald's universalism, as try to make us believe that MacDonald himself did not really believe it, was Lewis. As I have discussed elsewhere,[70] Lewis actually distorts MacDonald's views on this issue because they did not fit in with his own more conservative views. Although *Lilith* has disturbed some readers with its uncompromising presentation of cruelty and suffering, and apparent endorsement of patriarchy, it is nevertheless a deeply liberal book; its fundamental theme is the universality of the possibility of spiritual fulfillment, but only through a potentially painful process of 'unselfing'. MacDonald's universalism – according to which, if God could save the rich, then saving the heathen should not be a problem! – has bothered many Christian admirers of MacDonald, from his first (and only) congregation at Arundel, to Lewis. Whether MacDonald's kind of liberalism brings him close in spirit to Pullman's hostility to organized religion will be explored below.

There were personal reasons why MacDonald's late masterpiece seems obsessively concerned with death and the afterlife; his eldest and favourite daughter Lilia (the original of Lona in *Lilith*) died in her father's arms in 1991, between the first and final drafts of *Lilith*. However, the word 'after' in 'afterlife' suggests assumptions about temporal linearity that MacDonald is at pains to dismantle. In *Lilith* the basic ideas of 'whereness' and 'whenness' are fundamentally questioned in a way that harks back to post-Kantian German Romantic philosophers as well as forward to later thinkers in that tradition (including, arguably, Heidegger). When Mr. Vane, the main protagonist of *Lilith*, asks where he is after he has stumbled through a magic mirror, the raven (who mysteriously turns out to be not only a librarian, but also Adam) replies that it is impossible to answer such a question:

> "You know nothing about whereness. The only way to come to know where you are is to begin to make yourself at home."
> "How am I to begin that where everything is so strange?"
> "By doing something."
> "What?"
> "Anything; and the sooner you begin the better! For until you are at home, you will find it as difficult to get out as it is to get in."
>
> (*L* 13)

Such perplexing talk pervades *Lilith*, at times echoing the Alice books, though in a more existentially earnest way. There is also talk of multiple dimensions, anticipating the later scientific theories that Pullman uses in *HDM*. Thus in 'the region of the seven dimensions', the raven tells Vane, it is possible for different entities to exist in the same place at the same time; to deny this is a great mistake: ' "No man of the universe, only a man of the world would have said so" ', the raven sardonically remarks (*L* 23). What Greville MacDonald may have meant by 'the faculty of *bi-local existing*' that he found in his father's and Hoffmann's writings (*GMAW* 298), occurs when the raven shows Vane the coexistence of both his breakfast-room and a garden – with an admixture of synaesthesia apposite to the late Romantic/Symbolist context of *Lilith*: ' "Those great long heads of wild hyacinth are inside the piano, among the strings of it, and give that peculiar sweetness to her playing . . . There! I smell Grieg's Wedding March in the quiver of those rose-petals" ' (*L* 23).

Lilith has other fin-de-siècle resonances, including a nod towards Rider Haggard's *She*, published in 1887. But its central thrust is essentially Romantic, and although it may differ in some respects from *Phantastes*, *Lilith* is in many ways a companion piece to MacDonald's first fantasy novel. Significantly, *Phantastes* begins with a quotation from Novalis and *Lilith* ends with another: 'Our life is no dream, but should and will perhaps become one' – a line that also served as epigraph to the final chapter of *Phantastes*. The final chapter of *Lilith* contains an extended brooding on the nature of dreams and their relation to 'reality', echoing the question in *Through the*

Looking-Glass: 'Which Dreamed It?'[71] It also echoes the Romantic belief in the creative power of the unconscious as articulated in MacDonald's earlier essay on the imagination, which, as was suggested above, is the key to *Phantastes*. At the conclusion of *Lilith*, MacDonald writes about the origins of dreams, and indeed about fantasy itself ('fantasia'):

"Whence then came thy dream?" answers Hope.
   "Out of my dark self, into the light of my consciousness."
   "But whence first into thy dark self?" rejoins Hope.
   "My brain was its mother, and the fever in my blood its father."
   "Say rather," suggests Hope, "thy brain was the violin whence it issued, and the fever in thy blood the bow that drew it forth. – But who made the violin? and who guided the bow across its strings? Say rather, again – who set the song birds each on its bough in the tree of life, and startled each in its order from its perch? Whence came the fantasia? and whence the life that danced thereto? Didst *thou* say, in the dark of thy own unconscious self, 'Let beauty be; let truth seem!' and straightway beauty was, and truth but seemed?"
   Man dreams and desires; God broods and wills and quickens.
   When a man dreams his own dream, he is the sport of his dream; when Another gives it him, that Other is able to fulfil it.

(*L* 251)

The unconscious is central to MacDonald's vision. His work, like that of his fellow Scot, Robert Louis Stevenson, lies right on the cusp between the Romantic understanding of the unconscious and the psychoanalytical inter-pretation developed by Freud and Jung. MacDonald and Stevenson share the same metaphor for the location of the unconscious – in the garret. Poking fun at Descartes's views on the conscious ego, Stevenson confesses in his essay about the genesis of *Strange Case of Dr Jekyll and Mr Hyde*, 'A Chapter on Dreams' (1888), that 'the whole of my published fiction [may] be the single-handed product of some Brownie, some Familiar, some unseen collaborator, whom I keep locked in a back garret, while I get all the praise and he but a share (which I cannot prevent him getting) of the pudding'.[72] In *Lilith* Mr Vane is confident he knows who he is: '"How could I help knowing? I am myself and must know"' (*L* 14). But this Cartesian self-certainty is soon dis-mantled by the raven's relentless questioning (Vane's uncomfortable dia-logue with the raven is similar to Alice's interview with the Caterpillar in chapter 5 of *Alice in Wonderland*). A disorientated Vane stumbles back through the magic mirror into his own garret, which terrifies him, he says, with its '*uncanny* look' (*L* 16). Vane reflects in horror that '"[i]f I know noth-ing of my own garret . . . what is there to secure me against my own brain? Can I tell what it is even now generating? . . . What is at the heart of my brain? What is behind my *think*? Am *I* there at all? – Who, what am I?"' (*L* 16).

This fear of the unconscious remains even at the end of the novel, when Vane and his adopted family of Little Ones finally come home. In Chapter 45, whose title 'The Journey Home' is surely an allusion to Novalis's 'immer nach Hause' ('always going home') and in which there is an explicit quotation from Dante's *Paradiso*, there is a sense of paradise regained: 'The world and my being, its life and mine, were one. The microcosm and macrocosm were at length atoned, at length in harmony! I lived in everything; everything entered and lived in me . . . I was a peaceful ocean upon which the ground-swell of a living joy was continually lifting new waves; yet was the joy ever the same joy, the eternal joy, with tens of thousands of changing forms. Life was a cosmic holiday' (L 243–4). Nevertheless, even in midst of such bliss, the shape-shifting horrors of the Bad Burrow (itself borrowed from Dante) have not entirely disappeared, but remain in a state of suspended animation:

> We came to the fearful hollow where once had wallowed the monsters of the earth: it was indeed, as I had beheld it in my dream, a lovely lake. I gazed into its pellucid depths. A whirlpool had swept out the soil in which the abortions burrowed, and at the bottom lay visible the whole horrid brood: a dim greenish light pervaded the crystalline water, and revealed every hideous form beneath it. Coiled in spires, folded in layers, knotted on themselves, or 'extended long and large,' they weltered in motionless heaps – shapes more fantastic in ghoulish, blasting dismay, than ever wine-sodden brain of exhausted poet fevered into misbeing. He who dived in the swirling Maelstrom saw none to compare with them in horror: tentacular convolutions, tumid bulges, glaring orbs of sepian deformity, would have looked to him innocence beside such incarnations of hatefulness . . . Not one of them moved as we passed. But they were not dead. So long as exist men and women of unwholesome mind, that lake will still be peopled with loathsomenesses.
>
> (L 244)

These horrors of the imagination, which MacDonald suggests outdo even the nightmares of Poe, are held in check by the power that MacDonald refers to simply as 'Another'. It is this 'Other' who, through the imagination, makes heaven or hell on earth. At the heart of MacDonald's intense awareness of the power of fantasy, in both a Romantic and a psychoanalytical sense, is a theological commitment. This is not necessarily an orthodox theological commitment, since to refer to the divine as simply 'Other' sounds decidedly Gnostic. However that may be, MacDonald's commitment to the mythopoeic imagination as being of divine origin and power, and as carrying responsibilities as well as risks, is central to twentieth century debates about fantasy literature.

3

J.R.R. Tolkien and the Love of Faery

The closet Romantic

Tolkien's reticence about the very personal and essentially Romantic core of his myth-making resembles that of his friend, C.S. Lewis, whom Owen Barfield once described as being, if not actually insincere, then 'voulu' or studied in his self-presentation.[1] Lewis's need to maintain a persona, and his emphasis on impersonality in literature,[2] mask an intensely personal desire, or Romantic longing, of which he once said: 'In speaking of this desire . . . I feel a certain shyness. I am almost committing an indecency. I am trying to rip open the inconsolable secret in each one of you . . . the secret we cannot hide and cannot tell, though we desire to do both.'[3] Such desire of 'almost sickening intensity' was triggered in the young Lewis by the lines:

> I heard a voice that cried
> Balder the beautiful
> Is dead, is dead.[4]

Tolkien also acknowledges such experiences of what Lewis called 'Northernness' (*SBJ* 20) as when writing about his reader-responses as a child in *OFS*:

> [B]est of all [was] the nameless North of Sigurd of the Völsungs, and the prince of all dragons. Such lands were pre-eminently desirable . . . The dragon had the trade-mark *Of Faërie* written plain upon him. In whatever world he had his being it was an Other-world. Fantasy, the making or glimpsing of Other-worlds, was the heart of the desire of Faërie. I desired dragons with a profound desire.

> (*MCOE* 135)

Like Lewis, Tolkien kept his fantasies strictly private. It was only after three years of attending the 'Coalbiters' (from the Icelandic *kolbítar*) – an informal

61

Oxford club dedicated to the reading of the Icelandic sagas in the original – that, in 1929, Tolkien and Lewis met privately in Lewis's rooms for a conversation lasting into the small hours in which they confessed their mutual addiction to Norse mythology (*Inks* 28; *LL1* 838). It was a case, in Lewis's words, of declaring: 'What? You too? I thought I was the only one'.[5]

A few days after this meeting Tolkien took the unprecedented step of showing Lewis 'The Gest of Beren and Lúthien', the version in rhyming couplets of a tale he had been writing in different forms since 1917.[6] Lewis wrote to Tolkien expressing delight at the work, and soon afterwards provided a mock academic review (referring to articles by Professors Peabody and Pumpernickel in the pages of *Gestestudien*), pretending that Tolkien's poem was an ancient and anonymous manuscript in various redactions.[7] For a number of Tolkien's fantasy works, Lewis was the first reader, and for some years the only one (*Inks* 32). The secretive nature of Tolkien's early fantasy writing – which only Lewis succeeded in persuading him was more than a private obsession (*Inks* 32) – presumably led, as in Lewis's case, to a range of self-protective mechanisms or postures, such as his claim to know nothing about English literature after Chaucer (also a reflection of English departmental politics in the earlier part of last century[8]). Disparaging remarks about Romanticism in general, and Wagner in particular, should not distract us from the widely recognized indebtedness of Tolkien to Romanticism, or at least a particular Romantic tradition.[9]

Two caveats are necessary, however. Firstly, Tolkien was suspicious of discussing any work of art in terms of the 'influences' detectable in it. The 'bones-and-soup' metaphor (which Tolkien wrests from Dasent's introduction to his *Popular Tales of the North*) has a general applicability: what matters crucially, Tolkien argues in *OFS*, is the 'soup' or story as set before us by the author, and not the 'bones' of its sources (*MCOE* 120). Any attempt to substitute an exploration of sources for proper attention to the work as it is served up is a distraction. However, this by no means precludes an exploration of *how* a tale or a teller has *used* these sources. Appreciation of a good serving of soup by no means precludes discussion of its ingredients, and the cook's skill in blending them. Secondly, in this context the word 'Romanticism' is being used broadly, and is not restricted to writers working roughly between 1790 and 1830. A sense of what the word 'Romanticism' meant to Tolkien and Lewis can be gained from the Preface to the third edition of Lewis's *The Pilgrim's Regress* (=*PR*), where he discriminates between (at least) seven different ways of being 'romantic'. Presumably echoing Lovejoy's famous essay 'On the Discrimination of Romanticisms',[10] Lewis makes the typically hyperbolic claim that the term 'Romanticism' has been used in such varying senses that 'it has become useless and should be banished from our vocabulary' (*PR* 5). Lewis nevertheless finds it necessary to define these several uses of the word; what is striking is that the examples offered derive from a broad historical spectrum, ranging from Malory to Proust. Only his final category of Romanticism – 'sensibility to natural objects, when solemn and enthusiastic' – has all its examples from the Romantic period proper. Ironically, the senses in which Tolkien can described as 'Romantic' would presumably include the last of Lewis's Romanticisms (given Tolkien's much-attested love of nature); however, it would be primarily the second kind of Romanticism which attracted Tolkien:

> [T]he marvellous is 'romantic', provided it does not make part of the believed religion. Thus magicians, ghosts, fairies, witches, dragons, nymphs, and dwarfs are 'romantic' . . . In this sense Malory, Boiardo, Ariosto, Spenser, Tasso, Mrs Radcliffe, Shelley, Coleridge, William Morris, and Mr E.R. Eddison are 'Romantic' authors.
>
> (*PR* 6)

This list naturally says more about Lewis's tastes than those of Tolkien, who disclaimed knowledge of some of these authors (once commenting half-seriously: 'I don't know Ariosto . . . and I'd loathe him if I did').[11] Tolkien also disliked at least aspects of other writers on Lewis's list, for example Spenser, who was, as Shippey wryly puts it, 'one of several authors with whom Tolkien had a relationship of intimate dislike' (*RME* 389).

Two observations about Lewis's category of the Romantic as 'the marvellous' are pertinent. Firstly, as in the passage quoted above[12] from *AOL* (published between the first edition of *PR* and its later revised edition with Preface), Lewis insists that examples of the Romantic 'marvellous' must not belong to 'the believed religion'. Secondly, he refers to William Morris, who greatly influenced both Tolkien and Lewis, despite being deeply unfashionable by the1930s.[13] Tolkien was by no means alone in taking some Morris into the trenches, according to Garth, though a prose romance was more usual than *The Earthly Paradise* that accompanied Tolkien.[14] Richard Mathews has claimed that WW1 was largely responsible for the eclipse of Morris's reputation.[15] Doubtless Morris had some role in the creation of the high diction about war which Wilfred Owen called 'the old Lie' in 'Dulce et Decorum Est', though Garth has warned that:

> the disenchanted view [of Owen et al.] has left us a skewed picture of an important and complex historical event; a problem only exacerbated by a cultural and academic tendency to canonize the best and forget the rest . . . The disenchanted view of the war stripped meaning from what many soldiers saw as the defining experience of their lives.[16]

To problematize the canonization of 'the disenchanted school' of WWI poets such as Owen is obviously a sensitive issue. Whatever the origins of the pervasive use by the officer class of the term 'the Hun' in the context of WWI,[17] lines like the following from Morris's 1888 *The House of the Wolfings* (=*HOTW*) – a favourite of Tolkien's – can evoke ambivalent feelings: 'but the wrath rose up in my breast, / And the sword in my hand rose with it, and I leaped and hewed at the Hun'.[18]

Influence and the sense of 'depth'

Despite Lewis's memorable one-liner: 'No one ever influenced Tolkien . . . [y]ou might as well try to influence a bandersnatch' (*LL3* 1049), the greatest modern literary influence on Tolkien almost certainly *was* Morris (though the greatest influence of all was 'the author of *Beowulf*'). Lewis's distinction between 'source' and 'influence' is helpful here: 'A Source gives us something to write about; an Influence prompts us to write in a certain way . . . my own habit of immoderate quotation showed the Influence of Hazlitt, but not the influence of the authors I quote'.[19] Morris is not so much in Lewis's sense a 'source' for Tolkien: both writers derived many of their key ideas and motifs from their shared immersion in Norse literature and mythology. Only in one curious instance may Morris be regarded in some sense as a 'source'. Marjorie Burns has argued that Morris's *Icelandic Journals* provided Tolkien with several details in *The Hobbit*, including the figure of Bilbo himself. The latter's appearance is loosely based, Burns argues, both on Morris's self-descriptions in the *Journals*, and on cartoons of him by his travelling companion, Sir Edward Burne-Jones.[20] Morris's 'influence' on Tolkien is apparent in the archaic mannerisms of Tolkien's style, which, especially in his earlier works, is clearly based on that of Morris's prose romances. When Exeter College, Oxford, awarded Tolkien the Skeat Prize for English in 1914 (there was not a lot of competition that particular year), Tolkien chose several volumes by Morris, including his translation of the *Völsungasaga* and his prose-and-verse romance *HOTW* (*Biog* 99).

The texts Tolkien bought with his prize-money exemplify Lewis's distinction between 'source' and 'influence'. The translation of the *Völsungasaga* in a sense provides a 'source' in that the material relating to Sigurd and the dragon Fafnir (which Tolkien would already have known, not least from the version in Andrew Lang's *Red Fairy Book* of 1890) provided him not only with some of the key elements of Smaug in *The Hobbit*, but also details of the slaying of the dragon Glorund (Glaurung in later versions) by Túrin Turambar. The 'Tale of Turambar' was one of the three tales (the others are 'Beren and Tinúviel (later Lúthien)' and 'The Fall of Gondolin') that persisted in Tolkien's imagination from the original *Lost Tales* – elaborated at the end of WWI – through various versions (both in prose and in verse), and finally into the posthumously published *Silmarillion* and *Unfinished Tales*. The tale of Túrin Turambar, with the slaying of the dragon Glaurung, ultimately appeared as the climax of *The Children of Húrin*, a composite version of the Túrin story culled by Chrisopher Tolkien from his and his father's many versions, finally published in 2007.[21] The other key 'source' for the tale of Túrin, who unwittingly marries his sister and subsequently commits suicide, was the story of Kullervo from the Finnish *Kalevala*, which was itself a Romantic nationalistic collection/confection created by Elias Lönnrot: it first appeared in 1835 and was completed in 1849.[22] Tolkien deeply admired this (re)constructed national mythology, and like Margaret Schlegel in E.M. Forster's *Howard's End* (1910), bemoaned the lack of an English equivalent.[23] Tolkien's so-called 'legendarium' has often been interpreted as an attempt to do for England what Lönnrot did for Finland. In 1914 Tolkien wrote to his fiancée Edith Bratt that he was attempting 'to turn one of the [*Kalevala*] stories – which is really a very great story and most tragic [the tale of Kullervo] – into a short story somewhat on the lines of Morris's romances with chunks of poetry in between' (*TL* 7).[24] Here Morris's 'influence' on Tolkien is explicit, and presumably derives in considerable measure from *HOTW* that Tolkien had recently bought with his college prize-money.

Apart from works by Morris, the other items on that 1914 shopping list (courtesy of the disapproving shade of Walter Skeat[25]) were some books on mediaeval Welsh (*MCOE* 192). These Welsh books represent another 'influence' on Tolkien, in the sense that, in addition to whatever material he may have taken from Welsh legend as a 'source', it was the Welsh language itself that had a profound 'influence' on the way he would later write. Tolkien's first encounter with the Welsh language had been the names on the coal-trucks he saw on the railway line near the new home in industrial Birmingham where his mother had moved with her two young sons (*Biog* 43). These Welsh names fascinated the young Tolkien, and the later knowledge of Welsh he acquired was ultimately to provide the inspiration for one of the forms of Tolkien's invented Elvish language, called 'Sindarin'; the other form of Elvish – 'Quenya' – was modelled on Finnish (*RME* 275n). In fact it was Tolkien's experiences with the Welsh and Finnish *languages* that were decisive for his later elaboration of a 'mythology for England' – though this popular designation is actually 'a misnomer' according to Flieger (*IM* 145nl), since Tolkien's actual words in 1951 were that what he wished to '*dedicate* simply *to*: England; to my country' was 'a body of more or less connected legend, ranging from the large and cosmogonic, to the level of Romantic fairy-story' (*TL* 144, emphasis added). Of his first experience of Finnish, in a grammar he discovered in Exeter College library, Tolkien wrote to Auden in 1955:

> It was like discovering a complete wine-cellar filled with bottles of an amazing wine of a kind and flavour never tasted before. It quite intoxicated me; and I gave up the attempt to invent an 'unrecorded' Germanic language, and my 'own language' – or series of invented languages – became heavily Finnicized in phonetic pattern and structure . . . All this only as background to the stories, though languages and names are for me

inextricable from the stories. They are and were so to speak an attempt to give a background or a world in which my expressions of linguistic taste could have a function. The stories were comparatively late in coming.

(TL 214)

Not only the language of the Finnish *Kalevala*, but their mode of presentation as a *compilation* was to have a great influence on Tolkien. The fact that the *Kalevala*, like other compilations, are nineteenth century versions of older folk tales gives them a sense of historical *depth*.

This sense of historical depth is increased when, as in many mediaeval versions of mythical and/or legendary material, the mediaeval author is himself a (usually Christian) compiler of much older pre-Christian oral sources – as in the case of *Beowulf*. Tolkien sought to achieve this effect of historical depth in his invented mythology by providing multiple versions of the same story.[26] This may be to some extent a case of making a virtue of necessity (given Tolkien's tendency constantly to 'niggle' at, and rework, his stories). It also provides a kind of 'reality effect' that can be seen at work in *The Lord of the Rings* (=*LOTR*) and even in *The Hobbit*. Flieger argues that at least the dwarves' songs in *The Hobbit* appear to be 'obviously part of bardic tradition of preserved communal history and prophecy ... These songs become a mythic lead-in to *LOTR*, and serve retrospectively to fit *The Hobbit* into the larger history of the Silmarillion' (*IM* 64). Although originally developed as a 'stand-alone' fairy-story for Tolkien's children – and inhabiting the 'once-upon-a-time' region that is unconnected with 'real time' – *The Hobbit* was retrospectively linked to *LOTR* ('the new *Hobbit*', as Tolkien called it), and thus to the much older material in Tolkien's legendarium which underlies, and gives quasi-historical depth to *LOTR*. Even before the need to dovetail *The Hobbit* with its sequel, the earlier book already made a few allusions to Tolkien's legendarium, as John Rateliff shows in his detailed textual commentary in *The History of the Hobbit*.[27]

The illusion of depth is created by such devices as Tolkien's introduction into the second edition of *LOTR* of a 'Note on the Shire Records', which refers back to 'the Red Book of Westmarch' which 'has not been preserved, but many copies were made ... '.[28] This pseudo-historical contextualization of *LOTR* is a kind of pastiche of the scholarly work that formed part of Tolkien's 'day-job' as an Oxford professor. Indeed, it has been argued by Michael Drout that, in a process of 'cross-contamination of invention and deduction', Tolkien played aesthetically and fictively with ideas that solved actual scholarly problems relating to Anglo-Saxon history and literature:

In creating his mythology for Anglo-Saxon England Tolkien did not merely develop a speculative history of the Anglo-Saxon past but also indulged in the imaginative creation of pseudohistory that [he] himself did not believe to be factually true. But because this mythological history solved a number of historical and literary puzzles and was in itself aesthetically pleasing, Tolkien found it difficult to eschew it altogether. Therefore, while he explicitly and overtly severed the connections between real European history and Middle-earth, there remains a structural substratum of story-structure, names, and parallels that links early Anglo-Saxon and Germanic culture to Tolkien's imaginative creation.[29]

As further illustrations of the kind of scholarship that Tolkien is mimicking, Flieger cites the debates (well-known to Tolkien) surrounding the sources for the Welsh *Mabinogion*, which include the Red Book of Hergest and the White Book of Rhydderch.[30] Flieger develops her case in a later essay 'Tolkien and the Idea of the Book' where she discusses the probable impact on Tolkien of the discovery in 1934 in Winchester College Library of the manuscript underlying Caxton's printed version of *Le Morte D'Arthur*.[31] Unlike the modest quarto size of other significant medieval manuscripts (such as *Beowulf* and *Sir Gawain and the Green Knight*), the Malory manuscript was folio and contained some red as well as black lettering, thus making it an almost perfect fit with the 'great big book with red and black letters' that Sam envisages as an appropriate volume for his and Frodo's story in years to come (*LOTR* 712). Flieger speculates that Tolkien may even have privately entertained an analogy between the publication in 1947 of Vinaver's three-volume edition of Malory (based on the Winchester ms.),[32] and the dual publication of *LOTR* and *The Silmarillion* – an ambition that Tolkien had long (if rather unrealistically) nourished. Flieger argues that 'to position Bilbo as not just the narrator of *The Hobbit* and part of *LOTR*, but also, through "his researches at Rivendell", as the translator and redactor of the earlier "book" (whatever title it may have acquired by then), is to place that unassuming hobbit on a fictive editorial footing with Malory, and equally, to put Tolkien's Red Book on a Middle-earth par with the Winchester manuscript' (*Blackwelder* 294). Multiplying historical ironies, Flieger points out that despite Tolkien's acute disappointment that during his lifetime *The Silmarillion* was never published at all – let alone in a dual edition with *LOTR* – nevertheless this delay only served to intensify the resemblance of Tolkien's posthumously published oeuvre to some scholarly compilation of lost but found manuscripts. The editor was not any of the fictive editors Tolkien imagined, however, but his son Christopher, who oversaw the publication of the twelve-volume *History of Middle-earth* (*Blackwelder* 396).

Shippey compares Tolkien's technique of 'pastiche' to the linguistic procedure of 'calquing', where a word in one language is literally copied bit-by-bit into another, for example the French *haut-parleur* for 'loudspeaker' (*RME* 116). An example of calquing would be the name 'Rashbold' which Tolkien gives to an Oxford professor and his undergraduate son in *The Notion Club Papers* ('The Notion Club' itself being a kind of calque of 'The Inklings'): 'rash-bold' is a calque of Tolkien's name in the original German: '*toll-kühn*'

(*RME* 339). Thus for Shippey, the Shire is a kind of 'calque' of England (more specifically the West Midlands in the late nineteenth century), both like and unlike England, just as hobbits are both like and unlike English people (*RME* 116). Such 'calquing' is related to another linguistic technique: the reconstructing of lost words on the basis of known laws governing language change, for example 'Grimm's Law of Consonants' (*RME* 9; 12; 14). Such reconstruction can also work on the level of whole works and entire languages – and thus cultures – leading to the phenomenon of 'asterisk-realities', so named because of the convention in philology of placing an asterisk in front of a reconstructed word; for example, **manniz* is the reconstructed equivalent of 'men' (modern English) and '*Männer*' (modern high German) in Primitive Germanic – the linguistic ancestor of English, German and Norse. Tolkien's invented languages are like 'calques' of real languages such as Finnish, Welsh and Anglo-Saxon or Old English, while the countries which he mapped were 'calques' of North-Western Europe, and the peoples inhabiting them were 'calques' of real or reconstructed peoples (for example Anglo-Saxons, Lombards and Goths). Particularly in this last example of the Goths, Tolkien was again following Morris's *HOTW*. While Morris worked as it were by poetic instinct – informed by much reading – Tolkien's imagined languages, peoples and landscapes had a aura of quasi-scientific philological legitimacy as well as an assiduously rigorous attention to detail of the kind that Tolkien satirized in his allegorical story *Leaf by Niggle*.

This 'grounding' of Tolkien's work in a rigorous quasi-scholarly attention to detail is one of the elements that distinguish his work from that of a plethora of imitators. It also represents another inflection of the workings of the Romantic imagination; the brothers Grimm, whose collection of folk-tales was so closely associated with the development of the Romantic *Märchen* or fairy-tale, were also great pioneers in the science of philology. There is, however, a significant difference between the world of Morris's *HOTW* and Tolkien's *LOTR*. The former world did in some sense actually exist, and to that extent Morris's work is an imaginative historical reconstruction of real people in real places. Admittedly the historical context created by Morris (and his use of the term 'Goth') is vague and chronologically problematic, since it hovers uncertainly somewhere between the destruction of the legions of the Roman general Varus in 9CE by Arminius (leader of the Germanic Cherusci) and the arrival of the Huns some centuries later. Nevertheless, the event recounted in Chapter 6 of *HOTW* when a refugee Gael or Celt tells some 'Goths' about his experiences with the Romans is quasi-historical; something not entirely unlike this might actually have happened. Tolkien does something rather similar in his imaginative recreation of the aftermath of the Battle of Maldon in his 'play for voices', *The Homecoming of Beorhtnoth*. *HOTW* contrasts with other works by Morris such as *The Wood beyond the World* where the imagined world was never part of our world, and is more like the fantasy worlds of MacDonald; unlike the latter, however,

Morris's fantasy worlds tend to be 'stand-alone', requiring no 'portals' of any kind (such as magic mirrors) to enable movement between the imagined world and the real 'primary' world. *The Hobbit* initially took place in a largely 'stand-alone' fairy-tale world, even if Tolkien later developed its few tentative connections with the larger and older world of Middle-earth.

The so-to-speak ontological status of Middle-earth – with its vast history and mythology (Tolkien's 'legendarium') – is problematic. On the one hand, in being a kind of 'stand-alone' fairy-tale world, Middle-earth partly resembles the worlds of *The Hobbit* and *The Wood beyond the World* (worlds in other respects very different, with the former containing no sex, and the latter exuding it); but on the other hand, Middle-earth resembles the world of *HOTW* in that it is 'calqued' on reconstructed ancient – but in some sense 'real' – history. Tolkien seems to want to blur the ontological difference between the reconstructed 'asterisk-world' (which purports to be 'real') and his imaginary other world that *is* purely imaginary (similar in some respects to the Otherworld of Faërie). This ambiguity can arguably be seen in the tendency to *want* Tolkien to have said that his legendarium provided 'a mythology for England', when in fact, as Flieger has pointed out, he merely *dedicated* his imagined mythology *to* England. Of course the 'calqued' role of Tolkien as a compiler of 'a mythology for England', *à la* Lönnrot and the *Kalevala*, encourages the former interpretation. Fantasy is after all, as Tolkien knew, the province of *desire* – we *want* Middle-earth to be in some sense 'real'. It must also be admitted that, as Drout in particular has noted (see above), Tolkien himself had a strong tendency to such wishful thinking. The ontological difference between England and Middle-earth was something Tolkien created only gradually; at first there was, as we shall see, a disconcertingly strong overlap between England and Tolkien's Faërie island of 'Tol Eressëa', where we first hear the telling of 'the Lost Tales' that constitute Tolkien's legendarium. The distance between Tol Eressëa' (subsequently Middle-earth) and England increases as Tolkien's writing career develops. However, there always remains a connection between Middle-earth and our world (Drout's 'cross-contamination of invention and deduction') that is complex, ambiguous and problematic.

Time slips

(i) *The Lost Road*

The relation of his imaginative creations to reality was an issue that increasingly concerned Tolkien in the second half of the 1930s. On the one hand, the (more or less) 'stand-alone' fairy-tale world of *The Hobbit* was proving to be successful. On the other hand, Tolkien was also experimenting with ways in which his imaginary reconstructed 'asterisk-world' might actually be somehow related to our real 'primary' world. Early evidence for this is to be found in Tolkien's letter of February 1938 to Stanley Unwin, the publisher, expressing his gratitude to Unwin's son Rayner for his enthusiastic response to the first chapter of the sequel to *The Hobbit* (young Rayner's response to the manuscript of *The Hobbit* had been a decisive factor in its publication) (*TL* 29). Tolkien puts in a good word for Lewis's *Out of the Silent Planet* (=*OSP*) (which Unwin in the event passed to Bodley Head after the Allen & Unwin readers rejected it), alluding to a 'toss-up' between himself and Lewis to decide which one of them would write a 'thriller' about space-travel, while the other wrote about 'time-travel'. According to Christopher Tolkien, there is no evidence for the exact date of this celebrated 'toss-up', a phrase Tolkien uses in a letter of July 1964 (*TL* 347); Flieger calculates it must have been early in 1936.[33] Both of these 'thrillers' – each 'discovering Myth' in Tolkien's phrase – were begun, but only Lewis's was completed; Tolkien's fragment entitled *The Lost Road* (=*LR*) was turned down by Unwin (*TL* 29). However, Tolkien resurrected his 'time-travel' project a decade later, telling Unwin in July 1946 that he had 'written three parts of another book, taking up in an entirely different frame and setting what little had any value in the incohate *Lost Road* (which I had once the impudence to show you: I hope it is forgotten)' (*TL* 118). This second version of the 'time-travel' thriller was called *The Notion Club Papers* (=*NCP*). Although more substantial than its predecessor, it also remained unfinished. Very different from *LR*, and existing in various overlapping and conflicting drafts, *NCP* attempts like its predecessor to connect Tolkien's mythological world with 'true' history, or '*mythos* with *vera historia*', as Tolkien wrote to Unwin in March 1938, apropos Lewis's *OSP* (*TL* 33). To use the terms Tolkien elaborated in *OFS*, which he was also writing at about this time, he was seeking somehow to relate his 'secondary world' of myth and fantasy (or Faërie) to the 'primary world' of factual truth.

If the toss of a coin allocated to Tolkien the genre of 'time-travel' fiction, then the way the coin fell was fortunate, since this genre allowed Tolkien to address an issue that had haunted his fiction from the beginning: how to develop a narrative frame for his tales of an imagined mythological (or fantasy) world; and how to relate them to the 'primary' world of the reader in real history. The earliest version of Tolkien's mythology, written up by his wife in a school exercise book and dated February 1917, is entitled *The Cottage of Lost Play, which introduceth* [*the*] *Book of Lost Tales*. The key character is a traveller named Eriol who sails to the Lonely Island – 'Tol Eressëa in the fairy speech' – and finds his way to 'the Cottage of Lost Play' where he hears tales of the Valar (gods) and Eldar (elves) – in other words the beginnings of what would later be called 'the Silmarillion'.[34] At this stage there is an almost disconcerting blurring of the boundaries between Tolkien's private mythology and English history and legend. Christopher Tolkien tells us how in the notes to this very early version of his father's legendarium, Eriol 'adopted the name of *Angol*' and was called by this name 'after the regions of his home' by 'the Gnomes', as Tolkien still called the Elves or 'Noldor' at this point (though he later wisely abandoned the term, Paracelsus notwithstanding) (*BLT1* 24; 43–4). The reference here is clearly to 'the ancient homeland of the "English" before their migration across the North Sea to Britain' (*BLT1* 24). Eriol or *Angol* is thus an 'Angle', voyaging after the death of his first wife and sometime *before* the invasion of Britain by the Angles and other Scandinavian/Germanic peoples, to the Lonely Island, 'Tol Eressëa', that would later be called England. Back in his native Heligoland, Eriol had already fathered Hengest and Horsa (the semi-legendary leaders of the first Danish invasion of Britain, mentioned in *Beowulf*); however, in 'Tol Eressëa' he is rejuvenated, marries again and fathers Heorrenda. It is through Eriol, Tolkien says, that 'the *Engle* (i.e. the English) [who] have the true tradition of the fairies, of whom the *Iras* and the *Wéalas* (the Irish and the Welsh) tell garbled things' (*BLT2* 290). Here Tolkien's specifically English nationalism is taking revenge for his sense of the inferiority of English legends ('impoverished chap-book stuff') in comparison with those of the Celts (*TL* 144). Tolkien would later change his mythology radically and the Lonely Island, 'Tol Eressëa', would move much further West, to be visited (if such a thing proves possible at all) by voyaging *from* England. But at this earliest stage Tolkien did not hesitate to map his private mythology onto historical (or at least legendary) England. Thus the town in Tol Eressëa which Eriol visits is called 'Kortirion' and 'would become in after days Warwick . . . and Tavrobel, where Eriol sojourned for a while in Tol Eressëa, would afterwards be the Staffordshire village of Great Haywood' – both Warwick and Great Haywood were places of great personal significance for the Tolkiens (*BLT1* 25).

By the mid 1920s, however, Tolkien had begun to recast his mythology in a radical way, lessening the identification of Tol Eressëa with England, and increasingly replacing the figure (or at least the name) of 'Eriol' with that of 'Ælfwine'. This transition between Eriol and Ælfwine – both as narrator of, and participant in, the 'Lost Tales' – is for Christopher Tolkien 'the most difficult . . . part of the earliest form of the mythology . . . [N]o device of presentation can much diminish the inherent complexity and obscurity of the matter' (*BLT2* 278). The constantly changing differences between 'the Eriol story' and 'the Ælfwine story' (of which Christopher Tolkien offers a diagrammatic presentation (*BLT2* 303)) need hardly detain us; what is interesting is the emergence of a short work (again, in differing versions) entitled 'Ælfwine of England'. England was 'an island of the West' of which part had been broken off 'in the warfare of the Gods', although, as the narrator hastens to add, 'that part that was broken was called Ireland . . . and its dwellers come not into these tales' (*BLT2* 312). Elves still dwell in England, or 'Lúthien' (or 'Luthany') as they call it. 'Amidmost of that island', writes Tolkien in the archaic Morrisian prose of these 'Lost Tales of Elfinesse', lies the ancient town the Elves call Kortirion (*BLT2* 313). Here dwells Déor – the name of the exiled poet in the eponymous early Anglo-Saxon poem. In the latter, Déor has been supplanted by Heorrenda – the name of the son born to Eriol on Tol Eressëa, who in one version of Tolkien's legendarium compiles his father's writings in the 'the Golden Book of Heorrenda' (*BLT2* 290–1). Tolkien took only the names from the Anglo-Saxon poem – though he did not, his son claims, 'take the names at random' – often referring to the unknown poet of *Beowulf* as Heorrenda (*BLT2* 323). When the Vikings or 'the Men of the North whom the fairies of the island called Forodwaith' (*BLT2* 313) sack the town, killing Déor and his wife Éadgifu from Lionesse (or Lyonesse, the legendary drowned kingdom off Cornwall), their orphaned son Ælfwine is taken as a slave by the Vikings. But Ælfwine, who has inherited a longing for the sea from his mother, escapes and voyages widely before being shipwrecked on one of the Harbourless Islands, created to prevent anyone reaching Valinor, the country of the Valar (or gods) in the far West. Here Ælfwine meets the ancient Man of the Sea (Ulmo, the god of the Sea, in disguise), who miraculously releases from a sandbank a longship containing the dead Vikings who had killed Ælfwine's parents and taken him prisoner (*BLT2* 316–8). With the Man of the Sea as pilot and steersman, Ælfwine travels in the longship to further mysterious islands, where a strange people called the Ythlings build him a magic ship with the guidance (and spells) of the ancient Man of the Sea. The latter then leaps from a high cliff, disappearing into the surf to Ælfwine's consternation, but the unconcern of the islanders, who clearly know more than Ælfwine. The magic ship eventually finds its way to within sight and smell of Tol Eressëa, before it is driven back as the island disappears in mist. There are alternative endings to the tale of 'Ælfwine of England': in one, Ælfwine jumps overboard into the sea as the ship turns back; in another, Ælfwine returns home sadly.

Although this early tale is about 'Ælfwine of England', there is little to connect him to real history other than some very generalized references to legendary English figures. There are some more specific historical connections in a second version of the Ælfwine story – the one that formed the kernel of *LR*, the 'time-travel thriller' Tolkien started to write in the 1930s after the toss-up with Lewis. Tolkien gives a summary of this 'abortive book of time-travel' in a letter of July 1964:

> When C.S. Lewis and I tossed up, and he was to write on space-travel and I on time-travel, I began an abortive book of time-travel of which the end was to be the presence of my hero in the drowning of Atlantis. This was to be called *Númenor*, the Land in the West. The thread was to be the occurrence time and again in human families . . . of a father and son called by names that could be interpreted as Bliss-friend and Elf-friend. These no longer understood are found in the end to refer to the Atlantid-Númenórean situation and mean 'one loyal to the Valar, content with the bliss and prosperity within the limits prescribed' and 'one loyal to friendship with the High-elves'. It started with a father-son affinity between Edwin and Elwin of the present, and was supposed to go back

into legendary time by way of an Eädwine and Ælfwine of circa A.D. 918, and Audoin and Alboin of Lombardic legend, and so the traditions of the North Sea concerning the coming of corn and culture heroes, ancestors of kingly lines, in boats (and their departure in funeral ships). One such Sheaf, or Shield Sheafing, can actually be made out as one of the remote ancestors of our present Queen. In my tale we were to come at last to Amandil and Elendil leaders of the loyal party in Númenor, when it fell under the domination of Sauron. Elendil 'Elf-friend' was the founder of the Exiled kingdoms in Arnor and Gondor.

(*TL* 347)

In this remarkable passage Tolkien manages historically to connect figures in *The Hobbit*, *LOTR* and his wider legendarium with the (still, at the time of writing) 'present Queen'!

LR opens with Oswin Errol explaining to his twelve-year son Alboin that his name goes back to the grim times of Alboin son of Audoin, the Lombard king in the sixth century (*LR* 40). Alboin means 'Elf-friend', Oswin continues, and in Anglo-Saxon the name is Ælfwine, which is also the name of several figures in Anglo-Saxon history, including King Alfred's grandson who died in the Saxon victory over a Viking-led coalition at Brunanburh (937). Other examples include the Ælfwine killed at the Battle of Maldon (991) who appears in the eponymous Anglo-Saxon poem about the battle as well as in Tolkien's *The Homecoming of Beorhtnoth* (*LR* 41). The present-day Alboin suddenly and inexplicably says, while gazing at the sunset clouds from their holiday cottage in Cornwall: '"They look like the eagles of the Lord of the West coming upon Númenor"' (*LR* 41). Alboin is used to strange dreams and names, such as *Amon-ereb* and *Beleriand*, welling up from some kind of (Tolkienian) collective unconscious; he privately writes verse in a language he calls *Eressëan* (*LR* 44). We are told how, after a First at Oxford, Alboin goes on to develop an academic career very much like that of Tolkien himself, leading to a professorship at an early age. Like his father before him, Alboin is widowed young and has an intense relationship with his son Audoin. Both Alboin and Audoin suffer from 'dreams' in languages they barely understand, though they hide this from each other. Suddenly Alboin finds himself uttering again the words he had spoken as a boy about the eagles of the Lord of the West over Númenor, and (with overtones of Lewis) he is overcome by 'the old desire' which 'had been growing again for a long time, but . . . had not felt like this, a feeling as vivid as hunger or thirst . . . not since he was Audoin's age'. He falls asleep wishing there was a 'Time-machine' and involuntarily muttering about Númenor. In his dream he meets Elendil of Númenor, whose name means 'Elf-friend' in Eressëan, thus corresponding to Ælfwine in Anglo-Saxon, as well as to Alboin's own name (*LR* 52). Elendil offers Alboin the possibility of travelling back through time, but only if accompanied by Audoin (or Herendil in Eressëan) (*LR* 53).

The remaining two completed chapters of *LR* take place in Númenor, and focus on the debate between Elendil and Herendil about the crisis in Númenor following Sauron's arrival and his poisonous influence. The story ends there, apart from some fragmentary sketches, including two scenes including Ælfwine that were later incorporated into *NCP*. The first is set in North Devon in the tenth century: the Vikings have just been defeated at the battle of Archenfield in Herefordshire (914), but continue raiding the Devon coast. The scene opens with Ælfwine awakening in a hall filled with men from Wessex (under King Edward the Elder, son of King Alfred), the Welsh Marches and the Danish-controlled East Anglia (*LR* 91–2). Summoned to sing for the king, Ælfwine chants part of the Old English poem *The Seafarer*, but his performance is not well received (*LR* 92–3). The manuscript breaks off here, but both Tolkien's letter of July 1964 (quoted above) and *NCP* suggest that fragments relating to the *King Sheave* legend belong here. Ælfwine chants the ancient tale of *Sheave*, which Tolkien gives in both prose and verse (*LR* 94–100). Tolkien's versions of *King Sheave* have roots deep in Germanic legend, especially in *Beowulf*, as Christopher Tolkien explains in several pages of footnotes. The metrical version of *King Sheave* in *LR* concludes with a list of historical peoples begotten by Sheave:

> Sea-danes and Goths, Swedes and Northmen
> Franks and Frisians, folk of the islands,
> Swordmen and Saxons, Swabes and English,
> and the Langobards who long ago
> beyond Myrcwudu a mighty realm
> and wealth won them in the Welsh countries
> where Ælfwine Eadwine's heir
> in Italy was king. All that has passed.

(LR 100)[35]

This list of peoples is an echo – or 'calque' – of the lists in, for example, the Anglo-Saxon poem *Widsith*, 'the oldest [verses] in the English language, and . . . the earliest production in verse of any Germanic people';[36] this is especially true for the list concluding in line 70 of Widsith: 'I was with Ælfwine in Italy too'. 'Welsh' in this context has the older meaning, used also by Morris in *HOTW*, of 'Celtic or Roman foreigner'; while 'Myrcwudu' or Mirkwood, deriving particularly from the *Poetic Edda*, had by 1945 acquired a particular resonance in Tolkien's work.

(ii) *The Notion Club Papers*
Although *NCP* remained unpublished until its appearance in 1992 in *Sauron Defeated* (Volume 9 of *The History of Middle-earth*, edited by Christopher Tolkien), it is from several points of view a fascinating text. For one thing,

the eponymous 'Papers' are interesting as historical documents since they purport to be the minutes of an Oxford club whose name is a pastiche (or 'calque') of the real-life 'Inklings'. The game of 'spot-the-Inkling' is ultimately futile, however, since Tolkien avoids offering a *roman à clef* by blurring any too-definite likeness of characters to actual individuals. Although Tolkien's notes, published by his son in *Sauron Defeated*, contain the initials of real-life Inklings beside particular characters, these initials switch characters in different drafts, so that it becomes impossible to fix any character to any particular Inkling with absolute consistency. However, what is of literary-historical value is the documentation of the *atmosphere* and subject matter of an Inklings meeting. The discussion of the problems of writing 'time-travel' fiction is particularly interesting. Anticipating postmodern self-reflexive metafiction, *NCP* has the members of the 'Notion Club' discuss the narratological problems of the kind of book Tolkien was trying to write in *NCP*. Moreover, the members of the fictional 'Notion Club', including imaginary (if composite) figures based on Lewis and Tolkien, discuss the real book *OSP* by the real Lewis, which started with the 'toss-up' between Lewis and Tolkien that also led to the fiction (*NCP*) we are now reading.[37] A further intertextual gambit appears when the Tolkienesque Guildford refers to Lindsay's *VTA*, adding in a footnote (since Guildford, as the Club's reporter, takes the minutes): 'This book [*VTA*] had recently been rescued from oblivion by Jeremy's book on *Imaginary Lands*' (*SD* 164). Trewin Jeremy is another 'Notion Club' member, who later becomes central to the narrative when he goes in search of the imaginary lands in the West that lie at the heart of Tolkien's mythology. Finally, in what literary theorists call a *mise en abyme* (ironically the term derives from mediaeval heraldry), the editor of *NCP*, a Mr Howard Green, who in 2012 will find the papers dating from the 1980s among sacks of waste paper in the basement of Oxford's Examination Schools, quotes J.R. Titmass, 'the well-known historian of twentieth-century Oxford', to the effect that the name of the Club reporter, Nicholas Guildford, 'is certainly a fictitious name and derived from a mediaeval dialogue at one time read in the Schools of Oxford' (*SD* 156). We seem not a million miles away from Eco and Borges.

As Tolkien put it to Unwin, *NCP* takes up most of the content of *LR*, but 'in an entirely different frame and setting' (*TL* 118). While the frame for the events narrated in *LR* is the relationship between two father-son pairings (Oswin/Alboin and Alboin/Audoin), the frame in *NCP* is the Oxford club 'calqued' on the Inklings. In this latter frame for a tale of 'other worlds', the main topic of the opening discussion among the club members is – self-reflexively – the frame for a tale of 'other worlds'. After Ramer has read the group a tale set in another world (a tale the reader never hears), the ensuing discussion ranges over examples of the genres of space- and time-travel. But one member, Dolbear – who has an interest in psychoanalysis – realizes that no matter how slipshod the frame of Ramer's tale is, its central section – unlike the frame – is not 'made up' (*SD* 171). Ramer admits: '"I don't think our language fits the case. But there is such a world, and I saw it – once"' (*SD* 172). Ramer claims to have explored various means of travelling through time and space, including via telepathy and dreams, particularly the latter. Tolkien's references to dreams as a means of 'time-travel' owe much to J.W. Dunne's *An Experiment with Time* (1927), as Flieger has argued persuasively in *A Question of Time*. Dunne's ideas evidently lie behind Ramer's claim that '"a pretty good case ha[s] been made out for the view that in dream a mind can . . . move in Time: I mean, can observe a time other than that occupied by the sleeping body during the dream"' (*SD* 175). Like Dunne, Ramer has trained himself to use his dreams. Such experiments are, however, swept away by an experience that overwhelms Ramer. The dream, he says, was like '"a violent awakening"'; he continues: '"I was awake in bed, and I *fell wide asleep*: . . . suddenly and violently . . . I dived slap through several levels and a whirl of shapes and scenes into a connected and remembered sequence"' (*SD* 184). What Ramer calls '*my serious dreams*' are accompanied by very powerful emotional aftershocks, both positive ('"a happiness that brings tears, like the thrill of the sudden turn for good in a dangerous tale"'[38]) and negative ('"a dull sense of loss, as heavy as anything you felt in childhood when something precious was broken or lost"') (*SD* 184; 190; 191). One particular dream Ramer describes is of '"a Green Wave, white crested, fluted and scallop-shaped but vast, towering above green fields, often with a wood of trees"' (*SD* 194). As Christopher Tolkien notes, this is reminiscent of his father's letter to Auden about 'the terrible recurrent dream (beginning with memory) of the Great Wave, towering up, and coming in ineluctably over the trees and green fields. (I bequeathed it to Faramir.) I don't think I have had it since I wrote the "Downfall of Númenor"' (*SD* 217n45; *TL* 213).

At this point the significantly named Alwin Arundel Lowdham (Arry to his friends) begins to take an interest in Ramer's dreams, especially when Ramer links the Great Wave with Atlantis (*SD* 206). In Part Two of *NCP* (the manuscript of which carries the subtitle 'The Strange Case of Arundel Loudham') Lowdham starts to crack up, cursing 'Zigur' (or Sauron), and 'turning fiercely upon us as he cried aloud: *Behold the Eagles of the Lords of the West! They are coming over Númenór!*' (*SD* 231). When questioned, Lowdham denies knowing where the name comes from. Ramer says that *his* name for Atlantis is *Númenór*, a name Trewin Jeremy also suddenly admits to recognizing.

The next meeting begins with Lowdham's account of his father Edwin's mysterious disappearance in the Atlantic with his ship *The Éarendel*. The ship's name is significant: originally Edwin Lowdham had wanted to call his son Ælfwine Éarendel, but because of his mother's objections, he was named Alwin Arundel, with the unsuitable name passing to the ship (*SD* 234). Edwin Lowdham and *The Éarendel* disappeared in 1947, almost exactly forty years before the events depicted in *NCP*. The club members spot the allusions in the Edwin/Alwin::Éadwine/Ælfwine::Albuin/Auduin pairings, but *Éarendel* proves more difficult to place. The name comes from Cynewulf's Anglo-Saxon poem *Crist*: '*Eala Earendel engla beorhtast / ofer middangeard monnum sended.*' [Hail! Earendel brightest of angels / above the middle earth sent unto men.] – lines that greatly impressed the young Tolkien when he discovered them in 1914. Tolkien's reaction is transferred to Arry Lowdham in *NCP*: '"[w]hen I came across that citation . . . I felt a curious thrill, as if something had stirred in me, half wakened from sleep. There was something very remote and strange and beautiful behind those words, if I could grasp it, far beyond ancient English"' (*SD* 236). In 1914 Tolkien had been inspired to write the poem 'The Voyage of Éarendel the Evening Star', which opens: 'Éarendel sprang up from the Ocean's cup / In the gloom of the mid-world's rim'. Tolkien later wrote that with this poem '[Earendel] launched his ship like a bright spark from the havens of the Sun. I adopted him into my mythology – in which he became a prime figure as a mariner, and eventually as a herald star' (*TL* 385). *Éarendil* was to appear, Tolkien continues in this letter of 1967, 'in the earliest written (1916–7) of the major legends: *The Fall of Gondolin*'; and mindful of his desire to exclude explicitly Christian material from his 'legendarium', he adds: 'the use of *éarendel* in [Anglo-Saxon] Christian symbolism as the herald of the rise of the true Sun in Christ is completely alien to my use' (*TL* 386–7).

Besides the Anglo-Saxon connection, however, Lowdham claims to have heard *Éarendel* in another language and tells the Notion Club members of his 'visitations of linguistic ghosts', the linguistic equivalent of Ramer's Dreams (and Alboin's and Audoin's in *LR*) (*SD* 237). According to Lowdham the name *Éarendil* is 'Avallonian', whose 'simple and euphonious style' seems 'sacred and liturgical', leading him to call it 'Elven-Latin' (*SD* 241). Lowdham silences the scepticism and mockery of his fellow Notion Club members when at the next meeting he produces a text in 'Avallonian' and 'Adunaic' which has come to him in a dream. The text contains the names *Tar-kalion*, *Sauron* and *Zigur*; at the mention of the latter Jeremy becomes distressed and addresses Lowdham as 'Nimruzir' (or 'Elendil', as we discover) (*SD* 250). Staring out the window over Oxford, Lowdham shouts the fateful words: '"The Eagles of the Lords of the West are at hand!"'[39] A great storm erupts, the greatest storm in living memory, 'the terrible storm of June 12th 1987' (*SD* 251–2). Lowdham and Jeremy converse excitedly in a mixture of English and Adunaic as they evidently witness the Drowning of Númenór as if they were 'hanging over the side of a ship', before stumbling off, terror-stricken, into the stormy Oxford night.

What is striking about this dramatic (or melodramatic) climax is that characters and events in Tolkien's mythological world intrude into a 'realistic' (if fictional) Oxford, set in 1987. It is uncanny that in 1945–6 Tolkien should write about 'The Great Storm of 1987', setting it only a few months before the actual great storm of 1987. After witnessing this collision of mythology and (in some sense) real history, of *mythos* and *vera historia*,

Ramer comments to Guildford: ' "I have an odd feeling, Nick, or suspicion, that we may all have been helping to stir something up. If not out of history, at any rate out of a very powerful world of imagination and memory. Jeremy would say "perhaps out of both" " ' (*SD* 253). This refers to Jeremy's response, earlier in the evening, to Lowdham's guess that the linguistic fragments he has been 'receiving' relate to 'a record, or a legend, of an Atlantis catastrophe':

> 'Why *or*?' said Jeremy. 'I mean, it might be a record *and* a legend. You never really tackled the question I propounded at our first meeting this term. If you went back would you find myth dissolving into history or history into myth? Somebody once said, I forget who, that the distinction between history and myth might be meaningless outside the Earth, further back. Perhaps the Atlantis catastrophe was the dividing line?
>
> (*SD* 249)

The 'somebody' in question (though Christopher Tolkien omits this) is C.S. Lewis, Jeremy's research specialism. In the penultimate chapter of *OSP* (Lewis's part of the 'space- and time-travel' bargain and frequently mentioned in *NCP*), the hero Ransom reflects as the spacecraft rises above Malacandra (Mars) on the return voyage to Thulcandra (Earth):

> Seen from the height which the spaceship had now attained, in all their unmistakable geometry, [the 'canals'] put to shame his original impression that they were natural valleys. They were gigantic feats of engineering, about which he had learned nothing; feats accomplished, if all were true, before human history began . . . Or was that only mythology? He knew it would seem like mythology when he got back to Earth (if he ever got back) . . . It even occurred to him that the distinction between history and mythology might be itself meaningless outside the Earth.[40]

The relation of myth and history, and the relation of both to 'fact', is discussed at greater length in Lewis's *Perelandra*, the sequel to *OSP*. Because of the great importance of this issue to Lewis's conversion in 1931 (after intense discussion with Tolkien and Hugo Dyson), it will receive further attention in Chapter 4 below.

Meanwhile, the dramatic intrusion of elements from Tolkien's mythology into modern, 'real life' Oxford has a powerful impact – as do the Arthurian elements which erupt into modern England in Lewis's *That Hideous Strength* (= *THS*), the third of *The Cosmic Trilogy*. This was published in the same year that Tolkien was working on *NCP*, though its Preface is dated as Christmas Eve 1943. Tolkien had heard Lewis reading *THS* to the Inklings, but was unimpressed – 'Tripish, I fear', he commented (*Biog* 227n1). It had been spoiled, Tolkien felt, by the influence on Lewis of Charles Williams, which prevented the maturing of Lewis's invented mythology in the first two volumes of his Trilogy (*TL* 342; 361). Lewis's earlier mythology had much in common with Tolkien's, to the extent that Tolkien half-jokingly accused Lewis of plagiarizing the term 'Numinor' (*CT* 656), which Lewis had heard in passages from Tolkien's legendarium read to the Inklings (*TL* 224). Lewis had, to be fair, acknowledged Tolkien in the Preface to *THS*: 'Those who would like to learn further about Numinor [*sic*] and the True West must (alas!) await the publication of much that still exists only in the MSS of my friend, Professor J.R.R. Tolkien' (*CT* 354). Lewis's (misspelled) reference to Númenór and the terrifying irruption of mythological figures into contemporary (and specifically academic) life, link *THS* and *NCP*. It is ironical that the former, which many besides Tolkien have thought a disappointing sequel to the preceding volumes of the *Cosmic Trilogy*, should have been successfully published, while the arguably more promising *NCP* remained unfinished and unpublished for almost two decades after Tolkien's death, only appearing as part of a collection with the composite title *Sauron Defeated*.

After the cataclysmic storm scene and the disappearance of Jeremy and Lowdham, a mysterious manuscript is discovered, which according to Professor Rashbold of Pembroke ('calqued' on Tolkien) recounts the Fall of Númenór through the machinations of Zigur (Sauron). It is written in 'Old English of a strongly Mercian (West-Midland) colour, ninth century (*SD* 257) – a tongue to which Tolkien told Auden he was drawn more by blood and ancestry than any mere aptitude or academic inclination (*TL* 213). Lowdham and Jeremy eventually return to Oxford, and tell the assembled club how they sailed up and down the West coast of the British Isles (the 'Celtic Fringes'), ending up in Porlock, from where they walked to Culbone, whose 'magical geography' influenced Coleridge's early visionary poetry[41] (*SD* 267–8). At Culbone they are both overcome by a sense of the uncanny, Lowdham suddenly starts talking in Anglo-Saxon and he even refers to a Danish attack. We are thus returned to the scene from the end of *LR*, with references both to historical figures such as King Edward and King Alfred, and to figures from Tolkien's private mythology (Éadwine and Éarendel), all leading into the prose version of *King Sheave*. Also in this historical and mythological mix is a poem that 'came to' another Notion Club member Philip Frankley in his sleep, much like the 'Dreams' of other characters in *NCP* (and not unlike Coleridge's famous dream experience at Culbone). The poem Frankley dreamed – 'The Death of St. Brendan' – relates so closely to the experiences of Jeremy and Lowdham that the latter exclaims (referring to Ramer's dream-experiments): ' "Very odd! . . . Have you been in touch with our minds on the Ramer-system, Philip?" ' (*SD* 264). A key connection between 'The Death of St. Brendan' and the adventures of Jeremy and Lowdham is the quest for the old road to the uttermost West, or as Frankley's dream-poem puts it:

> The Star? Yes, I saw it high and far,
>   at the parting of the ways,

> a light on the edge of the Outer Night
>   like silver set ablaze,
> where the round world plunges steeply down,
>   but on the old road goes,
> as an unseen bridge that on arches runs
>   to coasts than [*sic*] no man knows.

(SD 264)

These lines are an unmistakeable reference to the fundamental shift in geography that occurred when Númenór fell into the abyss, and the shape of the world was changed, with the Western lands removed beyond 'the circles of the world' and 'beyond the reach of Men for ever' (*S* 315). The world itself was 'bent', yet the Straight Road to the Ancient West remained a tantalizing possibility for those (like Bilbo and Frodo at the end of *LOTR*) who 'by some fate or grace or favour of the Valar' were permitted to find it and 'come to the lamplit quays of Avalloné . . . and there look upon the White Mountain, dreadful and beautiful, before they died' (*S* 319). This is precisely the 'old road' of 'The Death of St. Brendan' and the eponymous 'lost road' of Tolkien's original 'time-travel' thriller, the predecessor of *NCP*.

More trouble with human history

The problems – geological, geographical and historical – caused by the cataclysmic sinking of Númenór/Atlantis and the 'bending' of the world, are mentioned in Tolkien's 1955 letter about Lewis's 'plagiarism' of the name 'Númenór':

> As for the shape of the world of the Third Age, I am afraid that was devised 'dramatically' rather than geologically . . . I do sometimes wish that I had made some sort of agreement between the imaginations or theories of the geologists and my map a little more possible. But that would only have made more trouble with human history.

(TL 224)

The phrase 'more trouble with human history' suggests the complex issues raised by the distinctive ways in which Tolkien's mythological world is related to 'true' history – his *mythos* to *vera historia*. In his essay '"And All the Days of Her Life Are Forgotten": *LOTR* as Mythic Prehistory' Rateliff makes a strong case for accepting in a fairly literal sense Tolkien's insistence that his legendarium is about the lost history of *our* world. In a way that distances him from his most slavish imitators, Tolkien sets his mythology not just in some imaginary Otherworld of fantasy or Faërie, or on some other planet, but in the imagined prehistory of *our* world. Middle-earth will ultimately become *our* earth: that is its (and our) tragedy (*Blackwelder* 67–8). Far from being a retreat into rustic jollity, as those who sneer at 'Hobbitry' sometimes assume (not without some justification, if one visits certain websites), Tolkien's world is actually very dark. Rateliff chooses his title from the 'Tale of Aragorn and Arwen' in Appendix A of *LOTR* (*LOTR* 1057–63). In this account of Arwen's choice to surrender her Elvish immortality in order to marry Aragorn (an explicit reprise of the Lúthien and Beren story), the words 'hard' and 'bitter' resonate throughout. The 'Gift' or 'Doom' of death to Men [*sic*)] which comes to Aragorn after 'six-score years [of] great glory and bliss' finds him ready, but not so Arwen. Her father Elrond had warned that ' "to Arwen the Doom of Men may seem hard at the ending" ' (*LOTR* 1061). As the narrator laconically puts it: 'Arwen become as a mortal woman, and yet it was not her lot to die until all that she had gained was lost' (*LOTR* 1062). Her sense of bereavement is overwhelming; she returns to the now deserted Lórien to await death alone. Until 'the world is changed' (Tolkien's eschatological hope for some cosmic *'eucatastrophe'*), 'all the days of her life are utterly forgotten by men that come after . . . ' (*LOTR* 1063). Tolkien's work exudes a powerful sense of loss. Rateliff chooses to refer to the tale of Aragorn and Arwen – almost the last word on the matter of *LOTR* – in order to stress that Tolkien's decision to locate his tales in the imagined prehistory of *our* world has 'a necessary consequence':

> Every wonder he creates is predestined to be destroyed, every race and creature he invents doomed to fade into extinction, every city and culture to pass away utterly, leaving no discernible trace. Only a word or two, a few vague legends and confused traditions, a smattering of lines of non-sense nursery rhyme, and perhaps a single, battered book would remain to testify of a time when we shared this world with other folk: the elves and dwarves and goblins, and others we have utterly forgotten (e.g. ents and hobbits).
>
> (*Blackwelder* 68)

If this is 'escapism', it is escapism of a particularly melancholy kind. The 'Objective Correlative' of *LOTR* is a kind of noble grief so powerful that the reader has to wonder about its sources. The latter presumably comprise both the life Tolkien led (the early loss of both parents; the Great War) and the literature he read, which tended to embody 'the northern heroic spirit, Norse or English . . . of uttermost endurance in the service of indomitable will', summed up in the famous lines from *The Battle of Maldon* ('Will shall be the sterner, heart the bolder, spirit the greater as our strength lessens'). Tolkien rendered these lines in *The Homecoming of Beorhtnoth* as: 'Mind shall not falter nor mood waver / though doom shall come and dark conquer'.[42]

It seems unlikely, then, that Tolkien's decision to focus on 'time-travel' depended solely on the toss of a coin, since not only the abortive *LR* and the incomplete *NCP*, but his entire oeuvre, are predicated on the construction of an imaginary *time*. As Tolkien wrote with reference to his legendarium in a letter of 1958:

> [As] 'history', it would be difficult to fit [its] lands and events (or 'cultures') into such evidence as we possess, archaeological or geological, concerning . . . what is now called Europe; though the Shire, for instance, is expressly stated to have been in this region. I could have fitted things in with greater verisimilitude, if the story had not become too far developed, before the question ever occurred to me . . . I hope the evidently long but undefined gap in time between the Fall of Barad-dûr and our Days is sufficient for 'literary credibility', even for readers acquainted with what is known or surmised of 'pre-history'. I have I suppose, constructed an imaginary *time*, but kept my feet on my own mother-earth for *place*.
>
> (*TL* 283)

Despite the admitted difficulties of aligning his 'feigned history' or legendarium with 'true' history, Tolkien is insistent that in some sense his works *are* history. Here Tolkien is repeating an emphasis that he had already expressed in a response (apparently written just for himself) to Auden's review of *The Return of the King* in 1956:

> I am historically minded. Middle-earth is not an imaginary world. The name is the modern form of *midden-erd>middel-erd*, an ancient name for the *oikoumenē*, the abiding place of Men, the objectively real world, in use specifically opposed to imaginary worlds (as Fairyland) or unseen worlds (as Heaven or Hell). The theatre of my tale is this earth, the one in which we now live, but the historical period is imaginary. The essentials of that abiding place are all there (at any rate for the inhabitants of N.W. Europe), so naturally it feels familiar, even if a little glorified by the enchantment of distance in time.
>
> (*TL* 239)

Rateliff claims that Tolkien criticism has tended to overlook Tolkien's insistence on the historical reality of his 'sub-created' world. Whatever chronological problems Tolkien may have had, for example with reconciling the time-frame in *The Hobbit* with the Shire calendar in Appendix D of *LOTR*, he insisted on 'working within our own past, however fictionalized and elaborated . . . [and] committed himself to a world that would end up just like the present' (*Blackwelder* 70). Although Rateliff recognizes that Tolkien did not explicitly claim to be creating 'a mythology for England', he argues that this contested term – apparently Carpenter's coinage (*Biog* 125) – is nevertheless 'extremely apt' (*Blackwelder* 94 notes 30 and 34). Thus for Rateliff:

> [Tolkien's] *legendarium* is not the lost English mythology but a substitute for it, having the same air, same tone, and the same elusive quality as the best of what had been lost. Tolkien wanted to create a new story to take the place of the lost tales, that would have the same function and feel as the stories he would have cherished if only they had survived . . . He wove in as many elements of the surviving fragments as he could – even Hengest himself became a son of Eriol the Wanderer in a version of his mythology – but the essential purpose is to create something new out of the surviving fragments.
>
> (*Blackwelder* 83)

To underline his point that Tolkien scholarship has neglected the quasi-historicity of Tolkien's fiction, Rateliff suggests that ironically Matthew Lyons's *There and Back: In the Footsteps of J.R.R. Tolkien* – an informed if hardly academic piece of travel-writing – is:

> probably nearer to grasping the essence of Tolkien's "mythology for England" than those who delve into lost myths. . . . Tolkien scholarship of the last twenty-odd years has given much attention to one aspect while ignoring the other. We need a balance: both are important, and the combination of the two is what makes Tolkien Tolkien. Middle-earth is not a Neverland or a Narnia or even a Dunsanian Dreamland but the good green earth beneath our feet, when it was enchanted.
>
> (*Blackwelder* 79)

Rateliff quotes part of Lyons's comment, after describing a visit to Cheddar Gorge (the 'original' of Helm's Deep): 'Tolkien was right to be wary about conceding such [information] about the relationship between real places and his imaginary ones, since it is the ambiguity of his world's relationship to England that generates meaning, not its explicitness. He had tried the more direct approach with *The Book of Lost Tales* and other unfinished works, and had failed'[43] (*Blackwelder* 89). Such a privileging of ambiguity almost seems like an appeal to some historicized version of Keats's 'negative capability'. The very ambiguity of the relation of Tolkien's imagined world to reality (specifically England) can arguably evoke a particular sense of mystery, an enchantment that bathes not only the imaginary world but also the real one. We also seem to be close here, as in *OFS*, to some theory of 'defamiliarization', Shelley's if not Shklovsky's.[44]

In the end, Rateliff's argument about the relation between the (for Tolkien divinely created) primary world and various 'sub-created' secondary worlds, comes back to what Rateliff calls 'Tolkien's sub-creative theology'. Rateliff points out that while it is true that Tolkien was a conservative Catholic and accepted traditional Catholic teaching, 'it would be truer to say that Tolkien believed everything the Church taught, *and more*' (*Blackwelder* 85, emphasis added). Though Rateliff insists that Tolkien was 'not a gnostic' (*Blackwelder* 84), he nevertheless emphasizes certain quasi-gnostic tendencies in the theory of 'sub-creation' that Tolkien shared with Lewis – tendencies which in Lewis's case arguably became a very definite Gnostic impulse, as we shall explore below. In ways that are not explicitly spelled out, Tolkien seems to be even closer to Lewis on this issue of the relation between primary and secondary creations than Rateliff indicates. The theory of 'sub-creation' first appeared in print in *OFS* where Tolkien introduces the notion of the writer as 'sub-creator' into his discussion of 'literary belief', and challenges Coleridge's famous idea of the 'willing suspension of disbelief' (*MCOE* 132). Insofar as an effort of will seems to be involved in Coleridge's notion, there must be, Tolkien suggests, a failure of art:

> The moment disbelief arises, the spell is broken; the magic, or rather art, has failed. You are then out in the Primary World again, looking at the little abortive Secondary World from outside. . . . [T]hen disbelief must be suspended (or stifled), otherwise listening and looking would become intolerable. But this suspension of disbelief is a substitute for the genuine thing, a subterfuge we use when condescending to games or make-believe . . . This suspension of disbelief may thus be a somewhat tired, shabby, or sentimental state of mind, and so lean to the 'adult'. I fancy it is often the state of adults in the presence of a fairy story.
>
> (*MCOE* 132)

However accurate Tolkien's criticism of Coleridge, may be it says much about 'the enchanted state' that Tolkien believed was engendered by genuine 'sub-creation'. The power of 'sub-creation' is analogous to that of the primary Creation, as Tolkien suggested in his poem 'Mythopoeia', from which he quotes a few lines in *OFS*:

> Man, Sub-creator, the refracted Light
> through whom is splintered from a single White
> to many hues, and endlessly combined
> in living shapes that move from mind to mind.
> Though all the crannies of the world we filled
> with Elves and Goblins, though we dared to build
> Gods and their houses out of dark and light,
> and sowed the seed of dragons – ' twas our right
> (used or misused). That right has not decayed:
> we make still by the law in which we're made.
>
> (*MCOE* 144)

The poem is described in *OFS* as coming from 'a letter I once wrote to a man who described myth and fairy-story as "lies"' (*MCOE* 143). The 'man' was C.S. Lewis, and the origins of the poem lie in the nocturnal discussion between Lewis and Tolkien (and Hugo Dyson) in the grounds on Magdalen College, Oxford, in September 1931 – the discussion that apparently clinched Lewis's conversion to Christianity. It began with Lewis's assertion that myths were untrue even if beautiful ('lies breathed through silver'). Tolkien's response was that since myths were human 'sub-creations', they participated in some way in the primary Creation of God, and therefore were in some derived sense 'true' (*Inks* 42–5).

Although in *OFS* Tolkien quoted from 'Mythopoeia', which was composed in various drafts in the early 1930s, the poem was not published in its entirety until 1988 when it appeared in an edition of *Tree and Leaf* (= *T&L*), accompanied by the two pieces which until then had been the main vehicles for its ideas: *OFS* and *Leaf by Niggle*. The latter had originally been published in 1945 in the *Dublin Review* and subsequently in the first edition of *T&L* (1964). This strange story originated, Tolkien claimed, 'virtually complete' in a dream in 1943 – an uncommon experience for him (*TL* 113). The story is a kind of allegory (notwithstanding Tolkien's dislike of allegories) that deals *inter alia* with the creative process. The amateur artist Niggle's painting of a great tree is miraculously transformed after he has died (we infer), and done time in a purgatorial 'Workhouse':

> Before him stood the Tree, his Tree, finished. If you could say that of a Tree that was alive, its leaves opening, its branches growing and bending in the wind that Niggle had so often felt or guessed, and had so often failed to catch. He gazed at the Tree, and slowly he lifted his arms and opened them wide.
>
> 'It's a gift!' he said. He was referring to his art, and also to the result; but he was using the word quite literally.
>
> (*T&L* 109–10)

In September 1954 Tolkien drafted – though never actually sent, since '[i]t seemed to be taking myself too importantly' (*TL* 196) – a long reply to Peter Hastings, manager of the Catholic Bookshop in Oxford, who had questioned Tolkien's orthodoxy at various points in *LOTR*. In his reply to Hastings – in effect a kind of apologia – Tolkien suggested an analogy between the 'subcreative' activity of Niggle and that of the Valar, the 'gods' of his mythology (*TL* 193–5). Like Niggle's Tree, the products of the 'sub-creation' of the Valar only acquire real Being through the miraculous activity of God or 'Ilúvtar' when he announces to the Ainur (or Valar): '"I know the desire of your minds that what ye have seen should verily be, not only in your thought, but even as ye yourselves are, and yet other. Therefore I say: *Eä! Let these things Be!"* . . . and [the Ainur] knew that Ilúvtar had made a new thing: Eä, the World that Is' (*S* 20–1).

Thus according to Tolkien's theory of 'sub-creation', human beings have the freedom – indeed the sacred duty – to create, in *imitation* (a term fraught with metaphysical complexities) of God's act of Creation. An essential difference between God's primary Creation and human 'sub-creation' is that the latter is not 'really real', although in the enchanted state we may feel it to be so. The product of 'sub-creation' could only become 'real' through the miraculous intervention of God, whose very essence is Being, according to traditional Catholic theology, which Tolkien alludes to in the letter previously quoted, referring to 'the sublimities of "I am that I am"' (*TL* 192). Such a divine intervention occurs in at the end of *Leaf by Niggle* and, *mutatis mutandis*, in the *Ainulindalë* section of *The Silmarillion*. Tolkien's theory allows for the possibility that the primary Creation we actually have is the one that God chose (for his own inscrutable reasons) to actualize; but this doesn't mean that God couldn't have actualized different worlds if He had so chosen. Hastings had expressed the concern that Tolkien had 'overstepped the mark in metaphysical matters', for example by making Treebeard claim that the Dark Lord had *created* the Trolls and the Orcs, and by granting reincarnation to the Elves, thereby failing to 'use those channels which [the 'sub-creator'] knows the [C]reator to have used already' (*TL* 187–8). This, however, is to miss the point of 'sub-creation' in Tolkien's view. Rather than being bound to 'the channels the [C]reator is known to have used already' – that is, to feel obliged always to replicate *this* world, more or less – Tolkien claims that precisely *liberation* from such previously-used channels is 'a tribute to the infinity of His potential variety, one of the ways in which indeed it is exhibited, as indeed I said in the Essay [*OFS*]' (*TL* 188). For the orthodox Judeo-Christian tradition there is nothing *inherently* sacred about *this* world other than the fact (the ultimate supernatural 'Fact') that God *chose* to actualize this particular possibility (or set of possibilities). Tolkien doesn't seem to think that it's necessary for a Christian to believe that this world is in any sense perfect; its flawed nature is not incompatible with our belief that this is the one God in His infinite wisdom has in fact chosen, though undoubtedly He could have chosen other worlds (rather like the line Izaak Walton quotes in *The Compleat Angler* about strawberries: 'Doubtless God could have made a better berry; but doubtless God never did').

We are returning here to the fundamental question of theodicy: *is* it the case that the (at best) imperfect creation is compatible with an all-powerful and all-loving God? One response to this is the Gnostic solution of severing the connection between God and the act of Creation: a truly good God would not create a world like ours. Tolkien certainly doesn't go very far down that road, but he does – at least by analogy – go part of the way when he separates the Ainur (who shape the world) from the Ilúvtar (who actually gives it Being, or 'lets it be' in the double sense of 'let' as both giving permission and making something happen – as in a 'fiat').[45] Such a distancing of Ilúvtar from the world emphasizes the fact that He did not in any immediate sense 'make' the world – the Ainur did that. The Ilúvtar only 'lets it be'. Whether such a slight – although noticeable – distance is entirely compatible with Roman Catholic orthodoxy is beyond the scope of the present study. What such a distancing does do, however, is to open up a space for the free play of the human imagination by adding the following kind of mental supplement to the Credo (Rateliff's *'and more'*): 'I believe in one God the Father almighty, maker of heaven and earth, and of all things visible and invisible [*however, having said that, it is nevertheless entirely possible that there might have been (and perhaps are) very different kinds of universe. Just supposing . . .*]'. Or as Rateliff puts it:

> Tolkien allowing for a sentient race like the Elves to experience a longevity that approaches immortality as well reincarnation within the world of time is not a heresy, as Hastings had charged, but simply *a proffered alternative* – a thought experiment, if you like, but fleshed out and given sub-creative power.
>
> (*Blackwelder* 85–6, emphasis added)

What Rateliff doesn't say is that Tolkien's 'proffered alternative' seems very close to Lewis's 'supposals'. As will be discussed below, Lewis developed the notion of 'supposals' in his discussion of allegory. As opposed to an allegory [which Lewis insisted *The Lion, the Witch and the Wardrobe* (=*LWW*) was *not*], Lewis proposed the idea of a 'supposal'. As he put it: 'If Aslan represented the immaterial Deity in the same way in which Giant Despair [in *Pilgrim's Progress*] represented Despair, he would be an allegorical figure.' However, according to Lewis, Aslan is actually the answer to the question: '"What might Christ become like, if there really were a world like Narnia and He chose to be incarnate and die and rise again in that world as he actually has done in ours?" This is not allegory at all. . . . This works out a *supposition . . .* but *granted* the supposition, He [Christ/Aslan] really would have been a physical object in that world' (*LL3* 1004–5).

Lewis seems ambivalent about the ontological status of 'the incarnation of Christ in another world'; it is 'a mere supposal', yet in Lewis's usage the term 'mere' can carry considerable freight. Lewis's claim here seems to resonate with the ambiguous status of Tolkien's legendarium. The latter is in one sense obviously not 'fact', yet Tolkien's sub-creation seems far more fleshed out and grounded (for example through the technique of calquing) than Lewis's. There is a paradox here, however: if Tolkien's sub-created world and its denizens seem more 'incarnate' than Lewis's, Tolkien strongly resisted Lewis's talk of the incarnation of Christ in another world as 'a supposal'. Lewis's explicit use of unmistakeably Christian material in *LWW* seemed distasteful and inappropriate to Tolkien; it blurred the ontological boundary between the primary world (where, for Tolkien, Christ had *in fact* become incarnate) and the secondary sub-created world which had to be kept free of any explicitly Christian ideas. This was important to Tolkien.

While Tolkien advocated (and convinced Lewis of) the God-given right – indeed duty – to sub-create, he insisted that these sub-creations should not contain any admixture of explicitly Christian material. This issue is really about the status of myth, which for Lewis is another way of talking about 'supposals'. Tolkien had persuaded Lewis back in 1931 that his delight in myth could lead to an acceptance of the Christian myth as 'fact'. But the transition from 'pagan' myth (for example, that of Balder) to Christian faith is one-way; it is an error, in Tolkien's view, to seek to Christianize myths retrospectively. 'Pagan' myths had their own appeal and their own truth, which was problematically related to the truth of the Christian myth. Tolkien seemed to think it necessary to live with this ambiguity, without seeking to resolve otherness prematurely. This is a far from merely theoretical issue, but one which goes to the heart of Tolkien's ambivalent attitude to 'pagan' myth and literature, an attitude in which Tolkien very much identified with that of the author of *Beowulf*. The latter, like later mediaeval compilers, was a Christian dealing sympathetically if guardedly with explicitly non-Christian sources. It is in this context that Tolkien's comments about other sub-creative possibilities should be viewed. While there may be other possible worlds and other possible myths, these must not, like Lewis's equivalents, contain too easily identifiable Christian elements. If there is a hidden Christ in Middle-earth, he has to be (unlike Aslan) pretty well hidden.

Fairy-tales, myth and Faery

OFS is not only about fairy-tales and fantasy, but also about mythology. Tolkien engages directly with the debate that dominated studies of myth and folklore during the nineteenth century: the methodological dispute between 'the comparative philologists' – led by Max Müller – and 'the evolutionary anthropologists', of whom a prominent representative was Andrew Lang. The fact that Tolkien's lecture *OFS* was delivered in honour of Lang by no means entailed his advocacy of Lang's position, though he did endorse Lang's criticism of Müller's thesis that mythology is 'a disease of language'. According to Müller's seminal essay 'Comparative Mythology' (1856), as summed up by Flieger:

> [M]yths as we have them arose through verbal misapprehension, the late misunderstanding of early, primarily Sanskrit Vedic names for celestial phenomena. In what he called the 'mythopoeic' age, the concepts arose that became the Aryan gods. As the migrations of the Indo-Aryan people splintered them into separate groups, so their language and its related mythology splintered into various offshoots. In this process, the original true, 'nature-solar' meanings were forgotten, surviving only in mythical words and phrases . . . According to Müller, 'The gods of ancient mythology were changed into the demigods and heroes of ancient epic poetry,

and these demigods again became at a later age the principal characters in our nursery tales'.

(IM 20–1)

For Tolkien, 'Müller's view of mythology as a "disease of language" can be abandoned without regret. Mythology is not a disease at all, though it may like all human things become diseased. You might as well say that thinking is a disease of the mind. It would be more near the truth to say that languages . . . are a disease of mythology' (*MCOE* 121–2). Müller's theory that mythology dwindles down through legend to folk-tales, *Märchen* or fairy-tales is – according to Tolkien – 'the truth almost upside down' (*MCOE* 123). It is actually the folk- or fairy-tale element which gives life to the mythology, Tolkien claims, giving as an example the relation of Thórr to thunder (*MCOE* 123–4). However, Müller's emphasis on language was not entirely mistaken, Tolkien insists. The problem is that Müller privileged language's power to abstract universal qualities from particular individuals (for example, the 'greenness' of grass), whereas Tolkien's focus is on the original creative power of language to generate the word 'green' in the first place: '[H]ow powerful, how stimulating to the very faculty that produced it, was the invention of the adjective: no spell or incantation in Faërie is more potent' (*MCOE* 122). If such ideas may seem to prefigure the so-called 'linguistic turn' in philosophy (they are perhaps reminiscent of the later Heidegger), they owe much to Owen Barfield, though both Barfield and Heidegger derive aspects of their philosophy from the Romantic tradition in different ways. Such ideas about language are in any case crucial to understanding fantasy. From this primary production of the infinitely potent 'word' (or 'Word') – specifically 'the adjective' in Tolkien's example – derives the power of creation. Tolkien claims: '[I]n such "fantasy", as it is called, new form is made; Faërie begins; Man becomes a sub-creator' (*MCOE* 122).

Though Tolkien endorsed Lang's criticism of Müller, he disagreed with Lang's alternative to comparative philology's obsession with high (and by preference Aryan) 'solar' mythology, – of which folk- and fairy-tales were merely the 'detritus'. Lang gives primacy to the folk- and fairy-tale material that tends to 'preserve an older and more savage form of the same myth, containing more allusions to cannibalism, to magic, or Shamanism, to kinship with the beasts, and to bestial transformations' (*IM* 22, quoting Lang's 'Mythology and Fairy Tales'). For Lang such 'primitive' material comes from the 'childhood' of the human race, therefore modern children appreciate folk- and fairy-tales more than 'civilised' adults. Regarding Lang's claim that in liking fairy-tales '[children's] taste remains like the taste of their naked ancestors thousands of years ago', Tolkien questions whether we really know much about these 'naked ancestors', other than 'that they were certainly not naked' and that 'our fairy-stories, however old certain elements in them may be, are certainly not the same as theirs' (*MCOE* 134). In rejecting Lang's argument,

Tolkien is in effect adopting the more modern stance of suspicion towards the theory that ontogeny recapitulates phylogeny. Besides the paucity of evidence for the literary tastes of 'primitive' human beings, there is also the available evidence of the tastes of modern children, who by no means universally enjoy fairy-stories. Lang's 'generalisations which treat [children] as a class' are, says Tolkien, 'delusory', and, in terms of Tolkien's own experience, counterintuitive. In his own case, famously, '[a] real taste for fairy stories was [only] wakened by philology on the threshold of manhood, and quickened to full life by war' (*MCOE* 135). In sum, Tolkien's view is that 'fairy-stories should not be *specially* associated with children' (*MCOE* 135). Such an association is:

> an accident of our domestic history. Fairy-stories have in the modern lettered world been relegated to the nursery, as shabby or old-fashioned furniture is relegated to the playroom . . . Children as a class . . . neither like fairy-stories more, nor understand them better than adults do . . . [I]n fact only some children, and some adults, have any special taste for them.
>
> (*MCOE* 130)

Tolkien accepts the truth of Lang's remark that 'He who would enter the Kingdom of Faërie should have the heart of a little child', but surmises that Lang is referring here to 'humility and innocence', rather than biological age. Such humility and innocence by no means entail 'uncritical wonder' and 'uncritical tenderness', Tolkien adds, quoting Chesterton's remark that: 'Children are innocent and love justice; while most of us are wicked and naturally prefer mercy' (*MCOE* 136–7).

Tolkien might well have introduced at this point MacDonald's distinction between 'children' and 'the childlike' in 'The Fantastic Imagination', an essay whose influence can be seen both explicitly and implicitly in Tolkien's lecture. Implicitly, MacDonald's insistence on the need for a fantasy writer to maintain consistency in 'a little world of his own, with its own laws . . . which is the nearest, perhaps, he can come to creation' (*CFT* 6) prefigures Tolkien's theory of 'sub-creation'. And there are two explicit references to MacDonald in *OFS*. One is Tolkien's insight that 'Death is the theme that most inspired George MacDonald' (*MCOE* 153). However profoundly true this remark may be of MacDonald, it also reveals much about Tolkien's own work when we look at the immediately preceding sentences: 'The human stories of the elves are doubtless full of the Escape from Deathlessness. . . . Few lessons are taught more clearly in them than the burden of that kind of immortality, or rather endless serial living . . . ' (*MCOE* 153). Tolkien wrote retrospectively of *LOTR* that 'it is only in reading the work myself . . . that I become aware of the dominance of the theme of Death' (*TL* 267). The other reference to MacDonald comes earlier in the lecture when Tolkien discusses the potential of fairy-stories to be 'the vehicle of Mystery', and comments: 'This at least is what George MacDonald attempted, achieving stories of power and beauty when he succeeded, as in *The Golden Key* (which he called a fairy-tale); and even when he partly failed, as in *Lilith* (which he called a romance)' (*MCOE* 125). Tolkien's appreciation of MacDonald is also indicated in passages in the original draft of *OFS* which were excised, but which still exist in the manuscript kept in Oxford's Bodleian Library. In one excised passage Tolkien acknowledged: 'For me at any rate fairy-stories are especially associated with Scotland . . . by reason of the names of Andrew Lang and George MacDonald. To them in different ways I owe the books which most affected the background of my imagination since childhood.'[46] In another omitted passage, relevant to our discussion of MacDonald in the previous chapter, Tolkien recognized that 'George MacDonald, in that mixture of German and Scottish flavours (which makes him so inevitably attractive to myself) has depicted what will always be to me the classic goblin. By that standard I judge all goblins, old or new' (*H&S2* 568).

Despite Tolkien's affirmation in *OFS* that in *GK* MacDonald had succeeded in achieving a story 'of power and beauty', he came to revise this judgment later in life. In 1964 Tolkien was invited, in place of the recently deceased C.S. Lewis, to write an introduction to a new American edition of *GK* for children. He wrote to the publisher (Pantheon Books): 'I am not as warm an admirer of George MacDonald as C.S. Lewis was; but I do think well of this story of his. I mentioned it in my essay *On Fairy-stories* . . . ' (*TL* 351). Tolkien's good opinion of *GK* did not survive the experience of re-reading it: 'I found that a highly selective memory had retained only a few impressions of things that moved me, and re-reading G.M. critically filled me with distaste. I had of course, never thought of *The G.K.* as a story for children (though apparently G. McD did).'[47] Tolkien was relieved when the project fizzled out (though it later came to fruition with a different publisher and an Afterword by Auden) (*SWM* 69). Had he continued, Tolkien confessed:

> I should only have written a severely critical or 'anti-' essay on G.M. – unnecessary, and a pity since G.M. has performed great services for other minds – such as Jack's [Lewis's]. But he was evidently born loving (moral) allegory, and I was born with an instinctive distaste for it. 'Phantastes' wakened him, and afflicted me with profound dislike.
>
> (*SWM* 69)

However, Tolkien did actually begin the introduction to the children's edition of *GK*, and after some preliminary remarks about MacDonald's beautiful beard, his marvellous waistcoats and his Scottishness, Tolkien goes on to warn his child readers that MacDonald preaches, 'not only on the platform or in the pulpit; in all his many books he preaches, and it is his preaching that is valued most by the grown-up people who admire him most' (*SWM* 69–70). It was apparently this so-called preachiness that gave rise to Tolkien's dig that MacDonald was an 'old grandmother' (though

MacDonald's fairy-grandmothers are powerful figures) (*H&S2* 570–1). Tolkien's characterization of MacDonald's typical readership (practically 'sermon fodder') no longer applies as generally as it once may have done, thanks, for example, to Knoepflmacher's edition of MacDonald's fairy-tales, where *GK* is currently most readily available. But if you are the right kind of reader for *GK*, Tolkien continues, then you will not forget it:

> Something . . . will remain in your own mind, as a beautiful or strange or alarming picture and will grow there, and its meaning, or one of its meanings – its meaning for you – will unfold itself, as you also grow. For me the chief picture that remained was the great valley encircled by hard towering mountains, with its smooth floor on which the shadows played, the sea of shadows cast by things that could not themselves be seen. When I went back to the story after some years, I was surprised to find what a lot more there was in it that I had forgotten. But it still remains for me the centre of the tale. I now find that it has of course stirred the imagination of other readers, though it does not seem to all of them as important as to me; nor does it have the same 'meaning' for them as for me. But that does not trouble me. These pictures or visions that come in such tales are large and alive and no one who sees them, not even the writer himself, understands the whole of them.
>
> (*SWM* 72)

This passage is slightly odd coming from someone who claims actively to dislike *GK*. Presumably Tolkien thought it possible to separate the 'speaking pictures' from the chaff of didacticism – though there's precious little of the latter in this fairy-tale by the writer who claimed in 'The Fantastic Imagination' that '[a] fairy-tale is not an allegory. . . . He must be an artist indeed who can . . . produce an allegory that is not a weariness to the spirit' (*CFT* 7–8). Both Tolkien's dislike of allegory and his openness to plurisignificance (or 'applicability') are explicitly prefigured in 'The Fantastic Imagination'; it seems uncharitable, then, for Tolkien to turn against MacDonald. The animus of the later Tolkien against MacDonald is further revealed in a snide aside in his notes for the introduction to his public reading of *Smith of Wootton Major* (=*SWM*) in Blackfriars, Oxford, in February 1965: 'The story was (as often happens) the result of an *irritant*. And since the irritant will in some degree affect the presentation of the movement of the mind that it sets going I will just say what the *irritant* was in this case. George MacDonald. A writer for whom I have a sincere and humble – dislike' (*H&S2* 945). In fairness, Tolkien was in later life also to turn against *The Hobbit* because of its overly intrusive narrator, though in a letter from 1959 he again seems unable to resist an implied sneer at MacDonald:

> When I published *The Hobbit* – hurriedly and without due consideration – I was still influenced by the convention that 'fairy-stories' are naturally

directed to children (with or without the silly added waggery 'from seven
to seventy'). . . . [T]he desire to address children, as such, had nothing to
do with the story as such in itself or the urge to write it. But it had some
unfortunate effects on the mode of expression and narrative method.

(*TL* 297)

In fact, in their playful use of narrative method, MacDonald's fairy-tales –
for example 'The Light Princess' – are considerably more sophisticated than
Tolkien's own early attempt at the fairy-tale genre in writing *The Hobbit*.

Tolkien's draft introduction to *GK* continues for about five pages. He discusses the nature of the 'fairy-tale', talking first of all about the 'tale'. What
Tolkien says here speaks volumes about his own writings, whatever relevance it may have to *GK*:

[T]he tale should tell something; a story, of related events, which should
interest a listener in themselves but especially as they are arranged in a
sequence from the chosen beginning to the chosen end. I say 'chosen',
meaning 'by the inventor', because the beginning and end of a story is
to it like the edges of the canvas or an added frame to a picture, say a
landscape. It concentrates the teller's attention, and yours, on one small
part of the country. But there are of course no real limits: under the
earth, and in the sky above, and in the remote and faintly glimpsed distances, and in the unrevealed regions on either side, there are things that
influence the very shape and colour of the part that is pictured. Without
them it would be quite different, and they are really necessary to understanding what is seen.

(*SWM* 73)

This effectively sums up the relationship between *The Hobbit* and *LOTR*,
and of both these narratives to *The Silmarillion* and Tolkien's legendarium
in general. As for the 'most important and also most misleading label *fairy*',
it is often misunderstood, continues Tolkien (*SWM* 73). Not only does it
not properly refer to pretty little creatures (as MacDonald well knew, says
Tolkien) – the term doesn't actually refer to a creature at all. It originally
meant 'enchantment or magic, and the enchanted world or country in
which marvellous people lived, great and small, with strange powers of
mind and will for good and evil' (*SWM* 74). Thus a fairy-tale is 'a tale about
that world, a glimpse of it; if you read it, you enter Fairy with the author as
your guide . . . [whether] a bad guide or a good one' (*SWM* 74). A bad guide
is one who does not take the adventure seriously, or who 'is just "spinning
a yarn" which he thinks is good enough "for children"' (*SWM* 74). But Fairy
is 'very powerful'. Even a bad guide cannot avoid making up his tale 'out
of bits of older tales, or things he half remembers, [that] may be too strong
for him to spoil or disenchant. Someone may meet them for the first time

in his silly tale, and catch a glimpse of Fairy and go on to better things' (*SWM* 74).

Then Tolkien suggests that what he has just said 'could be put into a "short story" like this. There was once a cook and he thought of making a cake for a children's party. His chief notion was that it must be very sweet, and he meant to cover it all over with sugar-icing . . . ' (*SWM* 75). This is the end of Tolkien's introduction to MacDonald's *GK* and the beginning of his own story that became known as *SWM*, though it is also a continuation by other means of his criticism of MacDonald: 'It is better anyway to preach by example than by criticism of others. But *Smith* remains as it were "an anti-G.M. tract"' (*SWM* 69–70). Not that there is any *allegory* in *SWM*, Tolkien hastened to tell Clyde Kilby, at least not in 'the Faery', he adds.[48] However, there is 'some trace of allegory in the Human part, which seems to me obvious though no reader or critic has yet adverted to it', Tolkien claims, with a condescension reminiscent of Vereker in Henry James's *The Figure in the Carpet*. Although 'as usual there is no "religion" in the story', Tolkien told Kilby, 'plainly enough the Master Cook and the Great Hall etc. are a (somewhat satirical) allegory of the village-church, and the village parson: its functions steadily decaying and losing all touch with the "arts", into mere eating and drinking – the last traces of anything "other" being left to children' (*SWM* 70). Tolkien elaborated this 'allegorical' reading in the essay he wrote on *SWM*, where he intimates that:

'Cooking' is a domestic affair practised by men and women: personal religion and prayer. The Master Cook [the Parson] presides over and provides for all the religious festivals of the year . . . The Great Hall is however no longer painted or decorated. If antique carvings, whether grotesques like gargoyles, or beautiful and of religious import, are preserved at all it is by mere custom. . . . Festivals are mere public assemblies . . . The church has been 'reformed'.

(*SWM* 100)

This passage suggests that while *SWM* may not be explicitly allegorical, it is certainly 'applicable', perhaps to the 'reform' introduced by the Second Vatican Council (1962–5), but more probably to the 'seizure' of the English Roman Catholic Church (and its buildings) by the Church of England during the Reformation – with the consequent loss of 'Mystery' in Tolkien's view.[49] It is even possible to suspect here a source for Tolkien's evident resentment of MacDonald. Both Tolkien and MacDonald were technically 'non-conformists' to the established Church of England, although MacDonald had felt able to leave his Congregationalist roots behind and find accommodation in the Anglican 'Broad Church'. The sense that, for Tolkien, MacDonald was 'all talk' – with the Protestant predilection for the ('pure') preached Word as opposed to ('colourful') Catholic ritual – would fit with

Tolkien's comment in his essay on *SWM* that 'Festivals are mere public assemblies for talk . . . Memory survives of "merrier" days, but most of the village would not approve of any revival of them' (*SWM* 100).

Other 'applications' of *SWM* have been proposed. Shippey, for example, wants to connect it with the feud between 'Lit and Lang' within English Studies.[50] However, Shippey also alludes to arguably the most convincing interpretation – given by Paul Kocher – that *SWM* is Tolkien's version of Shakespeare's *The Tempest*, with its 'Prospero speech' bidding farewell to the magic of his 'sub-creative' art[51] (*SWM* 65; *H&S2* 949). This is consistent with Tolkien's claim to Kilby that there was '*no* allegory in the Faery' (*SWM* 70); the allegory is rather *about* Tolkien's own relation *to* 'Faery'. Tolkien strongly resisted the reduction of Faërie to an allegorical expression of religious truths (as for example in Spenser's *FQ*). He insisted that in this sense there was no 'religion' in *SWM*, at least not in the sections set in 'Faery, which is conceived as having a real extramental existence' (*SWM* 70). This latter point is closely related to Lewis's arguments about the question of allegory in relation to *LWW*. After discussing how the part of the story set in the village of Wootton Major *is* allegorical (the Master Cook as Parson etc.), Tolkien goes on in his essay on *SWM* to emphasize that 'Faery is *not* religious. It is fairly evident that it is not Heaven or Paradise. Certainly its inhabitants, Elves, are not angels or emissaries of God (direct). The tale does not deal with religion itself. The Elves are not busy with a plan to reawake religious devotion in Wootton' (*SWM* 100). Tolkien then continues with what is one of his most important statements about Faërie:

> Faery represents at its weakest a breaking out (at least in mind) from the iron ring of the familiar, still more from the adamantine ring of belief that it is known, possessed, controlled, and so (ultimately) all that is worth being considered – a constant awareness of a world beyond these rings. More strongly it represents love: that is, a love and respect for all things, 'inanimate' and 'animate', an unpossessive love of them as 'other'. This 'love' will produce both *ruth* and *delight*. Things seen in its light will be respected, and they will also appear delightful, beautiful, wonderful even glorious. Faery might be said to represent Imagination . . . This compound – of awareness of a limitless world outside our domestic parish; a love (in ruth and admiration) for the things in it; and a desire for wonder, marvels, both perceived and conceived – this 'Faery' is as necessary for the health and complete functioning of the Human as is sunlight for physical life.
>
> (*SWM* 101)

This passage is clearly relevant to its primary referent, *SWM*, with allusions not only to Smith's transcendence of the small-mindedness epitomized by Nokes – and to the intense feelings of delight as well as bereavement generated by Smith's dealings with Faery – but also to Smith's discovery and ultimate acceptance of the fact that these experiences come only as a gift ('by grace'). Such experiences are not permanent possessions, but must be passed on, ironically in this case to Nokes's grandson Tim. The latter is 'not an obvious choice', comments Smith, to which Alf (secretly the King of Faery) replies: '"Neither were you"' (*SWM* 48).

However, the points made indirectly in *SWM* itself, and more explicitly in Tolkien's essay about his fairy-tale, also seem relevant to other works by Tolkien, not least *LOTR*. The far-from-obvious outcome of a selection process (the choice of Nokes's grandson Tim's to receive the 'fay-star') is even more strikingly exemplified in 'The Council of Elrond' chapter in *LOTR* where, after a lengthy debate among the high and mighty among Elves, Dwarves and Men (not to mention Gandalf, one of the Maiar, a lower order of the Valar or gods in Tolkien's mythology), it falls to Frodo to say in his small voice: '"I will take the Ring, though I do not know the way"' (*LOTR* 270). It is the very unexpectedness of choosing a hobbit for such a lofty action – in effect saving the world – that gives Frodo a chance of success. The quasi-Christian paradox (but only 'quasi-', since Tolkien sought to exclude explicitly Christian messages) that only the small, weak and humble can truly succeed is related to the further (quasi-Christian) paradox that in this context success means a kind of failure. Achievement here means surrendering the Ring, while winning involves losing it: the Lord of the Ring is the one who can throw it away. This crucial task of relinquishing the Ring proves infinitely difficult. Frodo, the anti-hero of Tolkien's heroic romance, finally manages to overcome the physical obstacles of his 'anti-quest' (to *lose* the Ring), largely thanks to Sam who, like some mediaeval saint, carries him on the final stages of the journey. The *spiritual* obstacles are, however, far more overwhelming than even the trek through Mordor's blasted plain of Gorgoreth to Mount Doom (with the obvious echoes of ravaged and desolate WWI landscapes). If Frodo succeeds physically (by actually reaching the Crack of Doom), in the end he fails spiritually, since he cannot ultimately surrender the Ring: '"I have come," [Frodo] said. "But I do not choose now to do what I came to do. I will not do this deed. The Ring is mine!"' (*LOTR* 945). Salvation, both of Frodo and of all Middle-earth, occurs through an event beyond Frodo's control, through the providential intervention of Gollum, whose final savage act of darkness and greed when he bites off Frodo's ring finger, secures universal release and the triumph of light. In an analogy of Catholic teaching (the term 'allegory' being off-limits), it takes an unanticipated intervention which seems providential, if not supernatural, to complete the work of Frodo and Sam. Grace, so to speak, completes nature, which can only go so far and do so much. Gollum's fall into the Crack of Doom is in a sense a miraculously fortunate or happy fall, in that it does what Frodo could not do and ends all the evil history of the Ring. There is also another sense in which Gollum's final fall into the abyss is a kind of happy fall, for it is almost a bizarre *Liebestod* or Romantic Love-death; as he dies Gollum cries ecstatically: '"Precious, precious, precious! . . . My Precious!

O my Precious!" . . . Out of the depths came his last wail *Precious*, and he was gone' (*LOTR* 946).

The reference in Tolkien's essay on *SWM* to the power of 'rings' ('the iron ring of the familiar . . . the adamantine ring of belief that is known, possessed, controlled') can hardly be accidental; 'the adamantine ring' in particular recalls Nenya, the Ring of Adamant, worn by Galadriel. These 'rings' are explicitly linked with the dangers of possessiveness when their power is contrasted with the 'unpossessive love' of what is 'other'. Such possessiveness is a kind of 'original sin' that runs through Tolkien's legendarium from its very beginning – the myth of Creation and Fall – narrated in the *Ainulindalë*. In this narrative Melkor (or Melko as he is known in the early version of *The Music of the Ainur* in *BLT1*), who 'had been given the greatest gifts of power and knowledge', began to weave into the cosmic music 'matters of his own imagining that were not in accord with the theme of Ilúvatar ['God']; for he sought therein to increase the power and the glory of the part assigned to himself', and the 'desire grew hot within him to bring into Being things of his own' (*S* 16). Melkor, like some existentialist hero, or indeed Milton's Satan, goes off alone into the void where he begins 'to conceive thoughts of his own unlike those of his brethren' (*S* 16). These subversive thoughts create discord in the music of the Ainur. However, Ilúvatar is able to create new music which overcomes Melkor's discordant music – 'loud and vain, and endlessly repeated . . . [with] little harmony, but rather the braying upon a few notes' – and takes it up ('sublates' it, in the arguably apposite Hegelian term) into a great harmony in which Melkor's most triumphant notes were taken by Ilúvatar's music and 'woven into its own solemn pattern' (*S* 17). Thus spoke Ilúvatar:

> Mighty are the Ainur, and mightiest among them is Melkor; but that he may know, and all the Ainur, that I am Ilúvatar, those things that ye have sung, I will show them forth . . . And thou, Melkor, shalt see that no theme may be played that hath not its uttermost source in me, nor can any alter the music in my despite. For he that attempteth this shall prove but mine instrument in the devising of things more wonderful which he himself hath not imagined.
>
> (*S* 17)

While not actually affirming a 'Fortunate Fall', this claim to bring ultimate good out of apparent (and deliberately willed) evil represents a kind of theodicy that echoes *inter alia* Goethe, Hegel and MacDonald. It also serves as a kind of gloss on *LOTR*, particularly the Mount Doom sequence. Frodo's sparing of Gollum earlier in the story has preserved the latter not so much for his own salvation, but as the vital cog in the machinery of Tolkien's grand narrative. As Frodo tells Sam at this *eucatastrophe*, the decisive turn of events on Mount Doom where Sam feels 'only joy, great joy': '"[D]o you remember Gandalf's words: *Even Gollum may have something yet to do*? But for him, Sam, I could not have destroyed the Ring. The Quest would have been in vain, even at the bitter end"' (*LOTR* 947). Or as Ilúvatar tells Melko, he who attempts to defy the divine plan only serves ultimately to enhance it in unforeseen ways.

Yet Tolkien's theodicy differs from more optimistic universalist scenarios – and arguably retains a particular kind of Christian bleakness – in its reluctance to agree (at least too readily) with Julian of Norwich that in the end 'All shall be well, and all manner of thing shall be well'; or indeed to affirm with Anodos at the end of *Phantastes* that: 'I know that good is coming to me – that good is always coming; though few have at all times the simplicity and the courage to believe it. What we call evil is the only and best shape, which, for the person and his condition at the time, could be assumed by the best good' (*Ph* 237). For at the end of *LOTR* all is not well, at least not wholly well. Although Sauron has been defeated and the Ring destroyed, irreparable damage has been done both to Frodo and to Middle-earth. The new Age of Men may be beginning in Middle-earth, but it is clearly a falling-off from earlier ages. The Elves will no longer have a home in Middle-earth, for at the end of *LOTR* they depart for the Blessed Realm of Aman, the Undying Lands of the Uttermost West. The destination of the Elves (and Bilbo and Frodo) lies, since the downfall of Númenor and the 'bending' of the world, beyond 'the circles of the world'. It can only be reached by the 'straight road' (the eponymous 'lost road'), as Tolkien insisted in a letter to Roger Lancelyn Green about the Elven ships leaving the Grey Havens at the end of *LOTR*:

> They only set out after sundown; but if any keen-eyed observer from the shore had watched one of these ships he might have seen that it never became hull-down but dwindled only by distance until it vanished in the twilight: it followed the straight road to the true West and not the bent road of the earth's surface. As it vanished it left the physical world. There was no return. The Elves who took this road and those few 'mortals' [e.g. Frodo and Bilbo] who by special grace went with them, had abandoned the 'History of the world' and could play no further part in it.
>
> (*TL* 410–11)

Although the Elves are going home, there is a strong sense of bereavement and defeat. As Galadriel had warned Frodo back in Lothlórien: '"[I]f you fail, then we are laid bare to the Enemy. Yet if you succeed, then our power is diminished, and Lothlórien will fade, and the tides of Time will sweep it away. We must depart into the West, or dwindle to a rustic folk of dell and cave, slowly to forget and be forgotten"' (*LOTR* 365). Here Galadriel echoes not only her earlier statement that '"through all the ages we have fought the long defeat"' (*LOTR* 357), but also the pessimistic words of Elrond at the

Council he summoned in Rivendell: '"[M]y memory reaches back even to the Elder Days. Eärendil was my sire, who was born in Gondolin before its fall . . . I have seen three ages in the West of the world, and many defeats, and many fruitless victories"' (*LOTR* 243). The outlook expressed here approximates (given that Middle-earth is so-to-speak pre-Christian) to the pre-Christian or pagan 'heroic code' of the North, summed up in the lines from *The Battle of Maldon* which Tolkien freely translated in *The Homecoming of Beorhtnoth* as: 'Mind shall not falter nor mood waver / though doom shall come and dark conquer' (*T&L* 141).

If the latter outlook might perhaps be characterized as 'non-optimistic' rather than 'pessimistic' (though Burns seems to regard the 'Norse' outlook as pessimistic when she claims that 'Tolkien, finally, is a pessimist and optimist both'),[52] such qualified pessimism is also a product of Roman Catholicism, as Tolkien wrote in a letter: 'Actually I am a Christian, and indeed a Roman Catholic, so that I do not expect '"history"' to be anything but a '"long defeat"' – though it contains (and in a legend may contain more clearly and movingly) some examples or glimpses of final victory' (*TL* 255). Tolkien claimed in a letter to Robert Murray, S.J. that *LOTR* is 'a fundamentally religious and Catholic work; unconsciously so at first, but consciously in the revision. That is why I have not put in, or have cut out, practically all references to anything like "religion", to cults or practices, in the imaginary world. For the religious element is absorbed into the story and the symbolism' (*TL* 172). Tolkien's rather paradoxical claim that precisely *because LOTR* is 'a fundamentally religious and Catholic work', he has *therefore* avoided all explicit references to religion, contrasts with what Tolkien believed was the overly explicit approach of Lewis, especially in *LWW*. In fact, as will be argued below, Tolkien's purveying of 'spilt religion' places him in the same broadly Romantic tradition as Lewis. A key difference, however, is that while Tolkien and Lewis shared an addiction to what might nowadays be called 'genre' fantasy literature (Haggard, Dunsany, Eddison), Lewis worked professionally with 'English Literature' (tending to focus on the Renaissance period), whereas, as Tolkien put it in the letter to Murray cited above: 'Certainly I have *not* been nourished by English Literature' (*TL* 172, emphasis added). While Lewis's expertise centred on more-or-less 'Christian' writers, this was less true of Tolkien. It was, after all, Tolkien who invited Lewis to join the 'Coalbiters' and in a sense converted him to studying (as opposed to reading versions of) Norse mythology (*Inks* 24–8). Indeed it was Tolkien who some years later more literally converted Lewis to Christian belief, precisely through Lewis's attraction (more emotional than informed) to pre-Christian mythology. Thus, whereas Lewis had a great admiration for Spenser's *FQ* – an allegory *inter alia* of Christian belief – Tolkien was much cooler, even declaring Spenser to be unreadable (*Inks25*).

Similarly, Tolkien claimed to have kept Arthurian 'Matter of Britain' elements out of his work because they were too explicitly Christian. In his previously-cited letter of 1951 to Milton Waldman of Collins, arguing for the joint publication of *LOTR* and *The Silmarillion* which together represent his mythology 'dedicated to England', Tolkien laments the poverty of English mythology, and adds:

> Of course there was and is all the Arthurian world, but powerful as it is, it is imperfectly naturalized, associated with the soil of Britain but not with English; and does not replace what I felt to be missing. For one thing its 'faerie' is too lavish, and fantastical, incoherent and repetitive. For another and more important thing: it is involved in, and explicitly contains the Christian religion. For reasons which I will not elaborate, that seems to me fatal. Myth and fairy-story must, as all art, reflect and contain in solution elements of moral and religious truth (or error), but not explicit, not in the known form of the primary 'real' world.
>
> (*TL* 144)

Flieger effectively shows the misjudged racial essentialism in this passage, as well as the fact that Tolkien's criticisms of the Arthurian literature are, so to speak, very much a case of 'the pot calling the kettle black' (*IM* 32–44). She also seeks to show that there are distinct, if perhaps sometimes unconscious, Arthurian echoes in Tolkien's work. The most explicit of these is the final departure of the wounded (or at least never-fully-recovered) Frodo in a ship bound for Tol Eressëa, known elsewhere in Tolkien's *oeuvre* as *Avallónë*. In relation to this scene Tolkien wrote to Waldman (in a passage omitted from the *Letters*): 'To Bilbo and Frodo the special grace is granted to go with the Elves they loved – an Arthurian ending' (*SD* 132). Such Arthurian echoes are less surprising when we realize that as late as 1955 Tolkien still harboured hopes of completing his alliterative poem *The Fall of Arthur*, begun in the 1930s (*TL* 219). However, according to Carpenter, Tolkien's Arthurian poem 'did not touch on the Grail' (the most obviously Christian motif) but offered 'an individual rendering of the Morte d'Arthur, in which the king and Gawain go to war in "Saxon lands" but are summoned home by news of Mordred's treachery' (*Biog* 224).

If, according to Carpenter, Tolkien went some way towards removing explicitly Christian elements in his Arthur poem, he also avoided another sort of explicitness. He told Waldman that one of the ideals of his proposed 'mythology dedicated to England' was that 'it should be "high" [and] purged of the gross' (*TL* 144). Flieger argues that, in the context of his criticisms of Arthurian mythology, Tolkien is here alluding to the adulterous triangles in 'the Matter of Britain' (*IM* 38). Yet Tolkien's (perhaps significantly) unpublished verse fragment 'The Fall of Arthur' contains what Carpenter claims is 'one of the few pieces of writing in which Tolkien deals explicitly with sexual passion, describing Mordred's unsated lust for Guinever [*sic*]: "His bed was barren; there black phantoms / of desire unsated and savage fury / in his brain had brooded till black morning"' (*Biog* 224–5). This is hardly bodice-ripping stuff, but its remarkableness nevertheless underlines the almost ubiquitous absence of the sexual body in Tolkien's works. Unless we go in for 'queer' readings of, for example, the Sam/Frodo/Gollum triangle along the lines of Lucie Armitt in her *Fantasy Fiction, LOTR* is, as Armitt remarks, a 'profoundly sexless narrative'.[53] In her Lacanian reading of *LOTR*, which compares the Ring to Poe's purloined letter (a 'pure signifier' – a literal O or nothing – whose circulation dominates the subjects in the tale), Valerie Rohy seeks to show how the displacement of the impossible homosexual relation between Frodo and Sam demonstrates the impossibility of all sexual relations. According to Lacan such relations (whether homo- or heterosexual) are foredoomed to inevitable failure. As in courtly love, the necessary obstacles to the consummation of sexual love only serve to mask (like the Freudian fetish) the fact that, according to Lacan, 'there is no sexual relation'.[54] As Rohy puts it: 'The radically limited relationships of Tolkien's universe differ little from our own; for all its fantastic, readily parodied elves and wizards, *LOTR* "realistically" – more realistically, even, than reality – describes the problem of human desire and the impasse of our own impossible sexuality'.[55]

Aside from such bleakly Lacanian interpretations of Tolkien's work,[56] Flieger suggests that in Tolkien's myth there is '[o]nly one love story, that of Beren and Lúthien, [that] is worthy of the name. Their love is neither forbidden nor illicit, and its successful outcome in Beren's quest for a Silmaril is a formative component of the entire legendarium' (*IM* 28). This story, perhaps based on MacDonald's 'Little Daylight' in *ABNW* – and certainly based on Tolkien's personal experience of his young wife dancing for him in a woodland glade (*TL* 420) – may be more sexually charged than Flieger recognizes. On Weathertop, Aragorn (at this point merely 'Strider') chants to the hobbits a verse form of the tale of Lúthien or Tinúviel, who at Beren's coming '*in his arms lay glistening*' (*LOTR* 192). The poem continues:

> Tinúviel the elven-fair,
>   Immortal maiden elven-wise,
> About him cast her shadowy hair
>   And arms like silver glimmering.

(*LOTR* 193)

Though hardly sexually explicit, these lines have perhaps a frisson of late Romantic eroticism. Admittedly the effect is rapidly neutralized by Strider's prose summary, jam-packed with information from Tolkien's mythology, and by the arrival of the Ringwraiths.

The tale of Beren and Lúthien is again explicitly invoked in the love story of Aragorn and Arwen, when Aragorn just happens to be singing 'The Lay of

Lúthien' when he first discovers Arwen dancing in the woods. Indeed, at this first encounter with Arwen he actually calls out the words '"*Tinúviel, Tinúviel!*"' from the song he will many years later sing to the hobbits on Weathertop. Perhaps significantly, the tale of Aragorn and Arwen is relegated to Appendix A of *LOTR*. The positioning of this tale outside the frame of the main story may be because it is not strictly necessary to the famously 'interlacing' structure of Tolkien's tightly woven narrative (though the banner sent to Aragorn by Arwen does play its role in the great battle of the Fields of Pelennor). Allusions to the tale of Aragorn and Arwen are, however, subtly woven into the main narrative, as Richard C. West has shown.[57] One effect – if not necessarily a cause – of the tale's relative exclusion from the primary narrative is the latter's focus on dramatic action rather than on any 'love-interest'. This may perhaps be a factor in the 'crossover' quality of *LOTR*. If *The Hobbit* is a children's book enjoyed by adults, then *LOTR* is an adults' book that has been enjoyed by younger readers.

However, despite its relegation to an appendix, the tale of Aragorn and Arwen is one of Tolkien's most moving pieces. It is a tale about enduring love, triumphing over seemingly impossible odds, and sealed with Arwen's sacrifice of her Elven immortality in order to live with her human husband for 'six score years of great glory and bliss' (*LOTR* 1062). Although not sexually explicit, this phrase does nevertheless suggest a deep and fulfilled sexual relationship. Arwen's grief at Aragorn's death is overwhelming. She returns alone to the spot where she and Aragorn had many years previously plighted their troth, the hill of Cerin Amroth in the now abandoned Lórien, where she now awaits death.[58] For Tolkien, the closet Romantic, deep sexual love and death seem somehow to be intimately connected. It is presumably no coincidence that, beside his and his wife's names on their gravestone in a North Oxford cemetery, is carved 'Beren' and 'Lúthien' (*Biog* 341–2).

The tale of Aragorn and Arwen may be in a sense marginalized in *LOTR*; nevertheless it reminds us that, as Tolkien put it in his statement of faith in Faërie in his essay on *SWM*: 'Faery . . . most strongly represents love'. This does not mean only sexual love, for despite the suggestions of Armitt and Rohy about the homosexual desire of Sam for Frodo, Sam's love is, on another reading, any one of (or indeed a blend of all) Lewis's 'Four Loves' *other than* 'eros'.[59] But for Tolkien love also has a broader sense of 'a respect for all things, "inanimate" and "animate", an unpossessive love of them as "other"' (*SWM* 101). This is presumably one of the reasons why Tolkien's work is so susceptible of 'Green' or ecological readings. As Kate Rigby puts it in her *Topographies of the Sacred*, which is an ecocritical recuperation of the Romantic tradition much indebted to Abrams's *NS*: 'The genre of fantasy . . . can be an effective vehicle for engaging with the question of our right relationship to the natural world, as it is, for example, in the work of J.R.R. Tolkien (a true inheritor of the romantic project of re-creating myth through literature)' (*TS* 106). The senses in which Tolkien saw *SWM* as being somehow 'an anti-G.M. tract' presumably include (perhaps unconsciously) the point that, unlike Mossy and Tangle who at the end of *GK* ascend the stairs in the rainbow to *somewhere else* ('the country whence the shadows fall'), Smith ends up back at home, and will 'not be going on journeys again . . . not on long ones, if you understand me' (*SWM* 51). The love at the heart of *SWM* is one that may have transcended the workaday world into the perilous realm of Faery, but it is a love that in the end returns to and embraces this earth. Such love produces 'both ruth [pity or sorrow] and delight'. In generating an awareness of an otherness beyond the 'adamantine rings' of egocentric control mechanisms, true love (if one dares to speak its name) tends to coincide with imagination, Tolkien claims. In linking 'true love' with the imagination, Tolkien is taking a line close to that of Iris Murdoch, whose 'warm fan-letter' in 1965 caused him the 'greatest surprise' (*TL* 353). 'Fantasy' in the bad sense described by Murdoch above all in *The Fire and the Sun* is precisely the opposite of Tolkien's 'Faery'.[60] Rather than being self-absorbed and 'escapist', fantasy for Tolkien can and should be about Faery, as defined in a passage already partly quoted but worth repeating:

> Faery might be said indeed to represent Imagination (without definition because taking in all the definitions of this word): esthetic; exploratory and receptive; and artistic; inventive, dynamic, (sub)creative. This compound – of awareness of a limitless world outside our domestic parish; a love (in ruth and admiration) for the things in it; and a desire for wonder, marvels, both perceived and conceived – this 'Faery' is as necessary for the health and complete functioning of the Human as is sunlight for physical life.
>
> (*SWM* 101)

This view of 'Faery', or fantasy, as essential to human completeness, is grounded in Tolkien's not entirely orthodox and (despite his criticisms of Coleridge) High Romantic theology of 'sub-creation', a theology of the imagination shared with Lewis and echoing MacDonald's. This is made explicit in the declaration of faith at the end of the section on 'Fantasy' in *OFS*, where 'Fantasy' does not so much refer to a literary genre as to 'a quality of strangeness and wonder in the Expression' that characterizes the fairy-tale: 'Fantasy remains a human right: we make *in our measure* and in our derivative mode, because we are made: and not only made, but made in the image and likeness of a Maker' (*MCOE* 139; 145, emphasis added).

4
C.S. Lewis: Reality and the Radiance of Myth

Allegories of desire

If Tolkien's writing was in a certain sense Romantic, Lewis was haunted by what he termed (*faute de mieux*) 'Romanticism' – a term he nevertheless proposed to abandon because it lacked a clear definition. This characteristically provocative gesture comes in the Preface to the second edition of *The Pilgrim's Regress* (=*PR*), the perhaps surprisingly tardy prose debut of such a prolific author of fiction and non-fiction (Lewis's two books of poetry had fallen stillborn from the press in the aftermath of WWI[1]). Not until his 35th year did Lewis compose, very rapidly and almost out of the blue, his first prose work, with the distinctly odd subtitle: *An Allegorical Apology for Christianity, Reason and Romanticism.* Although in the 1943 Preface to *PR*, appearing a decade after the first publication, Lewis subjects the term 'Romanticism' to a death of a thousand (or at least seven) qualifications, his retraction of the term was by no means final. When he came to write his spiritual autobiography *Surprised by Joy* (=*SBJ*) in the mid 1950s, Lewis used the term 'Romanticism' quite freely to describe the set of values, or *desires*, which were decisive in his development. The later autobiography covers almost the same ground as that mapped out in *PR* (which, like *Treasure Island*, seems to have begun with a map). In the Preface to *PR*, Lewis plays down the autobiographical element; the self-proclaimed addict of self-scrutiny has an almost obsessive wariness of autobiography: 'You must not assume that everything in the book is autobiographical. I was attempting to generalize, not to tell people about my own life' (*PR* 14).

PR is intensely personal, however; it focuses on a particular experience of intense longing (or 'Sweet Desire') which dominated Lewis's early life, and which he would later call 'Joy'. In the first edition of *PR* he used the term 'Romanticism' to refer to this experience. He tells us in the later Preface that what he had meant by 'Romanticism' was not one of the several discriminations of it he now offers; it was rather 'a particular recurrent experience which dominated my childhood and adolescence and which I hastily called

"Romantic" because inanimate nature and marvellous literature were among the things that evoked it' (*PR* 7). The experience is, he claims, 'common, commonly misunderstood, and of immense importance'; it is evoked in different people by different stimuli (*PR* 7). This intense longing differs from other longings because 'though the sense of want is acute and even painful, yet the mere wanting is felt to be somehow a delight' (*PR* 7). There is 'a peculiar mystery about the *object* of this Desire' since every supposed object of 'Desire' turns out to be inadequate to the strength of 'Sweet Desire' for 'the unnameable something, desire for which pierces us like a rapier at the smell of a bonfire, the sound of wild ducks flying overhead, the title of *The Well at the World's End*, the opening lines of *Kubla Khan*, the morning cobwebs in late summer, or the noise of falling waves' (*PR* 9–10). If this experience is universal, as Lewis suggests, then the triggers for it – or 'It', to use the private code of the young Lewis and Arthur Greeves (*LL1* 821n61) – are particular and personal. Lewis writes in *SBJ* that his earliest 'aesthetic experiences' (though he elsewhere resists calling such experiences merely 'aesthetic') were 'already incurably romantic'. The triggers were a toy garden his brother had constructed in a biscuit-tin lid and 'the Green Hills' – the Castlereagh Hills seen from the Lewis nursery window in Belfast. These hills, though not far off, 'were, to children, quite unattainable. They taught me longing – *Sehnsucht*; [and] made me for good or ill, and before I was six years old, a votary of [Novalis's] Blue Flower' (*SBJ* 12). These triggers for Lewis's 'Romantic' or 'aesthetic' experiences are arguably relevant to the discussion of Pullman's criticisms of Lewis's allegedly life-hating world-view (see below).

These decisive experiences recorded in *SBJ* were 'imaginative', Lewis claims, in the High Romantic sense of pointing towards some transcendent reality, rather than being merely egocentric fantasy or day-dreaming (*SBJ* 18). Lewis narrates the following very powerful early memory (or memory of a memory):

> As I stood beside a flowering current bush on a summer day there suddenly arose in me without warning, and as from a depth not of years but of centuries, the memory of that earlier morning at the Old House when my brother had brought his toy garden into the nursery. It is difficult to find words strong enough for the sensation which came over me: Milton's 'enormous bliss' of Eden (giving the full, ancient meaning to 'enormous') comes somewhere near it. It was a sensation of desire; but desire for what? Not certainly a biscuit-tin filled with moss, nor even . . . for my own past. . . . [A]nd before I knew what I desired, the desire was gone, the whole glimpse withdrawn, the world turned commonplace again, or only stirred by a longing for the longing that had just ceased.
>
> (*SBJ* 18–19)

A crucial phrase here is the 'longing for the longing', which echoes the fact that we are reading a 'memory of a memory'. This self-reflexive quality arguably echoes the German Romantic (and especially Hegelian) philosophy lurking behind the Idealism that still dominated Oxford philosophy when Lewis was an undergraduate.[2] Partly by temperament, and partly by historical and geographical accident, Lewis embraced this kind of philosophy, which he defended publicly until his defeat in Oxford's 'Socratic Club' in 1948 by Elizabeth Anscombe, a follower of Cambridge philosophy in general and Wittgenstein in particular (see below). Behind turn-of-the-century British Idealism and its German Romantic predecessors lay the Platonic tradition, including Plotinus and his one-time disciple Augustine of Hippo (as Abrams argued in *NS*). This fundamentally Platonic dimension to Lewis's thought pervades *The Chronicles of Narnia* (=*CN*), not only when Professor Kirke exclaims in *The Last Battle* (=*LB*): 'It's all in Plato, all in Plato!' (*LB* 160), but also, for example, in the scene in *The Silver Chair* (=*SC*) where the Witch tries to persuade Jill and Eustace that her realm of Underland is the only reality, an obvious reworking of Plato's cave allegory in *The Republic*. Lewis's quasi-Platonic 'dialectic of Desire', as he calls it in the Preface to *PR* (*PR* 10), is all about *memory*, which recalls Plato's fundamental claim that knowledge is memory (*anamnesis*). This emphasis on memory (suppressed and otherwise) also connects with psychoanalysis, although Lewis was scathing about what he saw as the reductionism of Freudian thought, for example in the chapter in *PR* entitled '*Poisoning the Wells*', featuring 'Sigismund Enlightenment'. Lewis arguably resembles (in some measure and in different ways) both Plato and Lacan in his emphasis that desire is defined by lack or want.[3] Lack or loss actually *constitutes* desire, as Lewis says in the Preface to *PR*:

> But this desire, even when there is no hope of satisfaction, continues to be prized, and even preferred to anything else in the world, by those who have once felt it. This hunger is better than any other fullness; this poverty better than all other wealth. And thus it comes about, that if the desire is long absent, it may itself be desired, and that a new desiring becomes a new instance of the original desire, though the subject may not at once recognize the fact and thus calls out for his lost youth of soul at the very moment in which he is being rejuvenated . . . not noticing that that even while we say the words the very feeling whose loss we lament is rising again in all its old bitter-sweetness. For this sweet Desire cuts across our ordinary distinctions between wanting and having. To have it is, by definition, a want: to want it, we find, is to have it.
>
> (*PR* 7–8)

This paradoxical (or dialectical) moment of desire is fleeting but overwhelming. It is a kind of religious experience, and Lewis is willing to see his kind of 'Romanticism' as 'spilt religion', as the anti-Romantic T.E. Hulme memorably put it.[4] Lewis's response to Hulme is to say that such spillage can be 'the beginning of a trail which, duly followed, will lead [someone] in the end to taste the cup itself' (*PR* 11).

What Lewis offered in *PR* and subsequently in *SBJ*, is a retrospective narrative of the 'lived dialectic of Desire' in which (and this practically defines 'dialectic') seemingly false moves are a necessary part of the total process. Insofar as their limitations are perceived and transcended, idols are important stages on the way to truth, which Lewis was old-fashioned enough to believe was worth searching for. Although he was not naïve and saw the likes of postmodernism coming, Lewis nevertheless believed in teleology, or a kind of grand narrative in which there was, if not a final end to desiring, then at least the 'good infinite' of a Platonic 'endless ending' as desire quests ever 'further up and further in' (*LB* 152ff). This contrasts with the 'bad infinite' of Lacanian desire, sliding ever further over and ever further out. The only authority Lewis claims for his account of the peregrinations of desire is that he has learned by repeated failure (*PR* 8). However, in true Platonic or dialectical fashion, the objects of desire are only false idols insofar as we misuse them by seeking to possess them. If they are properly seen as pointers to something 'further up and further in', the objects of desire can appear in their true light as images of something more glorious. Again, this is an issue to be discussed in the context of Pullman's criticisms of Lewis's allegedly world-hating outlook. We may anticipate here by asking whether Pullman has done justice to the *dialectical* nature of Lewis's – and indeed Plato's – quest for Joy.

As in *Pilgrim's Progress*, the narrator of *PR* dreams of a journey. A boy named John travels through an imagined world on a quest for a perfect island he has glimpsed, only in the end to discover – in a divine reversal of the direction of human seeking – that he must retrace his steps (the eponymous 'Regress'). While the running headlines Lewis added to the second edition of *PR* may be helpful, they can also interfere with the meanings a reader may derive from the story. To use E.D. Hirsch's terminology, the headlines give readers access to Lewis's original 'meaning', but they cramp the range of 'significance' they may find.[5] Because the story is explicitly an allegory, it is in Lewis's precise definition (discussed below), about the *author's* meaning; nevertheless, even a story specifically related to the intellectual climate of the 1920s and 1930s can have an 'applicability' (Tolkien's equivalent, roughly, of Hirsch's 'significance') beyond the author's intention. Some of Lewis's images are dated and some have worrying overtones (such as the pervasive use of 'brown girls' as a negative image for sexuality); but other images have a resonance that transcends their particular historical context and helps to create whatever impact *PR* has *as a story*. The headlines can then seem irritatingly redundant. When John hears sweet music and glimpses a perfect island with 'pale small-breasted Oreads', we may not wish to be told that 'He wakes to Sweet Desire; and almost at once mixes his own fantasies with it' (*PR* 24). Indeed the headline introduces the idea that sexuality does not belong in Paradise, something Pullman in particular would challenge.

The awakening of 'Sweet Desire' in John has an archetypal fairy-tale quality, an almost mythical resonance which strains away from allegorical specificity. After hearing a sweet musical note and a voice 'so high and strange that he thought it was very far away, further than a star', John comes across a strange gap or window in the wall beside the road:

> Through it he saw a green wood full of primroses; and he remembered suddenly how he had gone into another wood to pull the primroses, as a child, very long ago – so long that even in the moment of remembering the memory seemed still out of reach. While he strained to grasp it, there came to him from beyond the wood a sweetness and a pang so piercing that he forgot [everything] . . . All the furniture of his mind was taken away. A moment later he found that he was sobbing . . . and what it was that had happened to him he could not quite remember, nor whether it had happened in this wood, or in another wood when he was a child.
>
> (PR 24)

As in Lewis's first quasi-mystical experience beside a flowering currant bush, described in *SBJ*, the experience narrated in *PR* is inseparable from the *memory* – the infinitely distant memory – of a prior experience. The experiences in the woods in *PR* have more than a touch of William Morris about them. The second such experience described in *SBJ* also has a (less elevated) literary association: *Squirrel Nutkin,* and *only* this particular book by Beatrice Potter, Lewis adds (*SBJ* 19). The third quasi-mystical experience in *SBJ* has a literary trigger too: Lewis had read Longfellow's *Saga of King Olaf* in a 'shallow casual way for its story and its vigorous rhythms', but was not prepared for the impact of 'Tegner's Drapa' which begins:

> I heard a voice that cried,
> Balder the beautiful
> Is dead, is dead –
> And through the misty air
> Passed like the mournful cry
> Of sunward sailing cranes.
>
> I saw the pallid corpse
> Of the dead sun
> Borne through the Northern sky.
> Blasts from Niffelheim
> Lifted the sheeted mists
> Around him as he passed.

Lewis describes his reader-response as follows:

> I knew nothing about Balder; but instantly I was uplifted into huge regions of northern sky, I desired with almost sickening intensity something never to be described (except that it is cold, spacious, severe, pale and remote) and then, as in the other examples, found myself at the same moment already falling out of the desire and wishing I were back in it.
>
> (*SBJ* 20)

This experience was destined to be repeated several years later after a period of what might be called 'spiritual dryness' or even, given the association Lewis recognized between joy and sex, some kind of 'latency period'.[6] Repetition is also an expression of the structure of joy as memory. Lewis has an interesting aside here that echoes the 'ontogeny/phylogeny' debate (though he doesn't use these technical terms) when he claims that much of the character of the historical period called the Renaissance is actually a projection of the development of the individual beyond the 'Dark Ages' of boyhood. While Lewis's focus on 'boyhood' doubtless reveals a gender bias, it also reflects his specific horror of the English public school system. Thus, after the 'Dark Ages' of boyhood, a 'greedy, cruel, noisy and prosaic' period between childhood and adolescence, the young Lewis experienced a Renaissance of 'Joy' (*SBJ* 61). The specific trigger was again Nordic – the words *Siegfried and the Twilight of the Gods* and an illustration by Arthur Rackham. Although Lewis had at this point never heard of Siegfried, he says – let alone Wagner – that nevertheless 'pure "Nothernness" engulfed me: a vision of huge, clear spaces hanging above the Atlantic in the endless twilight of Northern summer, remoteness, severity' (*SBJ* 62). Of course memory is once more at the core of the experience: 'I knew that I had met this before, long, long ago in *Tegner's Drapa*, [and] that Siegfried . . . belonged to the same world as Balder and the sunward-sailing cranes' (*SBJ* 62). And again the experience seems largely constituted by *loss*:

> And with that plunge back into my own past arose at once, almost like heartbreak, the memory of Joy itself, the knowledge that . . . I was returning at last from exile and desert lands to my own country; and the distance of the Twilight of the Gods and the distance of my own past Joy, both unattainable, flowed together into a single, unendurable sense of desire and loss, which suddenly became one with the loss of the whole experience, which . . . had already vanished, had eluded me at the very moment when I could first say *It is*. And at once I knew . . . that to 'have it again' was the supreme and only object of desire.
>
> (*SBJ* 62–3)

The constant craving to have 'It' again became central to the life of the young Lewis, as can be seen from his correspondence with his confidant, Arthur Greeves and from his diary. In the latter, the 28 year-old Lewis noted in February 1927, with reference to his preparation for a session of Tolkien's 'Coalbiters':

> Spent the morning partly on the *Edda* . . . It is an exciting experience, when I remember my first passion for things Norse under the initiation of Longfellow (Tegner's 'Drapa' & 'Saga of K. Olaf') at about the age of nine; and its return much stronger when I was about 13, when the high priests were M. Arnold, Wagner's music, and the Arthur Rackham *Ring*. It seemed impossible then that I shd. ever come back to read these things in the original. The old authentic thrill came back to me once or twice this morning'.[7]

This diary entry comes almost two years before the late night conversation in which Lewis and Tolkien mutually confessed their shared addiction to Norse mythology (*LL1* 838). Something Lewis also shared with Tolkien was that their response to reading myths and fairy tales was to *write*. Lewis's response to reading Norse mythology was to compose, while still at school, a tragedy called *Loki Bound*, 'Norse in subject and Greek in form'. Lewis's Loki is: 'not merely malicious. He was against Odin because Odin had created a world though Loki had clearly warned him that this was a wanton cruelty. Why should creatures have the burden of existence forced upon them without their consent?' (*SBJ* 94). There is a strongly Schopenhauerian whiff to the young Lewis's pessimism; and if he had not yet read Nietzsche (certainly by 1924 he had read *Beyond Good and Evil*[8]), he seems to have caught at least the gist of certain ideas from *The Birth of Tragedy*.[9] Lewis discusses his early pessimism in *SBJ* (*SBJ* 95–6) and though he places it firmly in his pre-conversion past, it may nevertheless be relevant to Pullman's criticisms of a life-hating strain in Lewis. As a contemporary of Lewis's precursor St Augustine once said, the latter could change his life-hating Manichaeism as little as a leopard could change its spots.

Another factor relevant to the pessimism of the young (and, if Pullman is right, the not-so-young) Lewis – and also perhaps related to the overwhelming sense of loss which characterized his experiences of 'Joy' – is the nine-year-old Lewis's loss of his mother. The impact of his mother's death is perhaps best expressed in the following lines from *SBJ*:

> With my mother's death, all settled happiness, all that was tranquil and reliable, disappeared from my life. There was to be much fun, many pleasures, many stabs of Joy; but no more of the old security. It was sea and islands now; the great continent had sunk like Atlantis.
>
> (*SBJ* 23)

Lewis's image of the sinking of Atlantis for this cataclysmic loss was an image that also haunted Tolkien, who had lost his father when he was four and his mother ten years later. Perhaps Lewis derived the Atlantis image partly from Tolkien's use of the motif in many of his writings including *LR*, *NCP* and the various versions of the sinking of *Númenor* in his legendarium, all of which Lewis knew from readings to the Inklings.

A key element in the development of Lewis's mythology can be seen in his fascination with allegory. Three years after his 'creative' work in allegorical form (*PR*), he published his famous 'critical' masterpiece on allegory, *AOL*, which has set the agenda for critical discussion of Spenser's *Faerie Queene* (=*FQ*) for over seventy years. Even a critic with such radically different views from Lewis as Catherine Belsey not only orientates the argument of her book *Desire* by reference to Lewis's reading of *FQ*, but also finds it 'hard to resist the outlines of the story he tells'.[10] 'The Alligator of Love', as Lewis liked to call his famous book, is not only an erudite scholarly work, but also highly readable, written with a kind of gusto that exceeds the bounds of conventional scholarship. Although Lewis appealed to very different audiences with his literary criticism on the one hand, and his imaginative fiction on the other, there are some fascinating connections running between the different kinds of writing he practised.

One such connection is the concept of allegory, which was central to Lewis's work both as a critic and as a writer of imaginative fiction. Towards the beginning of *AOL* he offers a definition of allegory:

> On the one hand you start with an immaterial fact, such as the passions which you actually experience, and can then invent *visibilia* [visible entities] to express them. If you are hesitating between an angry retort and a soft answer, you can express your state of mind by inventing a person called *Ira* [Anger] with a torch and letting her contend with another invented person called *Patientia* [Patience]. This is allegory, and it is with this alone that we have to deal.
>
> (*AOL* 44–5)

This very precise and rather restricted definition of allegory is sharply contrasted by Lewis with another way of the relating the material to the immaterial, or the visible to the invisible:

> But there is another way . . . which is almost the opposite of allegory, and which I would call sacramentalism or symbolism. If our passions, being immaterial, can be copied by material inventions, then it is possible that our material world in its turn is the copy of an invisible world. The attempt to read [that invisible world] through its sensible [i.e. perceptible by the senses] imitations, to see the archetype in the copy, is what I mean by symbolism . . . The allegorist leaves the given – his

own passions – to talk of that which is confessedly less real, which is a fiction. The symbolist leaves the given to find another that is more real. To put the difference in another way, for the symbolist it is we who are the allegory.

(*AOL* 45)

This concept of symbolism, whose difference from allegory 'can hardly be exaggerated', Lewis says, 'makes its first effective appearance in European thought with the dialogues of Plato' (*AOL* 45). It finds its greatest expression, however, in the time of the Romantics, and this, Lewis suggests, 'is significant of the profound difference that separates it from allegory (*AOL* 46). Lewis does not elaborate on the connection with Romanticism here, yet it is important to make explicit what he leaves implicit, because his whole working definition of allegory, which opposes it sharply to symbol, is derived largely from the negative Romantic definition of allegory. The Romantic privileging of the vibrant, revelatory symbol over sterile and pedantic allegory may be a justified reaction to what allegory had become by the 18th century, but the very allegories which Lewis was approaching in *AOL* in terms of this unsympathetic Romantic definition of allegory often give the lie to that definition. There is a kind of inconsistency in *AOL* between the restrictive definition of allegory to which Lewis is theoretically committed, and his actual practice as reader and critic of allegory.

Lewis's theoretical commitment to the Romantic antithesis of symbol versus allegory is not loud but deep. 'Symbolism', he says, 'is a mode of thought, but allegory is a mode of expression. It belongs to the form of poetry, more than to its content' (*AOL*.48). This idea is further examined in a paper on metaphor that Lewis gave not long after the publication of *AOL*. 'Bluspels and Flalansferes: A Semantic Nightmare' is an essay whose bizarre title derives from Lewis's defamiliarizing tactic of inventing words to illustrate his discussion of 'dead' metaphors. The essay distinguishes between what Lewis calls 'the Master's metaphor' and 'the Pupil's metaphor'. Of these, he says:

The first is freely chosen; it is one among many possible modes of expression; it does not at all hinder, and only very slightly helps, the thought of its maker. The second is not chosen at all; it is the unique expression of a meaning that we cannot have on any other terms; it dominates completely the thought of the recipient; his truth cannot rise above the truth of the original metaphor.

(*SLE* 255)

This theory of the role of metaphor in language – which, like *AOL*, owes much to the latter's dedicatee, Owen Barfield – echoes the Romantic opposition between allegory and symbol. But the argument of the essay runs at the end into a kind of impasse, when Lewis writes:

> [A]ll our truth, or all but a few fragments, is won by metaphor. And thence, I confess, it does follow that if our thinking is ever true, then the metaphors by which we think must have been good metaphors. It does follow that if those original equations, between good and light, or evil and dark, between breath and soul and all the others, were from the beginning arbitrary and fanciful . . . then all our thinking is nonsensical. But we cannot, without contradiction, believe it to be nonsensical. And so, admittedly the view I have taken has metaphysical implications. But so has every other view.
>
> (*SLE* 265)

We are placed on the horns of a dilemma here, caught between some kind of essentialism and the only apparent alternative: a (to Lewis) unthinkable relativism. Lewis resorts to the typical Idealist manoeuvre of claiming that relativism is self-refuting ('we cannot, without contradiction, believe [our thinking] to be nonsensical'). Ironically, Lewis's particular philosophical training in British Idealism (and behind that the Hegelian tradition) meant that he was engaging in advance with some of the issues that underlie, *mutatis mutandis*, modern university courses in literary theory. There is something to be said for at least debating what sometimes seems to be the compulsory relativism (or anti-essentialism) of the academy. Lewis sees a contradiction (or perhaps a dialectic) between, on the other hand, the recognition that if language is fundamentally metaphorical, then 'truth' is imaginatively and aesthetically intuited rather than intellectually known (the 'Romantic' view); and, on the other hand the 'rationalist' demand for intellectual certainty. In other words, Lewis is caught between 'Myth' (as he increasingly began to call symbolism) and 'Fact'.

For Lewis the Romantic imagination did not *preclude* rationality, as is clear from the subtitle of *PR: An Allegorical Apology for Christianity, Reason and Romanticism. PR* is an allegory as subsequently defined in *AOL*: 'the allegorist [Lewis] leaves the given [his own intellectual and religious development] to talk of that which is confessedly less real, which is a fiction' (*AOL* 45). *PR* contains personifications such as Mr Halfways (Romanticism) and Sigismund Enlightenment (Freudianism). As noted above, Lewis added running headlines in later editions, though in the Preface to the third edition he admits that these stand in inverse proportion to its success *as a story*: 'when allegory is at its best, it approaches myth, which must be grasped with the imagination, not with the intellect' (*PR* 19). Lewis is working with such an impoverished concept of allegory that – for an allegory to succeed as a story – it must turn into what is defined as its opposite, i.e. myth or symbolism.

Lewis was aware of the problems relating to his definitions of allegory and myth/symbolism. In 1940 he wrote to E.M. Butler, Professor of German at Manchester and subsequently Cambridge:

> There are parts of that book [*AOL*] which I don't feel too happy about now and the passage on symbolism and allegory is one of them . . . If I had to do it again I shd. make the following distinction:
>
> 1. *Allegory* Each symbol, in isolation, has a meaning and the total meaning is built up out of these . . .
> 2. *Symbolical narrative or myth.* What has a meaning is the total story, and the separate characters or 'properties' are mere products of analysis. i.e. 'rescuing-Eurydice-from-Hell-and-losing-her-by-looking-back' has a meaning that neither Eurydice in isolation, nor Hell in isolation has . . . Also in a symbolical narrative the meaning usually cannot be stated in conceptual terms: it lives only *in the story*.
>
> (LL2 437–8, emphasis added)

However, Lewis continues, an odd thing follows:

> The same story may be mythical or symbolical to one person and allegorical to another. . . . When I read George MacDonald's stories as a boy I was overwhelmed with a sense of significance, but couldn't have identified any one thing in them with any idea, nor got the significance of the whole conceptually apart from the story. Now, when I re-read them, they are almost pure allegory to me – because, in the interval, I have discovered what they are 'about' by a quite different route.
>
> (LL2 438)

Here Lewis's readings of MacDonald appear more nuanced than Tolkien acknowledged when he said: '[Lewis] was evidently born loving (moral) allegory, and I was born with an instinctive distaste for it. *Phantastes* wakened him, and afflicted me with profound dislike' (*SWM* 69).

To resolve Lewis's unstable opposition between allegory and myth/symbolism, Paul Piehler has proposed a distinction between 'the allegory of vision' and 'the allegory of demystification'.[11] The latter – classically represented by Prudentius's depiction in *Psychomachia* of a battle between personified Virtues and Vices – was for Lewis originally a way of dealing with (by bringing to representation) forces which we would now call 'unconscious'. However, this kind of allegory as 'psychic defence by personification' seemed by the eighteenth century to have outlived its usefulness, and degenerated into the frigid personifications criticized by the Romantics. This concept of allegory, used by Lewis in *AOL*, is inappropriate to the medieval allegories he is considering there. Rather than abandon the concept of allegory, Piehler suggests we use the term 'allegory of vision' for such material. Whether or not one accepts Piehler's label of 'allegory of vision' for this 'other' kind of allegory that resists Lewis's narrowly prescriptive definition, one can see this 'other' 'other-speak' (the literal meaning of the Greek *allegoria*) taking shape between the lines of *AOL*. What emerges looks not only like what Lewis will describe as the second kind of Romanticism in the Preface to *PR*, but also like the imaginative fiction Lewis himself would write (the science-fiction and Narnia books) after his early attempt at an 'allegory of demystification' in *PR*. Of his 'Romanticism no.2' Lewis says: 'The marvellous is "romantic", provided it does not make part of the believed religion' (*PR* 10). Or as Lewis puts it in the passage from *AOL* already quoted in the Prelude above, the decline of the gods lets romance in, freeing poets to invent – under the pretext of allegory – regions of strangeness, beauty and 'the "other world" not of religion, but of imagination; the land of longing, the Earthly Paradise, the garden east of the sun and west of the moon' (*AOL* 75–6). Here, Lewis claims, 'we see the beginnings of that free creation of the marvellous which first slips in under the cloak of allegory. . . . For poetry to spread its wings fully, there must be, besides the believed religion, a marvellous that knows itself as myth' (*AOL* 82–3).

A marvellous that knows itself as myth

Lewis always denied that *CN* and his science-fiction trilogy were allegorical – to the puzzlement of many readers who felt instinctively that they were. His (perhaps disingenuous) denial rests on *AOL*'s narrow definition of allegory, still apparent in a letter of 1958 (cited in the previous chapter):

> By allegory I mean a composition . . . in wh. immaterial realities are represented by feigned physical objects; e.g. a pictured Cupid allegorically represents erotic love . . . or, in Bunyan, a giant represents Despair. If Aslan represented the immaterial Deity in the same way in which Giant Despair represented Despair, he would be an allegorical figure.
>
> (*LL3* 1004)

The idea that he 'drew up a list of basic Christian truths and hammered out "allegories" to embody them . . . is all pure moonshine', Lewis says elsewhere.[12] For Lewis, Aslan is not an allegorical figure at all; rather he is what he called a *supposal*, that is: 'an invention giving an imaginary answer to the question, "What might Christ become like, if there really were a world like Narnia and He chose to be incarnate and die and rise again in *that* world as He actually has done in ours?" This is not allegory at all. So in "Perelandra". This also works out a *supposition*' (*LL3* 1004). Lewis often reiterated this insistence that the Narnia books and the science-fiction trilogy were not allegories but supposals. A crucial difference between allegory and supposals is that:

> they mix the real and the unreal in different ways. Bunyan's picture of Giant Despair does not start from a supposal at all. It is not a supposition but a *fact* that despair can capture and imprison the human soul. What is unreal (fictional) is the giant, the castle, and the dungeon. The incarnation of Christ in another world is a mere supposal; but *granted* the supposition, He really would have been a physical object in that world and His death on the Stone Table . . . a physical event no less than his death on Calvary.
>
> (*LL3* 1004–5)

Lewis's attempt to maintain a clear division between 'fact' and 'fiction' is related to his similar attempt to divide 'literal' from 'metaphorical' language in his essay 'Bluspels and Flalansferes'. Allegory (in the narrow sense of Peihler's 'allegory of demystification') is the merely fictional decoration of statements of fact whose truth may be legitimated by reason alone; 'supposal' (or myth, the real 'other' of allegory), which differs *in principle* from factual truth, can only be 'received' in an 'imaginative embrace'. The latter phrase comes from Lewis's essay 'Myth Became Fact',[13] where he seeks sharply to demarcate two modes of apprehension – abstract intellectual understanding versus concrete imaginative experience ('knowing' versus 'tasting'). Paradoxically, these can only be united, he asserts, in the response to the unique event of the 'Incarnation' in which 'Myth became Fact'. This idea was central to Lewis's conversion to orthodox Christian faith. It was his momentous discussion with Tolkien and Hugo Dyson in 1931 which helped him to move from a merely intellectual assent to an abstract theism to a faith which was *both* an assent to real historical 'Fact' *and* an 'imaginative embrace' of a 'Myth' which loses none of its 'mythical radiance' for being also 'Fact' – 'Christ is more than Balder, not less', as Lewis later put it.[14] The examples of myth adduced in Lewis's decisive discussion with Tolkien and Dyson were pre-eminently Norse (Odin, Balder), though, in his account of it to Greeves, Lewis also mentions Adonis and Bacchus (*LL1* 976–7). This argument about the relation between concrete imaginative experience and abstract intellectual understanding must have resonated with the book Lewis was writing at this time, *AOL*. In the latter, Lewis is running an implicit argument *against* the reduction of allegory to a merely intellectual game (*The Faerie Queene* is not a *puzzle*), and *for* a view of allegory (Peiehler's 'allegory of vision') as inviting of an 'imaginative embrace'. The appeal of *FQ* – the focus of Lewis's concerns at this time – is not primarily to the abstracting intellect, though it does not for that reason make a *merely* sensual and emotional appeal. The whole point of the Christian humanism Lewis found in Spenser was to deploy attractive images in order to *train the emotions* into various virtues (Sidney's 'speaking pictures' to 'teach and delight'). What mattered was to know the truth with both the heart and the will *as well as* with the head (or 'wit'). In lines MacDonald took for the epigraph of Chapter XX of *Phantastes*, Spenser epitomizes the ideal that Lewis admired in the Christian humanist synthesis of Spenser and Sidney: 'The noble hart that harbours vertuous thought' (*FQ* 1.v.1).

This Christian humanist synthesis was repugnant to Tolkien, who disliked Spenser's style, language and anti-Catholicism. This dislike of Spenser's religion goes beyond Spenser's embroilment in the vicious religious politics of sixteenth-century Ireland. Lewis himself claimed that Spenser's involvement in the 'wickedness' of anti-Catholic politics began to corrupt his imagination in Book V of *FQ* (*AOL* 349). Such a direct moral judgment on the relation of politics to literature is perhaps rather unexpected in *AOL*, and may be worth recalling when looking at Pullman's criticisms of Lewis. However, the divide between Tolkien's Catholicism and Lewis's Protestantism is much more than political in this context. Lewis always felt a Protestant freedom to synthesize religion, philosophy and literature in a way that rankled with Tolkien's traditional Catholic sense that theology is best left to the priests and that if religion is to appear in literature, it should do so only indirectly and very discreetly. *CN* must on many counts have been a nightmare for Tolkien, not least because they are Lewis's miniature *FQ*.[15] Yet Lewis also felt that the presence of specific religious themes in literature should not be too explicit. He writes in relation to the question of the supposed pantheism in certain passages in the 'Mutability' Cantos at the end of *FQ*:

> The modern reader is tempted to enquire whether Spenser . . . equates God with Nature: to which the answer is, 'Of course not. He was a Christian, not a pantheist'. His procedure in this passage would have been well understood by his contemporaries: *the practice of using mythological forms to hint at theological truths was well established* and lasted as late as the composition of *Comus*. It is, for most poets and in most poems, by far the best method of writing poetry which is religious without being devotional . . . In the medieval allegories and the renaissance masks, God, if we may say so without irreverence, appears frequently, but always *incognito*. Everyone understood what was happening, but the occasion remained an imaginative, not a devotional one. The poet thus retains liberties which would be denied him if he removed the veil.
>
> (*AOL* 366, emphasis added)

Lewis's claim that 'everyone understood what was happening' ties in with his view that the roots of Spenser's imagination lie in the popular culture of the period, rather than in any recondite intellectual fashions:

> We have long looked for the origins of *The Faerie Queene* in Renaissance palaces and Platonic academies, and forgotten that it has humbler origins

of at least equal importance in the . . . chap-book, the bedtime story, the family Bible and the village church. What lies next beneath the surface in Spenser's poem is the world of popular imagination: almost, a popular mythology.

(AOL 312)

This linking of *FQ* with 'world of popular imagination: almost, a popular mythology' is a theme that Lewis often comes back to in his many writings on Spenser, of which perhaps the most revealing is his brief 'On Reading *The Faerie Queene*'. It begins: 'Beyond all doubt it is best to have made one's first acquaintance with Spenser in a very large – and, preferably, illustrated – edition of *The Faerie Queene*, on a wet day, between the ages of twelve and sixteen . . .'[16] There are, Lewis says, many aspects to *FQ*, including a 'luxurious, Italianate and florid' Renaissance element, but:

> it is best to begin with a taste for the homespun . . . and to keep your *The Faerie Queene* on the same shelf with Bunyan and Malory . . . and even with *Jack the Giant-Killer* . . . For this is the paradox of Spenser's poem; it is not really medieval – no medieval romance is very like it – yet everyone who has really enjoyed it . . . has enjoyed it as the very consummation of the Middle Ages.'

(SMRL 147)

In a previous essay Lewis had argued that what *FQ* requires of the reader is not critical acumen, but a 'childlike attention to the mood of the story' *(SMRL* 137), because 'its primary appeal is to the most naive and innocent tastes: to that level of our consciousness which is divided only by the thinnest veil from the immemorial lights and glooms of the collective Unconscious itself. It demands of us a child's love of marvels and dread of bogies, a boy's [*sic*] thirst for adventures' *(SMRL* 132). *FQ* is 'a great palace, but the door into it is so low that you must stoop to go in . . . It is of course much more than a fairy-tale, but unless we can enjoy it as a fairy-tale first of all, we shall not really care for it' *(SMRL* 133). In showing us what he loves about *FQ*, Lewis is, according to Wilson, 'actually writing a recipe for how to construct the Narnia Chronicles'.[17]

Regions of strangeness and beauty

While one can see with hindsight glimpses of Narnia in Lewis's writing about *FQ*, it easier to find Lewis's science-fiction trilogy between the lines of *AOL*. In the first book of the trilogy, published two years after *AOL*, Lewis shows at least as much interest in the medieval past as in any technological future. Although, as we have seen, the genesis of *OSP* purportedly lies in a toss-up between Tolkien and Lewis to decide which of them should write about space-travel and which about time-travel, there is also a sense in which *OSP* originates in Appendix I of *AOL*, which discusses the term *Oyarses* used by the medieval Platonist Bernardus Sylvestris. Lewis here refers to the advice given him on this subject by Professor C.C.J. Webb. In Chapter XXII of *OSP*, where the narrator explains how he came to be writing up Ransom's adventures on Mars ('Malacandra'), he quotes a paragraph from a letter he once wrote to Ransom; the paragraph is virtually identical to the relevant paragraph in *AOL*, even including a reference to 'C.J.' (*CT* 137).

The science-fiction trilogy transgresses any established definitions of genre, however. Although Lewis admits he had a 'ravenous lust' for the 'scientifiction' of writers in the tradition of H. G. Wells, this had little to do with any 'romantic spell' or joy, he says; his own 'planetary romances' were not so much the gratification as the 'exorcism' of that 'peculiar, heady attraction' for other planets (*SBJ* 34). The exorcism worked, Lewis suggests, by combining the 'coarse strength' of the 'fierce curiosity' inherent in science fiction with a 'more elusive, and genuinely imaginative, impulse' (*SBJ* 34). Such a transformation of science fiction into a new literary genre, which could carry a *spiritual* weight, did not originate with Lewis himself but with Lindsay's *VTA*. As Lewis wrote in a letter of 1947, he first learned from Lindsay that 'other planets in fiction are good for *spiritual* adventures. They can satisfy 'the craving that sends our imaginations off the earth' (*LL1* 753). In Lindsay he saw 'the terrific results' produced by combining two kinds of fiction hitherto kept apart – 'the Novalis, G. MacDonald sort' and 'the H. G. Wells, Jules Verne sort' (ibid.). This Novalis/MacDonald tradition is clearly identifiable with 'a marvellous that knows itself as myth', and unlike other kinds of science fiction, it is unconcerned about technological plausibility. In *OSP* Lewis transports his hero Ransom to Mars by means of a space-ship, a topic debated with some heat in *NCP*, where Guildford (the Tolkien figure) insists: 'An author's way of getting to Mars (say) is part of *his* story of *his* Mars; and of *his* universe, as far as that particular tale goes' (*SD* 163). Or as Lewis put it a decade later in his 1955 paper 'On Science Fiction', referring to the journeys to Mars in *OSP* and to Venus in *Perelandra*: 'I took a hero once to Mars in a space-ship, but when I knew better I had angels convey him to Venus. Nor need the strange worlds, when we get there, be at all strictly tied to scientific probabilities. It is their wonder, or beauty, or suggestiveness that matters' (*OTOW* 91).

If the narrator of *OSP* and *Perelandra* is obviously 'Lewis', there is some discussion of who the hero Ransom is. The fact that Ransom is a philologist has led some to assume that he is based on Tolkien, who suspected he 'may have had some part in [Ransom]' (*TL* 89). However, there is a purely functional motivation for having a philologist-hero who can rapidly acquire 'Old Solar', the language spoken on Malacandra and Perelandra. Other factors suggest that, in the first two books of the trilogy, Ransom is based on Lewis himself as much anyone, while in *THS* Ransom strikingly resembles Lewis's friend Charles Williams. Despite such speculation about the 'identity' of Ransom, he is referred to in the opening of *OSP* simply as 'the Pedestrian', perhaps hinting at *Pilgrim's Progress* and *Everyman*. The first two chapters see Ransom kidnapped by Devine, an unscrupulous entrepreneur, and Weston, the archetypal mad scientist, who need an earthling to take to the *sorns* of Malacandra. Devine and Weston – for whom the inhabitants of Malacandra are merely savages – assume that the latter want a human sacrifice, to which end they have brought Ransom. Actually they have misinterpreted the message from the Oyarsa (or tutelary spirit) of Malacandra who had merely wanted a Thulcandrian [earthling] to inform him about 'Maleldil's [God's[18]] strange wars there with the Bent one [Satan]' (*CT* 109). Thulcandra is the eponymous 'Silent Planet' because after its Oyarsa [Lucifer] had become 'bent' – and had almost destroyed Malacandra – he was banned from 'the Heavens' and confined to Thulcandra, with which all contact has been lost. Thus elements of Christian 'salvation history' have been transposed into a different mythological frame as 'supposals'.

The Oyarsa of Malacandra also wants to know why the Thulcandrians – Weston and Devine – have turned up on his planet. Ransom tells him that Devine's only motivation is 'the sun's blood' [gold]; however, Weston's motivation is less crude. 'Westonism', as Lewis elsewhere calls it, is the theory that the development of human technology would allow humans to colonize other planets, and so to live forever as 'they leap from world to world . . . always going to a new sun when an old one dies' (*CT* 110). Lewis told a correspondent that what started him writing *OSP* 'was the discovery that a pupil of mine took all that dream of interplanetary colonization quite seriously, and the realization that thousands of people in one way or another depend on some hope of perpetuating and improving the human race for the whole meaning of the universe – that a 'scientific' hope of defeating death is a real rival to Christianity' (*LL2* 262). *OSP* is a kind of counter-propaganda. As Lewis put it elsewhere:

> What immediately spurred me to write [*OSP*] was Olaf Stapledon's *Last and First Men* and an essay in J.B.S. Haldane's *Possible Worlds*, both of wh. seemed to take the idea of such travel seriously and to have the desperately immoral outlook wh. I try to pillory in Weston. I like the whole interplanetary idea as a *mythology* and simply wished to conquer for my own (Christian) pt. of view what has always hitherto been used by the opposite side.
>
> (*LL2* 236–7)

The fact that Lewis chose to oppose 'Westonism' with *myth* is significant. While Lewis used rational argumentation against the likes of 'Westonism', he was also ready to trade myths in defence of Christianity. As noted above, Lewis's essay 'Myth Became Fact' contrasted intellectual knowing with imaginative 'tasting'. Perhaps the most striking feature of *OSP* is the way it lets the reader 'taste' and 'feel' the beauty of the Heavens, and of Malacandra, in a way which reveals the poverty of Weston's desiccated worldview. Ransom's first numinous experience comes on the voyage to Malacandra:

> A nightmare, long engendered in the modern mind by *the mythology that follows in the wake of science,* was falling off him. He had read of 'Space': at the back of his thinking for years had lurked the dismal fancy of the black, cold vacuity, the utter deadness, which was supposed to separate the worlds . . . now that very name 'Space' seemed a blasphemous libel for this empyrean ocean of radiance in which they swam. He could not call it 'dead'; he felt life pouring into him at every moment. How indeed could it be otherwise, since out of this ocean the worlds and all their life had come? He had thought it barren; he saw now that it was the womb of worlds, whose blazing and innumerable offspring looked down nightly upon the Earth . . . No: Space was the wrong name. Older thinkers had been wiser when they named it simply the heavens – the heavens which declared the glory – the
> 'happy climes that ly
> Where day never shuts his eye
> Up in the broad fields of the sky.'[19]
> He quoted Milton's words to himself lovingly, at this time and often.
>
> (*CT* 26–7, emphasis added)

'Older thinkers had been wiser' is a typical Lewis comment. More specifically, as he argues in *The Discarded Image*: 'Nothing is more deeply impressed on the cosmic imaginings of a modern than the idea that the heavenly bodies move in a pitch-black and dead-cold vacuity. It was not so in the Medieval Model.'[20] Although Ransom quotes Milton, 'Milton here is medieval', as Lewis puts it when quoting the same lines in his essay 'Imagination and Thought in the Middle Ages' (*SMRL* 53).

It is Lewis's evocation of the sheer strangeness and beauty of Malacandra that remain with the reader. In a Postscript to *OSP*, 'Dr Ransom' admits he is disappointed by the narrator's attempts to portray his adventures:

> How can one 'get across' the Malacandrian *smells*? Nothing comes back to more vividly in my dreams . . . especially the early morning smell in those purple woods, where the very mention of 'early morning' and 'woods' is misleading because it must set you thinking of . . . the smell of our own planet, but I'm thinking of something totally different. More 'aromatic' . . . yes, but then it is not hot or luxurious or exotic as that word suggests. Something aromatic, spicy, yet very cold, very thin, tingling at the back of the nose – something that did to the sense of smell

what high, sharp violin notes do to the ear . . . I am homesick for my old Malacandrian valley when I think of it.

(*CT* 139)

There is also talk in *Perelandra* of homesickness for another planet, though this homesickness goes much further back than any sense of interplanetary exile; it is 'Sweet Desire' itself:

It was strange to be filled with homesickness for places where his sojourn had been so brief and which were . . . so alien to our race. Or were they? A cord of longing which drew him to the invisible isle seemed to him at that moment to have been fastened long, long before his coming to Perelandra, long before the earliest times that memory could recover in his childhood, before his birth, before the birth of man himself, before the origins of time. It was sharp, sweet, wild, and holy, all in one.

(*CT* 235)

As a mythical embodiment of 'the land of longing, the Earthly Paradise' (*AOL* 75), *Perelandra* is for many readers one of Lewis's greatest achievements. Elements of the traditional science-fiction story – such as a spaceship and some suspense – featured in *OSP*, but they barely figure in *Perelandra*, which is partly prose-poem, partly philosophical dialogue and as Lewis suggested, partly opera (*LL2* 630).

Perelandra opens on Earth, with 'Lewis' fighting his way past 'bent eldila' [fallen angels] to reach Ransom's cottage; Ransom is then transported in a 'celestial coffin' to Perelandra, which is covered in water, apart from one area of 'Fixed Land' and some floating islands. Like other stories by Lewis, *Perelandra* originated in a mental picture (*OTOW* 79) – in this case of floating islands – and developed into a story about 'an averted fall' (*OTOW* 181). The writing of *Perelandra* overlapped with Lewis's lectures on *Paradise Lost*, published as *A Preface to Paradise Lost* (=*PPL*) in 1942, a year before *Perelandra*. Lewis claimed that *Perelandra*, like the Narnia books, 'works out a *supposition*. ("Suppose even now, in some other planet there were a first couple undergoing the same that Adam and Eve underwent here, but successfully")'(*LL3* 1004). In the Perelandrian Fall story, the tempter is Weston. A genuinely eerie element in the book is the uncertainty as to whether it is Weston speaking through the mouth of what Ransom calls 'the Un-man', or Satan himself. Prior to Weston's possession by Satan, it had been apparent in his dialogue with Ransom that he had progressed beyond 'mere Westonism'. The goal of interplanetary colonization having been in principle achieved on Malacandra, Weston has developed an interest in 'spirituality' (*CT* 225–30). He preaches to Ransom a doctrine of 'emergent evolution', a mishmash of Life-philosophies with echoes of Bergson, Nietzsche and Hegel, culminating in the cry: 'I *am* the Universe. I, Weston, am your God and your Devil. I call that Force into me completely . . . ' (*CT* 230).

Already in this first encounter between Ransom and Weston, some of the technical problems relating to the book's form begin to emerge. Early in the dialogue Ransom is 'filled with a sense of crazy irrelevance' and reflects: 'Here were two human beings, thrown together in an alien world under conditions of inconceivable strangeness; . . . Was it sane – was it imaginable – that they should find themselves at once engaged in a philosophical argument which might just as well have occurred in a Cambridge combination [=common] room?' (*CT* 223). Lewis's acknowledgement of the craziness of his whole scenario hardly makes it more credible. However interesting the dialogues may be philosophically, they sometimes *do* seem incongruous and frankly unimaginable. Such incongruity results from Lewis's failure to balance two very different impulses: while Lewis the philosopher wants to argue rationally, Lewis the poet is committed to the power of myth and the Romantic imagination. His books of the 1930s and 1940s are dominated by this tension: some, such as *OSP*, tend towards the 'myth' pole; others, especially Lewis's apologetic writing, seek to convince by rational argument. Much of Lewis's writing falls somewhere between and is a mixture of both. *The Screwtape Letters* (=*SL*) and *The Great Divorce* (=*GD*) present highly imaginative settings for discussion of religious issues, but only *GD* contains genuinely mythical elements. *Perelandra* is an at times an uneasy mixture of myth and philosophical argument, as for example when Ransom and Weston engage in an extended discussion of death and nihilism while riding on dolphin-like fish over the boundless Perelandrian ocean.

Nevertheless there are in *Perelandra* powerful elements of myth on which the philosophical and theological discussions are superimposed. Lewis several times presents the idea that 'what was myth in one world might always be fact in some other', a thought prompted by Ransom's encounter with mermen and mermaids (*CT* 235). Ransom had earlier awakened on Perelandra to find something happening to him 'which perhaps never happens to a man until he is out of his own world: he saw reality and it was a dream. He opened his eyes and saw a strange heraldically coloured tree loaded with yellow fruits and silver leaves. Round the base of the indigo stem was coiled a small dragon covered with scales of red gold. He recognized the garden of the Hesperides at once' (*CT* 182). Ransom not only feels that he is living – quite literally – 'in Paradise' (*CT* 281); he also has the sensation 'not of following an adventure, but of enacting a myth' (*CT* 185). Repeating the suggestion made in *OSP* – and alluded to in Tolkien's *NCP* (*SD* 249) – that 'the distinction between history and mythology might be itself meaningless outside the Earth' (*CT* 129), Ransom concludes that 'the distinction between fact and myth is purely terrestrial' (*CT* 277); as the result of the Fall, it applies only on Earth:

Long since on Mars, and more strongly since he came to Perelandra, Ransom had been perceiving that the triple distinction of truth from myth and of both from fact was purely terrestrial – was part and parcel of that unhappy division between soul and body which resulted from the Fall . . . The Incarnation had been the beginning of its disappearance. In Perelandra it would have no meaning at all. Whatever happened here would be of such a nature that earth-men would call it mythological. All this he had thought before. Now he knew it.

(*CT* 273–4)

According to Lewis's essay 'Myth Became Fact', published a year after *Perelandra*, the distinction between 'knowing' and 'tasting' is only overcome on Earth by the Incarnation. But on Perelandra the distinction literally does not apply, as the narrator points out when Ransom eats some seaweed on Perelandra: 'while Ransom was on Perelandra his sense of taste had become something more than it was on Earth: it gave knowledge as well as pleasure, though not a knowledge that can be reduced to words' (*CT*.291).

Such an overcoming of the distinction between myth and fact is a bold gesture on Lewis's part, both in theological and literary terms. While every attempt is made in to emphasize the central place of the Incarnation in cosmic history, *Perelandra* pushes theological boundaries by proposing a scenario where an Incarnation is not necessary, because a Fall has not occurred. It is ironical that a writer so venerated by orthodox Christians could be accused of a kind of presumption in seeking to join together in his fiction the 'myth' and 'fact' that Lewis elsewhere says could only be reconciled by 'the Grand Miracle' of the Incarnation. Arguably Lewis is here setting his mythopoeic powers (doubtless unconsciously) alongside the mythopoeic powers of God. While Lewis strove in his apologetic writings to be an uncompromisingly orthodox Christian, perhaps Lewis the myth-maker is a sub-creator who has some problems with the 'sub'. Lewis might be considered a kind of modern Christian Gnostic, developing his own speculative mythology founded on (but going far beyond) the orthodox Christian story. Lewis was a Christian Platonist; but history shows that the line between Platonism and Gnosticism is far from clear.

The tradition in which Lewis stands goes back from Barfield through MacDonald, Novalis and Coleridge, to the Renaissance and Medieval Platonists, and back to Origen and the early Christian Platonists; it has always had strong Gnostic tendencies and therefore an uneasy relationship with Christian orthodoxy. It may be no accident that 'archons' – the mighty rulers who are standard features of Gnostic mythology – should appear in the penultimate chapter of *Perelandra*. As discussed above, though Rateliff insists that Tolkien was 'not a gnostic' (*Blackwelder* 84), he claims that while Tolkien was a conservative Catholic and accepted traditional Catholic teaching, 'it would be truer to say that Tolkien believed everything the Church taught, *and more*'. (*Blackwelder* 85, emphasis added). There is arguably a similar '*and more*' in Lewis's case, though here it is perhaps more problematic (or at least more obvious) because Lewis – in contrast to Tolkien's reserve – unabashedly *mixes* the mythological supplement with the primary Christian myth. Unlike Tolkien's, Lewis's mythical sub-creation is not kept separate from the religion believed as fact. Lewis's 'marvellous that knows itself as myth' needs – according to his own argument in *AOL* – to be 'disinfected of belief'; it has to be based on 'the old marvellous which was once taken as fact' – but no longer so (*AOL* 83). The '"other world" not of religion but of imagination', 'the regions of strangeness and beauty' (*AOL* 75), depend precisely on the decline of belief in the elements that comprise them. But in Lewis's science-fiction trilogy – and especially in *Perelandra* – he mixes 'romantic supposals' with myth that precisely *is* believed as fact.

This confers on Lewis's myth, and specifically on his hero Ransom, a problematic status for orthodox Christians. However, Christians who find the Gnostic tradition enriching rather than threatening may readily embrace Lewis's myths, since they contain little that is not at least implicitly in Novalis or in George MacDonald. Readers for whom the Christian God is as dead as the gods of the ancient world, may enjoy Lewis's myths in the same way that Lewis himself enjoyed the romantic marvellous he described in *AOL*. However, more politically motivated 'suspicious' readers may see in Lewis's writing a late version of 'Romantic ideology', and a problematic obliteration of the distinction between 'myth' and 'fact'. From this latter perspective, Lewis *would* want to show unpalatable (to Lewis) political 'facts' transfigured by consoling (to Lewis) 'myths'; and the overcoming of the 'fallen', terrestrial distinction between fact and myth, between literal and metaphorical uses of language, is just another version of the old Romantic nostalgia for an 'organic unity' falsifying the actual divisions of experience. To make matters worse, the mythological vision presented by Lewis is unashamedly hierarchical and deeply essentialist, not least in relation to gender. In a remarkable passage, all the more striking in light of later developments in feminist criticism (at which Lewis could hardly have guessed), Ransom encounters 'the real meaning of gender' (*CT*.327). Gender is not, we are told, 'an imaginative extension of sex'; on the contrary, '[g]ender is a reality, and a more fundamental reality than sex. Sex is . . . merely the adaptation to organic life of a fundamental polarity which divides all created beings. Female sex is simply one of the things that have feminine gender; there are many others, and Masculine and Feminine meet us on planes of reality where male and female would be simply meaningless' (*CT* 327). This almost seems written to exemplify the 'dual, *hierarchized* oppositions' that Hélène Cixous describes in her famous essay 'Sorties'.[21]

Lewis's adherence to what Cixous calls 'the Old order' is entirely explicit; indeed the existing order is not nearly old enough for Lewis. The order he longs for is not obviously identifiable with any power structure in the modern world. His 'discarded image' or worldview is medieval, essentialist and hierarchical, but by no means rigid; it is Platonist, but draws on that current in the Platonic (and especially neo-Platonic) tradition which is open to the *dialectical play* of the complex and differentiated structure of reality. This vision of 'the Great Chain of Being' is expressed above all in the operatic conclusion of *Perelandra*, where the eldila [angels] sing the praises of the 'Great Game' or 'Great Dance'. The latter is certainly hierarchical: '"All is righteousness and there is no equality. Not as when stones lie side by side, but as when stones support and are supported in an arch, such is his order"' (CT 340–1). Conversely, in a passage relevant to Pullman's idea of 'Dust', the very dust itself: '"which is scattered so rare in Heaven . . . is at the centre . . . as sparks fly out of a fire, He utters in each grain of it the unmixed image of his energy. Each grain, if it spoke, would say, I am the centre; for me all things were made"' (CT 342). The plan of the 'Great Game' is so grand that it escapes the human mind:

> "All that is made seems planless to the darkened mind, because there are more plans than it looked for. In these seas [of Perelandra] there are islands where the hairs of the turf are so fine and so closely woven that unless a man looked long at them he would see neither hairs nor weaving at all, but only the same and the flat. So with the Great Dance. Set your eyes on one movement and it will lead you through all patterns and it will seem to you the master movement. But the seeming will be true . . . There seems no plan because all is plan; there seems no centre because it is all centre".
>
> (CT.344)

Such passages could be compared with similar passages in Plotinus, the great neo-Platonist philosopher (and arguably a fountainhead of Romanticism). The negative theology of 'the Abyss' in the following passage is not only reminiscent of Valentinus, a Gnostic Christian contemporary of Plotinus, but also of Jacob Boehme, who influenced Romantic thinkers such as Novalis, Blake and Coleridge:

> "Yet this seeming also is the end and final cause for which He spreads out Time so long and Heaven so deep; lest if we never met the dark, and the road that leads no-whither, and the question to which no answer is imaginable, we should have in our minds no likeness of the Abyss of the Father, into which if a creature drop down his thoughts for ever he shall hear no echo return to him".
>
> (CT 344)

While Lewis could be an aggressively dogmatic Christian in the context of apologetic argument, as a myth-maker his position is more ambiguous, and in his mythology he entertains imaginatively ideas on the margins of Christian orthodoxy.

The uses (and abuses) of mythology are by no means the prerogative of the Right. William Blake is only one example of a writer who presented his radical vision through the medium of myth. Another example might be Pullman, though the radicalism of Pullman's message remains a moot point. Alongside Blake, Pullman's main literary influence is another political radical, Milton, and especially *Paradise Lost*. There is thus a close encounter between Pullman and Lewis that almost amounts to a family feud. If *HDM* is (starting with the title) deeply indebted to *Paradise Lost*, the writing of *Perelandra* overlapped with the writing of Lewis's *PPL*. Both *Perelandra* and *HDM* are, like their great predecessor *Paradise Lost*, centrally concerned with the myth of the Fall (whether, and however, that myth is conceived of as being 'true'). Pullman, Lewis and Milton have all been linked with Gnosticism. The great difference is that while Lewis, like Tolkien, wrote a mythological supplement (the '*and more*') to orthodox Christian doctrine, Pullman reads the Bible story *against the grain* – also a venerable Gnostic strategy. The particular focus of Pullman's counter-reading is the Fall – that cataclysmic moment in the history of this and other worlds, which is at the centre of *Perelandra* (and *The Magician's Nephew*), *HDM* and above all *Paradise Lost*.

In the Prelude above I argued that Pullman's re-writing of the Fall myth in terms of a 'Fortunate Fall' stands in the Romantic tradition outlined by Abrams in *NS*. Pullman's 'high argument' rehearses, I suggested, Wordsworth's Romantic re-writing of Milton's theodicy as a kind of internal evolution of consciousness and its relation to Nature. A more detailed reading of Pullman's version of the Fall myth, echoing not only Romantic ideas but also the neo-Platonic and Gnostic traditions lying behind some key Romantic themes, will be offered in the chapter on Pullman below. At this point it is worth looking more closely at Lewis's re-writing of the Fall myth in *Perelandra*, in order to highlight the key differences between Lewis and Pullman on this fundamental point. The central issue for both Lewis and Pullman is the relation between freedom and authority, or in broader terms, between free play and rigid structure. Lewis's Milton, unlike Blake's, is certainly not of the devil's party. Lewis spends a chapter of *PPL* seeking, if not to convert those who after Blake and Shelley have admired Satan, then at least 'to make a little clearer what it is they are admiring' (*PPL* 94–5). There is little to admire in the Satan of *Perelandra*. In a grotesque parody of the incarnation, Satan has assumed Weston's body and become 'the Un-man'; it (no longer 'he') shocks and disgusts Ransom with its trivial obscenities and cruelties, such as randomly mutilating Perelandrian frogs (a particular horror for the anti-vivisectionist Lewis) (*CT* 241–2). Satan comes in the form of Weston to tempt the Green Lady (the Eve of Perelandra) to transgress Maleldil's [the Lord's] command not to settle on the 'Fixed Land'. In a sense the whole point of this command is that it has no point, other than as an opportunity for obedience for its own sake. Similarly, according to Lewis in *PPL*, the apple in the Garden of Eden has for Milton (who here follows Augustine) no *intrinsic* importance (*PPL* 68–9).

However the commandment not to settle on the Fixed Land is more than an empty rule, set just to make a theological point; it also has a symbolic resonance. Perhaps surprisingly, given Lewis's alleged conservative tendencies, the stability of living on the Fixed Land is not what Maleldil has ordained for the inhabitants of Perelandra; rather they are to have a life on the open wave. Since the contours of the Perelandrian islands are constantly changing in response to the shape of the waves on which they float, life on the islands means literally 'going with the flow'. Symbolically there is a tension between the desire to be in control of one's own life, and a willingness to respond flexibly to whatever is sent by God. The idea of even wishing to be in control of one's experience comes as a shock to the Green Lady. One of the most interesting features of *Perelandra* is Lewis's subtle psychological descriptions of the way in which the Lady gradually loses a certain innocence or sense of immediacy, and begins to acquire self-consciousness and reflection – what she calls '"stepping out of life into the Alongside and looking at oneself living as if one were not alive"' (*CT*197). This movement from innocence to experience in both life and thought is of course a key Romantic theme, and one that greatly interests Pullman (especially Kleist's version). This key transition also seems to resonate with Lacan's famous essay on 'the Mirror Stage', when Weston (or Satan) produces a mirror and says to the Lady: '"Hold it further away and you will see the whole of the alongside woman – the other who is yourself"' (*CT*269). Lewis seems to be after a kind of fluid selfhood achieved by avoiding the fall into a fixed, alienated self-consciousness (also a Romantic desideratum). One is reminded of Kristeva's 'subject-in-process' which, by the power of 'the semiotic' (a pre-intellectual 'taste' of 'the real'), can resist enclosure into 'the Symbolic order'.

Lewis refuses, then, to countenance any post-Romantic sympathy for the Devil, or any valorization of the Fall as a hidden blessing. The idea of the 'Fortunate Fall', central to Romantic thought as delineated by Abrams (and echoed by Pullman), is specifically addressed in the repetition of the Edenic temptation scene re-enacted on Perelandra. The 'Tempter', in the form of Weston, tries with subtle arguments to persuade the Perelandrian Eve to disobey the divine command not to settle on the Fixed Land. When Ransom intervenes in the dialogue between Weston and the Green Lady, telling the latter about the tragic consequences of the temptation and Fall on Earth, Weston counters: '"[Ransom] has not told you that it was this breaking of the commandment which brought Maleldil to our world and because of which He was made man"' (*CT* 253). Ransom is overcome by doubt:

> What if the enemy where right after all? *Felix peccatum Adae*[Happy sin of Adam]. Even the Church would tell him that good came of disobedience in the end ... Progress passed before his eyes in a great momentary vision: cities, armies, tall ships, libraries and fame, and the grandeur of

poetry spurting like a fountain out of the labours and ambitions of men. Who could be certain that Creative Evolution was not the deepest truth?

(*CT* 253)

Then Ransom recovers himself and delivers what is in effect Lewis's response to the 'Fortunate Fall' argument:

"Of course good came of it ... Whatever you do, [Maleldil] will make good of it. But not the good He had prepared for you if you had obeyed Him. That is lost for ever. The first King and the first Mother of our world did the forbidden thing; and He brought good of it in the end. But what they did was not good; and what they lost we have not seen. And there were some to whom no good came nor ever will come".

(*CT* 253)

Then, turning to the body of Weston, the 'Un-man', Ransom adds: '"What good came to you? Do *you* rejoice that Maleldil became a man? Tell her of *your* joys, and of what profit you had when you made Maleldil and death acquainted"' (*CT* 253–4). In response to this, 'the body that had been Weston's threw up its head and opened its mouth and gave a long melancholy howl like a dog' (*CT* 254).

Lewis clearly feels that Ransom has clinched his case against the 'Fortunate Fall' argument (though, as we will discuss below, his insistence is partly undermined by a later passage in the 'Great Dance' sequence (*CT* 341)). Lewis insists that, far from being fortunate, the Fall is disastrous. As he puts it in *PPL*, the Fall of Satan, and the subsequent Fall of Man, far from being a fine thing, 'fails to be a roaring farce only because it spells agony' (*PPL* 103). The phrase 'Fall of Man' in the previous sentence was used deliberately, because, as discussed above, in *Perelandra* Lewis strongly affirms a kind of gender essentialism. This is significant because the myth of the Fall is often seen by feminist writers as symbolically encoding a gender hierarchy.[22] If Lewis in his exotic yet deliberately traditional treatment of the Fall myth reinforces a hierarchical gender essentialism, then Pullman, in his alternative re-telling of the myth, not only subverts the view (endorsed by Lewis) that the Fall represents an act of disobedience with catastrophic consequences; he also challenges the representation of Eve as a weak-minded and sinful subordinate who misleads her lord and master, Adam. As I will discuss below, Pullman instead presents an Eve-figure who is the hero of a Romantic myth of human (and indeed cosmic) development towards freedom and higher consciousness.

The final volume of the science-fiction trilogy, *THS*, differs from the others because, although it refers to Ransom's interplanetary travels, it does not itself depict such a voyage. *THS* marks a transition from science fiction proper to a different genre; its subtitle 'A modern fairy-tale for grown-ups' is doubtless influenced by that of MacDonald's *Phantastes: a Faerie Romance for Men and Women*. Not only are MacDonald's *Curdie* books mentioned in *THS* : just a year after the latter's publication, Lewis also published his MacDonald anthology. However, even *Phantastes* is about a journey to the other world of Fairyland (and indeed contains an account of 'a far-off planet'). The real model for *THS* is Charles Williams's 'supernatural thrillers', where supernatural forces intervene dramatically into contemporary England – perhaps foreshadowing Susan Cooper's *The Dark is Rising* sequence, or even in some respects the Harry Potter series.

On one level *THS*, like *AOL*, is about marriage, specifically that of the Studdocks; their problems are resolved through the influence of Ransom and his heavenly companions, the eldila. Jane Studdock is a doctoral student, working on Donne; her husband Mark is a pushy sociology don, whose education, Lewis says, 'had been neither scientific nor classical – merely "Modern". The severities both of abstraction and of high human tradition had passed him by' (*CT* 540). This connects with Lewis's claim in the Preface to *THS* (where he refers to Tolkien's 'Numinor [*sic*] and the True West') that behind his own 'tall story' lies a serious 'point', which had already been made in his book *The Abolition of Man* (=*AOM*) (*CT* 353–4). Mark Studdock embodies everything Lewis hated in the 'modern' education system that he attacked in *AOM*. The particular target of *AOM* is the influence on English Studies of the kind of theory that entails the loss of objective values; for the anti-relativist Lewis, such values are the condition for the possibility of being truly human. Although he could only have guessed at the hegemony in English Studies of the explicitly anti-humanistic varieties of structuralism and post-structuralism, nevertheless Lewis's argument against the 'the abolition of Man' and the nihilism at the heart of a thorough-going relativism is, *mutatis mutandis,* relevant to contemporary debate. Anticipating philosophers such as Gadamer, Lewis emphasises the primacy of tradition (or the 'Tao', as he calls it, to distance himself from the accusation of special Christian pleading) as the enabling medium of all human thought and value, and he is deeply suspicious of the methods and motivations of the project of modern scientific enquiry.

These ideas are embodied in *THS*. Mark's lack of what Lewis considered a proper education leaves him defenceless against the seductive power of the N.I.C.E. (National Institute of Co-ordinated Experiments) whose 'inner ring' is consciously nihilistic. Only the most inner ring of all, however, knows that the 'Head' of the N.I.C.E. – literally the head of the guillotined scientist Alcasan – is being kept alive not by the scientific apparatus attached to it, but by the powers of darkness, the 'Macrobes', as Lewis calls the 'bent eldils' or fallen angels. The N.I.C.E. wants to revive Merlin to help them complete their project of world domination and the eventual – literal – abolition of man. But Merlin is recruited by the other side, the community headed by Ransom, now Mr Fisher-King, the Pendragon. Merlin reluctantly agrees to let the Oyeresu take possession of him, and thereby becomes the agent of the final cataclysm at a banquet at the headquarters of the N.I.C.E. First, in a parody of the Biblical story of the tower of Babel ('that hyddeous strength', as Sir David Lyndsay's old Scots poem calls it), Merlin produces pandemonium through a crazy confusion of language; then he causes carnage by releasing the animals kept for the purpose of vivisection. At the end of the book Ransom returns to Perelandra to join Arthur and other heroes on the island of Aphallin (Avalon), while Mark and Jane go to bed to enjoy matrimonial bliss.

If *Perelandra* has its moments of incongruity, the conjunction of the mundane and the supernatural in *THS* can seem contrived in a different way. Its Arthurian theme, partly a tribute to Charles Williams – whose Arthurian poem *Taliessin through Logres* is mentioned in the book (*CT* 550) – is a not entirely successful attempt to introduce 'strangeness and beauty' into modern England. While Tolkien's comment on the sections read to the Inklings – 'Tripish, I fear' (*Biog* 227n1) – may seem harsh, and possibly reflects some personal issues between Tolkien, Lewis and Williams, it does target Lewis's tendency to *mix* elements of myth and fantasy in a way Tolkien felt harmed the coherence of Lewis's 'secondary world'. Tolkien thought that Williams's influence on Lewis (as opposed, presumably, to Tolkien's) had prevented the maturing of Lewis's invented mythology as expressed in the first two volumes of his science fiction trilogy. In a letter of 1965, Tolkien writes: '[Lewis's] own mythology (incipient and never fully realized) . . . was broken to bits before it became coherent by contact with C.S Williams and his 'Arthurian' stuff – which happened between *Perelandra* and *THS*. A pity, I think' (*TL* 361). Writing with the benefit of hindsight and the success of *LOTR*, Tolkien apparently forgets that his own fantasy writing contemporary with *THS* (that is, *NCP*) was quite similar, mixing legendary and mythological elements (Anglo-Saxon and Atlantean/Númenórean rather than Arthurian and 'Old Solar') with contemporary university life. Perhaps Tolkien's single-minded dedication to the more (if not entirely) self-contained world of Middle-earth was assisted by his failure to complete and publish *NCP*.

It is nevertheless true that, far from seeking to stress the autonomy of fantasy as a genre, Lewis was in the 1940s ready to put fantasy to a variety of uses, deploying fantastic elements in a range of texts. A decade previously *PR* had carried the subtitle 'An Allegorical Apology'. Such 'mixed genre' texts containing fantasy elements include *The Screwtape Letters* (1942) and *The Great Divorce: A Dream* (1946). Although *Screwtape* is often classified by critics as an apologetic work, Lewis himself included it as one of the works in which he had sought 'to embody my religious belief in symbolical or mythopoeic forms, ranging from *Screwtape* to a kind of theologized science-fiction' (*LL3* 517). Clearly *Screwtape* is at the opposite end of the range from *OSP*. It is essentially a witty and at times penetrating tract on moral theology, set in the imaginative framework of a correspondence between a trainee devil, Wormwood and his mentor, Screwtape. There is no evocation of the kind of symbolic landscape that figures so prominently in Lewis's properly mythopoeic writings. Within its fantastic framework, *Screwtape* seeks to guide the reader to moral insight by means of critical reflection.

However, *The Great Divorce* (=*GD*), published the year after *THS*, has divided critics as to whether it is primarily an apologetic work directed to the reader's reason, or essentially a fantasy, offering itself as myth to the reader's 'imaginative embrace'. Perhaps Barfield gets closest to the truth when he writes: '*The Great Divorce* . . . is a kind of myth and in that book, as perhaps not quite in any other, this ever diverse pair – rational Lewis and mythopoeic Lewis – I will not say unite, but they do at least join hands.'[23] In the Preface to *GD*, Lewis reminds the reader that, while he intended *GD* to have a moral, it is essentially a fantasy or 'an imaginative supposal' (*GD* 9). Among the acutely observed vignettes of moral and spiritual failure, often reminiscent of *Screwtape*, there are also moments of genuine imaginative power. Lewis is at his mythopoeic best when describing symbolic landscapes, 'regions of strangeness and beauty', inhabited by mythological figures. The terrifyingly beautiful landscape of 'the Valley of the Shadow of Life' is realized with considerable power. Indeed, because it is far more 'real' than the insubstantial ghosts who are on a day-trip from Hell, it is for them diamond-hard: from the smallest blade of grass to the river itself. Lewis had got this general idea, as well as the particular idea of raindrops that would pierce the ghosts like bullets, from an American pulp science fiction magazine (*GD* 9). The landscape and the mythological figures such as the herd of unicorns (*GD* 58) are realized much more fully than is the case, for example, in *PR*; on the other hand, the sketches of the quotidian miseries of human relationships are at times devastatingly 'realistic'. There is here a fine balance between fantasy and didacticism.

GD is also relevant to the central argument of the present book with its allusions to Blake's *Marriage of Heaven and Hell*. Lewis admits in the Preface that, although in his book he is not attacking Blake directly (not being 'a fit antagonist for so great a genius'), he is nevertheless writing against what he thinks Blake stands for – that is, a kind of perennial philosophy based on the belief:

> that reality never presents us with an absolutely unavoidable 'either-or'; that, granted skill and patience and (above all) time enough, some way of embracing both alternatives can always be found; that mere development and adjustment or refinement will somehow turn evil into good, without our being called on for a final and total rejection of anything we should like to retain.
>
> (*GD* 7)

In other words, as in *Perelandra*, Lewis is attacking precisely the kind of Romantic 'high argument' about the Fortunate Fall described in Abrams's

NS. Blake is made to stand for a belief that is for Lewis 'a disastrous error', because it seeks prematurely to move via philosophical theory and/or mystical vision to a God's eye view beyond the proper limits of human knowledge – a kind of retrospective overview according to which 'good is everything and Heaven everywhere' (*GD* 7–8; 115). According to Lewis such an approach can lead us 'to embrace the false and disastrous converse and fancy that everything is good and everywhere is Heaven' (*GD* 8).

Lewis's attack on Blake (or what he thinks Blake stands for) has relevance to our discussion below of Pullman's criticisms of Lewis. Another version of the 'disastrous error' Lewis is attacking in *GD* is the doctrine of Universalism, the belief that all will in the end be saved. A problem here is that Lewis's guide in *GD* – the Virgil to his Dante in this tour of the next world – is George MacDonald, and MacDonald was explicitly a Universalist. I have written elsewhere about the complex relation between Lewis and MacDonald, in which Lewis seems to misread MacDonald.[24] In *GD* 'Lewis' addresses 'MacDonald': 'In your own books, Sir, . . . you were a Universalist. You talked as if all men would be saved' (*GD* 114). 'MacDonald' is then made to give a long and rather obfuscatory reply containing what Lewis wanted MacDonald to have said, but contradicting what MacDonald actually did say. As Catherin Durie puts it in her paper 'George MacDonald and C.S. Lewis':

> As *GD* ends, Lewis can only have his MacDonald abjure universalism by explaining the limitations of earthly knowledge, and suggesting that all formulations distort; the important choice is the one to be made now. It is a device which allows the book to close, but it does not resolve the differences between Lewis and his master.[25]

Durie demonstrates how Lewis systematically misreads MacDonald's theology. One important aspect of MacDonald's theology that Lewis 'quietly drops' is 'the childlikeness of God', and its corollary that 'theology misrepresents God when it portrays him as the great king' – a view of God that is 'a long way from the hierarchical and authoritative images that move Lewis'.[26] Lewis's misreadings of MacDonald culminate in *GD* when, as we have seen, he makes the character 'George MacDonald' express views directly opposite to views the real MacDonald actually held. As Durie wryly sums up:

> Lewis and MacDonald are here made to change places; but the MacDonald who makes such forceful points is a ventriloquist's dummy. It is Lewis's voice which subverts the real MacDonald's belief in hell as a temporary purifying force, and heaven as the home of every one of God's children.[27]

Lewis's misreadings of MacDonald bear directly on issues that Pullman has raised in relation to Lewis. Firstly, Pullman's idea of 'the republic of heaven' depends precisely on his opposition to the idea of God as king (an opposition which MacDonald shared, but Lewis edited out). Secondly, on the issue of universal salvation, Lewis actively misrepresents MacDonald by making him reject the Universalism that MacDonald actually espoused, and according to which not only the mildly rebellious Susan, but also the seriously rebellious Satan (or 'Samoil', as he appears in *Lilith*[28]), will ultimately be saved (*L* 217–18). So even if, as Pullman has objected, Lewis lets Susan be damned (in both senses of 'let'), MacDonald certainly would not. This raises the possibility that Pullman may have more in common with MacDonald than we would expect if we assumed that MacDonald and Lewis shared the same (offensive to Pullman) theological views. Both MacDonald and Pullman share a closeness to Blake and the Romantic tradition that Lewis finds suspect.

Seeing pictures: Narnia and the Christian imaginary

Almost the last words that 'MacDonald' offers to 'Lewis' in *GD* are: ' "Do not ask of a vision in a dream more than a vision in a dream can give" ' (*GD* 116). Five years later, the delicate balance of fantasy and didacticism that characterised *GD* had swung decisively away, if not from didacticism as such, then from overt and rationally argued didacticism, and towards fantasy, specifically 'fantasy-for-children'. In his 1952 essay 'On Three Ways of Writing for Children', written nearly fifty years before Pullman and Rowling and the boom in so-called 'crossover' fantasy fiction, Lewis comments:

> Of course as all children's literature is not fantastic, so all fantastic books need not be children's books . . . But there may be an author who at a particular moment finds not only fantasy but fantasy-for-children the exactly right form for what he wants to say. The distinction is a fine one. His fantasies for children and his fantasies for adults will have very much more in common with one another than either has with the ordinary novel or with what is sometimes called 'the novel of the child life'. Indeed the same readers will probably read both his fantastic 'juveniles' and his fantastic stories for adults . . . I am not quite sure what made me, in a particular year of my life, feel that not only a fairy tale, but a fairy tale addressed to children, was exactly what I must write – or burst.
>
> (*OTOW* 62–3)

In discussions of what precisely produced in Lewis this intense need to write a 'fantasy-for-children', one suggestion is that his defeat in 1948 at Oxford's 'Socratic Club' by Elizabeth Anscombe precipitated his turn to communicating through fantasy and fairy tale rather than reasoned argument. The Socratic Club was one of Oxford's best-attended debating societies, and Lewis was both its President and star, regularly demolishing (preferably atheist) opponents to the delight of his fan club. His dominance lasted until he met his nemesis in Anscombe, a pupil of Wittgenstein and later Professor of Philosophy at Cambridge. Far from being an atheist, Anscombe was a devout Roman Catholic and an admirer of St Thomas Aquinas, but she offered a robust critique of chapter III of Lewis's recently published book *Miracles* (1947). This chapter, entitled 'The Self-Contradiction of the Naturalist', is only available in the original 1947 edition, since Anscombe's criticisms led Lewis to revise subsequent editions. Chapter III was pivotal to Lewis's overall argument, which sought to demonstrate the rationality of a supernatural interpretation of reality. Such 'supernaturalism' claims only that miracles are possible – not necessarily that they occur – and that for the universe to be rationally intelligible, there must be some principle or reality beyond 'nature', that is, beyond the 'Total System' explicable (in principle) by science. 'Naturalism' is thus self-refuting, according to Lewis, and 'supernaturalism' triumphant.[29] But as Anscombe, trained in the discipline of fine philosophical analysis, pointed out, the terms of Lewis's 'nice knock-down argument' did not withstand close scrutiny. However, if the terms in which Lewis discusses the claims of science appear crude, that is partly because Logical Positivism *was* crude in its dismissal of any value claims whatsoever, never mind religious claims. And the hostility to religion to which Lewis was responding has not disappeared; it is alive and well and living in Oxford in the person of Richard Dawkins, in whose writings Pullman has taken a keen interest.[30] Notwithstanding their antithetical presuppositions, Lewis and Pullman share a willingness to grapple with the philosophical implications of science.

Accounts of the Socratic Club debate vary – Anscombe herself thought the reports of Lewis's philosophical demise exaggerated. Most likely Lewis had simply underestimated the extent to which the ground-rules of professional philosophy had changed since he himself had studied philosophy. His pupil George Sayer commented: '[Lewis] could not cope with such developments and really had no desire to. They made what he regarded as philosophical thinking almost impossible. '"I can never write another book of that sort", he said to me of *Miracles*. And he never did.'[31] In a footnote towards the end of *Miracles*, however, Lewis hints at another way of presenting the truth he believed in. Dismissing reductionist views that see myth as either 'misunderstood history', 'diabolical illusion' or 'priestly lying', Lewis says that myth is, 'at its best, a real though unfocused gleam of divine truth falling on human imagination'.[32] Myth invites an 'imaginative embrace', and offers a 'taste' of truth, rather than any merely cognitive assent. Sometimes what an author seeks to communicate may be too subtle, too elusive, too *close*, to be caught in rational concepts. As Lewis says in his essay 'On Stories', sometimes only the net of narrative can get near to catching the bird – in this case – of paradise (*OTOW* 45). The footnote in *Miracles* anticipates Lewis's later and more successful attempt to talk about miracles, and indeed 'the Grand Miracle' of the incarnation itself, in the form of *stories*: 'The *story* of Christ demands from us, and repays, not only a religious and historical but also an *imaginative* response. It is directed to the child, the poet, and the savage in us as well as to the conscience and to the intellect. One of its functions is to break down dividing walls.'[33]

However traumatic the Anscombe affair of 1948 was for Lewis (Alan Jacobs has recently challenged the view that Anscombe's criticisms led Lewis to resort to fairy-tales[34]), by the late 1940s and early 1950s there is clearly a shift on Lewis's part away from apologetic writing, and towards the genre of the fairy-tale. There was much in Lewis's life during these years to drive him to seek the 'recovery, escape and consolation' that Tolkien said were characteristic of the fairy-story.[35] Whether we interpret such a resort to fairy-tale images in the face of acute stress as a form of 'escapism', or as a sane and healthy response to a situation that had led in 1949 to Lewis's physical collapse, in fact it seems as if Lewis had little conscious control over the images; he says they just came to him.

The accounts Lewis subsequently gave of the composition of *CN* emphasize his passive role in the process. 'Making' a story is not the best way to describe a process that Lewis said was more like bird-watching (*OTOW* 68). He continues: 'I see pictures. Some of these pictures have a common flavour, almost a common smell, which groups them together. Keep quiet and watch and they will begin joining themselves up' (*OTOW* 68). In Lewis's experience these pictures never joined themselves up to form a complete story; there were always 'gaps' which needed to be filled by 'some deliberate inventing' (*OTOW* 68). Nevertheless, he insists, 'the images always came first'. In the case of *LWW* the images or 'mental pictures' that 'bubbled up' were 'a faun carrying an umbrella, a queen on a sledge, [and] a magnificent lion'. 'At first,' he adds, 'there wasn't even anything Christian about them' (*OTOW* 73). As these images sorted themselves into events (i.e. became a story), they demanded a form, and the form that presented itself, and with which Lewis says he 'fell in love', was that of the fairy-tale. (ibid.) For Lewis a great advantage of the fairy-tale genre is that it circumvents the overly reverential attitude of conventional religious belief, which, he says, can 'freeze feelings' and (with its 'lowered voices') make the whole business of religion seem 'almost something medical'. (Ibid.) The fairy-tale form has an 'inflexible hostility to all analysis, digression, reflections and 'gas' (Ibid.). Although the latter features are probably intended by Lewis to be seen as elements of the realist novel, they might also be seen as characteristic of his own apologetic writing. But by casting his religious beliefs into an imaginary world, where vivid pictures are caught in the net of a fantastic narrative, might not some of these beliefs, asks Lewis, 'appear in their real potency?' 'Could one,' he continues (and one wonders whether Elizabeth Anscombe is still at the back of his mind), 'steal past those watchful dragons?' (Ibid.).

The Lion, the Witch and the Wardrobe

Regarding the best order in which to read *CN*, the consensus favours the order of publication, since the impact of a first reading of *LWW* is lost if the reader is already familiar with Narnia. The question of the very existence of Narnia dominates the early chapters of *LWW*. Lucy's first stumbling into Narnia through the wardrobe is a moment of real magic, equalling anything in Carroll or MacDonald. Like the existence of the Princess's great-great-grandmother in *PAG*, the existence of Narnia is a matter of faith. Lucy becomes distressed, as not only the villainous Edmund, but also Susan and Peter, will not take her discovery seriously. Peter and Susan, concerned about Lucy's mental health, seek the advice of the mysterious professor, who, unknown both to the children and to readers (unless they have previously read *MN*), had visited Narnia as a boy. The professor conceals his own acquaintance with Narnia, but in a piece of self-parody on Lewis's part, insists on the reign of logic in questions of belief in the supernatural. Echoing Lewis's knock-down argument in *Mere Christianity* that Jesus was 'bad, mad or God', the professor insists: ' "Either your sister is telling lies, or is mad, or she is telling the truth" ' (*LWW* 47). Experience rendering the first two unlikely, logic demands belief in Narnia, on the basis of the available evidence. ' "What *do* they teach them at these schools?" ' the professor mutters (*LWW* 49). Eventually all the children find their way into Narnia through the wardrobe, not through their own seeking, but because 'some magic in the house . . . was chasing them into Narnia' (*LWW* 52). Like joy, which it embodies, Narnia is never under our control; even when it is actively sought by calling upon Aslan, as at the beginning of *SC*, that seeking is in reality a response to the prior calling of Aslan (*SC* 25).

Tolkien was critical of *CN*, partly because the stories did not sufficiently conform to his criteria for 'sub-creation'. Nevertheless *CN* do exhibit some of the main features of Tolkien's account of the fairy-story. Above all, they express the 'Joy' that is for Tolkien 'the mark of the true fairy-story' (*MCOE* 155). In Lewis's essay 'On Three Ways of Writing for Children', which pays homage to Tolkien's *OFS* – 'perhaps the most important contribution to the subject that anyone has yet made' (*OTOW* 61) – Lewis writes of a boy reading a fairy tale:

> [F]airy land arouses a longing for he knows not what. It stirs and troubles him (to his life-long enrichment) with the dim sense of something beyond his reach, and far from dulling or emptying the actual world, gives it a new dimension of depth. He does not despise real woods because he has read of enchanted woods: the reading makes all real woods a little enchanted. This is a special kind of longing . . . the boy reading the fairy-tale desires and is happy in the very fact of desiring.
>
> (*OTOW* 65)

This affirmation by Lewis that, far from making the reader 'despise real woods', the fairy tale actually 'makes all real woods a little enchanted' is worth remembering in discussions of Pullman's accusation that the world-view expressed in Lewis's fantasy writing is essentially 'life-hating'. The desire or longing evoked by the fairy tale is of course ultimately for joy, which, when experienced, offers in Tolkien's words a 'fleeting glimpse . . . beyond the walls of the world, poignant as grief' (*MCOE* 153). It is particularly associated with the tale's sudden 'turn' towards the happy ending or *eucatastrophe*: 'In such stories when the sudden "turn" comes we get a piercing glimpse of joy, and heart's desire, that for a moment passes outside the frame . . . and lets a gleam come through' (*MCOE* 154). Such a joyous 'turn' comes in *LWW* when the stone table on which Aslan had been sacrificed cracks loudly, and the resurrected Aslan suddenly appears to Lucy and Susan. Tolkien calls such a glimpse of joy *evangelium* (good news or 'gospel') and explicitly links it with what for him is the greatest fairy-tale of all: 'The Gospels contain a fairy-story, or a story of a larger kind which embraces all the essence of fairy-stories' (*MCOE* 155). For Tolkien there is an *analogy* between the Gospel story (authored by God (*MCOE* 155n2)) and the fairy-story, between Creation (God's story) and sub-creation (a human story). But in Lewis's fairy-stories (and this partly explains Tolkien's unease with them) the *difference* essential to the analogical identity-in-difference between 'the Christian story' and the fairy-story seems in danger of being obliterated. The death and resurrection of Aslan have a more powerful impact than any mere *analogy* to the death and resurrection of Christ; they do not merely '*partake* of reality' (*MCOE* 155, emphasis added) so much as they *are* in some sense that reality.

Lewis's first Narnian fairy-tale has, of course, an happy ending. After the wicked Witch is killed by the resurrected Aslan, the children are made Kings and Queens of Narnia, and 'long and happy was their reign'. Initially they are busy 'seeking out the remnants of the White Witch's army and destroying them' (*LWW* 166), but once the threateningly 'other' has been eliminated, the children get on with promoting Lewis's version of 'the good life', with its embryonic concerns for ecology and animal rights: '[T]hey made good laws and kept the peace and saved good trees from being unnecessarily cut down, and liberated young dwarfs and young satyrs from being sent to school, and generally stopped busybodies and interferers and encouraged ordinary people who wanted to live and let live' (Ibid.). Such a vision is hardly utopian, but Lewis's message is not really about social justice or good citizenship. It is about the communication of joy. Readers of *LWW* may have their own moment when they get 'a piercing glimpse of joy'. It might be Lucy's first discovery of the snowy wood through the magic wardrobe; or the moment when the changing appearance of the wood forces the Witch's dwarf to exclaim: '"This is no thaw . . . This is *Spring*"' (*LWW* 112); or the girls' exhilarating ride on Aslan from the stone table to the Witch's castle; or the moment when the children finally reach Cair Paravel, the castle where they will be crowned and from which they will rule Narnia:

> The castle at Cair Paravel on its little hill towered up above them; before them were the sands, with rocks and little pools of salt water, and sea-weed, and the smell of the sea and long miles of bluish-green waves breaking for ever and ever on the beach. And oh, the cry of the sea-gulls! Have you heard it? Can you remember?
>
> (*LWW* 164)

The note of memory here is crucial. Joy is always a *remembered* experience.

Prince Caspian

LWW contains most of the triggers of joy that Lewis described, especially in *SBJ*: myth (whether Greek or 'Northern'), medieval romance and a Romantic delight in nature. These elements are even more apparent in Lewis's next fairy-tale, *Prince Caspian* (=*PC*). A medievalism reminiscent of Malory and Spenser is marked with detailed attention not only to the armour, the weapons and the fighting, but also to Caspian's medieval education and the stylized wording of Peter's challenge to Miraz. The sense of 'medievalness' is intensified because not only is Narnia in itself always already 'medieval' – there is also within the story itself a nostalgia for a lost medieval past. Over a thousand Narnian years have elapsed since the children's last visit, but only one of *our* years has passed, so that the children have the uncanny experience of discovering the ruins of their own castle. The children have become legendary figures in the Narnian world they return to, just as if, as Peter says, '"we were Crusaders or Anglo-Saxons or someone coming back to modern England"' (*PC* 34). It is noticeable however that there is no *cultural* change in Narnia, which during its entire history remains in a loose sense 'medieval' or pre-technological (apart from the lamp-post in Lantern Wood). The world of Narnia lives and dies without being exposed to the (for Lewis) horrors of modern civilization.

However, Lewis does not merely oppose 'nature' to 'culture' (as in Romanticisms 6 and 7 in the Preface to *PR*). Rather, he privileges one culture (the medieval) over others, both in his theoretical writing (especially *The Discarded Image*) and in his fictional works. Yet there is in *PC* a strong 'nature versus culture' theme, culminating in the 'liberation' of the river-god of the Great River of Narnia from 'his chains', i.e. the Bridge of Beruna (*PC* 169f). There is an anarchic wildness in *PC* that is perhaps closer to the heart of Lewis than the conservative tendencies of which he is often accused. The power that destroys the bridge and a couple of schools is Bacchus, a.k.a. Bromius, Bassareus and the Ram (*PC* 137). For reasons we can only guess at, Lewis does not give him his original name, Dionysus. Although Aslan has to be seen to be in control, Bacchus or Dionysus is a powerful presence in *PC*. Even the refrain that 'in all stories Aslan comes from over the sea' is an echo of the motif in Greek literature that the Stranger God, Dionysus, comes from over the sea. And when he comes, he comes with a vengeance. The epidemic of mania and violence brought by Dionysus, who is also, paradoxically, called the bringer of peace, is most powerfully expressed in Euripides's *Bacchae*, which had a great effect on the young Lewis. In a sentence that recalls the targeting of schools in the Bacchanalian 'Romp' in *PC*, Lewis says that he 'orgiastic drum-beat' of the *Bacchae* 'was perhaps unconsciously connected with my growing hatred of the public school orthodoxies and conventions, my desire to tear and break it all' (*SBJ* 93). Edmund's description of a ' "chap who might do anything – absolutely anything" ' (*PC* 137) is similar to Euripides's Dionysus; he is dressed only in a faun skin and his face is slightly effeminate, 'almost too pretty for a boy's, if it had not looked so extremely wild' (*PC* 136).

The conclusion of *PC* takes us very close to the heart of Lewis. One of those about to be liberated 'looked out of the window and saw the divine revellers singing up the street and a stab of joy went through her heart' (*PC* 172). In a scene that anticipates the miraculous healing of Digory's mother in *MN* (though here the dying woman is simply called 'Auntie'), Aslan has to squeeze into, and finally burst open, the woman's tiny cottage in order to reach her. Although it is Aslan who cures her, Bacchus makes a significant entry at this point: ' "Here you are, mother," said Bacchus, dipping a pitcher in the cottage well and handing it to her. But what was in it now was not water but the richest wine' (*PC* 174). Interestingly it is *Bacchus* who turns the water into wine. In his discussion in *Miracles* of the water-into-wine miracle at Cana, Lewis refers to 'the false god Bacchus'.[36] There he is emphasizing that Christ is the 'end' – in the sense of the *abolition* – of Bacchus. Here in *PC* he seems to be emphasizing that Aslan, 'the (not so) unknown Christ of Narnia', is the 'end' – in the sense of the *fulfilment* – of Bacchus. As Lewis put it elsewhere, discussing the 'mythical radiance' of 'pagan' gods and heroes: 'Christ is *more* than Balder [or Bacchus], not less'.[37]

The Voyage of the Dawn Treader

Greek mythology would never again dominate a Narnian Chronicle to the extent it does in *PC*. Though the episodic plot of *The Voyage of the Dawn Treader* (=*VDT*), with its loosely linked adventures at sea, is partly based on the *Odyssey*, it also owes much to the medieval Irish *Voyage of St. Brendan* that figured in Tolkien's *NCP*. *VDT* is also close in spirit to Spenser, being transparently 'allegorical' in its treatment of 'sanctification and the disciplines of the Christian life'.[38] The children's arrival on the *Dawn Treader* via a magic picture in a Cambridge bedroom and the sea east of Narnia can be read as entry into the 'ship' or 'ark' of faith through baptism. The voyagers – especially Eustace, the new recruit to the English friends of Narnia – are given a series of lessons in Christian virtue, particularly in temperance – in the broad sense of 'moderation' (as in *FQ* II) and not in the narrow sense of 'teetotalism'. The latter is one of the failings of the odious Eustace Clarence Scrubb, who, as Lewis says in a memorable opening line, almost deserved his name. Other (for Lewis) heinous faults in Eustace include being a vegetarian, a pacifist, a non-smoker and wearing a special kind of under-clothes. He also takes vitamin supplements and does not read 'the right books' (about dragons, for example) (*VDT* 7).

On one of the islands the *Dawn Treader* visits, Eustace sneaks off to avoid helping to repair and replenish the ship. Getting lost and caught in a torrential downpour, he takes refuge in a dead dragon's lair and falls asleep. Eustace awakes to find that he has turned into a dragon: 'Sleeping on a dragon's hoard with greedy, dragonish thoughts in his heart, he had become a dragon himself' (*VDT* 73). While Eustace is no doubt a 'record stinker', the particular punishment of dragonization seems harsh. There is also a disturbing cruelty in the manner of his cure. Eustace is led by Aslan to a pool and told to 'undress'. Eustace gradually realizes that he is expected to tear his own skin off. Three times Eustace peels it off, only to find another dragon-skin underneath. ' "You will have to let me undress you" ', commands Aslan, who painfully ' "peeled the beastly stuff right off" ', until, continues Eustace: ' "I smooth and soft as a peeled switch . . . Then he caught hold of me – I didn't like that much for I was very tender underneath now that I'd no skin on – and threw me into the water" ' (*VDT* 86). While the above scenario can doubtless be given a respectable allegorical interpretation, it also has sado-masochistic connotations.[39]

Arguably the real hero of *VDT* is Reepicheep, the talking mouse. He is given the highest destiny in the book, for it is he who is on a quest for joy. Reepicheep finds his heart's desire in the utter East, where 'quivering with happiness', he sails in his coracle over the wave at the 'End of the World', into Aslan's country (*VDT* 185). The book might well have ended with this moment of genuine climax. However, Lewis chose to add a final scene in which the children come to the 'End of the World', where they meet a Lamb who 'in its sweet milky voice' invites them (as in John 21:9–12) to come and breakfast on fish cooked on a fire. Some readers may find this an unfortunate shift of tone from 'allegory' in a good sense (the diminutive Reepicheep's story has an almost mythic grandeur) to 'allegory' in the bad sense of the didactic intrusion of edifying material from the Christian story, clumsily assimilated. Once again, Lewis's proclivity to mix 'neat' elements of the Christian story in with his own story tends to weaken the power and authenticity of both. Lewis seems determined to err on the side of obviousness, despite his knowledge that the best stories are elusive, that their narrative nets never quite catch what the story is *really* about (*OTOW* 44–5) – as Lucy discovers with the Magician's Book, when the loveliest story she has ever read fades irretrievably from her mind, and 'ever since that day what Lucy means by a good story is a story which reminds her of the forgotten story in the Magician's Book' (*VDT* 122).

The Silver Chair

The 'cured' Eustace, along with another new friend of Narnia, Jill Pole, is the hero of *SC*. The unpleasant 'co-educational' school, which had made such a 'record stinker' of Eustace, figures significantly at the beginning and end of the tale. *SC* begins on a dull autumn day with Jill crying behind the gym. The narrator denies that this is going to be 'a school story', but in a sense it is. The answer to the Professor's question '"What do they teach them in these schools?"' is of course: 'Not enough Plato'. *SC* seeks to remedy that deficiency. The influence of Plato's cave allegory is clear in the crucial dialogue between the Queen of Underland and the children, Puddleglum and Prince Rilian, but the whole book is about 'knowing'.

The real theme of SC is not so much the getting as the keeping of knowledge. Unlike Plato's allegory, the story does not begin underground, but after the prologue in school, in Heaven. Hounded by the bullies of 'Experiment House', Jill and Eustace invoke Aslan. They are transported not to Narnia itself, however, but directly to Aslan's country, that is, Heaven. Heaven is located on top of an enormously high cliff, from which Jill foolishly causes Eustace to fall. Eustace is saved, however, by Aslan's breath, which blows him to Narnia. Aslan then sets Jill and Eustace the task of seeking Prince Rilian, the lost son of Caspian. To guide them on this quest, Aslan gives them four signs, which he makes Jill learn by heart. Much of the plot of *SC* centres round whether Jill (and subsequently Eustace and Puddleglum, a froglike creature called a Marshwiggle) remember these signs, which Aslan drills into Jill in an example of the kind of rote learning that is presumably woefully lacking in Experiment House. Jill is told to repeat the signs morning, noon and night, because: '"Here on the mountain, the air is clear and your mind is clear; as soon as you drop down into Narnia, the air will thicken . . . [and] confuse your mind"' (*SC* 27).

The idea of falling from Heaven into the world with the task of remembering, despite appearances, the true and the real, is essentially Platonic. But the Biblical emphasis on revelation and obedience is also present, so that it is a *Christian* Platonism to which the reader is being introduced. As in the Renaissance Christian Platonism of Sidney and Spenser, it is more a matter of knowing truth with the heart than of understanding it with the head, more a matter of 'will' than of 'wit'.[40] It is *poetry* that touches the parts mere philosophy cannot reach, by setting forth captivating images of virtue. As Lewis puts it in *AOM*, 'without the aid of trained emotions the intellect is powerless' (*AOM* 19). The Narnia books follow in the tradition of Spenser in embodying 'in moving images the common wisdom'.[41] In contrast to I.A. Richards, Lewis *welcomes* 'stock responses' to literature; creating them is primarily what literature is *for* (*PPL* 54–7). All the Narnia books can be seen as attempts to train the reader's emotions by means of captivating images, by letting 'the pictures tell you their own moral' (*OTOW* 69).

SC is also the most *literary* of the Chronicles. Its atmosphere and at times diction are reminiscent of Malory and Spenser. Prince Rilian is explicitly compared with Hamlet (*SC* 123). The whole Underland sequence is strongly reminiscent of MacDonald's *PAG*, and the Really Deep Land of Bism, a kind of underground Paradise, connects, via MacDonald, with the German Romantic fascination with mines and underground mysteries (for example Hoffmann's *The Mines of Falun*). But the most sustained and important intertext for *SC* is *FQ*. The 'silver chair' itself appears in the Cave of Mammon sequence, when Guyon is led to the Garden of Proserpina (goddess of the Underworld), in the midst of which stands 'a siluer seat' (*FQ* II vii 51–3). Guyon resists the temptation to take the golden fruit of the garden and to sit on the 'siluer stoole' that is 'the chair of forgetfulness' (*FQ* II vii 63). The struggle between Rilian with the Green Witch, transformed into a serpent, echoes that between the Red Crosse Knight and the monstrous half-woman, half-serpent Error (*FQ* I i 18–19). As well as a taste of Heaven, and of virtue, Lewis in this Chronicle is giving younger readers a taste of literature.

And of philosophy – for although *SC* makes it plain that reason alone is not enough, clear thinking is nevertheless required. The crucial dialogue between the Witch and the heroes of *SC* is about appearance and reality, with the Witch representing a reductionist materialism, according to which anything outside of Underland (including the sun and Aslan) are merely imagined copies of the 'realities' of Underland (in this case, lamps and cats). The Witch does not rely on the force of logic, however, but on the hypnotic effect of her playing on a mandolin, and the fumes from a magic powder she throws on the fire, both of which make it 'harder to think' (*SC* 238). The Witch is on the brink of victory, with Rilian and the children having lost almost all memory of 'the real world', when Puddleglum saves the day, not by any decisive turn of argument, but by *doing* 'a very brave thing'. He stamps out the fire. This action is effective not only because it stops the befuddling fumes, but also because 'the pain itself made Puddleglum's head for a moment perfectly clear and he knew exactly what he really thought' (*SC* 144). The action also has a symbolic resonance because in Plato's allegory it is the fire in the cave that produces illusion. The clear-headed Puddleglum then addresses the Witch as follows:

"Suppose we *have* only dreamed, or made up, all these things – trees and grass and sun and moon and Aslan himself. Then all I can say is that . . . the made-up things seem a good deal more important than the real ones. . . . We're just babies making up a game, if you're right. But four babies . . . can make a play-world that licks your real world hollow. That's why I'm going to stand by the play-world. I'm on Aslan's side even if there isn't any Aslan to lead it. I'm going to live as like a Narnian as I can even if there isn't any Narnia".

(SC 145)

Just as Plato provided an explanation of his Cave allegory, Lewis could be seen as providing an explanation of this scene in *SC* in his paper 'On Obstinacy in Belief', where he discusses the place of logic and evidence in religious belief. He concludes with a sentence that sums up in cold prose what Puddleglum says with unaccustomed passion:

> They [critics of religious belief] cannot be expected to see how the *quality* of the object [God] which we think we are beginning to know . . . drives us to the view that if this were a delusion then we would have to say that the universe had produced no real thing of comparable value and that all explanations of the delusion seemed somehow less important than the thing explained.[42]

This is a far cry from the confident rationalism of the 'The Self-Contradiction of the Naturalist' in the original version of *Miracles*, and closer than Lewis perhaps realized to the Pragmatism rejected there.

The Magician's Nephew

The Horse and His Boy was written before *SC*, but published after it in order to maintain the continuity of the three Chronicles relating to Caspian. It appears as a tale-within-a-tale when in *SC* the 'grand old tale of Prince Cor and Aravis and the horse Bree' is recited by a blind poet at a banquet in Cair Paravel (*SC* 41); it is the slightest of the Chronicles when compared with the weightier narratives of the creation and end of Narnia in *MN* and *LB* respectively. *MN* is haunted by the impending death of Digory's mother. Between the introduction in Chapter 1 of the tear-stained boy whose mother is dying, and the moment in Chapter 11 when Digory finally asks Aslan for something 'to make Mother well', there are regular reminders of his mother's frail condition. Despite momentous events such as the death and birth of worlds (Charn and Narnia respectively), the reader is never allowed to forget that the story is intimately connected with Lewis's attempt somehow to come to terms with the death of his mother.

Lewis locates *MN* in the Edwardian world of Sherlock Holmes and Nesbit's Bastable children, and also of course in the personal history of the young Jack Lewis.[43] Digory Kirke's father is abroad, but his Uncle Andrew is no father-substitute, being vain, dangerous, and something of a magician. Digory meets Polly, the girl next door, and they accidentally stumble into Uncle Andrew's secret chamber where, before they realize what is happening, Uncle Andrew makes Polly disappear by means of a magic ring. Digory is compelled to follow her with the ring that will bring them both home, since, to Digory's disgust, Uncle Andrew is unwilling to try out his own magic rings. Before going after Polly, Digory hears the history of the rings. Uncle Andrew had inherited from a Mrs Lefay – literally his fairy godmother ('one of the last mortals in this country who had fairy blood in her') – a box of Atlantean origin. As we have seen, Atlantis was significant for Lewis as well as for Tolkien; *SBJ* (published the same year as *MN*) compares the loss of security Lewis experienced at his mother's death to the sinking of Atlantis (*SBJ* 23). According to Uncle Andrew, '"the Atlantean box contained something that had been brought from another world when our world was only just beginning"' (*MN* 23). On a literal level, the box contains dust (perhaps prefiguring Pullman's Dust[44]) from another world – actually from 'the Wood between the Worlds'. Uncle Andrew has made this dust into magic rings. On a symbolic level 'the Atlantean box' suggests the 'primary maternal matrix' or Kristeva's semiotic *chora*, from which the beginnings of all human being and identity emerge.[45]

Putting on the ring, Digory finds himself not in another world, but in 'the Wood between the Worlds', which, like Cittàgazze in *HDM*, is a kind of crossroads between worlds.[46] The children decide to explore some of the worlds accessible via the many pools in the Wood. Their first stop is the dead world of Charn, where Digory cannot resist ringing an obviously magical bell, thus awakening the terrifying witch Jadis from an enchanted sleep. If on one level Jadis owes something to the Queen of Babylon in Nesbit's *The Story of the Amulet* as well as to Rider Haggard's *She*, she can also be read in psychoanalytical terms as the 'split-off' 'Bad Mother', the epitome of rejecting cruelty. She is of course the White Witch of *LWW*, who, we have suggested elsewhere, embodies the feelings of rejection the young Lewis may have experienced at his mother's death.[47] After a bizarre interlude back in London, Jadis and the children – now accompanied by Uncle Andrew, a cabby and a horse named Strawberry – find themselves in utter darkness, in a place 'without form and void'. Here they witness the creation of the world of Narnia. It begins with a voice singing. The voice seems to come from all directions at once, and even out of the earth: 'Its lower notes were deep enough to be the voice of the earth herself [*sic*]. There were no words. There was hardly even a tune. But it was, beyond comparison, the most beautiful noise [Digory] had ever heard. It was so beautiful he could hardly bear it' (*MN* 93). As in Tolkien's *Song of the Ainur*, the creation narrative of *The Silmarillion*, the Voice sings into existence first stars and then a sun. While this scene echoes the Biblical Creation myth, there are also echoes of another myth of origins – told by psychoanalysts such as Winnicott and Kristeva – where the individual comes into being in the play of the mother's voice, eyes and body. Lewis seems here to going back into 'the semiotic', the living pulse of song, to find a joyous new beginning.

The joy created by Aslan is expressed in a later passage which echoes Lewis's first encounter with 'Holiness' in *Phantastes*, experienced as an intangible, elusive presence connected with 'the voice of my mother or my nurse' (*SBJ* 145):

> Both the children were looking up into the Lion's face [which] all at once . . . seemed to be a sea of tossing gold in which they were floating, and such a sweetness and power rolled about them and over them and entered them that they felt that they never been happy or wise or good, or even alive and awake, before. And the memory of that moment stayed with them always.
>
> (*MN* 165)

When Digory finally asks Aslan to cure his dying mother, Aslan shares Digory's grief, but promises nothing. He offers Digory the opportunity to redeem himself by averting the evil he brought into Narnia in the form of the Witch. From the garden at the Western end of the World, Digory must bring to Aslan an apple whose seed will grow into a tree that will ward off the Witch. On reaching the garden and plucking the silver apple, Digory encounters the Witch, who vainly tempts him to eat it himself, and live forever. The next temptation – to take the apple to his dying mother, not Aslan – is much harder to resist. Here, as in *Perelandra*, obedience for its own sake, against all that seems reasonable and humane, seems required of Digory. As in *Perelandra*, temptation is resisted and a kind of Fall averted. But the price for Digory is terrible; he must accept the inevitability of his mother's death. This is a re-enactment of Lewis's childhood trauma, when he had to come to terms with the fact that his prayers for his mother's recovery would remain unanswered. In this reprise of Lewis's own experience, Digory comes to accept that 'there might be things more terrible than losing someone you love by death' (*MN* 163). Although Digory wins through to acceptance, he is spared the ultimate trial that the young Lewis had to face. Aslan tells him to pluck an apple that *will* heal his mother. For Digory 'it is as if the whole world had turned inside out and upside down' (*MN* 163). This is Tolkien's 'joyous turn' or *eucatastrophe*, which brings consolation to the reader; what kind of consolation it brought to the writer is another question.

The Last Battle

LB is a profoundly melancholy book. By the second chapter we are warned by Roonwit the Centaur that: '"there have not been such disastrous conjunctions of the planets for five hundred years . . . [S]ome great evil hangs over Narnia"' (*LB* 19). The discussion between Roonwit, King Tirian and Jewel the Unicorn about the rumours of Aslan's presence in Narnia are interrupted by the arrival of a dying Dryad bringing news of the felling of talking trees. These are being sold, apparently on Aslan's orders, to the Calormenes (whose stereotypically oriental appearance and behaviour are evidence of Lewis's racism, according to Pullman). Then 'a really dreadful thing' happens. Tirian and Jewel come across two Calormenes whipping a Talking Horse; enraged, they kill the Calormenes without warning. Tirian feels dishonoured, and decides to surrender himself to the Calormenes to be brought before Aslan. He realizes he is going to his death, but asks: '"Would it not be better to be dead than to have this horrible fear that Aslan has come and it is not like the Aslan we believed in and longed for? It is as if the sun rose one day and were a black sun"' (*LB* 29). This image of 'the black sun', taken by Kristeva from Nerval's poem 'El Desdichado' ['The Disinherited'] for the title of her *Black Sun: Depression and Melancholia*, would certainly have been known to Lewis from *Phantastes*.[48] Kristeva's analysis of the melancholy inscribed in Nerval's poem seems to fit Lewis uncannily well. Nerval's prince is disinherited not of a 'property', but of 'an unnameable domain . . . the secret and unreachable horizon of our loves and desires . . . [which] assumes, for the imagination, the consistency of an archaic mother'.[49] The loss being mourned in *LB* is not just that of Narnia but also that of Atlantis, the 'archaic mother', whose sinking caused Lewis inconsolable grief.

LB depicts a losing battle against despair. Hope keeps reviving, only to be dashed. The real villains are the dwarfs. Tirian, Jill, Eustace et al. rescue a party of dwarfs being marched off to the Calormene mines. Instead of rejoicing at their liberation and the news that the new 'bad' Aslan is just Puzzle the donkey dressed up in a lion-skin, the dwarfs are cynical: '"No more Aslan, no more Kings, no more silly stories about other worlds"', they say (*LB* 72). During the eponymous Last Battle, the Talking Horses arriving as reinforcements for the hard-pressed Narnians are destroyed by the archery of the dwarfs. This really is the end. Our heroes are forced into the stable at the centre of the battlefield, which contains Tash, the Calormenes' bloodthirsty god.

This seems to signal the annihilation of Narnia and all the joy it has brought. However, in a final turn of 'sudden and miraculous grace', this *dyscatastrophe* (in Tolkien's phrase) is turned into 'the joy of deliverance', a deliverance which 'denies (in the face of much evidence, if you will) universal final defeat and in so far is *evangelium* [good news], giving a fleeting glimpse of Joy . . . ' (*MCOE* 153). But this is to be no mere glimpse of Joy; while the stable contains Tash, who rapidly disappears with the Calormene chief tucked under two of his four arms, it also contains Heaven itself, Aslan's country. In a reprise of Lucy's first experience in the wardrobe, the stable's inside turns out to be bigger than it is outside. It seems, however, that this cannot be Narnia, because the stable door leads *from* Narnia *to* somewhere else; in a pastiche of the Biblical Apocalypse, the children witness the end of Narnia as they look back through the door. Yet the 'somewhere else' is strangely reminiscent of Narnia. As Professor Digory Kirke, who has mysteriously turned up along with the other friends of Narnia, realizes, this world is in Platonic terms 'the real Narnia' of which the vanished Narnia was only the shadow or copy (*LB* 159f). The company of true

Narnians rushes 'further up and further in' until they arrive at the 'real' Narnian equivalent of the Western garden that the young Digory had visited in *MN*. Once again 'the inside is larger than the outside', for the garden contains yet another 'Narnia' which is even more beautiful and more real than the Narnia they've just left, just as *that* Narnia was more beautiful and real than the Narnia left behind through the stable door (*LB* 169).

This journey from glory to glory, ever further up and further in, embodies the vision of Christian Platonism. Behind this grand theological finale, however, lurks the heart-broken boy from Belfast who haunts the pages of *CN*, until at the end of *MN* his mother is restored to life by the goodness of Aslan and the power of Narnian magic. But in *LB* the goodness of Aslan is called into question, and Narnia itself falls. The main doubters of Aslan and his goodness are the dwarfs, who are also pivotal in the fall of Narnia. They too come through the stable door, but refuse to believe in the wonderful new world that the friends of Narnia find. For them, it is simply a pathetic illusion. They are the converse not only of the radical theologian in *GD* who thinks that the 'mean streets' of Hell are ' "in a sense, Heaven, if only we have eyes to see it" ' (*GD* 36), but also of the monk in Pullman's suburbs of the dead who claims that the barren wasteland is a ' "paradise which to the fallen soul seems bleak and barren, but which the eyes of faith see as it is, overflowing with milk and honey" ' (*AS* 336). Despite appearances, there is according to the dwarfs, no 'healing of harms'. For them, the children's vision of their dead mother and father waving to them across the valley – as if 'from the deck of a big ship when you are waiting on the quay' (*LB* 170) – would be one more piece of wishful thinking, like 'all that stuff about family reunions "on the further shore" . . . out of bad hymns and lithographs . . . it rings false. We *know* it couldn't be like that'. The voice here, however, is not that of the dwarfs, but that of the narrator (or Lewis himself) in *A Grief Observed*.[50] It seems that the dwarfs are never entirely left behind.

Till We Have Faces: A Myth Retold

The problem posed by the disbelieving dwarfs reappears in Lewis's next (and final) piece of imaginative writing, *Till We Have Faces: A Myth Retold* (=*TWHF*). The myth is that of Cupid and Psyche, classically told by Apuleius in his *Metamorphoses* (or *The Golden Ass*), though according to Lewis's Note to *TWHF*, Apuleius was the myth's 'transmitter, not its inventor'. Morris also retold the myth in verse in *The Earthly Paradise*, where the first line of his 'Cupid and Psyche' sets the tale '[i]n the Greek land of old'. But Lewis's version – 'a work of (supposed) *historical* imagination' – takes place not in the 'Greeklands' but in 'a little barbarous state on the borders of the Hellenistic world with Greek culture just beginning to affect it' (*LL3* 830). In terms of genre, Lewis's 'Cupid and Psyche' resembles Morris's prose romances more than the poem in *The Earthly Paradise*.

Lewis's retelling of the myth transforms it in several ways. Firstly, in Lewis's version Psyche's beautiful palace is invisible to mortal eyes. Echoing his account of the genesis of the Narnia stories in 'pictures', Lewis claims in the Note to *TWHF* that this idea of the palace's invisibility 'forced itself on [him] at the [his] first reading of the story, as the way things must have been'. For 35 years '[t]his re-interpretation of an old story ... lived in the author's mind, thickening and hardening over the years, ever since he was an undergraduate' (*TWHF* 8; cf. *LL3* 715). Lewis's response to the myth therefore predates his conversion to Christianity, and always privileged the point of view of Psyche's elder sister, though 'of course in [his] pre-Christian days she was to be in the right and the gods in the wrong' (*LL3* 715).

Not only are the events described in the myth transposed by Lewis into quasi-historical facts (a historical *supposal*) – in the course of the narrative the 'historical' facts *become* myth. The turning point of the narrative comes when Psyche's elder sister, Orual, stumbling across a secluded temple dedicated to Psyche, hears a priest recite the myth of Cupid and Psyche. This retelling as myth of 'the facts' that Orual had herself witnessed many years previously, enrages her. A significant difference between the myth and 'what really happened' lies in the diverging accounts of what had led Psyche to disobey Cupid's command never to look at his face – a disobedience which caused Psyche to lose her divine lover. In the myth, Psyche's disobedience is prompted by her jealous sisters, whereas 'in fact' Orual was never, she insists, motivated by jealousy of Psyche's lover and grand palace. Orual claims only ever to have acted out of love for Psyche. The crucial 'fact' that the myth omits is that Psyche's palace was *invisible* to Orual, who therefore believed that Psyche needed to be rescued from madness. This omission from 'the sacred story' wipes out 'the very meaning, the pith, the central knot, of the whole tale', says Orual (*TWHF* 252). She therefore resolves to retell the myth 'as it really happened', and this retelling forms the bulk of *TWHF*. Since Orual holds the gods responsible for the false myth of Cupid and Psyche, her retelling is also an indictment of the gods. In seeking to demonstrate the divine *injustice*, Orual's account is literally the opposite of theodicy. It is written as it were 'in defence of the dwarfs', that is, in defence of those who do not, or will not, see the reality of 'real Narnias', or magical palaces, or (in Curdie's case) mystical great-great-grandmothers.

While the idea of re-writing the old myth of Cupid and Psyche had been with Lewis for 35 years, he says that the most appropriate literary form had eluded him: 'I tried it in all sorts of verse-forms in the days when I still supposed myself to be a poet' (*LL3* 833). The breakthrough came early in 1955 when he and Joy Davidman 'kicked a few ideas around till one came to light' (*LL3* 589). Whatever the contribution made by Joy, a published poet and novelist in her own right, *TWHF* is in form, if not in content, almost unrecognisable as Lewis's work. The Narnia books and the science-fiction trilogy have either an omniscient narrator, or something close to it; there is little questioning of narrative authority. By contrast, *TWHF* has that most characteristic device of the modern novel, an unreliable narrator. Orual's resolve to set the record straight results of course only in her version of events. Lewis's awareness of the presence of selectivity and bias in any account of 'the facts' was perhaps heightened by his experience of writing his own story in *SBJ*, published the year before *TWHF*. Commentators have seen in Orual's story sometimes echoes of Lewis's life, sometimes of Joy Davidman's. More likely Orual is a kind of 'Everyman' figure: in the text itself her identity is fluid – under the veil she always wears she is imagined to be an infinite variety of things, from an animal, to a great beauty, to nothing at all (*TWHF* 237). Like the faceless image of Ungit in the temple, and like the text itself, she is open to interpretation.

More precisely, it is the nature of Orual's *love* which is open to interpretation, and which is the 'central knot in the tale'. In Orual's version, her love for Psyche and indeed for other characters such as her Greek tutor, 'the Fox' and Bardia (her General), is presented as innocent and selfless. By the end of the book, however, her love for each of these characters can be seen as selfish and manipulative. *TWHF* could be said to embody in fictional form the gist of Lewis's later book, *The Four Loves*. In this book Lewis argues that the three natural loves – that is: affection (Greek *storge*), friendship (Greek *philia*) and *eros* – all tend to become perverted unless redeemed by the fourth love, divine charity. Orual's love for 'the Fox' exemplifies friendship, her love for Bardia has an erotic dimension and her love for Psyche is what Lewis calls affection; but in each case Orual's natural human love is shown to have been perverted by her selfishness.

Orual's love for Psyche is the central issue of the book. When Psyche's mother died giving birth to her, Psyche's stepsister Orual acted as a mother-substitute to the preternaturally beautiful child. The possessiveness of Orual's quasi-maternal love for Psyche, her 'ravenous need to be needed', had been anticipated in the ghastly mother in *GD*. Orual's jealousy is masked by her justified fears for Psyche when the priest of Ungit demands Psyche's exposure on the mountain as an offering to 'the Shadowbrute' or god of the mountain. Orual cannot endure the faint hope Psyche entertains that the god of the mountain may turn out to be the divine lover for whom she has always longed. Psyche's hope for a love-death that will fulfil her *Sehnsucht* evokes intense hostility in Orual (*TWHF* 82–4). When Orual subsequently discovers Psyche alone but happy on the mountain, she is predisposed to disbelieve her claim that she has indeed come home to her divine lover. The trouble is that this 'home', a fabulous palace, is invisible to Orual. Rather than believe that the palace is real but invisible to her, Orual decides that Psyche is either 'bad' (playing games) or more likely 'mad'.

This 'central knot' of the tale is given a further twist when Orual fleetingly *does* see a fabulous palace, which promptly vanishes (*TWHF* 141–3). This apparent glimpse is rationally explicable given the swirling mist and Orual's distraught, half-awake condition. Orual is faced with more ambiguous evidence than are the dwarfs or Lucy's siblings in the Narnia books, where failure to see the 'real Narnia' or Aslan is presented as a culpable lack of faith. However, the form and the content of *TWHF* foreground ambiguity in a way that is new for Lewis. Orual finds that she has to retell her retelling of the myth of Psyche. In terms that echo Lewis's own experience of writing *SBJ*, she says: 'What began the change was the very writing itself. Let no one lightly set about such a work. Memory, once waked, will play the tyrant' (*TWHF* 263). Subsequent revelations make Orual despair of catching the truth in 'trim sentences' that are in reality merely 'the babble we think we mean' (*TWHF* 305). Truth is only available to mortals in the indeterminacy of language, where 'like all these sacred matters, it is and is not' (*TWHF* 279). In the end, shortly before her death, after a series of dreams and visions in which she becomes identified with Psyche, Orual encounters the god:

> The air was growing brighter and brighter about us; as if something had set it on fire. Each breath I drew let into me new terror, joy, overpowering sweetness. I was pierced through and through with the arrows of it. I was being unmade. I was no one. But that's little to say; rather, Psyche herself was, in a manner, no one. I loved her as I would have once thought it impossible to love; would have died any death for her. And yet, it was not, not now, she that really counted. Or if she counted (and oh, gloriously she did) it was for another's sake. The earth and stars and sun, all that was or will be, existed for his sake. And he was coming. The most dreadful, the most beautiful, the only dread and beauty there is, was coming.
>
> (*TWHF* 318–19)

When Lewis referred in a letter to this scene as 'the numinous breaking through' (*LL3* 630), he perhaps had in mind Rudolf Otto's account of the numinous in *The Idea of the Holy*,[51] a book whose influence he acknowledged (*LL3* 980). Notwithstanding Lewis's scepticism about 'existential' interpretation (*LL3* 1012), he was arguably not too far removed from the attempts of some modern religious thinkers to reinterpret myth in order to bring about – amid the nightmarish ambiguity and chaos of history – an encounter with 'the Wholly Other': the *mysterium tremendum et fascinans*. Far from producing the allegories of Christian doctrine that *CN* are popularly supposed to be, Lewis sought in this re-telling of a pagan myth in *TWHF* to confront his readers with an *experience* which, by being presented historically, that is, located (as a 'supposition') in *this* world, powerfully calls in question, transcends and yet glorifies this world – even if only ambiguously and in a glass darkly.

5

Measuring Truth: Lyra's Story

True stories and fantasies

Discussion of Philip Pullman in a book about fantasy literature can hardly avoid the issue of his explicit disavowal of fantasy. In various interviews Pullman has bluntly expressed his dislike of fantasy literature, and has sought to distance his own work from it. For example, in his reply to the question 'Did you write *HDM* as "fantasy"?' Pullman claimed:

> I don't like fantasy. The only thing about fantasy that interested me when I was writing this was the freedom to invent imagery such as the daemon; but that was only interesting because I could use it to say something truthful and realistic about human nature. If it was just picturesque or ornamental, I wouldn't be interested.[1]

With apparent reluctance, Pullman acknowledged in a radio discussion in 2002 that 'there probably is a . . . tradition of writing that one has to call for want of a better word, fantasy . . . and there is undoubtedly a fine tradition of the sort of fairy-tale fantasy kind in England in particular which is where I find myself I suppose.'[2] However, Pullman is quick to make his customary moves in such discussions of his relation to fantasy: he expresses his dislike of the genre, contrasts it with what he claims is the essential 'realism' of his own writing, and gives a derogatory caricature of what passes for 'fantasy':

> The more fantastical something is the less interesting I personally find it. By realistic I mean if it is talking about human beings in a way which is vivid and truthful and tells me things about myself and my own emotions and things which I recognize to be true . . . I don't often encounter that sort of thing in fantasy because a lot of fantasy writing seems to me preoccupied with one adventure after another and improbable sorts of magic and weird creatures like orcs and elves and so on who don't have any connection with the sort of human reality that I recognize so I am a

little bit wary of fantasy and what I was trying to do in my 'fantasy' – and you can probably hear the inverted commas there – was to tell a realistic story by means of the fantastical sort of machinery of the stories.[3]

There is in the above response another move typical of Pullman, that of claiming merely to use the *techniques* of fantasy fiction ('the fantastical sort of machinery') for other ends than those of writers who in Pullman's view are merely 'preoccupied with one adventure after another and improbable sorts of magic and weird creatures' that don't have any connection with the sort of human reality he recognizes. Whatever the justice of Pullman's description of sub-Tolkienian 'genre' fantasy (ironically it was Terry Brooks, doyen of American 'genre' fantasy, who provided the introduction to the first American mass-market Del Rey/Ballantine paperback edition of *The Golden Compass*), the suggestion that writers of 'high' or 'epic' fantasy such as Lewis and Tolkien have abandoned any connection with human reality (recognizable to Pullman) is a complex issue; it is entangled with philosophical (if not theological) questions in the discussion of which oversimplifying binary oppositions are not helpful.

In a recent interview Pullman's condemnation of 'fantasy' seems even more outspoken:

I always took a dim view of fantasy – still do in fact. Most of it is trash, but then most of everything is trash. It seemed to me writers of fantasy in the Tolkien tradition had this wonderful tool that could do anything and they did very little with it. They were rather like the inventors of the subtle knife who used it to steal candy when they could have done much more.[4]

The aside that 'most of everything is trash' is a little odd (or unguarded) from someone so stridently critical of the supposedly world-hating tradition of Platonism. Interestingly it is to a late and distorted form of Platonism (the 'Black Platonism' of David Lindsay[5]) that Pullman goes on to allude:

The first book I think really did what fantasy can do, besides *Paradise Lost*, was a book published in 1920 called *The* [*sic*] *Voyage to Arcturus* by David Lindsay. It's a very poorly written, clumsily constructed book which nevertheless has the force, the power, the intensity of genius. He uses fantasy to say something profound about morality – none of Tolkien's imitators do this.[6]

In what seems a further twist in the network of Oedipal relations (*à la* Harold Bloom) that I have argued connect Pullman and Lewis and George MacDonald,[7] Pullman makes almost exactly the same move *vis-à-vis* Lindsay that Lewis makes *vis-à-vis* MacDonald. The claim that Lindsay's work is poorly written, clumsy but 'nevertheless has the force, the power, the intensity of genius' is precisely what Lewis claimed about MacDonald. According to Lewis, the texture of MacDonald's writing as a whole was 'undistinguished, at times fumbling', even if as a maker of myths MacDonald was 'the greatest genius' creating 'fantasy that hovers between the allegorical and the mythopoeic'.[8] A further irony is that Lindsay's *VTA* was probably more inspired by MacDonald than by any other writer. *VTA* was also, as noted in the previous chapter, a decisive influence on Lewis's 'science-fiction' trilogy. Thus in seeking to distance himself from the fantasy tradition he associates especially with Tolkien, Pullman is (perhaps unconsciously) allying himself with a fantasy tradition running from MacDonald (with arguably Carlyle and the German Romantics in the background) through Lindsay and on to Lewis. Tolkien himself read *VTA* 'with avidity' and compared it favourably with Lewis's *OSP* (which he admired): 'it is both more powerful and more mythical (and less rational, and also less of a story – no one could read it merely as a thriller and without interest in philosophy, religion and morals)' (*TL* 34).

The concern for the 'story' here evinced by Tolkien is something that Pullman too has made much of. One of the surprisingly numerous ideas that Pullman actually *shares* with Lewis and Tolkien (despite his frequent criticisms of them) is a deep suspicion of what he sees as the modernist contempt for 'the story'. As he puts in the *Literary Review* interview with Claudia FitzHerbert:

> At the beginning of the twentieth century, with the modernists, we lost confidence in storytelling – think of Joyce, and Woolf to some extent, and E M Forster with his 'oh dear – yes, the novel tells a story' as if it were a shameful thing to do. Suddenly the novel became self-conscious about itself and about the process of storytelling, and a huge awkwardness set in that resulted in a split between the people who tell stories – the middlebrow – and the others who would do anything rather than tell a story . . . – the highbrow.[9]

As with Lewis and Tolkien, Pullman's concern for 'the story' is not merely a literary predilection but has moral and philosophical implications. Pullman has acknowledged that his differences with Lewis and Tolkien have more to do with their actual stories (and especially the stories' *messages*, as Pullman reads them), than with the more theoretical writings by Tolkien and Lewis *about* the power and necessity of 'the story' as a literary phenomenon – indeed as something more fundamentally important than a literary phenomenon. Lewis's claim that 'Sometimes Fairy Stories May Say Best What's to be Said' is echoed by Pullman in his Carnegie Medal Acceptance Speech: 'There are some themes, some subjects, too large for adult fiction; they can only be dealt with adequately in a children's book.'[10] Pullman admitted in a radio discussion: 'I have read [Tolkien's "On Fairy-Stories"] and I have also read C. S. Lewis on . . . fairy stories and I find what both of them have to say when they are writing about fiction much better than what they say when they are writing fiction to be frank. They are both fine critics.'[11]

Thus the title of Lewis's piece 'Sometimes Fairy Stories May Say Best What's to be Said'[12] seems to anticipate Pullman's Carnegie Prize acceptance speech. It also appears that Lewis's claim in this piece that the Narnia stories began not as allegories, but rather as mental pictures or images, subsequently connected by 'some deliberate inventing' (*OTOW* 72–3; 68), is closely echoed by Pullman's parting shot in his 2002 Guardian interview: 'I don't have a theme – I have a series of disconnected pictures or scenes, which I think about in order to find out what connects them; and I discover more as I write the whole thing, and revise it later.'[13] Perhaps this is merely a common experience among creative writers; however, the almost verbatim repetition of Lewis's words about the genesis of the Narnia books by a writer who arguably misreads and rewrites Lewis's work (*à la* Bloom) is curious. Of Pullman's literary relationship with Lewis, one is tempted to use the adage: 'Can't live with him, can't live without him'. Another of Lewis's writings that Pullman has presumably read more sympathetically than the Narnia books is Lewis's 'On Stories'. First published in 1947 in the same volume as Tolkien's *OFS*,[14] it was originally read to an undergraduate literary society in Oxford in 1940, that is, well before later developments in the discipline of 'narratology'; the only theorists of Story that Lewis adduces are Aristotle, Boccaccio and Jung. The paper also predates Lewis's own published stories, apart from *OSP*. Interestingly, this paper by Lewis makes particular reference to *VTA*, anticipating Pullman's views when it pays homage to Lindsay's 'remarkable achievement' despite being 'unaided by any special skill or even any sound taste in language', and indeed 'while writing in a style that is (to be frank) abominable' (*OTOW* 35; 43). Thus, in a kind of uncanny relay, Pullman's views on Lindsay precisely mimic those of Lewis on both Lindsay and MacDonald.

However, whatever Pullman may have to say in speeches and interviews about stories being 'the most important thing in the world', without which 'we wouldn't be human beings at all'[15] (Pullman's '*homo fabulator*' to Marx's '*homo faber*'?), it is *within* his stories themselves that the power and importance of stories is most strikingly affirmed. Apart from Pullman's brilliant metafictional exploration of 'the story' in *Clockwork*,[16] the idea of 'the story' is also at the heart of *HDM*. The turning point in Lyra's story is also the turning point for her world, and ultimately for the universe (or perhaps 'multiverse'). This crucial turning point is the moment in the land of the dead when all seems lost, with the harpies threatening to turn what is already a wasteland into hell if Will uses the subtle knife to cut an escape-route for the ghosts. However, Tialys, the tiny Gallivespian, suddenly takes the initiative and offers the harpies a bargain. What in effect turns a looming catastrophe into something resembling Tolkien's *eucatastrophe* is Tialys's offer of a new deal to the harpies. The harpies' role, assigned to them thousands of years ago by 'the Authority', is to seek out the worst in the ghosts in the land of the dead, feeding on the wickedness till their 'blood is rank with it and [their] very hearts sickened' (*AS* 331); and to remind the dead constantly of their worst faults during their lifetime, literally *ad nauseam* (*AS* 323). In what might be read as a kind of self-referential allusion by Pullman to his own writing practice and fear of criticism, the first story Lyra tells the harpies reworks her fantastic tale of the previous evening 'shaping and cutting and improving and adding', before she is literally savaged by her audience screaming '"*Liar!*"' – which sounds to Lyra like her own name (*AS* 307–8). While the harpies easily and scornfully see through the rather silly, over-confident fabrications in Lyra's first tale, they are nevertheless attentive to the true stories she subsequently tells about her life in her Oxford (the Oxford in 'Brytain'). Tialys spots the significance of this, and asks the harpies why they attacked Lyra when she told her first story, to which they chorus: '"Lies and fantasies!"' (*AS* 332). However, Lyra's true stories are 'nourishing', according to the leading harpy No-name (later renamed by Lyra as 'Gracious Wings') (*AS* 332). Like some miniature Greek hero, the wily Tialys then proposes that instead of battening on the wickedness, cruelty and greed of the ghosts, the harpies instead demand from them the story of their lives, '"the truth about what they've seen and touched and heard and loved and known in the world"' (*AS* 333). The harpies are won over by this proposal, together with the suggestion from Salmakia, Tialys's fellow Gallivespian, that they exchange the task which they perform for the Authority (subjecting the dead to mental torture) for the more honourable task of guiding the ghosts through the land of the dead to the opening to be cut by Will into the out-side world (*AS* 334). However, the harpies will still exercise a form of post-mortem judgment in that they retain the right to refuse to guide any ghosts who lie, or withhold anything, or have no story to tell (*AS* 334). As No-name declares, evidently speaking for Pullman: '"If they live in the world, they *should* see and touch and hear and love and learn things"' (*AS* 334).

Everything hinges on this deal with the harpies, crucially brokered by the diminutive Gallivespians. The plan to release the dead, not just with the col-lusion of the harpies, but with their active co-operation, changes every-thing. As Tialys says: '"This will undo everything. It's the greatest blow you could strike. The Authority will be powerless after this"' (*AS* 326). This release of the dead is a kind of 'Harrowing of Hell' and the parallels with Christian teaching are underlined when Lyra quotes her father Lord Asriel's saying that '"*Death is going to die*"' (*AS* 325). The very idea that redemption from death is the result of a kind of *bargain* is an ancient one in the Christian tra-dition.[17] Pullman's re-writing of the Fall story is explicit and often discussed; what is perhaps less obvious is that he also has a kind of Redemption story. In Pullman's version the crucial factor is not a death (as in the Christian story, repeated in *LWW*) but a *discussion*: a deal struck between, on the one hand, the harpies (the agents of the Authority) and, on the other, Lyra (whose idea it is) and Will (who will ultimately enact the idea with the subtle knife). This bargain, set up by the Gallivespians, does not involve an exchange of lives so much as an exchange of *stories*, of *lived* stories. But only real stories about real lives in the real world will do.

This crucial opposition between 'true stories' and 'lies and fantasies' is not essentially one between 'fact and fiction', despite the quotation from Byron at the head of the chapter containing the harpies' denunciation of Lyra's 'lies and fantasies': 'I hate things all fiction . . . There should always be some foundation in fact [for the most airy fabric – and pure invention is but the talent of a liar]'[18] (*AS* 291). Both sides of Pullman's opposition are 'stories'. The kind of 'true stories' which are desirable are not merely factual reportage, but rather *evoke* the texture of the natural world. Lyra tells the ghosts (and the harpies clustering in the background):

> about the willow trees along the river's edge, with their leaves silvery underneath . . . and how when the sun shone for more than a couple of days, the clay began to split up into great handsome plates, with deep cracks between, and how it felt to squish your fingers into the cracks and slowly lever up a dried plate of mud, trying to keep it as big as you could without breaking it . . . And she described the smells . . . the smoke from the kilns, the rotten-leaf-mould smell of river when the wind was in the south-west, the warm smell of the baking potatoes the clay-burners used to eat; and the sound of the water slipping slickly over the sluices . . . As she spoke, playing on all their senses, the ghosts crowded closer, feeding on her words, remembering the time when they had flesh and skin and nerves and senses, and willing her never to stop.
>
> (*AS* 330)

Such an evocation of the physical world is not simply factual but *imaginative*. Its imaginative grasp of the real world (literally groping in the mud in this case) offers the antithesis of the fantasizing of which Lyra is accused not only by the harpies but, on an earlier occasion, by Tialys himself: ' "You're a thoughtless irresponsible lying child. Fantasy comes so easily to you that your whole nature is riddled with dishonesty, and you don't even admit the truth when it stares you in the face" ' (*AS* 280).

The opposition here is not, then, between fiction and fact, but rather between fantasy (in a negative sense) and the imaginative intuition of reality. Pullman has claimed that 'the subtle power of the imagination is that it deals directly with the real world'.[19] In other words, the opposition in question seems to echo the distinction made by Coleridge in his *Biographia Literaria* between fancy and the imagination. A deeper echo might be the opposition between the fire and the sun in Plato's allegory of the cave in *The Republic*, especially as interpreted by Iris Murdoch, for example in *The Fire and the Sun*, where she argues that the fire symbolizes self-serving egotistical fantasy, while the sun symbolizes the true and the real seen in an act of imaginative intuition.[20] If the suggestion of a Platonic filiation for Pullman's thinking seems to go against his declared anti-Platonism, this only underlines the point I have made elsewhere that Pullman may be operating with a rather undialectical version of Platonism, or more bluntly put, with a kind of caricature of Platonism. Pullman's high Romantic view of the imagination as the antithesis of fantasy (or fancy) in the negative sense emerges explicitly towards the end of *AS* when the angel Xaphania tells Lyra and Will of another way of 'travelling' into other worlds, known to Will's shamanistic father:

> 'It uses the faculty of what you call the imagination. But that does not mean *making things up*. It is a form of seeing.'
> 'Not *real* travelling, then,' said Lyra. 'Just pretend . . . '
> 'No,' said Xaphania, 'nothing like pretend. Pretending is easy. This way is hard, but much truer.'

This connection of the cult of the imagination to shamanism does not seem too far away from the Romantic exaltation of the poet as seer and prophet, above all in a figure such as Blake. It is also related to Platonism, if there is any truth in the controversial ideas in E.R. Dodds's (according to Harold Bloom 'superb'[21]) book *The Greeks and the Irrational*, which argues that the origins of Platonism are shamanistic.[22]

To return to C.S. Lewis – an acquaintance of Dodds from student days – the antithesis suggested by Pullman between imagination and fantasy, or between fantasy in a creative sense and fantasy in a negative sense, echoes a distinction made by Lewis in one of those critical essays of which Pullman has not entirely disapproved. In 'On Three Ways of Writing for Children' Lewis distinguishes between fantasy as giving a new dimension of depth to our experience, and fantasy as egocentric wish-fulfilment. He goes on to discuss the charge that fairy-tales and fantasy teach children 'to retreat into a world of wish-fulfilment – "fantasy" in the technical psychological sense of the word – instead of facing the problems of the real world' (*OTOW* 64). The fulfilment offered by this kind of fantasy is according to Lewis 'in very truth compensatory: we run to it from the disappointments and humiliations of the real world: it sends us back to the real world undivinely discontented. For it is all flattery to the ego' (*OTOW* 64). By contrast, in a passage quoted above, Lewis believes that the fairy-tale can arouse a longing in the reader:

> It stirs and troubles him (to his life-long enrichment) with the dim sense of something beyond his reach and, far from dulling or emptying the actual world, gives it a new dimension of depth. He does not despise real

woods because he has read of enchanted woods: the reading makes all real woods a little enchanted.

(OTOW 65)

Here Lewis's Platonism is ultimately dialectical, I would argue, despite his own polemical tendency to force an 'either-or' rather than settling for any consoling 'both-and', as we saw in his (warily non-specific) criticisms of Blake's *Marriage of Heaven and Hell* in *GD*. By 'dialectical' I mean the search to overcome static dualisms by bringing seemingly fixed and irreconcilable oppositions into the transforming interplay of reciprocal criticism.[23] Fantasy stirs an imaginative longing that does not reject or flee from the world, but actively seeks to transfigure it. Lewis's essentially Romantic and Platonic vision seems quite close to Pullman's, despite Pullman's attempts to disavow both Lewis and Platonism – or more precisely, to disavow Lewis because of what Pullman interprets as Lewis's 'Platonism'. Except that the 'Platonism' of which Lewis (as well as Tolkien) stands condemned is very one-sided and undialectical. Lewis's 'Romantic Platonism' is actually, I suggest, not entirely unlike what Pullman himself is offering in his fiction. While Pullman seems to recognize glimpses of himself in Lewis's critical writings, he evidently feels a need (as I have discussed elsewhere) to misread Lewis's fantasy fiction systematically – in a way that arguably turns it into something that is rather different from what Lewis actually wrote (in my reading). The outlook of Pullman's 'Lewis' (arguably a caricature) is only apparently the opposite, I propose, of a certain kind of Romantic and (dialectical) Platonic vision of truth that Pullman seems in some respects actually to share with Lewis.

On the discrimination of Platonisms

Clearly it is controversial to claim that, notwithstanding Pullman's explicit anti-Platonism, he is in some sense close to what I have called Lewis's 'dialectical' Platonism. The key issue here is that the latter by no means necessarily implies a devaluation, let alone a hatred, of this world, but rather a certain care in our dealings with it. There is always a danger (which arguably Pullman has not avoided) of conflating Platonism and Manichaeism. The latter seems historically to have been 'world-hating', since from this point of view Creation in some sense actually *is* the Fall, and consequently the world and the flesh are merely snares (or indeed 'tombs') from which the Manichaean adept seeks to escape. That famous ex-Manichaean, Augustine of Hippo, was acutely aware of the importance of discriminating between on the one hand Manichaeism – which was profoundly anti-Christian, notwithstanding the claims of its adherents – and on the other hand Platonism, which was in Augustine's view compatible with Christian faith, if insufficient on its own.[24] It was of course claimed even during Augustine's lifetime that he could as little slough off his early Manichaeism as a leopard can change its spots.[25] Augustine's residual Manichaeism is arguably evident above all in his doctrine of Original Sin, transmitted by concupiscence or sexual desire at the moment of conception. The idea of Original Sin – one of Augustine's particular contributions to the Christian tradition[26] – symbolizes everything that Pullman is writing against. This does not, however, necessarily invalidate Augustine's role as a mediator of a tradition of Christian Platonism; it rather shows how vulnerable that tradition is to a particular kind of distortion.

C.S. Lewis stands, then, in a long line of Christian Platonists for whom the world and the body – as the good creations of a good God – are capable of expressing divine beauty and wisdom. The fact that human beings are perennially prone to idolize, degrade and exploit that which should reflect the divine glory is the problem of sin or evil. It can also result in the kind of distorted over-correction that fears and loathes both the body and sexuality (and, notoriously, female sexuality). But the fact that historically the Christian church has countenanced all sorts of neurotic repression (as Pullman has often, and rightly, pointed out, not least in his depiction of the Church in Lyra's world) does not necessarily mean that such repression is in any sense the essence of Christianity. The Christian church has no monopoly on repression and neurosis, though, to be fair, it has had its fair share. The point is that some versions of Christian Platonism are far from being world-hating, but rather advocate the proper respect for, if not celebration of, the world and the body as images of the divine life. In this sense Christian Platonism can be world affirming. The difficulty is that Platonism, like Christian faith itself, is *dialectical*, that is, always on the move and so always potentially volatile; the very desire which it claims leads ultimately to God is dangerously powerful and always prone to short-circuiting the spiritual (and not only the spiritual) system by seeking premature fulfilment or joy. And joy prematurely grasped inevitably turns out to be mere pleasure or 'thrills', as Lewis insists above all in his deeply Augustinian spiritual autobiography *SBJ*, which narrates the '*lived dialectic*' of what Lewis believed was his archetypal experience.[27]

There is one strong piece of evidence for the claim that Pullman is in some sense in tune with a radically dialectical version of Christian Platonism – his much-publicized alignment with William Blake. As Northrop Frye sums up Blake's historical position:

> To understand Blake's thought historically, we must keep in mind an affinity between three Renaissance traditions, the imaginative approach to God through love and Beauty in Italian Platonism, the doctrine of inner inspiration in the left-wing Protestants, and the theory of creative imagination in occultism. In these traditions, again, we should distinguish certain elements which, though often found in the vicinity of Blake's type of thinking, were either ignored or condemned by him. The Renaissance development of [Plato's] *Symposium* is Blakean: the Pythagorean tendencies derived from [Plato's] *Timaeus* and the Cabbala are not. The occult idea that man can

create a larger humanity from nature is Blakean: magic, sympathetic healing and evocation of spirits are not. The belief that the Bible is understood
only by an initiated imagination is Blakean: the secret traditions of
Rosicrucians and the rest do not lead us to Blake whatever they may be.[28]

The works of Pullman, one is tempted to add, are Blakean: the works of J.K.
Rowling, whatever else they may be, are not (though Rowling does, like Blake,
have a sense of humour[29]). It is through Blake that Pullman is in direct and
indirect contact with the heterodox strand of the Christian Platonist tradition
that runs from Gnosticism and Neo-Platonism through Boehme to the
strange but highly influential symbolism of Swedenborg (a tradition to which
MacDonald was also attracted). Of Blake's relation to Swedenborgianism,
Kathleen Raine – who seeks to distance herself from the *Road to Xanadu* kind
of source hunting which Wimsatt and Beardsley criticise in 'The Intentional
Fallacy'[30] – has written: 'while Blake's attitude to Swedenborg may have
changed – perhaps more than once – the mark of Swedenborgian doctine and
symbolism went deep'.[31]

A key section of Raine's magisterial (if unconventional) *Blake and the
Tradition* is her interpretation of Blake's 'Little Girl Lost' – an earlier version
of which (entitled 'The Little Girl Lost and Found and the Lapsed Soul')
Lewis called in a letter to Raine 'an absolute stunner: one of the most important discoveries (of that kind) made in our times' (*LL3* 893). Raine claims
that Blake's 'Little Girl Lost' poems – which, with their lost little girl called
Lyca, are clearly alluded to in *HDM* – are versions of the myth of Persephone
or Kore, the young girl who is abducted (or does she voluntarily go?) to the
world of the dead. According to Raine:

> the story of Lyca in the two poems *The Little Girl Lost* and *Found* is . . .
> Blake's version of the myth of Persephone and Demeter. Blake's poems are
> symbolic on several levels, like the Mysteries themselves. The rape of
> Proserpina, as we know from Apuleius . . . was exhibited among the sym-
> bolic shows of the Mysteries . . . Blake's Lyca, like the figure of Persephone,
> is at once the human soul and the soul of the earth. The sleeper is Lyca;
> but it is 'earth' who will awake. This alone should tell us that we are to
> read what follows as myth . . . Blake has beautifully combined a classical
> and a biblical allusion in the flowering of the desert that is to follow the
> wakening of the earth.[32]

The myth of Persephone (or Proserpina) was also interpreted by Neo-
platonist philosophers as the descent of the soul into the material world in
order ultimately to redeem it:

> the 'descent of intellect into the realms of generation becomes . . . the
> greatest benefit and ornament which a material nature is capable of

receiving; for without the participation of intellect in the lowest regions of matter, nothing but irrational soul and a brutal life would subsist in its dark and fluctuating abode'.[33]

This myth of the redemption of matter through the work of Persephone/Lyca seems to connect with Pullman's myth of Lyra's redemption of the world through the saving of Dust, that is, matter-become-conscious. The Persephone/Lyca myth is also related to the Christian myth of the Harrowing of Hell and the freeing of the imprisoned souls, 'for it is said that on the night of the marriage of Persephone all the souls in Hades rejoiced, that no souls descended into the underworld, and that Charon the ferryman [who appears in *AS*] rowed his empty boat on the river of Lethe, singing'.[34]

There is no need to make the claim that Pullman is consciously echoing the Persephone myth, let alone its neo-Platonist interpretations cited by Raine. Of the persistent influence of myth, Raine comments:

As to that common ground of all souls which Jung calls the collective unconscious, no poet can go far in that region without discovering that all mythologies are its language and its realizations embodied in whatever symbolic inheritance he may himself possess. Tradition is the record of imaginative experience, and its myths and symbols provide a language in which such knowledge may be expressed and transmitted.[35]

All that I am suggesting is that when Pullman allows his writing to come under the influence of Blake, and particularly the 'Little Girl Lost' poems, this involves a larger complex of symbolic and mythical resonance than he may consciously realize. Part of that larger complex of traditional symbolism derives from the tradition of heterodox Christian Platonism in which Blake himself was immersed, both consciously and unconsciously. The power of Pullman's myth, then, may derive partly from sources beyond his conscious control. The extent to which Pullman *is* conscious of this mythological background may be interesting as a matter of authorial biography, but is ultimately neither here nor there with regard to how his story actually *works*. In his essay 'Neoplatonism in the Poetry of Spenser' Lewis was critical of what calls 'that deadly outlook . . . which treats a poet as a mere conduit pipe through which "motifs" and "influences" pass by some energy of their own' (*SMRL* 149). On the other hand, approaches such as those of Raine and Frye, which stress the power of underlying myths and archetypes at work in literature, connect with more recent postmodern theories of intertextuality – Julia Kristeva, for example, has described reading Frye's *Fearful Symmetry* as 'a "revelation" in its insertion of the poetic text into Western literary tradition' (*NATC* 1443). However postmodern (or not) we may believe Pullman to be, certainly his work in very explicitly intertextual.

Reading like a butterfly

Pullman's intertextual inclinations are especially apparent in *AS*, with its chapter epigraphs (in the UK edition, if not the American), and the *Acknowledgements* section at the end of the book, where Pullman – giving as his motto 'Read like a butterfly, write like a bee' – makes particular mention of Kleist's *On the Marionette Theatre*, Milton's *Paradise Lost* and the works of William Blake (*AS* 549–50). The first of these was mentioned in our Prelude above in connection with Abrams's claim that Kleist's essay 'merely epitomized what had become one of the most familiar of [Romantic] philosophical commonplaces. [Kleist] uses the figure to support his paradox (derived from Schiller) that puppets, acting by pure necessity, exhibited a grace beyond the reach of human dancers, since these latter are inescapably self-divided and self-conscious. The key to this disparity between puppet and dancer . . . lies in a just understanding of the third chapter of Genesis' (*NS* 221). While Kleist's essay may be for Abrams merely one example among others of the Romantic motif of the Fortunate Fall seen as a creative evolution from innocence to experience, it nevertheless focuses these issues for Pullman in particular ways that have proved fruitful in generating key passages in his books. The anecdote in Kleist's essay about fencing with a bear flows directly into Chapter 13 of *NL* ('Fencing') where, like the character in Kleist's anecdote, Lyra is frustrated by her inability to trick Iorek the bear with any kind of feint. This idea that bears cannot be tricked is crucial to the narrative of *NL*, for in the mortal combat between Iorek and Iofur in Chapter 20 ('à Outrance') it is Iofur's desire no longer to be a bear, but a human with a daemon, that makes him fatally vulnerable to Iorek's trickery. Pullman describes this moment very powerfully, offering the second example in almost as many pages of an extended Homeric or epic simile (Pullman's years of teaching Homer, as well as of reading Milton, are clearly in evidence):

> You could not trick a bear, but . . . Iofur did not want to be a bear, he wanted to be a man; and Iorek was tricking him.
>
> At last he found what he wanted: a firm rock deep-anchored in the permafrost. He backed against it, tensing his legs and choosing his moment.
>
> It came when Iofur reared high above, bellowing his triumph, and turning his head tauntingly towards Iorek's apparently weak left side.
>
> That was when Iorek moved. Like a wave that has been building its strength over a thousand miles of ocean, and which makes little stir in the deep water, but which when it reaches the shallows rears itself high into the sky, terrifying the shore-dwellers, before crashing down on the land with irresistible power – so Iorek Byrnison rose up against Iofur,

exploding upwards from his firm footing on the dry rock and slashing with a ferocious left hand at the exposed jaw of Iofur Raknison.

(*NL* 353)[36]

In the earlier 'Fencing' chapter which echoes Kleist's essay, Iorek tells Lyra that the bears have the power to see in a way that humans have forgotten, and that this relates to Lyra's capacity to read the aliethiometer (*NL* 227). Lyra's ability (and subsequent inability) to read the aliethiometer are figurative of that movement or 'fall', at the heart of Kleist's essay, from innocent grace into self-consciousness. Like the ending of Kleist's essay, the ending of *HDM* offers the hope that the consequences of this fall can be overcome, and that what came through innocent grace can be recuperated through diligent work. In the pregnant conclusion of Kleist's essay, which according to Abrams epitomizes German Romanticism, and specifically the historical *dialectic* of German Romanticism, the narrator asks:

> 'Does that mean', I said in some bewilderment, 'we must eat again of the tree of knowledge in order to return to the state of innocence?'
> 'Of course,' he said, 'but that's the final chapter in the history of the world.'[37]

There is a sense in which this eschatology ('the final chapter in the history of the world'), which is anticipated in Kleist, actually appears in *HDM*[38] when, in a recapitulation of the Biblical Fall, Lyra and Will eat of 'the little red fruit' and experience some kind of incipient carnal knowledge, while '[a]round them there was nothing but silence, as if all the world were holding its breath' (*AS* 492). The world is holding its breath partly because the angel Balthamos is desperately struggling to prevent Father Gomez (armed with a rifle and 'preemptive absolution') from murdering Lyra to prevent her eating of the fruit in a second 'Fall'. In an intertextual allusion of a less literary kind (Pullman claims that the cowardly Balthamos's last ditch heroics are a reprise of the Robert Vaughn character in the already intertextual film *The Magnificent Seven*[39]), Balthamos does save the day, and much more than the day. For when Lyra is saved, she and Will 'fall', and, in a reversal of the Biblical Fall, they *restore* 'the true image of what human beings always could be, once they had come into their inheritance' (*AS* 497). This restoration of the true image of humanity (in contrast to the image of God in man *lost* in traditional Christian accounts of the Fall) also has cosmic consequences, like its orthodox original.[40] At the very moment of Will and Lyra's 'fall', the flow of Dust out of the universe into the abyss is reversed: 'The Dust pouring down from the stars had found a living home again, and these children-no-longer-children, saturated with love, were the cause of it all' (*AS* 497). To borrow an analogy sometimes used in discussions of Christian 'Salvation History', this great turning point is, so to speak, the 'D-Day' of the war between the forces of good and evil.

Final victory (for Pullman presumably 'the republic of heaven') is still in the future, and has to be patiently worked for.

The so-called Fall of Christian tradition is thus presented by Pullman as a decisive, if ultimately provisional, victory; if the Fall is the great *catastophe* of traditional (and especially Augustinian) Christianity, then in Pullman's version it is the great *eucatastophe*. More accurately, we should speak of the Fall as interpreted by the dominant strand of the Christian tradition, since the strategy of reversing the orthodox understanding of the Fall has a very long *alternative* history. To engage with this alternative Christian history is to explore a tradition with which Pullman is widely held to be at least conversant: that is, Gnosticism.[41] The alternative Gnostic version of the Genesis story, though never entirely lost, resurfaced in the texts discovered at Nag Hammadi in Upper Egypt in 1947, and was popularized by Elaine Pagels in *The Gnostic Gospels* (as well as in Michèle Roberts's novel *The Wild Girl*,[42] loosely based the Nag Hammadi texts). One of the defining characteristics of the Gnostic movement (prefiguring Blake's line about the need to 'create a System, or be enslaved by another Man's'[43]) is its resistance to the orthodox compulsion to define, and its valorization of interpretative diversity as a sign of spiritual maturity. As Irenaeus, an orthodox opponent of Gnosticism, complained: 'every one of them generates something new every day, according to his ability; for no one is considered initiated . . . unless he develops some enormous fictions.'[44] Although it is thus in principle impossible to present 'Gnosticism in a nutshell', it is nevertheless possible to outline some characteristic features.[45] One typical Gnostic move is to read the Genesis narrative otherwise that in the orthodox tradition, generally by demoting the God of Genesis and particularly by promoting the serpent; one Gnostic group – the Ophites, named after the Greek *ophis* or 'serpent' – particularly venerated the serpent as Wisdom (*sophia*) or even Christ himself.[46] The God of Genesis is an ignorant and arrogant usurper who has no rightful claim to exclusive status, let alone worship.[47] This is clearly echoed in the account Balthamos gives to Will of the Authority:

> the Authority, the Creator, the Lord, Yahweh, El, Adonai, the King, the Father, the Almighty – those were all names he gave himself. He was never the creator. He was an angel like ourselves – the first angel, true, the most powerful, but he was formed of Dust as we are . . . He told those who came after him that he had created them, but it was a lie. One of these who came later was wiser than he was, and she found out the truth, so he banished her. We serve her still. And the Authority still reigns in the Kingdom, and Metatron is his Regent.
>
> (*AS* 33–4)

There is an unmistakable reprise here of the story told in several of the Nag Hammadi texts (in two of which the 'Authority' figure is called 'Samael'[48]), and a clear connection between Metatron and the Jewish Gnostic or Kabbalistic tradition.[49] There is rather more mystery surrounding the wiser angel who was banished. She may be identified as Xaphania, but this is far from certain.[50] She might also be identified with the figure of Wisdom or Sophia who appears in so many Gnostic myths (including those of Novalis). This female figure of Wisdom is related to the serpent (not least by means of verbal resemblances in Aramaic generating 'a four-way pun that includes Eve (Hawāh)'): 'Sophia [literally, "wisdom"] sent Zoe [literally, "life"], her daughter, who is called Eve, as an instructor to raise up Adam'.[51] Another Gnostic account of the Fall runs as follows:

> And the spirit-endowed Woman came to [Adam] and spoke with him, saying, 'Arise, Adam.' . . . Then the Female Spiritual Principle came in the Snake, the Instructor, and it taught them saying, ' . . . you shall not die; for it was out of jealousy that he [the "Authority" figure] said this to you. Rather, your eyes shall open, and you shall become like gods, recognizing evil and good.' . . . And the arrogant Ruler cursed the Woman . . . [and] the Snake.[52]

Thus Pullman follows the Gnostic model fairly closely when his 'tempter' is a female figure, Mary Malone, who comes to 'instruct' the new Eve, Lyra. The reversal continues in that what Mary instructs Lyra about is precisely the mysteries of the female body. And it is Mary's initiation of Lyra into the mystery of sexuality that prepares the way for her 'Fall' with Will, which in Pullman's myth is simultaneously the restoration of everything.

It is instructive to compare Pullman's restaging of the temptation in Eden with that of Lewis in *Perelandra*. In both cases the re-run of Eden happens in another world. In both cases the 'tempter' or the 'instructor' is appropriately enough a scientist, prompting the question whether Pullman is deliberately reworking Lewis's version[53]. However, crucially, while Lewis's 'tempter' is a deranged and profoundly evil male scientist, Pullman's scientist is a woman, perhaps a little cranky in orthodox scientific terms (with the *I Ching* pinned to the back of her office door), though that is presumably the point; and though a lapsed nun (again, that is presumably the point), she is in Pullman's terms a 'good' character: brave, generous and loyal, as well as responsible for initiating Lyra into the mysteries of her body. Mary Malone is manifestly the opposite of Weston, both in his previous appearance in *OSP* where his colonizer's contempt for 'the natives' contrasts with Mary's co-operation with, and affection for, the *mulefa*; and in his appearance in *Perelandra* as the 'Un-Man'. There are, nevertheless, some curious echoes running between Weston and Mary. Both are in scientific terms unorthodox: Weston seems even to anticipate some of the more adventurous ideas related to modern science which seem to verge on the mystical, and in which Mary (and Pullman) are interested.[54] In a conversation (discussed above) on Perelandra (*CT* 223),

Weston informs Ransom that during his convalescence after his journey to Malacandra (or Mars) – recounted in *OSP* – he has developed a keen interest in 'spirituality'. This has taken him beyond mere 'Westonism' (the dream of interplanetary colonization) and has led him to question the traditional dualism of 'Man' and 'Nature': a binary opposition that breaks down when we contemplate 'the unfolding of the cosmic process' (*CT* 224). Weston has immersed himself in 'biological philosophy' and is now 'a convinced believer in emergent evolution', according to which:

> "The stuff of mind, the unconsciously purposive dynamism, is present from the beginning . . . The magnificent spectacle of this blind, inarticulate purposiveness thrusting its way upward and ever upward in an endless unity of differentiated achievements towards an ever-increasing complexity of organisation, towards spontaneity and spirituality, has swept away all my old conception . . . The forward movements of Life – growing spirituality – is everything".
>
> (*CT* 224–5)

This spirituality (which seems in some respects to foreshadow Pullman's idea of 'Dust') has led Weston to penetrate the crust of 'outworn theological technicalities' that surrounds organised religion (*CT* 225). The underlying 'Meaning' and the 'essential truth of the religious view of life' is 'pure Spirit', ' "a great, inscrutable Force, pouring up into us from the dark bases of being" ' that has chosen Weston as its instrument (*CT* 225–6). According to Weston's vitalism – which perhaps anticipates what might pass for (post)modern spirituality in at least some Cambridge common rooms – such binary opposites as God and the Devil, or heaven and hell, are 'pure mythology', 'doublets [that] are really portraits of Spirit, of cosmic energy' (*CT* 227). Weston castigates Ransom's obtuseness and timidity in clinging to 'the old accursed dualism', and failing to see that 'Without Contraries [there] is no progression':[55]

> "*Your* Devil and *your* God . . . are both pictures of the same Force. Your heaven is a picture of the perfect spirituality ahead; your hell a picture of the urge . . . which is driving us on . . . Hence the static peace of one and the fire and darkness of the other. The next stage of emergent evolution, beckoning us forward, is God; the transcended stage behind . . . is the Devil. Your own religion, after all, says that the devils are fallen angels".
>
> (*CT* 227–8)

There is at least a family resemblance between such a vision and the Romantic (and more specifically Blakean) vision that can be sensed in *HDM*, especially when the latter is laced with a dash of the more adventurous ideas in contemporary scientific thinking. Such a vision is also compatible with (and arguably derived historically from) the kind of Gnostic and alchemical

ideas that influenced not only Blake but also many other thinkers and sci-
entists including Newton himself (the 'inscrutable Force, pouring up into us
from the dark bases of being' is reminiscent of Boehme). It is almost as if
Lewis's seemingly uncanny prescience of intellectual movements which
only emerged fully after his death,[56] has allowed him a glimpse of the sort
of Blakean or Gnostic vision with which Pullman is associated – and which
Lewis seems to be criticizing in advance.

This is aligned with the fact that, as noted in the previous chapter,
Ransom/Lewis in this scene in *Perelandra* explicitly criticizes the Fortunate
Fall idea which was central, Abrams argues, to a main trajectory of Romantic
thought (though as previously noted, and also discussed below, Ransom's
argument is partly undermined by a later passage (*CT* 341)). Lewis is fighting on several fronts, though his different engagements derive from a fundamental opposition to any mode of thought that in his view conjures away
the primary realities of good and evil, sin and atonement. Thus Lewis resists
not only the Fortunate Fall idea, which for him underestimates both the
great weight of sin and the greatness of what was lost at the Fall (as well as
the cost of redeeming that loss); he also resists any collapsing of the opposition of good and evil into some productive clash of contraries. Lewis also
resists the broadly Gnostic tradition from which such views derive (though
the strength of his resistance is arguably in inverse proportion to a kind of
Gnostic tendency in his own creative writing). In Lewis's other treatment of
the Fall, *PPL*, composed about the same time as *Perelandra*, he explicitly
takes issue with the attempt by Dennis Saurat to connect *Paradise Lost* with
the (to Lewis heretical) Kabbalistic or Jewish Gnostic tradition.[57] Lewis
opposes any 'Gnosticization' of the Fall story; the latter is for him a bulwark
of Christian orthodoxy. Pullman's opposition to Lewis could hardly be more
complete; however, in a curious echo effect, it almost feels as if it is Lewis
who is criticizing Pullman in advance.

Pullman is thus directly opposed to Lewis's orthodox interpretation of the
Fall, which for Lewis is also in agreement with Milton's interpretation. In following Blake's reading of Milton as 'a true Poet and of the Devil's party without knowing it',[58] Pullman appears to be explicitly taking a position in the
great debate about the interpretation of *Paradise Lost*. In this debate between
on the one hand the 'orthodox' approach not only of Lewis but also (in a subtly different way) of Stanley Fish,[59] and on the other hand the 'Romantic'
interpretation of *Paradise Lost*, for example by Blake and Shelley, the crux of
the matter is the status accorded to Satan *vis-à-vis* God. In *HDM* the Romantic
Satan-figure is clearly Lord Asriel, who wages war on heaven – or more precisely on the Almighty, the ruler of the Kingdom of Heaven – in order to estab-
lish a new republic of heaven. There seems to be an explicit allusion to Satan
when it is stated that Asriel's army is greater than 'the one that fought the
Authority before, and it's better led' (*SK* 284). Thus Asriel is an improvement
on Satan, or so the suggestion seems to be. However, Asriel is not the main

focus of attention (or the 'hero') in *HDM* in quite the same way that Satan appears to be in *Paradise Lost*. Although Asriel figures largely in *HDM*, the trilogy literally begins and ends with Lyra, and the initiative for the instauration of the republic of heaven lies with Lyra and Will. Through his sacrificial death (along with Marisa Coulter), Asriel causes the literal downfall of Metatron into the abyss (*AS* 430), thus saving Lyra, who subsequently saves the world(s). Immediately after the narrative of the downfall of Metatron, the Regent of the Authority, the death of the latter is recounted. But the Authority is not in the end so much defeated by Asriel, as liberated by Lyra and Will from the crystal cage which had preserved the 'demented and powerless' Ancient of Days (*AS* 431). It is not hard for Lyra and Will to help the Authority out of the crystal litter once it has been opened with the subtle knife, known (ironically, given this no-contest) as 'Aesahaettr' or 'god-destroyer' (*SK* 286):

> for he was as light as paper, and he would have followed them anywhere, having no will of his own, and responding to simple kindness like a flower to the sun. But in the open air there was nothing to stop the wind from damaging him, and to their dismay his form began to loosen and dissolve. Only a few moments later he had vanished completely, and their last impression was of those eyes, blinking in wonder, and a sigh of the most profound and exhausted relief.
>
> Then he was gone: a mystery dissolving in mystery.
>
> (*AS* 432)

The gift of annihilation comes to the Authority just as it had earlier come to the ghosts whose release from the world of the dead would, according to Tialys, spell the end of the Authority's power (*AS* 326). In both cases Lyra and Will bring about the relief of extinction which seems to be the fulfillment of Asriel's prophecy that ' "*Death is going to die*" ' (*AS* 325). Again, this is a Romantic re-interpretation of orthodox Christian teaching which is this case substitutes some kind of pantheistic mystical absorption for the resurrection of the body. Elsewhere I have (perhaps ungenerously) called this Pullman's 'Happy Hour' version of mystical release,[60] presented at least in Roger's case as a moment of intoxication – 'he was gone, leaving behind such a vivid little burst of happiness that Will was reminded of the bubbles in a glass of champagne' (*AS* 382).

This would have satisfied neither Lewis nor Milton as an acceptable version of the Christian hope that 'the last enemy that shall be destroyed is death',[61] presumably the original of Asriel's ' "*Death is going to die*" '. Ironically, Paul's First Letter to the Corinthians is, in one interpretation, precisely *about* Gnosticizing Christians who are seeking to turn the promise of resurrection into a merely 'spiritual' experience.[62] Paul's insistence on the resurrection of the dead (as opposed to any Platonic immortality of the soul)[63] is not just a case of first-century fundamentalism, but rather an insistence that the

Christian Gospel is inescapably to do with bodies and history.[64] Whatever version of the Christian story (or myth) you are interpreting – and all reading and telling is an interpretation – Paul seems to be saying that the story has to be about bodies and history; the latter are not to be conjured away into some mystical experience. This is an emphasis that Blake would have recognized. But one can discuss the extent to which other Romantic retellings of the Christian story remove it from the body and history by 'spiritualizing' it. You do not have to be a fundamentalist Christian to ask about what might be getting lost in the Romantic transposition of the Christian myth into a myth of evolving consciousness or 'Spirit'. One of the paradoxes of Pullman's attraction to the Gnostic tradition is that the latter does tend to pull away from the body and history into a realm of spiritual enlightenment. Ironically Pullman's this-worldly slogan 'there en't no elsewhere' echoes a key emphasis of the orthodox Christian doctrines of Incarnation and Resurrection when they insist, in opposition to any Gnostic or Neo-platonic 'flight of the alone to the alone', on the central importance of the body and history.

The hatred of theologians

Lest I be suspected of imposing some theological agenda on Pullman's work, it is worth insisting that there must inevitably be some theological discussion of a writer who so explicitly foregrounds his relationship with Milton and Blake and (especially via Kleist) with German Romantic thought, and who goes out of his way (implicitly in his fiction, and explicitly elsewhere) to criticize the Christian Church and Christian writers such as Lewis and Tolkien. The references to theology adduced in the present book are intended to elucidate and discuss the ideas Pullman explicitly presents, rather than score particular theological points. Moreover, apart from specifically theological discussion, the question of the relation of private spiritual experiences to history and the body politic is also a key issue in Romantic studies. In addition to (and in certain respects in contrast with) Abrams's *NS* – whose reading of Romantic literature we used above to locate Pullman's 'high argument' – more recent critical works on Romantic literature also use religious thought to contextualize their arguments.[65] Thus Pullman has deliberately positioned himself at the heart of some ongoing theological debates – even his title *His Dark Materials* connects with theological discussion of Milton's orthodoxy.[66]

The difficulty is that when Pullman gets involved in the game of theological hardball, some problems and inconsistencies begin to emerge. According to Hugh Rayment-Pickard, what he paradoxically calls Pullman's *'religious reaction against religion'* in many ways 'does not stand up to scrutiny: it fails to engage with human tragedy, for example, or the crisis of moral authority that follows from the death of God'.[67] At which point Pullman will no doubt claim that he's just writing stories, not doing theology. But as Rayment-Pickard has pointed out, what one might call Pullman's (not so) 'hidden theology' takes the form of an attempt to 'out-narrate' the Christian story itself[68] – and not just the derivative 'little narratives' by the likes of Lewis and Tolkien, whose 'fairy-stories' (or fantasy fictions) are derivative of, and analogically related to, the Great (Fairy) Story of the Gospel, according to Tolkien.[69] Pullman is competing with that grand narrative itself, 'the Great Code' in Blake's phrase. This raises the question of the precise relation of Pullman's myth to the Christian myth: is Pullman's myth an *alternative version* of the Christian myth, along the lines of Carlyle's 'new Mythus' of 'natural supernaturalism' or (arguably) Blake's revision of the Christian myth? Or is Pullman offering a *different myth* from the Christian one? The latter alternative parallels the dilemma of feminist theologians (or *thealogians*, though this may beg the question): should they offer a radically revised version of the Christian message (the Rosemary Ruether kind of approach[70]), or should they abandon and replace the irredeemably flawed patriarchal myth of Christianity?[71] This issue also relates to the much-debated question of the identity of Gnosticism. Is Gnosticism an alternative version of Christianity? Or is it a different religion?[72]

Traditionally such issues of Christian identity have been bedevilled by so-called *'odium theoligicum'* ('the hatred of theologians') – that peculiarly virulent kind of hatred that theologians seem to have for those who disagree with them. To use the sad old theology professor's joke: for Calvin (who is of course alluded to in Lyra's world) the doctrine of the Trinity was a burning issue. Pullman is undeniably possessed by 'the hatred of theologians' in the (objective genitive) sense of an understandable hatred *of* theologians such as Calvin or (collectively) the Inquisition; however, he may also perhaps himself have become infected by the *condition* of *odium theoligicum* ('the hatred of theologians') in the (subjective genitive) sense that he too seems possessed by a kind of virulent theological hatred of those he disagrees with. At times Pullman might perhaps even be accused of the same kind of inflexible and ungenerous attitude toward his religious opponents that he is quick to condemn. Pullman may not burn anyone, but he does in the figure of Father Gomez create a caricature of a ruthless zealot, whose cruelty is legitimated by a doctrine invented by Pullman ('pre-emptive absolution') – on the basis of which he is consigned to a particularly unpleasant death. Gomez is arguably the victim of a kind of 'pre-emptive damnation' engineered by Pullman. Pullman the 'Author-God' (to borrow Barthes's phrase[73]) might be held to be as guilty of a kind of authorial absolutism as the God he condemns. He might even be accused of exercising the literary equivalent of Calvinist 'double predestination', with Lyra predestined to salvation and Gomez to perdition. Does the reader ever really feel that the outcomes could have been otherwise? There is arguably a kind of 'staged' feel to the narrative, and as has not infrequently been pointed out, Pullman's ecclesiastical villains have a distinctively pantomime feel.

Criticisms of the Christian Church pervade *HDM*, and though Pullman may claim that his criticisms are directed at *any* repressive institution,[74] one may suspect here a hint of disingenuousness. Pullman would be hard-pressed to deny that that there is something approaching a personal vendetta in his attacks on the Christian Church. Evidence for this would be Pullman's apparent need to invent (over and above the dismally long list of actual Church atrocities) some nefarious Church doctrines and practices such as 'pre-emptive penance and absolution' and 'intercission'. Although the latter practice is explicitly related to the Church's condoning of the castration of choristers (*NL* 374), the concept of intercission is all Pullman's own. He carefully avoids calling the Church in Lyra's world 'Christian', and the allusions to actual or quasi-Christian institutions are carefully scrambled so that, for example, we have the (Roman Catholic) Magisterium with its various competing branches such as the Consistorial Court of Discipline and the General Oblation Board – set up in (Protestant) Geneva after the death of 'Pope John Calvin'. The implication presumably is that no Christian tradition has a monopoly of institutionalised oppression; and just to be even-handed, the Russian Orthodox tradition is represented by the unpleasant and implicitly paedophilic priest Semyon Borisovitch. The latter is one of the triad of unadulterated clerical villains in the trilogy, alongside the fanatical Fathers Gomez and MacPhail.

Pullman has claimed some affinity with the dissenting tradition (not least through his professed admiration of Milton and Blake). However, the criticisms of the Church made in this tradition usually contrast the failings of the human institution with the life and teachings of Jesus. But Jesus is only referred to once in the entire trilogy, in Mary Malone's account of her vocation to become a nun (*AS* 465). Pullman has, to be fair, hinted that his next book (*The Book of Dust*) will deal with Jesus as 'one of these great prophets, great religious geniuses whose teaching is too revolutionary . . . too hard to live up to, and so is perverted and altered and controlled and led into safe channels by the human organisation which is set up in his name'.[75] In a sense, then, the jury is still out on the question of Pullman's entitlement to claim his descent from the tradition of Christian dissent.

Pullman's myth

Pullman is of course perfectly entitled to criticise the (by implication Christian) Church from whatever viewpoint he chooses to adopt. The difficulty is that in many respects Pullman's narrative is parasitic on the Christian myth. It seems too intimately related to the latter to be an *alternative* myth, and seems more like some kind of *revision* of the Christian myth. It is instructive to compare Pullman with Tolkien and Lewis at this point. Superficially Pullman is like Tolkien in that he doesn't mention Christianity explicitly, apart from the one reference to Jesus by Mary Malone (*AS* 465). But unlike Tolkien (or Ursula Le Guin, for that matter), Pullman does not create a completely different mythology. This assertion must be qualified firstly by conceding Pullman's creation of the very different world and culture of the *mulefa* (though *mulefa* history is in some sense related to ours with a common, and in their case unmistakably Fortunate Fall); and secondly by recognising that Tolkien's creation myth (the *Ainulindalë*) is clearly based in considerable measure on the Judeo-Christian creation narrative. But in general Pullman is much more like Lewis in that Christianity is unmistakably present (if never explicitly named) in the *HDM* trilogy. In contrast to Lewis, however, the ever-present but never-named Christianity is presented in an exclusively negative light. Whatever Pullman's myth is, it seems to be dependent on the myth of a totally depraved Christianity. Even without Christian preconceptions it seems unlikely that – whatever the appalling mental and physical suffering caused by the Church down through the centuries – this is the whole story. There is something slightly disturbing in a myth that has to invest so much energy in demonizing its significant other. In more than one sense, then, 'daemons' seem to be at the centre of Pullman's myth.

So what precisely *is* Pullman's myth – apart from its dependence on the Christian myth that is reversed with an alternative version of the Fall? In a bold move Pullman does literally give an alternative *version* (rather than an alternative *interpretation*) of the Fall narrative in Genesis. By adding new material into the Genesis narrative Pullman is in effect changing Jewish and Christian sacred scripture. To put this into perspective, one has only to recall the furore provoked by Salman Rushdie's *The Satanic Verses*, published seven years before *NL*. The so-called 'Satanic Verses' – introduced (or restored) into the Koran – at least have some kind of historical warrant (even if contested); Pullman's 'daemonic verses' are entirely his own invention. The accusation of heresy usually centres on the *interpretation* of scripture, or on whether certain texts count *as* scripture; that Pullman can unilaterally *alter* scripture, and then amicably discuss his ideas with the Archbishop of Canterbury, says a great deal about our contemporary society (which is clearly *not* subject to the Magisterium).

I referred above to Pullman's 'daemonic verses' because the additional material he smuggles into the canon of scripture all concerns daemons. When Asriel reads aloud Genesis 3:5 (in the King James Version, evidently still in use in Lyra's world – one of Pullman's private fantasies?), Pullman adds: 'For God doth know that in the day ye eat thereof, then your eyes shall be opened, *and your daemons shall assume their true forms*, and ye shall be as gods, knowing good and evil' (*NL* 372, Pullman's additions italicized). The following verse runs in Asriel's Bible: 'And when the woman saw that the tree was good for food, and that it was pleasant to the eyes, and a tree to be desired *to reveal the true form of one's daemon*, she took of the fruit thereof and did eat . . . '. The next verse which Asriel reads (Genesis 3:7) runs: 'And the eyes of them both were opened, *and they saw the true form of their daemons, and spoke with them.*' Pullman then makes a more substantial insertion:

> *But when the man and the woman knew their own daemons, they knew that a great change had come upon them, for until that moment it had seemed that they were as one with all the creatures of the earth and air and there was no difference between them.*
> *And they saw the difference, and they knew good and evil; and they were ashamed,* and they sewed fig leaves together *to cover their nakedness.*
>
> (NL 372)

In terms of style, how convincing we find Pullman's attempt to vie with scripture must be a matter of individual reader-response; in terms of *content*, the major innovation is the introduction of his invention of 'daemons'. Daemons are clearly a strikingly original component of Pullman's alternative myth; however, the material difference they make to Pullman's myth overall is debatable. Daemons are undoubtedly a brilliant invention, narratologically and otherwise.[76] But in terms of actually generating significant new ideas, arguably it is doubtful whether they amount to more than a clever device which (besides its narratological usefulness) allows Pullman to spell out his particular interpretation of the Fall story. The very fact that in our world we have daemons 'on the inside' tends to suggest that they don't actually *add* very much to the basic myth Pullman is telling, though they greatly increase the interest of the way he tells it.

There is, however, another passage that Asriel reads from his Bible which, although it is the same as the version on our world, is nevertheless susceptible of a radically different interpretation in the world of Asriel and Lyra: 'In the sweat of thy face shalt thou eat bread, till thou return into the ground: for out of it wast thou taken: for dust thou art, and unto dust shalt thou return' (Genesis 3:19) (NL 373). This is the key text for interpreting the idea of 'Dust', which is arguably the linchpin or hinge of Pullman's myth. I use the word 'hinge' deliberately, because 'hinge' ('*brisure*') is an important term in Derrida's writing, and Ann-Marie Bird has made a strong case for interpreting the role of Dust on *HDM* in terms of Derrida's work. (*L&S* 188–98) For Derrida, the effect of 'hinge-words' is to 'break down the oppositions by which we are accustomed to think . . . matter/spirit . . . veil/truth, body/soul, text/meaning, interior/exterior, representation/presence, appearance/essence etc'.[77] Although Bird does not, as far as I am aware, make use of Derrida's word 'hinge', the term expresses what she sees as the function of the word 'Dust' to 'disturb the traditional Christian hierarchies . . . the value-laden binaries of innocence-experience, good-evil, and spirit-matter that lie at the core of the Fall myth' (*L&S* 189). Another of Derrida's key 'hinge-words' is the Greek word *pharmakon* which can mean both 'poison' and 'remedy', a drug which can kill and/or cure; that undecidable (but rather important) 'and/or' is in a crude sense what 'deconstruction' is about. Pullman's 'Dust' may be in a similar sense 'undecidable' or 'double': the 'Dust-hunters' in the Church and especially at Bolvangar are 'as frightened of it as if it were deadly poison' (*NL* 18); and yet it is also what allows the 'alethiometer' ('truth-measure') to work and ultimately enables conscious life in the universe to be saved. In a sense 'Dust' *is* conscious life in the universe, yet it is also closely associated with death and 'dark matter' (some philosophers have suggested a necessary link between consciousness and awareness of death[78]). Using the verse quoted by Asriel (Genesis 3:19), the Church in Lyra's world has linked the so-called Rusakov Particles with Original Sin and death (*NL* 273).

As Frost points out, '[t]he mystery of Dust – its nature, cause, effects, and origins – is arguably the subject of *His Dark Materials*, determining the movement of its plots and defining its themes.'[79] Not only the so-called 'Dust-hunters', but all the main characters in *HDM* are in different ways in search of Dust. Mrs. Coulter and her 'Gobblers' want to find Dust to destroy it as the source of all evil. Lyra wants to find it because, as her daemon Pantalaimon tells her, reversing the binary opposition, 'if *they* ["the Oblation Board and the Church and Bolvangar and Mrs Coulter and all"] all think Dust is bad, it must be good' (*NL* 397). Asriel wants to find it, but his intentions are dark. At the end of *NL* he tells Mrs Coulter that he wants to destroy Dust, but later admits in *AS* that he had lied in order to persuade her to accompany him into the new world; his intention was always, she realizes, to preserve Dust (*AS* 401). At this point there is a decisive, if barely mentioned, moment in which, like the spinning coin which generates possible worlds, the whole narrative of *HDM* might have been otherwise: 'Moving like someone in a dream, [Mrs Coulter] . . . picked up the rucksack . . . and reached inside it for her pistol; and what she would have done next, no one knew, because at that moment there came the sound of footsteps running up the stairs' (*AS* 401–2). Here we seem to have both narrative uncertainty and narratorial omniscience; it could be postmodern narratological knowingness, or just old-fashioned authorial heavy-handedness.

Dust, then, both focuses and 'decentres' Pullman's myth. As Bird has suggested, Dust enables Pullman to proclaim the death of God (if not the Author-God), without necessarily falling into some modernist or Enlightenment grand narrative. Of the great atheistic 'masters of suspicion' (as Ricoeur puts it[80]) – Marx, Freud and Nietzsche – Asriel seems closest to the Nietzschian persona: aristocratic and apparently beyond good and evil (Lewis's Uncle Andrew in his dreams). The republic of heaven is hardly communist, and the psychoanalysis implied by *HDM* is more Jungian than orthodox Freudian. But there do seem to be similarities between Asriel and Nietzsche's *Übermensch*. The moment when Asriel climbs the bridge into a new world in the sky has strong connections with Nietzsche and German neo-Romanticism, not only with the rainbow bridge to Valhalla at the end Wagner's *Rheingold*, but also with

Schoenberg's setting of the Nietzschian Stefan George's poem 'Entrückung', which Pullman quotes when Asriel talks of feeling the wind from another world (*NL* 395). And there seems an echo of Wagner's *Götterdämmerung* when Asriel, united in death with his lover Marisa Coulter, precipitates the downfall of Metatron at the same time as the Authority dissolves with Will's application of the 'Subtle Knife', 'Aesahaettr' or 'god-destroyer'.

However, as Nietzsche insisted, the death of God is only the beginning. The real problem is how to *replace* God, given that non-replacement is structurally and linguistically inconceivable (belief in God being for Nietzsche coterminous with belief in grammar[81]); Derrida's term for this God-replacement is the 'centre' which organizes thought, and which has had many names (for example, *eidos* [Idea], *arche* [Origin], *telos* [End] *ousia* [Essence], *aletheia* [Truth], consciousness[82]). Pullman's proposal for a God-replacement, a centre which according to Bird is not a centre, seems to be Dust, that is, consciousness informing matter. From Dust derives all conscious life, including not only the angels, but also the Authority himself (though he denied it). But while Dust may look like a Derridean paradox, deconstructing the mind/matter binary opposition, actually it is an idea which is equally at home in monistic and pantheistic systems such as that of Spinoza, which Bird mentions (*L&S* 191). What Bird doesn't mention in this context, however, although Pullman explicitly does, is Augustine's definition of angels: 'from what they are, spirit, from what they do, angel' (*SK* 260). Bird comments that 'in an overt attempt to disturb the spirit-matter binary, [Pullman's] angels claim: "From what we are, spirit; from what we do, matter. Matter and spirit are one" (*SK* 260) – an incongruous statement made possible only if we envisage everything as part of a single whole' (*L&S* 191).

The reference to Augustine that Bird skips over is, however, not insignificant, for it connects Pullman's idea of Dust with another tradition of pantheistic and/or monistic thought: that of Platonism. How familiar Pullman is with the writings of Derrida is a moot point. But he is almost certainly acquainted with the version of mystical Christian Platonism presented by Lewis in certain passages in *Perelandra*, which seem to be one of the sources for Pullman's idea of Dust.[83] There is a resemblance to Pullman's Dust in the following description in *Perelandra* of what Lewis calls 'the Great Dance':

"That Dust itself which is scattered so rare in Heaven, whereof all worlds, and the bodies that are not worlds, are made, is at the centre. [Dust] is farthest from [the Holy One] of all things, for it has no life, nor sense, nor reason; it is nearest to Him of all things for without intervening soul, as sparks fly out of a fire, He utters in each grain of it the unmixed image of his energy. Each grain, if it spoke, would say, I am the centre; for me all things were made".

(*CT* 342)

Some of the key ideas – paradox, decentring, even the 'weave of differences' – which Bird derives from Derrida (though she concedes they can be found also in Spinoza) are present in the extended account of the mystical Great Dance in *Perelandra* (*CT* 340–5). Of course Lewis's vision is explicitly hierarchical, though that hierarchy is somewhat at odds with its monism. What is of particular relevance to the present discussion is that although Lewis prefaces it with an orthodox caveat ('"though the healing what was wounded and the straightening what was bent is a new dimension of glory, yet the straight was not made that it might be bent nor the whole that it might be wounded"' (*CT* 341)), nevertheless he seems to affirm the idea of the Fortunate Fall which he is elsewhere at pains to reject:

> "All which is not itself the Great Dance was made in order that He might come down into it. In the Fallen World He prepared for Himself a body and was united with the Dust and made it glorious for ever. This is the end and final cause of all creating, and the sin whereby it came is called Fortunate and the world where this was enacted is the centre of all worlds".
>
> (*CT* 341)

This suggests that, despite Ransom's rebuttal (after some hesitation) of the Fortunate Fall in *Perelandra*, nevertheless Lewis's thought strains away from the orthodox rejection of the Fortunate Fall idea that is so central to Romanticism (and Pullman). Similarly (and paradoxically) Lewis's thought can also be seen straining *towards* the kind of monistic/pantheistic vision that he caricatures in Weston's ideas, and which seems close to that Romantic dimension of Pullman's thought that Bird connects with Spinoza.

And what of the *truth* of Pullman's myth? Truth, or in Greek *aletheia*, was one of the terms in Derrida's list of God-replacements which ground systematic (or 'structural') thought, but which have now, he claims, become redundant.[84] Truth, apparently, has gone the way of grand (or meta-) narratives in our so-called postmodern condition.[85] Yet Pullman has the audacity to create what he calls an 'alethiometer', an instrument which *measures truth*. Pullman is not unaware of the claims of theory, which he wickedly refers to as an 'intellectual endeavour, or if you prefer mystery-cult [which] is a source of great fascination and enormous fun and considerable professional advantage to those who know how to play it', adding that, after a talk with a leading post-structuralist, one of Derrida's famous maxims proved 'a mystery too profound for my feeble understanding'.[86] In the same lecture Pullman acknowledges as helpful an idea in Karen Armstrong's *The Battle for God*, where (*pace* 'theory'):

> she sets out the difference between 'mythos' and 'logos', different ways of apprehending the reality of the world. Mythos deals with meaning,

with the timeless and constant, with the intuitive, with what can only be fully expressed in art or music or ritual. Logos, by contrast, is the rational, the scientific, the practical; that which is susceptible to logical explanation. Her argument is that in modern times . . . people in the Western world 'began to think that logos was the only means to truth, and began to discount mythos as false and superstitious'.[87]

These ideas are certainly not new, and are indeed commonplaces of the broadly Romantic tradition; but they have clearly struck a chord with Pullman. What they indicate is that Pullman sees myth as a means to, and expression of, truth, which links him (their differences notwithstanding) with the tradition of mythopoeic writers such as MacDonald, Tolkien and Lewis.

What Pullman objects to even more than 'theory' is theocracy, as he makes clear at some length in the same lecture; his opposition to 'fundamentalism' of any sort is apparent from *HDM*. I am not entirely convinced by Bird's argument that, despite his apparent attraction to some kind of pantheistic monism à la Spinoza (or 'Romanticism'), Pullman has an at least implicitly postmodern incredulity towards grand narratives and a suspicion of the ineluctable tendency of 'totalizing' thought to become 'terroristic' (*L&S* 193). Maybe; but I suspect that his objections to fundamentalism are more straightforward and old-fashionedly liberal than that. The alethiometer *does* measure truth. It accesses truth not only by scholarly method but also by the kind of intuition that the Romantics generally called 'imagination', and Keats in particular called 'negative capability': that state of mind that is capable, as Mary Malone informs Lyra, 'of being in uncertainties, mysteries, doubts, without any irritable reaching after fact and reason'[88] (*SK* 92). Shelley King gives a sustained reading of the alethiometer as a device for foregrounding the reading process itself, which can work (or perhaps 'play') with the 'innocent' immediacy of childhood, as well as working with the mediated and laboriously acquired knowledge of experience (King relates the former to George MacDonald's trust in the child reader) (*L&S* 108–11). Lyra will eventually experience both ways of reading the alethiometer; at the conclusion of *HDM*, having lost the 'grace' of intuitive reading with the onset of puberty, she plans to study to become a trained 'alethiometrist'. How the alethiometer works is a mystery, but it is in some unexplained way linked to Dust. Bird connects the idea of Dust with Derrida and deconstruction, but I am more convinced by King's attempt to link the alethiometer to the tradition of hermeneutics (though I don't think King explicitly uses that term). The reading of the alethiometer, with its intuitive to-and-fro between 'readerly' questions and 'textual' responses, sounds rather like what is called 'the hermeneutical circle' in a tradition running from the German Romantic thinker Schleiermacher through to Heidegger and Gadamer. If Pullman's work inevitably raises philosophical questions, then he seems to me to be more in tune with the broadly Romantic and hermeneutical tradition that still believes in some kind of truth (even if, as Gadamer insists, that truth is not subject to scientific method).[89]

The most explicit 'event of truth' (to use a term from the hermeneutical tradition just referred to) occurs at the end of *HDM* with the appearance of the angel Xaphania in a kind of epiphany – or even annunciation, given the salvific role assigned to Lyra, the second Eve. Xaphania appears as Lyra sobs 'with desperate abandon', having just discovered that she has lost her ability to read the alethiometer (*AS* 518–19). Although Xaphania has come to ask Will how to close the openings made by the subtle knife, she also comes, like the figure of Sophia or Wisdom in many a Gnostic myth, to deliver truth. After having explained to Lyra that although she has lost the ability to read the alethiometer 'by grace' she can regain this ability by a lifetime of work, Xaphania announces:

> "Understand this: Dust is not a constant. There's not a fixed quantity that has always been the same. Conscious beings make Dust – they renew it all the time, by thinking and feeling and reflecting, by gaining wisdom and passing it on . . . And if you help everyone else in your worlds to do that, by helping them to learn and understand about themselves and each other and the way everything works, and by showing them how to be kind instead of cruel, and patient instead of hasty, and cheerful instead of surly, and above all how to keep their minds open and free and curious . . . Then they will renew enough to replace what is lost through one window".
>
> (*AS* 520)

Clearly the Didactic Author is not dead. Xaphania's moral message blends a Gnostic emphasis on knowledge with what looks suspiciously like a liberal humanism that is not only unexceptionable – as Pullman has regularly insisted in response to those who condemn him as 'dangerous'[90] – but also rather unexceptional (and arguably Christian-based).

However, Xaphania's message is not merely a general code of conduct for all right-minded people. It implicitly requires a specific sacrifice on the part of Lyra and Will: the window that can be kept open my means of the Dust generated by all the good works required by Xaphania is not for the benefit of Lyra and Will, as Will initially hopes. Rather, as Lyra immediately sees, it should be for the dead to use to escape from the land of the dead; and, given that long-term survival in a different world is impossible, Will and Lyra must abandon any hope of ever being together (*AS* 520–1). What is required of them is infinite *renunciation*. This at first sight seems rather odd given Pullman's strictures on Lewis's apparent refusal of adolescent sexuality, especially in the notorious case of Susan Pevensie. But such renunciation is very much in the Romantic tradition epitomised by Wagner's *Tristan and Isolde* and derives, according to Lewis and Denis de Rougemont, from the ideal of

Courtly Love which was decisively shaped, de Rougemont argues, by the mediaeval form of Gnosticism known as Catharism.[91] Unlike the clichéd fairy-tale ending, Pullman's young heroes don't live together happily ever after; but *like* that conventional ending, the reader isn't actually *shown* Lyra and Will living apart unhappily ever after, although Pullman has already published a short work called *Lyra's Oxford* and a further related novel is promised. The sacrifice of Will and Lyra is a noble gesture whose consequences we are hardly (as yet) permitted to see being lived out; in a sense we are *told* of their sacrifice rather than *shown* it (though the metaphor of 'great wave of rage and despair' which engulfs Will is developed in an extended and very powerful way (*AS* 521–2)).

However that may be, an even nobler gesture perhaps is the great sacrifice of Lord Asriel and Marisa Coulter; in what might be seen as their love-death, they plunge together into the abyss embracing not only Metatron but each other. But here too there is an issue as to how this grand gesture is related to lived moral experience. Ironically, given his criticisms of fantasy writers such as Tolkien and Lewis for their lack of 'realism' in terms the psychological development of characters, there is surprisingly little to prepare the reader of *HDM* for the final self-sacrifice of Lyra's parents. More could arguably have been made of whatever process of moral and spiritual development *transformed* Asriel and Marisa Coulter from cruel, ambitious and self-obsessed figures into models of self-sacrifice. However, such questions about novelistic 'realism' (which Pullman has directed at Tolkien and Lewis) are perhaps ultimately inappropriate insofar as Pullman – like Tolkien and Lewis – is arguably offering a *myth*. 'Character' analysis – Lewis's 'analysis, digression, reflections and "gas"' (*OTOW* 73) – is arguably not the primary concern of myth-makers. Milton's Satan may be convincing as a 'character', but he is more compelling as a powerful mythical figure.

Heroes

When Nietzsche overthrew the Christian myth (though it has been argued that the title of his book *Der Antichrist* should really be translated 'The Anti-Christian' rather than 'The Anti-Christ' – an outlook Pullman would presumably share[92]), he offered alternative mythical figures to Jesus, whether Zarathustra or Dionysus (versus 'the Crucified').[93] However, although Lord Asriel – the most Nietzschean character in *HDM* – cuts a grand figure, and although he is partly modelled on Milton's Satan, in the end he hardly achieves the status of the trilogy's 'hero' (or 'anti-hero'). Marisa Coulter embodies, as Mary Harris Russell has shown (*L&S* 213–17), not only features of Eve, but also of the 'anti-Eve' Lilith who powerfully dominates MacDonald's eponymous novel. But like Asriel, Coulter is too ambiguous a figure to carry off the role of hero. As was suggested above, their joint sacrifice is too sudden and unexpected, and smacks too much of the *'deus ex machina'* to earn them the status of heroes. Perhaps in our postmodern condition there can be no more heroes, or only heroes of a very different kind – such as Lyra and Will.

HDM literally begins and ends with Lyra, who like Harry Potter, her rival in the best seller lists (and not only for children's books), seems almost ostentatiously ordinary, but is also 'the chosen one'. Some critics have been suspicious of the elitism (to say the least) that goes with Harry's special status in Wizarding circles.[94] Lyra has thus far escaped such suspicion, though like Harry she has an impressive pedigree. She is in effect an orphan like Harry, and one in reality by the end of the trilogy. This is all classic Freudian 'family romance' material, and can frequently be linked with similar motifs in fairy-tales.[95] Of course Lyra is not a boy, though at first she does her best to be one. She is a wilfully wayward intertextual relative of Lucy Pevensie, with a penchant for hiding in wardrobes and a special relationship with a menacingly large regal carnivore. Lyra is also a kind of Alice with attitude and the common touch, actually giving her name at one point as 'Alice' (*NL* 101); Alice is the prototype of the 'deconstructed' hero, according to Hourihan, who subverts hero conventions and gender dualisms.[96] And Lyra is a shocking liar. This arguably goes beyond the customary resourcefulness of heroes in fairy-tales and Greek myths. Lyra is a borderline case of compulsive lying or mythomania; Pullman is arguably creating a new mythology round a mythomaniac.

Lyra, then, is not 'morally . . . as pure and innocent as traditional fantasy prescribes' according to Maria Nikolajeva in her essay 'Harry Potter – A Return to the Romantic Hero'.[97] Nikolajeva offers readings of various examples of 'crossover fantasy fiction' using the analyses of myth by Northrop Frye in *The Anatomy of Criticism* and Joseph Campbell in *The Hero with a Thousand Faces* (with Jung's 'archetypes' in the background). She suggests that although historically children's literature comes after 'myth as such' (i.e. the mythic figure as 'cultural hero' teaching his people to use fire, hunt and cultivate land), nevertheless 'the mythic hero is a major source of inspiration for children's writers . . . even though contemporary authors [who] may lean heavily on myth . . . will inevitably deconstruct it in some way'.[98] In contrast to the relatively unambiguous Harry Potter, Nikolajeva argues that the young protagonists of *HDM* have 'dubious moral qualities' and that '[t]he utter ambiguity of character in Pullman's trilogy is based on the postmodern concept of indeterminacy, of the relativity of good and evil'.[99]

However, as I have argued above, the case that Pullman is a signed-up postmodernist has yet to be proved. Certainly his hero Lyra is morally flawed, and certainly there are acute ironies in the doubling of Lyra as the wannabe back-street kid and Lyra as the second Eve (and indeed the saviour of the world). But Pullman's story could arguably be related to yet another genre, the *Bildungsroman*, whose name reflects it origins during the German Romantic period. For it seems that although Lyra is a liar, she *learns* the value of truth. She has to go on a great journey, and specifically to the Underworld – the land of the dead – in order to find this out. And it is precisely her *moral insight* which determines the ending of the trilogy: Lyra *sees*, as Will initially does not, that the dead need the window-between-the-worlds even more than she and Will do. The trilogy ends with moral insight, self-sacrifice and the dedication to a scholarly search for the truth obtainable from the alethiometer. *HDM* is literally about Lyra's moral and spiritual formation (*Bildung*). While in her search for truth Lyra may have to grapple with moral ambiguity (she discovers that she has to *reverse* – more than once – what she thinks she knows both about Dust and about her parents), this does not speak to me of moral relativism or indeterminacy.

There is a sense then that Lyra's story is about her *initiation* into the *mystery* of truth. In terms of this reading the Fall is precisely the great rite of passage, the initiation into the journey towards maturity and wisdom, both sexual, intellectual and spiritual. This latter triad seems to echo (if not replicate) the Christian triad of 'body-soul-spirit' that Mary Malone thinks corresponds to the tripartite human nature that Lyra and Will have worked out for themselves (*AS* 462–3). Initiation is also the central movement of the great mythic pattern (departure-initiation-return) that according to Joseph Campbell underlies all the various myths about 'The Adventures of the Hero' – as Part I of *The Hero with a Thousand Faces* is entitled – while the first section of the chapter on 'Initiation' (entitled 'The Road of Trials') describes various accounts of the descent into the underworld. If it is possible – as Deborah De Rosa has proposed – to blend the *Bildungsroman* with Campbell's initiation myth in a reading of the Harry Potter stories,[100] then a similar reading of *HDM* seems promising. The turning point in Lyra's moral development occurs in the land of the dead, which in the absence of her daemon is indeed a 'road of trials'. The hero with whom Campbell begins the 'Initiation' chapter is Psyche, though he could just as well have mentioned Persephone or Kore – interestingly in terms of *HDM*, Campbell moves rapidly on to discuss 'the shamans of the farthest north (the Lapps, Siberians, Eskimo, and certain American Indian tribes), when they go to seek out and recover the lost or abducted souls of the sick'.[101] If Lyra can be read as the female hero questing for knowledge, then Will is much more Campbell's 'Hero as Warrior' – as his shaman father, at this point unbeknown to Will (and in flagrant antithesis to any postmodernist anti-essentialism), declares: 'Then you're a warrior. That's what you are. Argue with everything else, but don't argue with your own nature' (*SK* 335).

In a sense, Campbell's (no doubt seductively oversimplifying) universal myth of 'departure-initiation-return' had already been synthesized with the *Bildungsroman* in the work of German Romantic writers, above all Novalis. *Heinrich von Ofterdingen* – a *Märchen* or myth about (in Abrams's words[102]) 'the circuitous journey through alienation to reintegration' – is an explicit riposte to the original and archetypal *Bildungsroman*: Goethe's *Wilhelm*

Meister's Apprenticeship. As noted in the Prelude above, Novalis is for Abrams 'an author who conveniently brings together . . . the Scriptural story of Eden and the apocalypse; pagan myths and mystery cults; Plotinus, Hermetic literature, and Boehme; the philosophical and historical doctrines of Schiller, Fichte, Schelling, and contemporary *Naturphilosophie;* the exemplary novel of education, *Wilhelm Meisters Lehrjahre* – and fuses them . . . ' (*SN* 245–6). A similar, and similarly grand, range of themes and intertextual references is arguably to be found in Pullman's myth. A major difference from Novalis, however, is that Pullman's hero is a girl: she is the seeker rather than the sought. To make the hero a girl is not unprecedented. Humphrey Carpenter does not seem to realize the remarkableness of his claim that 'Alice is Everyman', according to Hourihan.[103] Tangle may arguably have a more significant role than initially appears in George MacDonald's 'The Golden Key' – the only MacDonald tale that Pullman admits to having read. And E. Nesbit certainly subverts the idea of the male hero, especially in her 'Dragon' stories. But it was arguably only around 1990 that we had fantasy novels explicitly foregrounding female figures who are in the full sense heroes, for example *Tehanu* (1990), Ursula Le Guin's supplement to her Earthsea trilogy.[104]

Is Lyra then, like Alice, 'Everyman' [*sic*]? By reversing the relation between Adam and Eve, Pullman opens up the possibility that, just as Adam in the Bible is an inclusive figure (for example 'As in Adam all die . . . ' (1 Corinthians 15:22)), so Lyra is a kind of inclusive figure. If Jesus is for Christians a 'second Adam', then Lyra might be seen in the same way as 'a second Eve', a conclusion that Mary Harris Russell explicitly draws (*L&S* 220). Pullman's reversal of the patriarchal order embodied in the Adam and Eve relation implies a reversal of the order of salvation, so to speak. As Russell boldly puts it: 'Our new common life, in Pullman's *HDM* trilogy, begins in a garden and must, therefore, begin with Lyra, mother of us all, the new Eve' (*L&S* 221). It is piously to be hoped that *The Book of Dust*, Pullman's promised sequel to the *HDM* trilogy, will clarify the relation between the Jesus myth and the Lyra myth, because a salvific 'Lyra myth' appears to be precisely what Pullman is offering – as Russell again makes explicit: 'Lyra, the new Eve, is breaking through [the Authority's] boundaries. Freeing the dead, she breaks out of an enclosed territory instead of being expelled from one, as was the traditional Eve' (*L&S* 220).

If Pullman is ambitious as a myth-maker, and prone to neither reticence nor false modesty, nevertheless his short piece 'A word or two about myths' ends on a note of humility as well as – with the suggestion of an allusion to Tolkien and Lewis – joy:

[E]ach new writer does bring something never seen before to a story that might have been told a thousand times. It might never have been seen from quite this angle, it might never have been suffused with quite this emotional tone; the intelligence that plays over the events might never have glittered with quite this silvery wit. This is what makes the telling, and retelling, and retelling of myths such an endlessly refreshing struggle, such a demanding privilege, such a humbling joy.[105]

A couple of paragraphs before this, Pullman acknowledges Lewis's idea that 'a myth is a story whose power is independent of its telling. Our first experience of the story of Orpheus and Eurydice would effect us just as strongly in whatever version we came across it, because it's the shape of the events that contains the power, and not merely the language.'[106] I have discussed elsewhere the implications of such a separation of 'myth' from 'its telling', particularly in relation to film versions (which Lewis mentions in *An Experiment in Criticism*), for example of *LOTR* and *LWW*.[107] Whether Pullman's myth of Lyra is as powerful in its film version is unclear at the time of writing. The loss of the final three chapters of *NL* in the film *The Golden Compass* certainly diminishes the final impact of the book. A subsequent film may restore that sublime (if no longer climactic) moment when, at the end of the novel, 'Lyra and her daemon turned away from the world they were born in, and looked toward the sun, and walked into the sky' (*NL* 399). And to return to the beginning: by displacing the attempt to poison Asriel from the Master of Jordan onto the Magisterium's Fra Pavel, the film dissipates the intriguing ambiguity of the Master, a fact that hardly encourages confidence that the overall complexity of Pullman's myth will be retained. Thus far the screenplay editor's knife has not been subtle.

Postscript: Harry Potter, Hogwarts and All

Although passing reference has been made to the Harry Potter series (=*HPS*) at several points above, the extent to which Rowling's work properly belongs in the present book remains an open question. What place can Harry have in our (suspiciously grand) narrative of high Romantic fantasy? One possibility might be to see the *HPS* in Bakhtinian terms as analogous to the classical 'fourth drama' that (rather like Cerberus appearing as 'Fluffy' in *The Philosopher's Stone*) parodies the high seriousness of the preceding tragic trilogy[1] – in this case the mythopoeic canon of MacDonald, Tolkien and Lewis. The crude playground- (and, in the case of Moaning Myrtle, literally toilet-) humour of the *HPS* – complete with vomit- and bogey-flavoured Bertie Bott beans – contrasts with the high seriousness of the mythopoeic canon (though Gandalf too will have his little joke).[2] In some respects the *HPS* recalls the anarchic madness and 'rampant magic'[3] of Hoffmann's *The Golden Pot*, and its treatment of the Dursleys echoes Hoffmann's ridicule of conventional 'philistine' values. The *HPS* doesn't, however, parody high fantasy in the manner of Terry Pratchett or even Diana Wynne Jones,[4] and on one level Rowling does take her story-telling seriously – if perhaps not quite so seriously as Pullman, the heir apparent of Lewis et al. ('Move over Tolkien and C.S. Lewis . . . '[5]). It has been argued that Rowling uses a kind of postmodern self-mockery to deflect attention from the ultimate seriousness of the *HPS*, which under its garish exterior offers a postmodern version of Lewis's Christian faith and philosophical Realism or Platonism.[6] Though Pullman can be extremely funny (for example, in *I was a Rat!*[7]), self-mockery is not generally one of the varieties of postmodernism he has adopted.[8]

The decision to relegate Harry to a Postscript (putting him metaphorically under the stairs) is over-determined. Partly it is an issue of space: though *HDM*, *CN*, and *LOTR* may be 'big reads', they are dwarfed by the seven-volume *HPS*. There is so much going on in these seven volumes, and such a blend of genres,[9] that to do them justice would exceed the scope of the present book. While the works by Lewis, Tolkien and Pullman examined above may contain elements of the *Bildungsroman*, the *HPS* derives much more specifically from the genre of the 'School Story'.[10] Though different from the genre of fantasy, such stories, set in (private) British boarding schools, were ironically always already a fantasy for the vast majority their readers – an irony only intensified with the world-wide reception of Rowling's stories based on the conventions of the very British Public School system (House rivalry, dorms, common rooms etc). Gradually the *HPS* has moved away from Hogwarts, so that in *Deathly Hallows* we *return* to Hogwarts, which really only figures as the setting for Rowling's 'Last Battle'.

Much ink has been spilled (and blogs divided) over the question of Rowling's relation to the fantasy tradition discussed above. Like Pullman, Rowling makes the claim (seemingly *de rigueur* for contemporary writers of crossover fantasy fiction) that she neither likes nor reads fantasy novels,[11] even claiming that it was only after the publication of *The Philosopher's Stone* that she realized she'd written one.[12] Asked in the Scholastic interview about her relation to Tolkien, Rowling replied:

> I didn't read *The Hobbit* until after the first Harry book was written, though I read *LOTR* when I was nineteen. I think, setting aside the obvious fact that we both use myth and legend, that the similarities are fairly superficial. Tolkien created a whole new mythology, which I would never claim to have done. On the other hand, I think I have better jokes.

With these latter two comments (winningly modest and witty, respectively) one can only concur. Regards the relationship between Rowling and Lewis, the situation is rather more complex. In an early interview Rowling claimed to love Lewis's work: 'Even now, if I was in a room with one of the Narnia books I would pick it up like a shot and re-read it.'[13] But nine years later, she claimed in a *Time Magazine* interview that she hadn't read all the Narnia books and that something about Lewis's sentimentality gets on her nerves. Echoing Pullman's attacks on Lewis, she rounds up the usual suspect: 'There comes a point where Susan . . . is lost to Narnia because she becomes interested in lipstick. She's become irreligious basically because she has found sex. I have a big problem with that.'[14]

Also reminiscent of Pullman is Rowling's increasing willingness to speak her mind in interviews, both live and on-line, most controversially with her recent 'outing' of Dumbledore. However, regarding this and other questions of interpretation, it seems wisest to maintain a certain reserve about 'consulting the oracle'.[15] Not only the gayness of Dumbledore, but also the religious and possibly mythic dimensions of the *HPS* are best elucidated by scrutiny of the text. An immediate issue here is that of the quality of Rowling's prose, which has suffered by comparison with Pullman's fine writing. However that may be, literary quality is not in itself an insurmountable obstruction to the power of the mythopeic writing, as Lewis and Pullman recognized in the cases of MacDonald and Lindsay. Harold Bloom also accepts this in his harsh (and hardly convincing) criticism of the first Harry Potter novel: 'Though [it] is not well written, that is not in itself a crucial liability. It is much better to see the movie, *The Wizard of Oz*, than to read the book upon which it was based, but even the book possessed an authentic imaginative vision. *Harry Potter and the Sorcerer's Stone* does not . . . '[16] The latter is in effect, according to Bloom, the 'quite readable' *Tom Brown's Schooldays* 're-seen through the magical mirror of Tolkein [sic]'. Bloom misses the 'authentic imaginative vision' he finds in 'superior fare' such as *The Wind in the Willows* and the Alice books. At least in A.S. Byatt's attack on the *HPS* the examples used to highlight Rowling's inadequacies come from the second part of the twentieth century (Alan Garner, Susan Cooper, Diana Wynne Jones, Ursula Le Guin).[17] Unlike the work of these writers, the *HPS* lacks for Byatt a sense of mystery and the numinous. But here, as in case of Bloom, we are dealing with matters of taste. Bloom may have a weakness for the film version of *The Wizard of Oz*, and Byatt a penchant for Georgette Heyer and Terry Pratchett, but in the Latin phrase (in this case used by Kant rather than Ms. Rowling): *de gustibus non est disputandum* [there's no disputing about taste].[18] Indeed, the real target of both Bloom and Byatt is not so much the *HPS* itself as the world that has allowed it to be so successful. They particularly abhor the dominance in the academy of a kind of 'dumbing down' approach in 'cultural studies' that subverts any distinction between 'high' and 'low' culture, and even – horrible to relate – allows the likes of the *HPS* onto university curricula.

Both Bloom and Byatt have been criticized for the literary elitism of their attacks on Rowling. But is there also perhaps lurking in the background the echo of a certain kind of religious elitism? As respectively a Gnostic and a Quaker (whether lapsed or 'practising'), neither Bloom nor Byatt would seem to have much time for the *catholicity* (if not Catholicism – Rowling is in fact a Protestant) of Rowling's work and its reception. The open-mindedness regarding the *aesthetic form* of myth professed by Pullman, Lewis and perhaps Tolkien is paralleled by a tolerance about the readerly reception of a 'crossover' work that does not target a particular audience. As MacDonald puts it in 'The Fantastic Imagination', what matters is not so much the meaning that the author puts into a fairy-tale as the meaning the reader takes out (*CFT* 7). This is structurally similar to the attitude of mass religions such as Roman Catholicism and Hinduism, which tend to be tolerant of the proliferation of (to more austere tastes) 'vulgar' imagery and apparently 'superstitious' practices. If Rowling has a message (and perhaps the *HPS* isn't *just* about making money[19]), then presumably it's in the old Christian-humanist (and Lewisian) tradition of Sir Philip Sidney's speaking pictures that teach and delight.

The moral or 'spiritual' message concealed in J.K. Rowling's Every Flavour Beans may not be to every critical theorist's taste, but it looks in effect like a version of the Christian-based liberal humanism also promulgated (*mutatis mutandis*) by Pullman. A major difference, however, is that while Pullman ostentatiously distorts orthodox Christian symbolism in his myth (the Fall is, as the Gnostics always said, actually the opposite), Rowling slips apparently orthodox Christian symbols into her narrative. In this regard her position is somewhere between Lewis and Tolkien. Like Tolkien, Rowling avoids referring explicitly to Christian material, though like Lewis in *LWW*, she alludes to Christmas, with carol-singing in the little church in Godric's Hollow, and (unattributed) Biblical texts inscribed on the gravestones, though it is stressed that Harry doesn't recognize these and finds them hard to understand.[20] Yet as in Lewis's Narnia stories, Rowling's Christian meaning is hard to miss; you don't have to employ John Granger's esoteric 'literary alchemy' to get a Christian meaning out of the *HPS* (though Rowling does admittedly share with Hoffmann an indebtedness to the alchemical tradition[21]). The scene in *Deathly Hallows*, for example, where Hagrid carries the apparently dead Harry, who has willingly allowed himself to be put to death by the Dark Lord, is like a kind of grotesque *pietà*:

> Someone slammed Harry's glasses back onto his face with deliberate force, but the enormous hands that lifted him . . . were exceedingly gentle. Harry could feel Hagrid's arms trembling with the force of his heaving sobs, great tears splashed down upon him as Hagrid cradled Harry in his arms, and Harry did not dare, by movement or word, to intimate to Hagrid that all was not, yet, lost.[22]

Of course this passage will evoke the (not necessarily opposite) criticisms of being sentimental mush and theologically problematic, and not only from the Christian Right. On the other hand, it is a powerful evocation in popular culture of a potentially moving Christian image of the power of a willing sacrificial death to overcome death. To call it trite may perhaps smack of a cultural and spiritual elitism. As Tolkien said of MacDonald (and it is also true, I argued above, of Lewis's Narnia books), Rowling's theme is fundamentally about death: the death of her mother and the need to come to terms with mortality. Voldemort is defined by his inability to accept his mortality – his name means 'flight (or theft) from death'. Mortality is an issue we all have to face, whatever our aesthetic predilections: death is also in this respect a great leveller. And if the *HPS* is on one level a myth about confronting personal issues (whether moral, religious or psychological[23]), then neither its poor aesthetic quality (if such be the case), nor its popularity, is necessarily a *problem*. Perhaps it is Byatt, Bloom et al. who have the problem.

Notes

Prelude: Pullman's 'High Argument'

1. Or sub-genre, according to Harold Bloom in '*Clinamen*: Towards a Theory of Fantasy', in E. Slusser, E. Rabkin and R. Scholes (eds), *Bridges to Fantasy* (Carbondale: Southern Illinois UP, 1982), p. 2 (the whole passage is cited below). [Hereafter *Clinamen*].
2. 'Children' is here 'understood in the broadest sense of the term . . . to encompass the period of childhood up through late adolescence', as Jack Zipes puts it in his General Editor's Foreword to the Children's Literature and Culture Series (Garland Publishing). The implied readership also includes adults, as in the phenomenon of so-called 'crossover' or 'kidult' fiction.
3. M.H. Abrams, *Natural Supernaturalism: Tradition and Revolution in Romantic Literature* (New York: Norton, 1971). [Hereafter *NS*]. Though strongly critiqued from the first, *NS* was recuperated by ecocritic Kate Rigby in her *Topographies of the Sacred: The Poetics of Place in European Romanticism* (University of Virginia Press, 2004), which includes references to myth and fantasy. See the end of Chapter 3 below.
4. While Thomas Carlyle (1795–1881) mainly belongs to the Victorian period, his work most relevant to the argument below was published by 1830, and his *Sartor Resartus* (from which Abrams's title derives) was written by 1832. In a broad sense, to be discussed below, Carlyle can be considered 'Romantic'.
5. A rather different – and like my own, avowedly selective – approach is that of John Stephens and Robyn McCallum in *Retelling Stories, Framing Culture: Traditional Story and Metanarratives in Children's Literature* (New York: Garland, 1998).
6. Modern discussion could be seen to begin with A.O. Lovejoy's 'Milton and the Paradox of the Fortunate Fall' (*ELH* 4 (1937)). See also Chapter III section (iv)' 'The Fortunate Fall' of A.D. Nuttall's *The Alternative Trinity: Gnostic Heresy in Marlowe, Milton and Blake* (Oxford: Clarendon: 1998).
7. F.D.E. Schleiermacher, *On Religion: Speeches to Its Cultured Despisers* [1799] (ed. R. Crouter) (Cambridge: CUP, 1996).
8. Thomas Carlyle, *Sartor Resartus* (ed. McSweeney and Sabor) (Oxford: OUP, 1999), p. 147. [Hereafter *SR*].
9. 'Prospectus to *The Recluse*', line 71.
10. See Wendy Parsons and Catriona Nicholson, 'Talking to Philip Pullman: An Interview', *The Lion and the Unicorn*.23: 1 January 1999.
11. See Andrew Bowie, *From Romanticism to Critical Theory* (New York: Routledge, 1997); *Aesthetics and Subjectivity* (2nd ed.) (Manchester: Manchester University Press, 2003).
12. On the issue of canonicity in the area of Romanticism see for example the Introduction to Edward Larrissy (ed.), *Romanticism and Postmodernism* (Cambridge: CUP, 1999), pp. 3–4.
13. Paul Hamilton, 'The New Romanticism: Philosophical Stand-ins in English Romantic Discourse', *Textual Practice* 11 (1997): 109, quoted in Kooy (see next note).
14. See Michael John Kooy, 'After Romantic Ideology – A Special Issue of *Romanticism On the Net.*' *Romanticism On the Net* 17 (February 2000) [10 July 2006] (http://users.ox.ac.uk/~scat0385/guest8.html)
15. Ibid.

16. The conclusion of Shelley's *A Defence of Poetry* (1821–40). Pullman's Carnegie Prize acceptance speech concludes: 'Thou shalt not is soon forgotten, but Once upon a time lasts forever.' (http://www.randomhouse.com/features/pullman/philippullman/speech.html.)

17. On Pullman's 'postmodernism' see Deborah Thacker and Jean Webb, *Introducing Children's Literature: from Romanticism to Postmodernism* (London: Routledge, 2002) pp. 42–4; 140–2.

18. See Lyn Haill, ed., *Darkness Illuminated* (London: National Theatre/Oberon Books, 2004) p. 101.

19. See Anne-Marie Bird, 'Circumventing the Grand Narrative: Dust as an Alternative Theological Vision in *His Dark Materials* ' in Millicent Lenz with Carole Scott (eds.), *His Dark Materials Illuminated* (Detroit: Wayne State UP, 2005). [Hereafter *L&S*].

20. See Prawer in Siegbert Prawer (ed.), *The Romantic Period in Germany* (London: Weidenfeld and Nicolson, 1970), p. 10. Pullman too is interested in the technicalities of late Romantic music – see child_lit LISTERV (27 July 2000); also *L&S*, pp. 5–6.

21. Prawer (ed.) (1970) p. 9.

22. C.S. Lewis in the Preface to *The Pilgrim's Regress: An Allegorical Apology for Christianity, Reason and Romanticism* (revised ed.) (London: Geoffrey Bles, 1943), p. 10. [Hereafter *PR*].

23. C.S. Lewis, *The Allegory of Love* (Oxford: Clarendon, 1936), pp. 75–6. [Hereafter *AOL*].

24. See Nuttall (1998).

25. *The Collected Letters of C.S. Lewis, Volume 1* (ed W. Hooper) (London: HarperCollins, 2004), p. 753. [This three-volume edition of Lewis's letters is hereafter cited as *LL1, 2* or *3*].

26. Personal correspondence (2005). On Lindsay's dark vision see Adelheid Kegler, 'Encounter Darkness: The Black Platonism of David Lindsay', *Mythlore* 19.2 (72) (1993): 24–33.

27. See Harold Bloom, *Omens of the Millennium: The Gnosis of Angels, Dreams, and Resurrection* (London: Fourth Estate, 1996).

28. See James Trainer's chapter on 'The *Märchen*' in Prawer (ed.) (1970), p. 107.

29. In a personal letter of April 2008, received after the first draft of the present book, Philip Pullman claimed to have been reading Hoffmann 'for most of [his] adult life', and to have read Novalis's *Heinrich von Ofterdingen* about 25 years ago; he continues: 'However, it's fifteen years since I began writing *His Dark Materials*, so there may well be some influence there.'

30. Personal correspondence (2005).

31. Ibid.

32. See Louis Althusser, *For Marx* (trans. Ben Brewster) (London: Allen Lane/Penguin, 1969), Chapter 7, 'Marxism and Humanism'.

33. See William Gray, 'Pullman, Lewis, MacDonald and the anxiety of influence', *Mythlore* 97–8 Vol. 25, No. 3–4, Spring/Summer 2007. See also William Gray, *Death and Fantasy: Essays on Philip Pullman, C.S. Lewis, George Macdonald and R.L. Stevenson* (Newcastle: Cambridge Scholars Publishing, 2008), Chapter 8.

34. Novalis, 'Klingsor's *Märchen*' in *Henry von Ofterdingen* (trans. Palmer Hilty) (Long Grove, IL: Waveland, 1990), pp. 142–3. [Hereafter *HvO*.]

1 German Roots and Mangel-wurzels

1. In *The Golden Pot* the evil apple-woman is the offspring of a mangel-wurzel and a dragon's feather.

2. See Jack Zipes, 'Cross-Cultural Connections and the Contamination of the Classical Fairy Tale', in Jack Zipes (ed.), *The Great Fairy Tale Tradition: From Straparola to the Brothers Grimm* (New York: Norton, 2001), p. 858.

3. See Jack Zipes, *Breaking the Magic Spell: Radical Theories of Folk and Fairy Tales* (London: Heinemann, 1979), p.186n26, on Rölleke's detailed philological work on the original manuscript of the Grimms' collection. See also Siegfried Neumann, 'The Brothers Grimm as Collectors and Editors of German Folktales' (trans. Donald Haase) in *The Reception of Grimms' Fairy Tales* (ed. Haase) (Detroit: Wayne State UP, 1993), reprinted in Zipes (ed.) (2001), pp. 969–80.

4. See Zipes, 'Cross-Cultural Connections' in Zipes (ed.) (2001), p. 862; also Harry Velten, 'The Influence of Charles Perrault's *Contes de ma Mère L'oie* on German Folklore', in Zipes (ed.) (2001), p. 958.

5. See Zipes, 'Cross-Cultural Connections' in Zipes (ed.), (2001), pp. 851–65.

6. Among the wealth of literature on this theme, Jerome McGann's *The Romantic Ideology: A Critical Investigation* (Chicago: Chicago UP, 1983) is seminal.

7. On this transition from folktale (*Volksmärchen*) to fairy tale (*Kunstmärchen*) see Zipes (1979) especially chapters 2 ('Might makes Right') and 3 ('The Romantic Fairy Tale in Germany').

8. Raymond Immerwahr, 'The word "*romantisch*" and its history' in Prawer (1970), pp. 58–9.

9. Letter to Henry Crabb Robinson quoted by Abrams (*NS* 278; 514n45).

10. See Rosemary Ashton, *The German Idea: Four English Writers and the Reception of German Thought 1800–60* (Cambridge: CUP, 1980), p. 187n4; see also E.S. Shaffer, 'Ideologies in Readings of the Late Coleridge:*Confessions of an Inquiring Spirit*', *Romanticism On the Net* 17 (February 2000) [19 July 2006]. http://users.ox.ac.uk/~scat0385/17confessions.html

11. S.T. Coleridge, *Biographia Literaria*, Chapter XIII.

12. See Roger Cardinal, *German Romantics in Context* (London: Studio Vista/Cassell & Collier Macmillan, 1975), pp. 50–2.

13. Heinrich Heine, *Die Romantische Schule*. See *The Romantic School and other essays* (ed. J. Hermand and R.C. Holub) (New York: Continuum, 1985). Robertson quotes Heine's essay in the Introduction to E.T.A. Hoffmann, *The Golden Pot and Other Tales* (Oxford: OUP, 1992), p. vii. [Hereafter *GPOT*].

14. Novalis, *Philosophical Writings* (trans. Margaret Mahoney Stoljar) (Albany: SUNY, 1997), p. 67.

15. George MacDonald, *The Complete Fairy Tales* (ed. U.C. Knoepflmacher) (Harmondsworth: Penguin, 1999), p. 133. [Hereafter *CFT*].

16. John Keats, letter to George and Georgiana Keats, 14 February – 3 May 1819.

17. Novalis, *Philosophical Writings*, p. 65.

18. For a fuller discussion than is usually given in surveys of German Romanticism, see H.J. Hahn, 'G.H. Schubert's Principle of Untimely Development (Aspects of Schubert's *Ansichten von der Nachtseite der Naturwissenschaft* and its Reverberations in Romantic Literature)', *German Life and Letters*, July 1984, pp. 336–53.

19. On Freud's connections with German Romanticism, especially Novalis, see Kenneth S. Calhoon, *Novalis, Freud and the Discipline of Romance* (Detroit: Wayne State UP, 1992).

20. Carlyle's translation of *Die Elfen* has been reprinted in Douglas Anderson (ed.), *Tales Before Tolkien: The Roots of Modern Fantasy* (New York: Ballantine, 2003).

21. Carol Tully (trans. and ed.), *Romantic Fairy Tales* (Harmondsworth: Penguin, 2000), p. xvii.

22. My distinction here between 'one-world' fairy tales and 'two-world' fantasies is sometimes expressed in terms of Bakhtin's genre-specific 'chronotopes'. See M.M. Bakhtin, 'Forms of Time and the Chronotope in the Novel', *The Dialogic Imagination* (ed. M. Holquist) (Austin: Texas UP, 1981); also Maria Nikolajeva, 'Fantasy Literature and Fairy Tales' in Jack Zipes (ed.), *The Oxford Companion to Fairy Tales* (Oxford: OUP, 2000), p. 152.

23. Novalis, *Schriften*, (ed. Kluckhohn), III, 98, #241. Cited in Robert Lee Wolff, *The Golden Key: A Study in the Fiction of George MacDonald* (New Haven: Yale UP, 1961), p. 392n8.

24. See footnote 29 to the Prelude above.

25. F.G. Ryder and R.M. Browning, *German Literary Fairy Tales* (New York: Continuum, 1992), p. 80.

26. This moment of hesitation is the mark of 'the fantastic' (as opposed to 'the marvellous') according to Tzvetan Todorov, *The Fantastic: A Structural Approach to a Literary Genre* (Ithaca: Cornell UP, 1975).

27. Zipes (1979), pp. 37–9.

28. See Neil Hertz, 'Freud and the sandman', in J.V. Harari (ed.), *Textual Strategies* (New York: Cornell UP, 1979).

29. Zipes (1979), p. 37.

30. Tully (ed.) (2000), p. 85.

31. Kenneth S. Calhoon uses Freud's 'Family Romance for Neurotics' [*Der Familienroman der Neurotiker*] (1908) to read *HvO*. See Calhoon (1992), pp. 6–14.

32. See Maria M. Tatar, 'Mesmerism, Madness and Death in E.T.A. Hoffmann's *Der Goldne Topf*', *Studies in Romanticism* 14 (1975), pp. 365–89.

33. Calhoon (1992), p. 5.

34. See Rosemary Jackson, *Fantasy: the Literature of Subversion* (London: Routledge, 1981), pp. 2; 9–10.

35. See Zipes (1979); also *Fairy Tales and the Art of Subversion* (London: Heinemann, 1983).

36. See Jack Zipes, *Sticks and Stones: The Troublesome Success of Children's Literature from 'Slovenly Peter' to 'Harry Potter'* (London: Routledge, 2002); also Suman Gupta *Re-reading Harry Potter* (Basingstoke: Palgrave Macmillan, 2003).

37. See Bakhtin (1981) on 'chronotopes' and Todorov (1975) on 'the marvellous'.

2   George MacDonald's Marvellous Medicine

1. For the argument (based partly on MacDonald's autobiographical novel *The Portent*) that Thurso Castle was the nobleman's mansion in the north of Scotland where the young MacDonald – employed as a tutor – discovered a wonderful library, see William Raeper, *George MacDonald* (1987), p.395n28.

2. Thomas Carlyle, 'Novalis', *Miscellaneous Essays* Vol. II (London: Chapman, 1872), pp. 201–6.

3. Glenn Sadler (ed.), *An Expression of Character: The Letters of George MacDonald* (Chicago: Eerdmans, 1994), p. 252.

4. Ibid., p. 107.

5. Greville MacDonald, *George MacDonald and His Wife* (London: George Allen & Unwin, 1924), p. 297. [Hereafter *GMAW*].

6. George MacDonald, *Phantastes, A Faërie Romance* (London: Dent Everyman's Library, 1915), p. vii. [Hereafter *Ph*].

7. See Neil Gaiman, *Stardust* (London: Headline, 1999); Susanna Clarke, *Jonathan Strange and Mr Norrell* (London: Bloomsbury, 2003).

8. Raeper, (1987), pp. 106–12; 237–63.

9. 'The Fantastic Imagination' is reprinted in U.C. Knoepflmacher (ed.), *George MacDonald: The Complete Fairy Tales* (Harmondsworth: Penguin, 1999). [Hereafter *CFT*].

10. George MacDonald, *A Dish of Orts* (Dodo Press, 2007), p. 1. [Hereafter *Orts*].

11. *Unspoken Sermons* (3rd series), p. 161; cf. Raeper (1987), p. 242.

12. Karl Barth, *Church Dogmatics* 1/1 (Edinburgh: T&T Clark, 1975), p. xiii (partially retracted in 2/1, pp. 80f).

13. See for example Gary Dorrien, 'The "Postmodern" Barth? The Word of God As True Myth', *The Christian Century*, April 1997; and Robert Jenson's essay on Barth in David Ford (ed.), *The Modern Theologians* (Oxford: Blackwell, 2000).

14. See Bowie (1997) and (2003).

15. After writing the above, I discovered two recent essays by Bonnie Gaarden also comparing MacDonald's approach with Abrams's version of Romanticism in general – and with Hegelianism in particular – and plotting the limits of MacDonald's attraction to pantheism: '*Die Aufhebung* in George MacDonald', *North Wind: A Journal of the George MacDonald Studies* 24, 2005; '"The Golden Key": a double reading', *Mythlore*, vol. 24, issue: 3–4, 2006.

16. See William Gray, *Robert Louis Stevenson: A Literary Life* (Basingstoke: Palgrave Macmillan, 2004), pp. 53–4. On the relation of Stevenson to MacDonald, see my 'Amiable Infidelity, Grim-faced Dummies and Rondels: RLS on George MacDonald' in *North Wind* 23: 2004; and 'A Source for the Trampling Scene in *Jekyll and Hyde*', *Notes and Queries*, December 2007. See also Gray, *Death and Fantasy*, Chapter 3.

17. Raeper (1987), p. 242–3.

18. Edmund Cusick, 'MacDonald and Jung' in William Raeper (ed.), *The Gold Thread: Essays on George MacDonald* (Edinburgh: Edinburgh UP, 1990).

19. William N. Gray, 'George MacDonald, Julia Kristeva and the Black Sun', *Studies in English Literature 1500–1900*, Autumn, 1996. See also Gray, *Death and Fantasy*, Chapter 1.

20. See Chapter 5 below; see also Gray (2007), and Gray, *Death and Fantasy*, Chapter 8.

21. It is unclear whether MacDonald was aware of similar ideas among the French Symbolists who knew the German Romantic tradition (see Marcel Raymond, *From Baudelaire to Surrealism* (London: Methuen, 1970)) and on whose work Kristeva partly based her *Revolution in Poetic Language* (New York: Columbia UP, 1984).

22. Roland Barthes, 'The Death of the Author' (1968), reprinted many times; originally translated by Stephen Heath in *Image, Music, Text* (London: Fontana, 1977).

23. On MacDonald and the Victorian fear of 'degeneration' see Geoffrey Reiter, '"Travelling Beastward": George MacDonald's Princess Books and Late Victorian Supernatural Degeneration Fiction' in Roderick McGillis (ed.), *George MacDonald: Literary Heritage and Heirs* (Wayne, PA: Zossima Press, 2008).

24. MacDonald (deliberately?) misquotes Phineas Fletcher's *Purple Island* Canto 6 (Fletcher's 'the first' becoming 'their fount') that derives from *FQ* II IX 52.

25. John Docherty, 'The Sources of "Phantastes"', *North Wind* 9 (1990), pp. 38–9.

26. See Gray (1996). See also Gray, *Death and Fantasy*, Chapter 1.

27. David S. Robb, *George MacDonald* (Edinburgh: Scottish Academic Press, 1987), pp. 83–4. Robb also sees *Phantastes* as a response to Arnold's 'Dover Beach' read in manuscript form (ibid.).

28. Wolff (1961), pp. 42–4.
29. Adrian Gunther, 'The Structure of George MacDonald's *Phantastes*', *North Wind* 12 (1993).
30. The 'incoherence' camp includes: Wolff (1961); Richard Reis, *George MacDonald* (New York: Twayne, 1972); Colin Manlove, *Modern Fantasy* (Cambridge: CUP, 1975); Raeper (1987). The critics arguing for 'coherence' are: John Docherty, 'A Note on the Structure and Conclusion of *Phantastes*', *North Wind* 7 (1988); and McGillis, 'The Community of the Centre' in McGillis (ed.), *For the Childlike* (Metuchen: Scarecrow, 1992). McGillis has more recently written: 'I am not going to defend the coherence of *Phantastes* here or argue for its productive incoherence, but . . . suggest that that the seeming contradiction between coherent and incoherent fits with MacDonald's sense of the fairy tale or fantasy as a form'. 'Fantasy as Miracle' in McGillis (ed.) (2008), p. 205.
31. Gunther (1993), p. 43.
32. Cf. Gray (1996), p. 886. See also Gray, *Death and Fantasy*, Chapter 1.
33. An even curiouser link between *Phantastes* and *Through the Looking-Glass* is that one of the three faults for which Alice holds Kitty up to the looking-glass as a punishment, is pulling the tail of Snowdrop, the name of the kitten belonging George MacDonald's daughter, Mary.
34. McGillis (ed.) (1992), p. 61.
35. See John Docherty, 'George MacDonald's *The Portent* and Colin Thubron's *A Cruel Madness*', *North Wind* 13 (1994), p. 22n4.
36. George MacDonald, *The Portent and Other Stories*, Chapter 17, 'The Physician' (Whitehorn, CA: Johannesen, 1994), pp. 97ff.
37. See for example Gilbert and Gubar, *The Madwoman in the Attic* (New Haven: Yale UP, 1979), pp. 53ff; and Elaine Showalter, *The Female Malady* (London: Virago, 1987).
38. George MacDonald, *Adela Cathcart* [1864] (Whitehorn, CA: Johannesen, 1994), pp. 12–13. Cited in *AC*.
39. Valeria Mosini, 'When the Interplay Between Evidence and Theory Becomes Tension: Dr Hahnemann's Homeopathic Medicine'. LSE Centre for Philosophy of Natural and Social Science, Discussion Paper Series (DP 72/04).
40. Raeper (1987), p. 222.
41. See F. Hal Broome, 'Dreams, Fairy Tales, and the Curing of Adela Cathcart', *North Wind* 13 (1994), p. 17n9.
42. Raeper (1987), p. 223.
43. See C.S. Lewis (ed. Walter Hooper), *Of This and Other Worlds* (London: Collins, 1982), p. 73.
44. See F. Hal Broome (1994), p. 12.
45. Ibid.
46. 'Introduction' to McGillis (ed.) (1992), pp. 7–13.
47. A. Waller Hastings, 'Social Conscience and Class Relations in MacDonald's 'Cross Purposes', McGillis (ed.) (1992), p. 75.
48. Michael Mendelson, 'The Fairy Tales of George MacDonald and the Evolution of a Genre', McGillis (ed.) (1992), pp. 38–9; 40.
49. George MacDonald, *Unspoken Sermons Series One* [1867], e-text published by Johannesen.
50. See Gray (2007). See also Gray, *Death and Fantasy*, Chapter 8.
51. Rolland Hein, *The Harmony Within: The Spiritual Vision of George MacDonald* (Grand Rapids: Eerdmans, 1982), p. 144.
52. McGillis (ed.) (1992), p. 31. I had already written the passages above about Carlyle and Abrams's *NS* before I read Mendelson's essay.

53. Personal correspondence (September 2005).
54. See Celia Catlett Anderson, '*The Golden Key*: Milton and MacDonald', in McGillis (ed.) (1992).
55. Wolff (1961), pp. 137–8.
56. Cynthia Marshall, 'Reading "The Golden Key"': Narrative Strategies of Parable', McGillis (ed.) (1992), p. 107.
57. J.R.R. Tolkien, 'On Fairy-Stories' in Christopher Tolkien (ed.), *The Monsters and the Critics and Other Essays* (London: HarperCollins, 3006), p. 110. [Hereafter *OFS* and *MCOE* respectively].
58. William Raeper 'Diamond and Kilmeny: MacDonald, Hogg and the Scottish Folk Tradition', McGillis (ed.) (1992), p. 142.
59. Humphrey Carpenter, *Secret Gardens: The Golden Age of Children's Literature* (Boston: Houghton Mifflin, 1985), p. 74.
60. U.C. Knoepflmacher, *Ventures into Childland : Victorians, Fairy Tales, and Femininity* (Chicago: University of Chicago Press, 1998), p. 244.
61. See, for example, William Gray, 'Wisdom Christology in the New Testament, its Scope and Relevance', *Theology*, November, 1986.
62. See for example, Deidre Hayward, 'The Mystical Sophia: More on the Great Grandmother in the *Princess* Books', *North Wind* 13 (1994).
63. George MacDonald, *At the Back of the North Wind* (Ware: Wordsworth, 1994), p. 45. [Hereafter *ABNW*].
64. See Gray (1996); see also Gray, *Death and Fantasy*, Chapter 1. See also Ruth Y. Jenkins, '"I am spinning this for you, my child": Voice and Identity Formation in George MacDonald's Princess Books', *The Lion and the Unicorn* Volume 28, No. 3 September 2004.
65. Philip Pullman, *The Ruby and the Smoke* (London; Scholastic. 1999).
66. George MacDonald, *The Princess and the Goblin* and *The Princess and Curdie* (ed. R. McGillis) (Oxford: OUP World's Classics, 1990), p. 5. [Hereafter *PGPC*].
67. See Julia Kristeva, 'Giotto's Joy'. *Desire in Language:a Semiotic Approach to Literature and Art*, (New York: Columbia UP, 1980), pp. 210–36, 224.
68. See Gray (1996) and Jenkins (2004).
69. See W. Gray, 'The Angel in the House of Death: Gender and Subjectivity in George MacDonald's *Lilith*' in Hogan and Bradstock (eds) *Women of Faith in Victorian Culture: reassessing 'The Angel in the House* (Basingstoke: Macmillan, 1998); see also Gray, *Death and Fantasy*, Chapter 2; and the discussion in *North Wind* 21 (2002) initiated by John Pennington's article 'Of "Frustrate Desire": Feminist Self-postponement in George MacDonald's *Lilith*'.
70. See Gray (2007). See also Gray, *Death and Fantasy*, Chapter 8.
71. See also the discussion between Alice, Tweedledum and Tweedledee about (the Red King's) dreams and reality in Chapter 4 of *Through the Looking-Glass*.
72. 'A Chapter on Dreams', *Further Memories*, vol. 30 of *The Works of Robert Louis Stevenson* (Tusitala Edition) (London: Heinemann, 1924), p. 50.

3 J.R.R. Tolkien and the Love of Faery

1. Owen Barfield in the Introduction to Jocelyn Gibb, ed., *Light on C.S. Lewis* (London: Geoffrey Bles, 1965); p. xi. Tolkien alludes to Barfield's comment in *The Letters of J.R.R. Tolkien* (ed. Humphrey Carpenter, assisted by Christopher Tolkien) (London: George Allen & Unwin, 1981), p. 363 451n. [Hereafter *TL*]. See also Humphrey Carpenter, *The Inklings* [1978](London: HarperCollins, 2006), p. 61 [Hereafter *Inks*]. Also William Gray, *C.S. Lewis* (Plymouth: Northcote House, 1998) p. 5.

2. Lewis anticipated Wimsatt and Beardsley's 'Intentional Fallacy' (1946) in *The Personal Heresy: A Controversy* (with E.M.W. Tillyard) (London: OUP, 1939), p. 18ff.
3. See the eponymous sermon in *The Weight of Glory and Other Addresses* (New York: HarperCollins, 2001), pp. 29–30 (where Lewis talks of 'the secret which hurts so much that you take your revenge by calling it names like Nostalgia and Romanticism . . . '). For discussion of 'desire' in Lewis, see Gray (1998), Chapter 2 and passim.
4. *Surprised by Joy: The shape of my early life* [1955](London: Collins Fontana, 1959), p. 18. Hereafter *SBJ*. Lewis's quest for 'Joy' is discussed in the following chapter.
5. Carpenter (*Inks* 28) applies to the first intimate encounter between Tolkien and Lewis this 'typical expression of opening Friendship' from Lewis's *The Four Loves* (London: Geoffrey Bles, 1960), p. 77. In *SBJ* Lewis describes a similar encounter in adolescence with Arthur Greeves apropos (presumably Guerber's) *Myths of the Norsemen* (*SBJ* 106), and uses almost identical words in the Preface to *SBJ* in relation to the experience of joy.
6. It first appears as 'The Tale of Tinúviel', posthumously published in *The Book of Lost Tales, Part Two: The History of Middle-earth, Volume 2* (ed. Christopher Tolkien) (London: HarperCollins, 1984) [Hereafter *BLT2*].Tom Shippey claims that Tolkien produced more than a dozen versions of this tale; see *The Road to Middle-Earth* (revised and expanded ed.) (London: HarperCollins, 2005), p. 292. [Hereafter *RME*].
7. J.R.R. Tolkien, *The Lays of Beleriand: The History of Middle-earth, Volume 3*, (ed. Christopher Tolkien) (London: HarperCollins, 1985), pp. 150–1; 315–29.
8. On the 'Lit. and Lang.' dispute within English; see Shippey, *RME*, Chapter 1 passim.
9. See for example Shippey, *RME* 219; John Garth, *Tolkien and the Great War* (London: HarperCollins, 2003), pp. 36; 64; 216; 229; 290; 294; Verlyn Flieger, *Splintered Light: Logos and Language in Tolkien's World* (London: Kent State UP, 2002), pp. 22–4; Brian Rosebury, *Tolkien: A Cultural Phenomenon* (Basingstoke: Palgrave Macmillan, 2003), pp. 147; 157; 191; Marjorie Burns, *Perilous Realms: Celtic and Norse in Tolkien's Middle-earth* (Toronto: Toronto UP, 2005), pp. 15–6. Michael Moorcock talks of Tolkien's 'corrupted romanticism' in *Wizardry and Wild Romance; A Study of Epic Romance* (Austin, TX: MonkeyBrain, 2004), p. 139.
10. Arthur O. Lovejoy, 'On the Discrimination of Romanticisms', *PMLA*, Vol. 39, No. 2. (Jun., 1924), pp. 229–53.
11. Humphrey Carpenter, *J.R.R. Tolkien: A Biography* [1977] (London: HarperCollins, 2002), p. 291. [Hereafter *Biog*].
12. See Prelude above.
13. See 'William Morris' in Lewis's *Selected Literary Essays* (Cambridge: CUP. 1969). [Hereafter *SLE*].
14. Garth (2003), p. 296, quoting Paul Fussell, *The Great War and Modern Memory* (Oxford: OUP, 1975), pp. 135; 138–9.
15. Richard Mathews, *Fantasy: The Liberation of Imagination* (New York/London: Routledge, 2002), pp. 87; 158n4.
16. Garth (2003), pp. 302–3.
17. One origin of the WWI use of the term 'the Hun' may be Kaiser Wilhelm II's order during the Boxer Rebellion (1899–1900) that his troops imitate the Huns of old ("let the Germans strike fear into the hearts, so he'll be feared like the Hun").
18. *HOTW*, Chapter 3, 'Thiodolf talketh to the Wood-Sun'.
19. 'The Literary Impact of the Authorised Version', *SLE*, pp. 133–4.
20. Burns (2005), pp. 75–92, especially p. 88.

21. J.R.R. Tolkien, *NARN I CHÎN HÚRIN: The Tale of the Children of Húrin* (ed. Christopher Tolkien) (London: HarperCollins, 2007).

22. On the collection/confection issue, see Tom Shippey's retraction (*RME* 395) of his earlier scepticism about Lönnrot in his *J.R.R. Tolkien: Author of the Century* (London: HarperCollins, 2000).

23. E.M. Forster, *Howard's End* [1910] (Harmondsworth: Penguin, 1973), p. 249. Cited by Verlyn Flieger, *Interrupted Music: The Making of Tolkien's Mythology* (Kent, Ohio: Kent State UP, 2005), p. 4. [Hereafter *IM*].

24. See also Tolkien's letter to Auden in 1955 (*TL* 214). Shippey suggests Tolkien may have been working on the Kullervo story as early as 1912 (*RME* 297).

25. As Tolkien jokes in his 1955 O'Donnell lecture 'English and Welsh'. (*MCOE* 192).

26. On 'creating depth', see Shippey's sub-section with that title (*RME* 351–61).

27. See John Rateliff, *The History of The Hobbit, Part One: Mr Baggins* (London: HarperCollins, 2007), for example pp. 54–5 and 63n26 on the allusions in the dwarves' second song at Bag-End.

28. J.R.R. Tolkien, *The Lord of the Rings* (50th Anniversary Edition) (London: HarperCollins, 2005), p. 14. [Hereafter *LOTR*].

29. Michael D.C. Drout, 'A Mythology for Anglo-Saxon England' in Jane Chance (ed.), *Tolkien and the Invention of Myth* (Lexington: Kentucky UP, 2004), pp. 240; 229–30.

30. Flieger (2005), p. 56–60.

31. Verlyn Flieger, 'Tolkien and the Idea of the Book', in *The Lord of the Rings 1954–2004: Scholarship in Honor of Richard E. Blackwelder*, ed. Wayne G. Hammond and Christina Scull (Marquette UP, 2006), pp. 290–6. [Hereafter *Blackwelder*].

32. For discussion of Vinaver and 'The Malorian Tradition' see Stephens and McCallum, pp. 130–4; 163n1.

33. J.R.R. Tolkien, *The Lost Road and Other Writings: The History of Middle-earth, Volume 5*, (ed. Christopher Tolkien) (London:HarperCollins, 1987), p. 8. [Hereafter cited as *LR*]. Verlyn Flieger, *A Question of Time: J.R.R.Tolkien's Road to Faërie* (Kent, Ohio: Kent State UP, 1997), p. 62.

34. J.R.R. Tolkien, *The Book of Lost Tales, Part One: The History of Middle-earth, Volume 1* (ed. Christopher Tolkien) (London:HarperCollins, 1983) pp. 13–20. [Hereafter *BLT1*].

35. These concluding lines of the metrical version in the published *LR* apparently originate in a prose version from the later *NCP*. See *LR* 100; *SD* 294n103.

36. *The Earliest English Poems* (trans. and ed. M. Alexander) (2nd ed.) (Harmondsworth: Penguin, 1991), p. 9.

37. J.R.R. Tolkien, *Sauron Defeated: The History of Middle-earth, Volume 9*, (ed. Christopher Tolkien) (London: HarperCollins, 1992), p. 164. [Hereafter *SD*].

38. A clear echo of Tolkien's description of the so-called '*eucatastrophe*' in 'On Fairy-Stories', delivered in 1938, but not published until 1947, after the writing of *NCP*.

39. *The Silmarillion* (London: Allen & Unwin, 1977), pp. 313–14. [Hereafter *S*].

40. C.S. Lewis, *OSP*, in *The Cosmic Trilogy* (Basingstoke: Pan/Macmillan, in association with The Bodley Head, 1990), p. 129. [Hereafter *CT*].

41. See Richard Holmes, *Coleridge: Early Visions* (Harmondsworth: Penguin, 1990), p. 164n. Christopher Tolkien doesn't note this connection of the North Devon coast with Coleridge.

42. J.R.R. Tolkien, *Tree and Leaf* (London: HarperCollins, 2001), pp. 124; 141. [Hereafter *T&L*].

43. Matthew Lyons, *There and Back: In the Footsteps of J.R.R. Tolkien* (Wimbledon: Cadogan Guides, 2004), p. 144. Lyons concludes his tour of 'Tolkien's England'

with the comment: 'I can see more clearly that [*LOTR*] is in itself an act of rescue for an England vanished from the record, woven together from almost random glimpses of the past, odd snatched phrases or broken monuments' (p. 196).

44. On 'defamiliarization' see Tolkien, *OFS* (*MCOE* 146); Shelley, 'A Defence of Poetry' in *The Norton Anthology of Theory and Criticism* (ed. V. Leitch) (New York: W.W. Norton, 2001), p. 714. [Hereafter *NATC*]. For a discussion of *OFS* and the Russian Formalist theory of defamiliarization see Clyde B. Northrup, 'The Qualities of a Tolkienian Fairy-Story', *MFS Modern Fiction Studies*, Vol. 50, no. 4, Winter 2004.

45. John Macquarrie has made much of this double meaning of 'let be' in his deeply Heideggerian philosophical theology. See *Principles of Christian Theology* (London: SCM, 2003).

46. Wayne Hammond and Christina Scull, *The J.R.R Tolkien Companion & Guide: Reader's Guide* (London: HarperCollins, 2006), pp. 567. [Hereafter *H&S2*].

47. '"Genesis of the story": Tolkien's Note to Clyde Kilby' in J.R.R. Tolkien, *Smith of Wootton Major* (Extended Edition) (ed. Verlyn Flieger) (London: HarperCollins, 2005), p. 69. [Hereafter *SWM*]. Flieger is quoting from The Tolkien Papers held at Oxford University's Bodleian Library.

48. On Tolkien's 'seemingly inconsistent and idiosyncratic spellings' of 'Fairy'; see Flieger's note in *SWM* 143.

49. For the Vatican II reading see reference to Derrick's review in *H&S2* 570–1; for the English Reformation reading see Flieger in *SWM* 147.

50. In terms of Tolkien's private symbolism, Nokes = 'at the oaks' > oaks = 'critics'; the birch in Faërie > birches = 'philologists'. See *RME* 209–12.

51. Paul Kocher, *Master of Middle-earth* (Boston: Houghton Mifflin, 1972), p. 203.

52. Burns (2005), p. 178.

53. Lucie Armitt, *Fantasy Fiction: An Introduction* (London: Continuum, 2005), pp. 91–100. The 'profoundly sexless' comment is on p. 95.

54. Jacques Lacan, *Feminine Sexuality* (ed. Juliet Mitchell and Jacqueline Rose) (New York: Norton, 1985), p. 143; quoted by Valerie Rohy in 'On Fairy Stories', *MFS Modern Fiction Studies*, Vol. 50, no.4, Winter 2004, p. 930.

55. Rohy (2004), p. 933–4.

56. I have argued elsewhere that the construction of desire in the work of Lewis (and arguably Tolkien) is fundamentally at odds with a Lacanian approach; see Gray (1998) pp. 15–16.

57. Richard C. West, '"Her Choice was Made and Her Doom Appointed": Tragedy and Divine Comedy in the Tale of Aragorn and Arwen' (*Blackwelder* 317–29).

58. For the theory that Arwen is not entirely alone at the end, but is visited by the spirit of Aragorn, see West. (*Blackwelder* 329n30).

59. The eponymous loves are: 'affection'; 'friendship'; '*eros*'; '*caritas*'. See C.S. Lewis, *The Four Loves* (London: Geoffrey Bles, 1960).

60. See Iris Murdoch, *The Fire and the Sun: Why Plato Banished the Artists* (Oxford: OUP, 1978), especially pp. 76–9.

4   C.S. Lewis: Reality and the Radiance of Myth

1. *Spirits in Bondage* (London: Heinemann, 1919); *Dymer* (London: Dent, 1926) (both under the pseudonym 'Clive Hamilton').

2. On this philosophical context see John Passmore, *A Hundred Years of Philosophy* (Harmondsworth: Penguin, 1968).

3. Plato, *Symposium* 203b.

4. 'Romanticism and Classicism', Greenblatt and Abrams (eds), *The Norton Anthology of English Literature* (vol. 2, 8th ed.) (New York: W.W. Norton, 2006), p. 2000.
5. See E.D. Hirsch, 'Objective Interpretation', *Validity in Interpretation* (New Haven: Yale UP: 1967).
6. Lewis discusses the relation between sex and Joy (or 'It', as he and Arthur Greeves called the experience) in a letter to Greeves in January 1930: 'If [the psychoanalyst] can say It is sublimated sex, why is it not open to me to say that sex is undeveloped *It*? – as Plato would have said' (*LL1* 878).
7. C.S. Lewis , *All My Road Before Me: The Diary of C.S. Lewis 1922–7* (ed. W. Hooper) (London: HarperCollins, 1993), p. 448.
8. Ibid., p. 314.
9. Cf. Silenus's response to King Midas in Chapter 3 of *The Birth of Tragedy*: 'What would be best for you is quite beyond your reach: not to have been born, not to be, to be *nothing*. But the second best is to die soon.'
10. Catherine Belsey, *Desire: Love Stories in Western Culture* (Oxford: Blackwell, 1994), p. 152.
11. Paul Piehler, 'Myth or Allegory? Archetype and Transcendence in the Fiction of C.S. Lewis' in P.J. Schakel and C.A. Hutter (eds), *Word and Story in C.S. Lewis* (Columbia: Missouri UP, 1991).
12. C.S. Lewis, 'Sometimes Fairy Stories May Say Best What's to be Said' in *Of This and Other Worlds* (ed. W. Hooper) (London: Collins, 1982), p. 72. [Hereafter *OTOW*].
13. C.S. Lewis, *God in the Dock* (Glasgow: Collins, 1979), p. 44.
14. Ibid.
15. Doris T. Myers, *C.S. Lewis in Context* (Kent: Kent State University Press, 1994), p. 126.
16. C.S. Lewis, *Studies in Medieval and Renaissance Literature* (Cambridge; CUP, 1966), p. 146. [Hereafter cited in parentheses as *SMRL*].
17. A.N. Wilson, *C.S. Lewis: A Biography* (London: HarperCollins, 1990). p. 145.
18. Literally 'the Lord's' in 'Old Solar' (*LL2* 666–7).
19. Milton, *Comus* 977–9.
20. C.S. Lewis, *The Discarded Image* (Cambridge: CUP, 1964). p. 111.
21. Often reprinted, Cixous's essay originally appeared in Cixous and Clément, *La Jeune Née* [*The Newly-Born Woman*] (1975, trans. 1986).
22. On the Fall as a 'Gender Paradigm' see Stephens and McCallum (1998), pp. 41–8.
23. In Schakel, Peter J. (ed.), *The Longing for a Form: Essays in the Fiction of C.S. Lewis* (Kent,Ohio: Kent State UP, 1977), p. 21.
24. See Gray (2007). See also Gray, *Death and Fantasy*, Chapter 8.
25. Raeper (ed.) (1990), p. 176.
26. Ibid.,p. 173.
27. Ibid.,p. 175.
28. See George MacDonald, *Lilith* (Eerdmans, 1981), p. 107, where 'Samoil' (probably to be identified with 'Sammael') is the name of the Shadow.
29. For a more detailed discussion of Lewis's argument see Gray, *C.S. Lewis*, pp. 56–8.
30. See Richard Dawkins, *The God Delusion* (London: Bantam, 2006).
31. George Sayer, *Jack: A Life of C.S. Lewis* (London: Hodder & Stoughton, 1997), p. 308.
32. C.S. Lewis, *Miracles* (London: Collins, 1960), p. 138n1.
33. Ibid. (emphasis added).
34. Alan Jacobs, in *The Narnian: The Life and Imagination of C.S. Lewis* (New York: HarperCollins, 2005), pp. 232–3, criticises this view, and the demonization of Anscombe as 'the White Witch'.

35. On Lewis's problems at this time, see Gray, *C.S. Lewis*, pp. 60–1.
36. Lewis (1960), p. 140.
37. Lewis (1979), p. 44, emphasis added.
38. Myers (1994), p. 140.
39. On Lewis's sado-masochistic tendencies see his letters to Arthur Greeves from 'Philomastix' ('Whip-lover'). (*LL1* 268–88).
40. C.S. Lewis, *English Literature in the Sixteenth Century Excluding Drama* (Oxford: Clarendon, 1954), p. 345.
41. C.S. Lewis (1954), p. 386.
42. C.S. Lewis, *They Asked for a Paper* (London: Geoffrey Bles, 1962), p. 196.
43. Lewis was known all his life as 'Jack'.
44. Hugh Rayment-Pickard, *The Devil's Account: Philip Pullman and Christianity* (London: Darton, Longman & Todd, 2004), pp. 63–4.
45. For a sustained Kristevan reading Lewis's oeuvre, see Gray (1998) passim.
46. Philip Pullman, *The Subtle Knife* (London: Scholastic, 1997), p. 208. [Hereafter cited as *SK*].
47. See Gray, *C.S. Lewis*.
48. See Gray (1996). See also Gray, *Death and Fantasy*, Chapter 1.
49. Julia Kristeva, *Black Sun: Depression and Melancholia* (New York: Columbia UP, 1989), p. 145.
50. C.S. Lewis *A Grief Observed* (London: Faber, 1964), p. 23.
51. Rudolf Otto, *The Idea of the Holy* (trans. J. Harvey) (London: OUP, 1923).

5   Measuring Truth: Lyra's Story

1. http://www.randomhouse.com/features/pullman/author/qa.html#q3
2. http://www.abc.net.au/rn/relig/enc/stories/s510312.htm
3. Ibid.
4. *Literary Review* Interview with Claudia FitzHerbert http://www.literaryreview.co.uk/pullman_08_07.html
5. See Kegler in *Mythlore* 19.2 (72) (1993).
6. FitzHerbert Interview.
7. See Gray (2007). See also Gray, *Death and Fantasy*, Chapter 8.
8. C.S. Lewis, *George MacDonald: An Anthology* (London: Geoffrey Bles, 1946), pp. 16; 14.
9. FitzHerbert Interview.
10. http://www.randomhouse.com/features/pullman/author/carnegie.html
11. http://www.abc.net.au/rn/relig/enc/stories/s510312.ht
12. First published in *The New York Times Book Review*, 18 November 1956.
13. http://books.guardian.co.uk/departments/childrenandteens/story/0,650988,00.html
14. C.S. Lewis (ed.), *Essays Presented to Charles Williams* (London: OUP, 1947).
15. http://www.randomhouse.com/features/pullman/author/author.html
16. Philip Pullman, *Clockwork or All Wound Up* (London: Doubleday, 1996).
17. See classically Gustav Aulen, *Christus Victor* (London: SPCK, 1931).
18. Letter to John Murray, 2 April 1817. Cited in Laurie Frost, *The Elements of His Dark Materials* (Buffalo Grove: The Fell Press, 2006), p. 514.
19. In his early novel *Galatea* (London: Victor Gollancz, 1978) p. 160; quoted by Rayment-Pickard (2004), p. 30.

20. Iris Murdoch (1978), p. 66; see also p. 79: 'As pictured in the *Republic*, the higher level is reflected as an image in the lower level. The high-temperature fusing power of the creative imagination, so often and so eloquently described by the Romantics, is the reward of the sober truthful mind which, as it reflects and searches, constantly says no and no and no to the prompt easy visions of self-protective self-promoting fantasy.'

21. Bloom (1996), p. 136.

22. E.R. Dodds, *The Greeks and the Irrational* (London: CUP, 1951).

23. This is not the place to engage in philosophical debate, but I should acknowledge that my use of the term 'dialectical' is decisively influenced by Hans-Georg Gadamer's reading of the history of philosophy from Plato through German Romantic philosophy to Heidegger. See especially his *Dialogue and Dialectic: Eight Hermeneutical Studies on Plato* (trans. P. Christopher Smith) (New Haven: Yale University Press, 1983) and *Hegel's Dialectic: Five Hermeneutical Studies* (trans. P. Christopher Smith) (New Haven: Yale University Press, 1982).

24. On Augustine, Platonism and Manichaeism see above all Peter Brown, *Augustine of Hippo* (London: Faber, 1967).

25. This remark is ascribed to Julian of Eclanum in Augustine's final unfinished work in response to Julian, *Opus Imperfectum Contra Julianum* ('Unfinished Work Against Julian') IV, 42. For discussion of Augustine, Julian and Manichaeism; see Elaine Pagels, *Adam, Eve and the Serpent* (Harmondsworth: Penguin, 1990), Chapter 6 passim.

26. See Pagels (1990), p. 109, especially note 55.

27. See Gray, *C.S. Lewis*, pp. 4–16. 'Lived dialectic' is also a phrase Lewis uses with reference to Lindsay's *A Voyage to Arcturus* (*OTOW* 35).

28. Northrop Frye, *Fearful Symmetry: A Study of William Blake* (Princeton: Princeton University Press, 1947), p. 155.

29. On Blake's sense of humour; see Nuttall (1998), pp. 192–4.

30. Kathleen Raine, *Blake and the Tradition* Volume 1 (Princeton: Princeton University Press, 1968), p. xxix.

31. Ibid., p. 4. See also Morton D. Paley's conclusion that 'one should take Blake's "Swedenborg" throughout not as a historical figure . . . but as the beliefs and attitudes that has accumulated around his name, as in the case of Blake's "Newton" of his "Locke"' (*Apocalypse and Millennium in English Romantic Poetry* (Oxford: OUP, 1999) p. 37).

32. Ibid., pp. 130–2.

33. Ibid., p. 142. Raine is quoting Thomas Taylor's *A Dissertation on the Eleusinian and Bacchic Mysteries*, pp. 129–30. For Blake's enthusiastic, if not uncritical, 'eclectic assumption of Taylor's Neoplatonism'; see Peter Ackroyd, *Blake* (London: Sinclair-Stevenson, 1995), pp. 88–90. See also Jon Mee, *Romanticism, Enthusiasm and Regulation* (Oxford: OUP, 2003), p.272n30.

34. Ibid., p. 143.

35. Ibid., p. xxvi.

36. The example of a Homeric simile three pages earlier is even more extended: 'Like two great masses of rock balanced on adjoining peaks and shaken loose by an earthquake . . . ' (*NL* 350).

37. Heinrich von Kleist, 'On the Marionette Theatre' [1810] (trans. Idris Parry, 1981), cited in Nicholas Tucker, *Darkness Visible: Inside the World of Philip Pullman* (Cambridge: Wizard Books, 2003), p. 207.

38. This seems structurally to echo Abrams's claim that the prophecy of the German Romantic Schelling is realized in Blake (*NS* 256).

39. http://www.powells.com/authors/pullman.html. *The Magnificent Seven* is famously based on Kurosawa's *Seven Samurai*.

40. For a classic account of the complex readings of this Genesis passage in Christian history see David Cairns, *The Image of God in Man* (Revised ed.) (Glasgow: Collins, 1973).

41. See for example Mary Harris Russell, '"Eve, Again! Mother Eve!" Pullman's Eve Variations' in *L&S*, p. 212.

42. Michèle Roberts, *The Wild Girl* (London: Minerva, 1991).

43. *Jerusalem* Plate 10, line 20. G.E. Bentley (ed.), *William Blake's Writings* (Oxford: Clarendon, 1978), vol. I, p. 435.

44. Irenaeus, *Libros Quinque Adversus Haereses* [Five Books Against Heretics], 1.18.1. Cited in Pagels, *The Gnostic Gospels* (Harmondsworth: Penguin, 1982), p. 48.

45. In addition to Pagels, see Hans Jonas, *The Gnostic Religion*, 2nd revised ed. (Boston: Beacon Press, 1963); James. M. Robinson, ed., *The Nag Hammadi Library in English* (Leiden: Brill, 1977); Kurt Rudolph, *Gnosis* (Edinburgh: T.&T. Clark, 1983); Bentley Layton, ed., *The Gnostic scriptures* (London: SCM, 1987); Giovanni Filoramo, *A History of Gnosticism* (Oxford: Blackwell, 1990). Alistair H.B. Logan, *The Gnostics* (London: T&T Clark, 2006) offers a helpful overview of recent scholarly discussion of 'Gnosticism'.

46. See Nuttall (1998), pp. 10–15.

47. Cf. Pagels (1982), pp. 56–7.

48. The *Hypostasis of the Archons* and *On the Origin of the World* (Pagels (1982), p. 56). Compare MacDonald's *Lilith* (Eerdmans, 1981), p. 107, where the Shadow is named as 'Samoil' (a variant of 'Sammael'). 'Sammael' is also related to the Satanic figure of 'Zamiel' in Pullman's *Count Karlstein or The Ride of the Demon Huntsman*, derived in turn from Carl Maria von Weber's definitively Romantic opera *Der Freischütz*.

49. See Bloom (1996), pp. 44–53; 202–7.

50. See Frost (2006), p.128.

51. Pagels (1982), p. 57, citing *On the Origin of the World* 115.31–116.8.

52. Pagels (1982), p. 57, citing *Hypostasis of the Archons* 89.11–91.1.

53. Pullman's knowledge of *Perelandra* is confirmed in personal correspondence (2008): 'As for C.S. Lewis's *Perelandra* and the other two, I read them avidly as a boy, because they were in my grandfather's study, where I was allowed to browse when he wasn't writing his sermons.'

54. See Mary and John Gribbin, *The Science of Philip Pullman's His Dark Materials* (London: Hodder, 2003).

55. *The Marriage of Heaven and Hell* Plate 3, paragraph 2, G.E. Bentley (ed.), (1978), p. 77. Lewis does not, to be fair, cite Blake. Blake's famous dictum seemed to me to fit here.

56. See A.D Nuttall, 'Jack the Giant-Killer' in George Watson (ed.), *Critical Essays on C.S. Lewis* (Aldershot: Scolar Press, 1992).

57. Lewis devotes the whole of Chapter XII of *A Preface to Paradise Lost* to a critique of Saurat's *Milton, Man and Thinker* (New York: Dial, 1925).

58. *Marriage of Heaven and Hell*, Plate 6, paragraph 22, G.E. Bentley (ed.) (1978), p. 80.

59. See Fish's *Surprised by Sin: The Reader in* Paradise Lost (Cambridge: Harvard UP, 1967) and *How Milton Works* (Cambridge: Harvard UP, 2001). In fact Fish's approach recognizes truth in both approaches, since the sympathy with the Devil

in the 'Romantic' interpretation is precisely the kind of response that the 'orthodox' Milton expects to evoke in 'fallen' readers.

60. Gray (2007), p. 122. See also Gray, *Death and Fantasy*, Chapter 8.
61. I Corinthians 15:26. This verse also appears on the gravestone of James and Lily Potter. See J.K. Rowling, *Harry Potter and the Deathly Hallows* (London: Bloomsbury, 2007), p. 268.
62. See Walther Schmithals *Gnosticism in Corinth* (Nashville/New York: Abingdon, 1971); Hans Conzelmann, *1 Corinthians* (Philadelphia: Fortress, 1975).
63. A classic account of this is Oscar Cullmann's *Immortality of the Soul or Resurrection of the Dead?* (London: Epworth, 1958). The binary opposition suggested by Cullmann's title has been challenged, especially by Martin Hengel, e.g. *Judaism and Hellenism* (Philadelphia: Fortress Press, 1974).
64. More technically, the 'horizon' of the Gospel preached by Paul is 'apocalyptic eschatology'.
65. For example Paley (1999) and Mee (2003).
66. See John Rumrich, 'Milton's God and the Matter of Chaos', *PMLA*, Vol. 110, No. 5 (October1995); Nuttall (1998); Rumrich and Dobranski (eds), *Milton and Heresy* (Cambridge: CUP, 1998).
67. Rayment-Pickard (2004), pp. 89–90.
68. Ibid., p. 62.
69. 'The Gospels contain a fairy-story, or a story of a larger kind which embraces all the essence of fairy-stories', Epilogue, 'On Fairy-Stories' (*MCOE* 155).
70. See e.g. Rosemary Ruether, *Sexism and God-Talk* (London: SCM, 1992).
71. See Pat Pinsent, 'Unexpected Allies? Pullman and the Feminist Theologians' in *L&S*, and my review in *IRSCL Newsletter* No. 52 Autumn/Winter 2006. (http://www.irscl.ac.uk/reviews/lenz_scott1.htm).
72. For a summary of recent discussion of these questions see the Introduction to Logan (2006).
73. See Roland Barthes, 'The Death of the Author', *NATC*.
74. See Pullman on theocracy in his University of East Anglia lecture 'Miss Goddard's Grave' (http://www.philip-pullman.com/pages/content/index.asp? Page ID=113).
75. Haill (ed.) (2004), p. 57.
76. Pullman speaks about the narratological usefulness of daemons in his 2003 *South Bank Show* interview with Melvyn Bragg.
77. Robert Young (ed.), *Untying the Text: A Post-Structuralist Reader* (London: Routledge, 1981), p. 18.
78. For example Heidegger, especially in *Being and Time* [1927] (trans. Macquarrie & Robinson) (New York: Harper, 1962). I have discussed possible links between Pullman and Heidegger's thought in '"Witches' Time" in Philip Pullman, C.S. Lewis and George MacDonald' in Pat Pinsent (ed.), *Time Everlasting: Representations of Past, Present and Future in Children's Literature* (Lichfield: Pied Piper, 2007). See also Gray, *Death and Fantasy*, Chapter 9.
79. Frost (2006), p. 319.
80. Paul Ricoeur, *Freud and Philosophy* (New Haven: Yale University Press, 1970), p. 32.
81. Friedrich Nietzsche, *Twilight of the Idols* (trans. Polt) (Indianapolis: Hackett, 1997), p. 21.
82. See Jacques Derrida, 'Structure, Sign and Play in the Discourse of the Human Sciences', *Writing and Difference* (trans. Alan Bass) (London: Routledge, 1978). It seemed appropriate to capitalize the English translation of these terms.
83. For Pullman's knowledge of *Perelandra* see footnote 53 above.

84. Derrida (1978).
85. Jean-Francois Lyotard, *The Postmodern Condition* (Manchester: Manchester UP, 1986).
86. 'Miss Goddard's Grave' (http://www.philippullman.com/pages/content/index.asp? Page ID=113).
87. Ibid.
88. Letter to George and Thomas Keats, 21 December 1817.
89. Hans-Georg Gadamer, *Truth and Method* (London: Continuum, 2004).
90. Peter Hitchens, 'This is the most dangerous author in Britain' *The Mail on Sunday* (27 January, 2002, p. 63) (http://home.wlv.ac.uk//~bu1895/hitchens.htm).
91. See *AOL* Chapter 1 ('Courtly Love') and Denis de Rougemont, *Love in the Western World* (Princeton: Princeton University Press, 1983).
92. Walter Kaufmann (ed.), *The Portable Nietzsche* (Harmondsworth: Penguin, 1976), p. 565.
93. Friedrich Nietzsche, *Ecce Homo*.
94. Shuman Gupta, *Re-reading Harry Potter* (Basingstoke: Palgrave Macmillan, 2003).
95. See Sigmund Freud, 'Family Romances' [1909] in *The Pelican Freud Library* (vol. 7) *On Sexuality* (Harmondsworth: Penguin, 1977); Maria Tatar, *The Hard Facts of the Grimms' Fairy Tales* (Princeton: Princeton University Press, 1987) also Wendy Doniger, 'Never Snitch: The Mythology of Harry Potter' (http://fathom.lib. uchicago.edu/1/777777121870/)
96. Margery Hourihan, *Deconstructing the Hero* (London: Routledge, 1997), pp. 207–9.
97. Maria Nikolajeva, 'Harry Potter – A Return to the Romantic Hero' in Elizabeth Heilman (ed.), *Harry Potter's World: Multidisciplinary Critical Perspectives* (London: RoutledgeFalmer, 2003).
98. Ibid., pp. 136–7. Nikolajeva cites Hourihan (1997).
99. Ibid., p. 136.
100. Deborah De Rosa, 'Wizardly Challenges to and Affirmations of the Initiation Paradigm in *Harry Potter*' in Heilman (ed.) (2003), p. 163.
101. Joseph Campbell, *The Hero with a Thousand Faces* [1949] (London: HarperCollins, 1993), pp. 97–100.
102. The title of Chapter 4 of *NS*.
103. Hourihan (1997), p. 207, citing Carpenter, *Secret Gardens: The Golden Age of Children's Literature* (Boston: Houghton Mifflin, 1985), p. 62.
104. The novels adduced in the section 'Retelling the Story of the Hero: A Female Hero Paradigm' in Stephens and McCallum (1998) (pp. 117–25) are all published in the late 1980s or early 1990s.
105. Philip Pullman, 'A word or two about myths', included in *The Myths Boxset* (Edinburgh: Canongate, 2005).
106. Ibid. Pullman doesn't reference this point made by Lewis in the Preface to *George MacDonald: An Anthology* (pp. 15–17) and reiterated in his late work *An Experiment in Criticism* (p. 41).
107. Gray (2007). See also Gray, *Death and Fantasy*, Chapter 8.

Postscript: Harry Potter, Hogwarts and All

1. See 'From the Prehistory of Novelistic Discourse' (section II) in Bakhtin (1981).
2. See Terri Doughtry, 'Locating Harry Potter in the "Boys' Book" Market' in Lana Whited (ed.), *The Ivory Tower and Harry Potter* (Columbia: Missouri UP, 2002), p. 255. On the paucity of irony in *LOTR* see Moorcock (2004), p. 111.

3. Greville MacDonald's words; see the second paragraph of Chapter 2 above.
4. See Diana Wynne Jones, *The Tough Guide to Fantasy Land* (London: Gollancz, 2004). Gollancz also publish the Harvard Lampoon's *Bored of the Rings* (2001) and Michael Gerber's *Barry Trotter and the Shameless Parody* (2002).
5. Back cover of UK paperback edition of *AS*.
6. See John Granger, *Unlocking Harry Potter: Five Keys for the Serious Reader* (Wayne, PA: Zossima Press, 2007).
7. Philip Pullman, *I was a Rat!* (London: Doubleday, 1999).
8. John Granger is the source of the rumour that the self-regarding Gilderoy Lockhart in *Harry Potter and the Chamber of Secrets* is based on Pullman. See his *Harry Potter and the Inklings: The Christian Meaning of the Chamber of Secrets* (http://www.digital-disciple.com/harry_potter_granger.htm).
9. According to Anne Alton 'much of the appeal [of the *HPS*] lies in J.K. Rowling's incorporation of a vast number of genres in the books.' See 'Generic Fusion and the Mosaic of *Harry Potter*' in Heilmann (ed.) (2003), p. 141.
10. See Pat Pinsent, 'The Education of a Wizard: Harry Potter and his Predecessors' in Whited (ed.) (2002).
11. Interview on Scholastic.com, 16 October 2000 http://www.scholastic.com/harrypotter/books/author/interview2.htm
12. Interview with Lev Grossman http://www.time.com/time/magazine/article/0,9171,1083935-2,00.html
13. de Bertodano, Helena, 'Harry Potter Charms a Nation' http://www.accio-quote.org/articles/1998/0798-telegraph-bertodano.html
14. http://www.time.com/time/magazine/article/0,9171,1083935-2,00.html
15. The concluding phrase of Wimsatt and Beardsley's 'The Intentional Fallacy'.
16. Harold Bloom, 'Can 35 Million Book Buters Be Wrong? Yes.' *Wall Street Journal*, 7 November 2000. See http://wrt-brooke.syr.edu/courses/205.03/bloom.html
17. A.S. Byatt, 'Harry Potter and the Childish Adult', *New York Times*, 7 July 2003 query.nytimes.com/gst/fullpage.html?res=9A02E4D8113AF934A35754C0A9659C8B63-52k
18. *Critique of Judgement*, Section 56.
19. Zipes (2002) and Gupta (2003) make critiques of the capitalistic motivation behind the *HPS* (see Note 36 for Chapter 1).
20. Rowling (2007), pp. 264–9. The texts are Matthew 6:21 and I Corinthians 15:26 (the latter is also alluded to by Lord Asriel (*AS* 325)).
21. Hoffmann's use of alchemical material derived from G.H. Schubert and *Le Comte de Gabalis* was discussed in Chapter 1 above. Rowling's use of the historical alchemist Nicolas Flamel in *The Philosopher's Stone* is quite explicit.
22. Rowling (2007), p. 582.
23. See Margaret Rustin and Michael Rustin, *Narratives of Love and Loss: Studies in Modern Children's Fiction* (London: Karnac, 2001), Postscript: 'The Inner World of Harry Potter'.

Bibliography

Abrams, A. H., *Natural Supernaturalism: Tradition and Revolution in Romantic Literature* (New York: Norton, 1971).

Armitt, Lucie, *Fantasy Fiction: An Introduction* (London: Continuum, 2005).

Bakhtin, M. M., 'Forms of Time and the Chronotope in the Novel', *The Dialogic Imagination* (ed. M. Holquist) (Austin: Texas UP, 1981).

Barthes, Roland (trans. Stephen Heath), *Image, Music, Text* (London: Fontana, 1977).

Blake, William (ed. G. E. Bentley) *William Blake's Writings* (vol. I) (Oxford: Clarendon, 1978).

Bloom, Harold, *The Anxiety of Influence* (New York: OUP, 1973).

Bloom, Harold, '*Clinamen*: Towards a Theory of Fantasy', in Slusser, E., Rabkin, E. and Scholes, R. (eds), *Bridges to Fantasy* (Carbondale: Southern Illinois UP, 1982).

Bloom, Harold, *The Flight to Lucifer: A Gnostic Fantasy* (New York: Farrar, 1979).

Bloom, Harold, *Omens of the Millennium: The Gnosis of Angels, Dreams, and Resurrection* (London: Fourth Estate, 1996).

Bowie, Andrew, *From Romanticism to Critical Theory* (New York: Routledge, 1997).

Bowie, Andrew, *Aesthetics and Subjectivity* (2nd ed.) (Manchester: Manchester UP, 2003).

Brown, Peter, *Augustine of Hippo* (London: Faber, 1967).

Burns, Marjorie, *Perilous Realms: Celtic and Norse in Tolkien's Middle-earth* (Toronto: Toronto UP, 2005).

Calhoon, Kenneth S., *Novalis, Freud and the Discipline of Romance* (Detroit: Wayne State UP, 1992).

Campbell, Joseph, *The Hero with a Thousand Faces* (London: HarperCollins, 1993).

Carlyle, Thomas, 'Novalis' in *Critical and Miscellaneous Essays* (vol. 2) (London: Chapman and Hall, 1899).

Carlyle, Thomas, *Sartor Resartus* (ed. McSweeney and Sabor) (Oxford: OUP, 1999).

Carpenter, Humphrey, *The Inklings* (London: HarperCollins, 2006).

Carpenter, Humphrey, *J. R. R. Tolkien: A Biography* (London: HarperCollins, 2002).

Carpenter, Humphrey, *Secret Gardens: The Golden Age of Children's Literature* (Boston: Houghton Mifflin, 1985).

Chance, Jane (ed.), *Tolkien and the Invention of Myth* (Lexington: Kentucky UP, 2004).

Derrida, Jacques, 'Structure, Sign and Play in the Discourse of the Human Sciences', *Writing and Difference* (trans. Alan Bass) (London: Routledge, 1978).

Drout, Michael, 'A Mythology for Anglo-Saxon England' in Chance (ed.) (2004).

Filoramo, Giovanni, *A History of Gnosticism* (Oxford: Blackwell, 1990).

Flieger, Verlyn, *Interrupted Music: The Making of Tolkien's Mythology* (Kent, Ohio: Kent State UP, 2005).

Flieger, Verlyn, *A Question of Time: J. R. R.Tolkien's Road to Faërie* (Kent, Ohio: Kent State UP, 1997).

Flieger, Verlyn, *Splintered Light: Logos and Language in Tolkien's World* (London: Kent State UP, 2002).

Flieger, Verlyn ,'Tolkien and the Idea of the Book' in Hammond and Scull (eds) (2006).

Frye, Northrop, *Fearful Symmetry: A Study of William Blake* (Princeton: Princeton UP, 1947).

Gadamer, Hans-Georg (trans. P. Christopher Smith) *Dialogue and Dialectic: Eight Hermeneutical Studies on Plato* (New Haven: Yale UP, 1983).

Gadamer, Hans-Georg (trans. Weinsheimer and Marshall) *Truth and Method* (new ed.) (London: Continuum, 2004).

Garth, John, *Tolkien and the Great War* (London: HarperCollins, 2003).

Gibb, Jocelyn (ed.), *Light on C. S. Lewis* (London: Geoffrey Bles, 1965).

Granger, John, *Unlocking Harry Potter: Five Keys for the Serious Reader* (Wayne, PA: Zossima Press, 2007).

Gray, William, 'The Angel in the House of Death: Gender and Subjectivity in George MacDonald's *Lilith*' in Hogan, A. and Bradstock, A. (eds), *Women of Faith in Victorian Culture: Reassessing 'The Angel in the House'* (Basingstoke: Palgrave Macmillan, 1998).

Gray, William, *C. S. Lewis* (Plymouth: Northcote House, 1998).

Gray, William, *Death and Fantasy: Essays on Philip Pullman, C. S. Lewis, George MacDonald and R. L. Stevenson* (Newcastle: Cambridge Scholars Publishing, 2008).

Gray, William, 'George MacDonald, Julia Kristeva and the Black Sun', *Studies in English Literature 1500–1900*, Autumn, 1996.

Gray, William, 'Pullman, Lewis, MacDonald and the Anxiety of Influence', *Mythlore* 97–8, vol. 25, no. 3–4, Spring/Summer, 2007.

Gray, William, *Robert Louis Stevenson: A Literary Life* (Basingstoke: Palgrave Macmillan, 2004).

Gray, William, '"Witches' Time" in Philip Pullman, C. S. Lewis and George MacDonald' in Pat Pinsent (ed.), *Time Everlasting: Representations of Past, Present and Future in Children's Literature* (Lichfield: Pied Piper, 2007).

Gupta, Suman, *Re-reading Harry Potter* (Basingstoke: Palgrave Macmillan, 2003).

Hahn, H. J., 'G. H. Schubert's Principle of Untimely Development (Aspects of Schubert's *Ansichten von der Nachtseite der Naturwissenschaft* and its Reverberations in Romantic Literature)', *German Life and Letters*, July 1984.

Hammond, Wayne G. and Scull, Christina, *The J. R. R. Tolkien Companion & Guide: Reader's Guide* (London: HarperCollins, 2006).

Hammond, Wayne G. and Scull, Christina (eds), *The Lord of the Rings 1954–2004: Scholarship in Honor of Richard E. Blackwelder* (Marquette UP, 2006).

Haill, Lyn (ed.), *Darkness Illuminated* (London: National Theatre/Oberon Books, 2004).

Heilman, Elizabeth (ed.), *Harry Potter's World: Multidisciplinary Critical Perspectives* (London: RoutledgeFalmer, 2003).

Heine, Heinrich, *The Romantic School and Other Essays* (ed. J. Hermand and R. C. Holub) (New York: Continuum, 1985).

Hertz, Neil, 'Freud and the Sandman', in J. V. Harari (ed.), *Textual Strategies* (New York: Cornell UP, 1979).

Hoffmann, E. T. A., *The Golden Pot and Other Tales* (trans. R. Robertson) (Oxford: OUP, 1992).

Holmes, Richard, *Coleridge: Early Visions* (Harmondsworth: Penguin, 1990).

Jonas, Hans, *The Gnostic Religion* (2nd revised ed.) (Boston: Beacon Press, 1963).

Jackson, Rosemary, *Fantasy: The Literature of Subversion* (London: Routledge, 1981).

Jacobs, Alan, *The Narnian: The Life and Imagination of C. S. Lewis* (New York: HarperCollins, 2005).

Kegler, Adelheid, 'Encounter Darkness: The Black Platonism of David Lindsay', *Mythlore* 19.2 (72) (1993).

Kleist, Heinrich von, 'On the Marionette Theatre' (trans. Idris Parry, 1981), in Tucker (2003).

Knoepflmacher, U. C., *Ventures into Childland: Victorians, Fairy Tales, and Femininity* (Chicago: University of Chicago Press, 1998).

Kooy, Michael John, 'After Romantic Ideology – A Special Issue of Romanticism On the Net', *Romanticism On the Net* 17 (February 2000) [accessed 10 July 2006] (http://users.ox.ac.uk/~scat0385/17hoeveler.html).

Kristeva, Julia, *Black Sun: Depression and Melancholia* (New York: Columbia UP, 1989).

Kristeva, Julia, 'Giotto's Joy', *Desire in Language: A Semiotic Approach to Literature and Art* (New York: Columbia UP, 1980).

Kristeva, Julia, *Revolution in Poetic Language* (New York: Columbia UP, 1984).

Lenz, Millicent with Scott, Carole (eds), *His Dark Materials Illuminated* (Detroit: Wayne State UP, 2005).

Lewis, C. S., *The Allegory of Love* (Oxford: Clarendon, 1936).

Lewis, C. S., *The Collected Letters of C. S. Lewis* (3 vols) (ed. W. Hooper) (London: HarperCollins, 2004).

Lewis, C. S., *The Cosmic Trilogy: Out of the Silent Planet; Perelandra; That Hideous Strength* (London: Pan Books in association with The Bodley Head, 1989).

Lewis, C. S., *The Discarded Image* (Cambridge: CUP, 1964).

Lewis, C. S., *The Four Loves* (London: Geoffrey Bles, 1960).

Lewis, C. S. (ed.), *George MacDonald: An Anthology* (London: Geoffrey Bles, 1946).

Lewis, C. S., *A Grief Observed* (London: Faber, 1964).

Lewis, C. S., *Miracles* (London: Collins, 1960).

Lewis, C. S. (ed. Walter Hooper) *Of This and Other Worlds* (London: Collins, 1982).

Lewis, C. S. (with E. M. W. Tillyard) *The Personal Heresy: A Controversy* (London: OUP, 1939).

Lewis, C. S., *The Pilgrim's Regress: An Allegorical Apology for Christianity, Reason and Romanticism* (revised ed.) (London: Geoffrey Bles, 1943).

Lewis, C. S., *A Preface to Paradise Lost* (London: OUP, 1942).

Lewis, C. S., *Selected Literary Essays* (Cambridge: CUP, 1969).

Lewis, C. S., *Studies in Medieval and Renaissance Literature* (Cambridge: CUP, 1966).

Lewis, C. S., *Surprised by Joy: The Shape of My Early Life* (London: Collins Fontana, 1959).

Lewis, C. S., *The Weight of Glory and Other Addresses* (New York: HarperCollins, 2001).

Lindsay, David, *A Voyage to Arcturus* (Edinburgh: Canongate Classics, 1998).

Logan, Alistair H. B., *The Gnostics* (London: T&T Clark, 2006).

Lovejoy, A. O., 'Milton and the Paradox of the Fortunate Fall', *ELH* 4 (1937).

Lovejoy, A. O., 'On the Discrimination of Romanticisms', *PMLA*, vol. 39, no. 2 (Jun., 1924).

MacDonald, George, *Adela Cathcart* (Whitehorn, CA: Johannesen, 1994).

MacDonald, George, *At the Back of the North Wind* (Ware: Wordsworth Editions 1994).

MacDonald, George (ed. U. C. Knoepflmacher) *The Complete Fairy Tales* (Harmondsworth: Penguin, 1999).

MacDonald, George, *A Dish of Orts* (Dodo Press, 2007).

MacDonald, George, *Lilith* (Eerdmans, 1981).

MacDonald, George, *Phantastes, A Faërie Romance* (London: Dent Everyman's Library, 1915).

MacDonald, George, *The Portent and Other Stories* (Whitehorn, CA: Johannesen, 1994).

MacDonald, George (ed. R. McGillis) *The Princess and the Goblin* and *The Princess and Curdie* (Oxford: OUP, 1990).

MacDonald, Greville, *George MacDonald and His Wife* (London: George Allen & Unwin, 1924).

Mathews, Richard, *Fantasy: The Liberation of Imagination* (New York/London: Routledge, 2002).

McGann, Jerome, *The Romantic Ideology* (Chicago: Chicago UP, 1983).

McGillis, Roderick (ed.), *For the Childlike* (Metuchen: Scarecrow, 1992).

McGillis, Roderick (ed.), *George MacDonald: Literary Heritage and Heirs* (Wayne, PA: Zossima Press, 2008).

Moorcock, Michael, *Wizardry and Wild Romance: A Study of Epic Romance* (Austin, TX: MonkeyBrain, 2004).

Murdoch, Iris, *The Fire and the Sun: Why Plato Banished the Artists* (Oxford: OUP, 1978).

Myers, Doris T., *C. S. Lewis in Context* (Kent: Kent State UP, 1994).

Nietzsche, Friedrich (ed. Walter Kaufmann) *The Portable Nietzsche* (Harmondsworth: Penguin, 1976).

Novalis, *Henry von Ofterdingen* (trans. Palmer Hilty) (Long Grove, IL: Waveland, 1990).

Novalis, *Philosophical Writings* (trans. Margaret Mahoney Stoljar) (Albany: SUNY, 1997).

Nuttall, A. D., *The Alternative Trinity: Gnostic Heresy in Marlowe, Milton and Blake* (Oxford: Clarendon: 1998).

Otto, Rudolf (trans. J. Harvey) *The Idea of the Holy* (London: OUP, 1923).

Pagels, Elaine, *Adam, Eve and the Serpent* (Harmondsworth: Penguin, 1990).

Pagels, Elaine, *The Gnostic Gospels* (Harmondsworth: Penguin, 1982).

Paley, Morton D., *Apocalypse and Millennium in English Romantic Poetry* (Oxford: OUP, 1999).

Parsons, Wendy and Nicholson, Catriona, 'Talking to Philip Pullman: An Interview', *The Lion and the Unicorn*,23: 1 January 1999.

Prawer, Siegbert (ed.), *The Romantic Period in Germany* (London: Weidenfeld and Nicolson, 1970).

Pullman, Philip, *The Amber Spyglass* (London: Scholastic, 2000).

Pullman, Philip, Carnegie Prize acceptance speech [accessed 24 July 2008] (http://www.randomhouse.com/features/pullman/author/carnegie.html).

Pullman, Philip, *Clockwork or All Wound Up* (London: Doubleday, 1996).

Pullman, Philip, *I was a Rat!* (London: Doubleday, 1999).

Pullman, Philip, *Northern Lights* (U.S. *The Golden Compass*) (London: Scholastic, 1995).

Pullman, Philip, *The Ruby and the Smoke* (London: Scholastic. 1999).

Pullman, Philip, *The Subtle Knife* (London: Scholastic, 1997).

Pullman, Philip, 'A Word or Two About Myths', *The Myths Boxset* (Edinburgh: Canongate, 2005).

Raeper, William, *George MacDonald* (Tring: Lion, 1987).

Raeper, William (ed.), *The Gold Thread: Essays on George MacDonald* (Edinburgh: Edinburgh UP, 1990).

Raine, Kathleen, *Blake and the Tradition* (vol. 1) (Princeton: Princeton UP, 1968).

Rateliff, John, *The History of The Hobbit, Part One: Mr Baggins* (London: HarperCollins, 2007).

Rayment-Pickard, Hugh, *The Devil's Account: Philip Pullman and Christianity* (London: Darton, Longman & Todd, 2004).

Robb, David S., *George MacDonald* (Edinburgh: Scottish Academic Press, 1987).

Rowling, J. K., *Harry Potter and the Chamber of Secrets* (London: Bloomsbury, 1998).

Rowling, J. K., *Harry Potter and the Deathly Hallows* (London: Bloomsbury, 2007).

Rowling, J. K., *Harry Potter and the Philosopher's* [U.S. *Sorcerer's*] *Stone* (London: Bloomsbury, 1997).

Rudolph, Kurt, *Gnosis* (Edinburgh: T&T Clark, 1983).

Sadler, Glenn (ed.), *An Expression of Character: The Letters of George MacDonald* (Chicago: Eerdmans, 1994).

Schakel, Peter J. (ed.), *The Longing for a Form: Essays in the Fiction of C. S. Lewis* (Kent, Ohio: Kent State UP, 1977).

Schleiermacher, F. D. E. (ed. R. Crouter) *On Religion: Speeches to Its Cultured Despisers* [1799] (Cambridge: CUP, 1996).

Shippey, Tom, *J. R. R. Tolkien: Author of the Century* (London: HarperCollins, 2000).

Shippey, Tom, *The Road to Middle-Earth* (revised and expanded ed.) (London: HarperCollins, 2005).

Stephens, John and McCallum, Robyn, *Retelling Stories, Framing Culture: Traditional Story and Metanarratives in Children's Literature* (New York: Garland, 1998).

Stevenson, Robert Louis, 'A Chapter on Dreams', *Further Memories*, vol. 30 of *The Works of Robert Louis Stevenson* (Tusitala Edition) (London: Heinemann, 1924).

Tatar, Maria M., 'Mesmerism, Madness and Death in E. T. A. Hoffmann's *Der Goldne Topf*', *Studies in Romanticism* 14 (1975).

Thacker, Deborah and Webb, Jean, *Introducing Children's Literature: From Romanticism to Postmodernism* (London: Routledge, 2002).

Todorov, Tzvetan, *The Fantastic: A Structural Approach to a Literary Genre* (Ithaca: Cornell UP, 1975).

Tolkien, J. R. R. (ed. Christopher Tolkien) *The Book of Lost Tales, Part One: The History of Middle-earth*, vol.1 (London: HarperCollins, 1983).

Tolkien, J. R. R. (ed. Christopher Tolkien) *The Book of Lost Tales, Part Two: The History of Middle-earth*, vol. 2 (London: HarperCollins, 1984)

Tolkien, J. R. R. (ed. Christopher Tolkien) *The Lays of Beleriand: The History of Middle-earth*, vol. 3 (London: HarperCollins, 1985).

Tolkien, J. R. R., *The Letters of J. R. R. Tolkien* (ed. Humphrey Carpenter, assisted by Christopher Tolkien) (London: George Allen & Unwin, 1981).

Tolkien, J. R. R., *The Lord of the Rings* (50th Anniversary Edition) (London: HarperCollins, 2005).

Tolkien, J. R. R. (ed. Christopher Tolkien) *The Lost Road and Other Writings: The History of Middle-earth*, vol. 5 (London: HarperCollins, 1987).

Tolkien, J. R. R. (ed. Christopher Tolkien) *The Monsters and the Critics and Other Essays* (London: HarperCollins, 2006).

Tolkien, J. R. R. (ed. Christopher Tolkien) *NARN I CHÎN HÚRIN: The Tale of the Children of Húrin* (London: HarperCollins, 2007).

Tolkien, J. R. R. (ed. Christopher Tolkien) *Sauron Defeated: The History of Middle-earth*, vol. 9 (London: HarperCollins, 1992).

Tolkien, J. R. R. (ed. Christopher Tolkien) *The Silmarillion* (London: Allen & Unwin, 1977).

Tolkien, J. R. R. (ed. Verlyn Flieger) *Smith of Wootton Major* (Extended Edition) (London: HarperCollins, 2005).

Tolkien, J. R. R., *Tree and Leaf* (London: HarperCollins, 2001).

Tucker, Nicholas, *Darkness Visible: Inside the World of Philip Pullman* (Cambridge: Wizard Books, 2003).

Tully, Carol (trans. and ed.), *Romantic Fairy Tales* (Harmondsworth: Penguin, 2000).

Whited, Lana (ed.), *The Ivory Tower and Harry Potter* (Columbia: Missouri UP, 2002).

William, Morris, *The Earthly Paradise: A Poem in Five Volumes* (vol. II) (London: Reeves and Turner, 1889).

Wilson, A. N., *C. S. Lewis: A Biography* (London: HarperCollins, 1990).

Wolff, Robert Lee, *The Golden Key: A Study in the Fiction of George MacDonald* (New Haven: Yale UP, 1961).

Zipes, Jack, *Breaking the Magic Spell: Radical Theories of Folk and Fairy Tales* (London: Heinemann, 1979).

Zipes, Jack, *Fairy Tales and the Art of Subversion* (London: Heinemann, 1983).

Zipes, Jack (ed.), *The Great Fairy Tale Tradition: From Straparola to the Brothers Grimm* (New York: Norton, 2001).

Zipes, Jack (ed.), *The Oxford Companion to Fairy Tales* (Oxford: OUP, 2000).

Zipes, Jack, *Sticks and Stones: The Troublesome Success of Children's Literature from 'Slovenly Peter' to 'Harry Potter'* (London: Routledge, 2002).

Index